The Formative Years of Benjamin Bird

MD GAGE

PAGE PUBLISHING, INC.
New York, NY

First originally published by Page Publishing, Inc. 2019

ISBN 978-1-64462-279-7 (Paperback)
ISBN 978-1-64462-278-0 (Digital)

Printed in the United States of America

This story is dedicated as an expression for tolerance.

Contents

Foreword

In response to a request by his extended maternal family at the 1977 annual Dalkens family reunion, Benjamin Ray Bird, at that time a forty-three-year-old history professor, committed himself to research and write the Dalkens family's genealogical history. From his earliest awareness, Ben believed he could not understand himself fully unless he saw himself in the context of his extended family. From his earliest known direct ancestors until his present time, all of Ben's support, sustenance, and sense of being loved seemed to come from them. His destiny seemed entwined totally and compatibly with his family, not just his immediate family, who loved and nurtured him, but also his lineage, as far back as could be known. No wonder he launched into genealogical research in 1977 with verve and dedication. Where a family comes from and the historical events that affect them help determine its character.

It was too late for Ben to gather much firsthand information on earlier generations because primary sources—grandparents and most great-aunts and great-uncles—were already gone. Nevertheless, he enjoyed conducting research, and he anticipated that researching his lineage would make him a better history professor, for he could draw upon personal family events in relating the British background to American history, the American Revolution, the taming of the frontier, race relations and the slavery issue, the Civil War, Reconstruction, Native American history, the westward movement, and the growth of industry within the economic and religious and social fabric of the nation.

Although Ben's adopted children and their offspring would not share the DNA genetics of his family, they would benefit from his research—their adoption placed them in the center of his heritage. Biological connections were overblown, anyway, for individuals descend from innumerable ancestors. Each person has two parents, four grandparents, eight great-grandparents. If one calculates twenty generations of ancestors, even considering the occasional mating of cousins, the mathematics is staggering: twenty generations of life provide one with over one million direct ancestors!

In a broader family, all people on earth are cousins, variously removed.

PART I

Roots Out of Dry Ground

Frontier Hopscotch

B en's 1977 research of his family history found his mother's ancestors embedded deeply in the heritage of the American frontier,
the Old South, Indian history, and Protestant fundamentalism. His
maternal great-grandfather, John Jay Dalkens, was born in Western
Tennessee in 1838 into an extended family of pioneer farmers who
moved onto public lands hoping to acquire the means to file claim to
the land after it was surveyed and made legally available. They built
cabins, dug wells, hunted and fished, trapped fur animals, cleared
fields, had babies, raised grain and corn for fodder, and perhaps cultivated small cotton patches for income. Unable to buy the homesteads they had squatted upon when the land became legally open,
they cursed the system, packed up, moved on, and repeated the process along the edge of the next frontier.

Growing up on a frontier farm where most of the family's needs
were met by their own craftsmanship, with hunting and farming
skills, John Dalkens was conditioned to a subsistence agrarian life.
When he was twenty years old, his father died and his widowed
mother moved her family to Jackson Parish, Louisiana, to be near
relatives. There John soon became acquainted with a beautiful young
schoolteacher, Lydia Godby, whom he married after a short courtship. Their first child, Thomas, was born in 1861.

There were few slaves in their community. The Dalkens family
owned none. Nevertheless, John Dalkens and three of his brothers

joined the Confederate Army's Twenty-Eighth Louisiana Regiment in 1862 to defend Louisiana from a threatened Union invasion. Following the fall of New Orleans to the Union Navy in 1862, their regiment was sent to Vicksburg, Mississippi, to defend the Confederacy's last stronghold on the Mississippi River.

Private John Dalkens received a leg wound at Vicksburg in 1863, an injury that was treated successfully and primitively with maggots to stop gangrene from destroying his leg. In order to escape capture at the Fall of Vicksburg, Dalkens and his brothers floated across the river at night, holding on to a log. They furloughed themselves to go home for a visit with their families, then rejoined a Confederate force at Mansfield, Louisiana, which in 1864 stopped the Union forces of General Nathaniel Banks from invading Texas. Their kid brother, Andrew Jackson Dalkens, aged fifteen, followed them to Mansfield and was mustered into the Confederate forces as a drummer boy.

John Dalkens and his brothers were discharged from the Confederate Army on June 14, 1865, when his unit learned that the war had ended. He returned from the war much older than his years, having witnessed and participated in the random waste of human life. Quickly he and Lydia resumed their young married life. He farmed near their relatives while she taught school. Boy-girl twins, Robert and Izora, were born to them in 1866. A black neighbor woman with a nursing infant babysat the Dalkens babies while Lydia taught school, and wet-nursed the twins along with her own.

Like clockwork, John and Lydia had a new baby every other year. Lydia's lactation was their birth control; weaning a child was almost always followed by getting pregnant again. Their fourth child, a son, Mitchell, was born in 1868, followed by another boy, Joseph, in 1871, and a daughter, Leticia, in 1874.

Like their Scotch Irish ancestors who immigrated to the Carolinas in the late 1700s, with strong backs and restless blood, John Jay Dalkens and his relatives followed the frontier into Texas in 1870, leaving Louisiana at a time when that state was experiencing a harsh federal Reconstruction program characterized by political graft and high taxes. They settled near Paris, one of the early towns to develop in Northeast Texas.

In June 1875, the last Plains Indian raiding party—a large band of Quahadi Comanches led by Quanah Parker—surrendered to federal troops and relocated onto the Fort Sill US Military Reservation in Southwestern Indian Territory. With the threat of Indian raids gone, within the next two years, the western line of the Texas farming frontier swept southwestward, encompassing Palo Pinto County and Erath County, Texas. In May 1876, John Dalkens and two of his married brothers moved their growing families to Southwestern Erath County, where they remained for a decade.

Erath County in the 1870s and 1880s was populated by small farmers who owned 50 to 160 acres, large cattle ranches that spanned several sections, and farm tenants who rented small farms from absentee landlords through a sharecropping system. Following the Civil War, which bankrupted the entire South, the ownership of land fell largely into the hands of absentee landlords, carpetbaggers from the North, bankers, and speculators. To put the land into production and to provide a place to live for countless displaced farm families and former slaves, sharecropping allowed landless subsistence farmers to occupy and cultivate a small farm, to get credit from the landowner or local banker to buy seeds and implements, to raise cotton or another cash crop. When the harvest was sold, the lender got the loan repaid with interest, and the landowner got a third or a fourth of the proceeds, depending on the crop. Finally, the farmer would get his share, if anything remained from the sale of the crop.

Often, because of bad weather conditions, poor farming practices, or lack of implements, the crop might not even pay the interest on the loan. Sharecroppers tended to work hard, optimistically put in a cash crop of cotton or corn, produce garden vegetables, milk, eggs, and pork for their own use, but fail to make a profit. After a year or two of struggling, they would then vacate their leases and move on to repeat the process in another community.

Close-knit extended families followed the sharecropping pattern for several generations. An elderly farmer and his married children with their families sought new sharecrop farms as close to one another as possible, because living near one another was their social security, their harvesttime labor pool, their insurance that someone helpful who cared about them in a crisis would always be nearby.

John Dalkens was one of those subsistence sharecroppers who farmed as much land as he and his children could operate, putting in a cotton crop, raising grain and fodder for a small herd of milk cows and draft animals. A staple diet for the Dalkens family included salt pork, corn bread, beans and potatoes, yams, molasses, fresh eggs, fish and wild game, milk, cheese, and strong black Louisiana coffee. Surplus foods harvested from garden crops were dried and stored.

The Dalkens family grew in Erath County, but they did not prosper. Their baby daughter Leticia died in the winter of 1875, then her place was taken by another daughter, Adesta, born in the spring of 1876. In 1879, their fifth son, James Nelson Dalkens (Benjamin Bird's maternal grandfather) was born. In 1881, another daughter, Jane, arrived, and in late 1882, Lydia delivered her tenth and last baby, a new daughter, Penny. There was a span of twenty-one years between the birth of their first child and their last child, not an unusual occurrence in those years because of the lack of birth control, and not an altogether unwelcome situation because of the great need for farm labor. It was an especially hard life for women. They tended to age rapidly and die young.

In 1887, following disastrous droughts and bitterly cold winters, John Dalkens moved his family near Lydia's relatives in Southwestern Louisiana. Lydia's health was failing, and John wanted her to enjoy a more moderate climate. The family Bible recorded her date of death, February 24, 1889, at the age of forty-nine. She was survived by nine children—five of them still living at home with their bereaved father, who outlived her thirty years.

Ten-year-old James Nelson Dalkens, Lydia's youngest son, held poignant memories of her throughout his life, remembering a compassionate, beautiful, industrious, intelligent, and devout mother who loved her children dearly.

*   *   *

In those years, a widower with children at home soon would seek a new mother for them and a new mate for himself. And so it was in the winter of 1889 when John Jay Dalkens, who was working as a peddler selling dry goods house to house until spring planting time arrived, called upon the Southwestern Louisiana farm home of Eliza Brown, a thirty-five-year-old widow with four children. Eliza's needs were many, her funds few. Although she was unable to buy any goods from John Dalkens, he visited with her for over an hour. A series of visits followed, each lasting about five hours, and made the Brown children realize Mr. Dalkens was "sparkin' and lookin' for a home."

In the spring of 1890, John Dalkens married Eliza Brown, moved his five remaining children in with her four, into her double log cabin, which had two rooms sixteen feet square, separated by a wide enclosed hallway, and a side room added on, which served as a kitchen. A long porch spanned the entire front of the house.

The intermingling of relationships was haphazard, hectic, but happy. The more kids, the merrier! All the boys slept on cots, pallets, or hammocks on the porch, except in cold weather, when they bedded down in the hall. The eldest Dalkens daughter, Adesta, fourteen, bore many of the housework responsibilities. Eliza's eight-year-old daughter, Hannah, was sandwiched between nine- and eight-year-old Dalkens sisters, Jane and Penny. Joseph Dalkens, eighteen, and Buford Brown, fourteen, could do a man's work in the fields. Eliza's six-year-old son, Lucas, and four-year-old son, Hubert, were constantly underfoot, pampered, loved, and teased.

At the age of eleven, Ben's grandfather, James Dalkens, was a happy-go-lucky family humorist and trickster who fit cohesively in the center of the children. He was born with a happy disposition, which he displayed his entire life. He loved his stepmother and his siblings, including the Brown children. His wit and good humor smoothed over many trying moments and turned a household of potential turmoil into a congenial family, despite the tendency for his practical jokes to get out of hand. One of his favorite tricks was to lock his sisters in the family's outhouse when they went to relieve themselves just before bedtime, or chase them yelling in the darkness as they ran laughing and screaming back to the cabin. James liked to hunt and fish, and his success brought many a good dinner of wild game to the table. When he got old enough to earn wages, James brought home dolls and toys for the youngsters and a sack of hard candy for the entire family.

Typical for that time and that region, John Dalkens raised cotton as a cash crop and corn as a food crop for the family and for the farm stock. With help from the children, Eliza tended to chickens and a vegetable garden and preserved food by the drying method. In 1891, Eliza gave birth to a son, Luger; in 1893, another son, Harold; and in 1895, a girl, Callie, the last of seventeen children overall. John Dalkens was fifty-seven and Eliza was forty-two when Callie was born. The Dalkens-Brown family truly became blood related, for each individual was now blood related to half-siblings who were blood related to them all.

*   *   *

In 1894, following the collapse of farm prices and other unsettling conditions related to the economic Panic of 1893, the family lost Eliza's Louisiana farm to foreclosure and moved via train to Hardin County, Texas, near Beaumont. John Dalkens and his son Joseph worked as lumberjacks in the southern pine forest. The younger children went to school when they could, and the family went to church when they could. Eliza was a devout Methodist; consequently, most of the family's descendants followed that persuasion. The Dalkens-Brown family had a reputation for always providing lodging, meals, and meeting places for Methodist circuit preachers.

The great hurricane that devastated Galveston in 1900, killing thousands, severely damaged the Dalkens-Brown home, fifty miles inland. Instead of rebuilding, John Dalkens decided to move his family north to Erath County, Texas, where the four eldest Dalkens children, Thomas, Robert, Izora, and Mitchell, had married, started families, and rented farms. Adesta, who had married a Louisiana man, stayed behind.

Gradually the extended Dalkens-Brown children grew up and dispersed across North Texas and Western Indian Territory, following opportunities, crop failures, and marriages. John and Eliza Dalkens brought their extended family together at Thanksgiving each year, establishing the practice of an annual reunion, an event that continued into the fifth and sixth generations. It was at the 1900 Thanksgiving reunion that James Dalkens, a restless twenty-one-year-old bachelor, went home with his older brother Robert to live and farm with him. James and Robert were very close and shared many characteristics and interests. Robert had filed on a 160-acre homestead in the Denim community in Day County, in Oklahoma Territory, on a quarter section located near the south bank of the Canadian River just a few miles from the Texas Panhandle. James helped Robert move his family and possessions to Oklahoma in two covered wagons.

Day County had been organized in 1892 as a result of a land run opening the Cheyenne and Arapaho Reservation to white settlement. After each member of the Cheyenne and the Arapahoe tribes had been granted personal ownership of 160 acres, the remaining surveyed sections were made available for homesteading. At high noon on April 19, 1892, soldiers fired their guns into the air, which was a signal for prospective settlers to rush in on horseback, in covered wagons, or on foot to place their individual stake with their marker on it on a desirable, unclaimed 160-acre tract. The homesteader would then need to secure a corner stake that surveyors had placed with the section number on it. After living on the land for five years and making improvements, the settler could "prove up" his claim and the deed would be granted. This was the third of five land runs into Oklahoma Territory.

In the eastern part of the Cheyenne and Arapaho Reservation, the quarter sections were quickly taken up by the initial land rush, but in the western sections near the Texas Panhandle, settlement went slowly, partly caused by the general knowledge of the dire experiences of settlers failing on similar lands in dry Western Kansas. Another significant factor slowing development in the greater part of the sections in Western Day County north of the Canadian River was that cattlemen from the Texas Panhandle and from No Man's Land (Oklahoma's future Panhandle) grazed the open range, using a territorial free-range herd law that would remain in effect until county settlers voted to end it. The cattlemen tended to ride roughshod over the settlers, tearing down fences, their herds eating up the crops, the cowmen fighting homesteaders and one another over grazing sites and water holes. In 1896, the Day County Courthouse was burned to the ground, destroying all records and thwarting a countywide election to end free grazing. In 1902, a posse of cattlemen lynched a farmer they suspected of poisoning water holes where many cattle had died.

By selecting his homestead on the more settled south side of the Canadian River, Robert Dalkens avoided the turmoil. He also was fortunate that a destructive tornado that lashed across Day County on May 28, 1903, missed his farm.

Adept at carpentry, James lived with Robert's family off and on for several years and helped Robert build a six-room two-story house for his wife and six children. They built barns, fenced the homestead pasture to hold a growing herd of cattle, and broke the sod for fields of corn, cotton, oats, and sorghum. Although as a single man James could have filed on a 160-acre quarter section near his brother's, he was too much a potential young lothario at that time to commit himself to settling down. His tall handsome physique, ready smile, wit, shock of wild brown hair, and love for fun opened many doors of access to single young ladies in the territory. He owned a guitar but could not play it well. The instrument was a ruse that he used to get someone else to provide the music for him while he danced with young ladies. He played the field, but his respect for the memory of his mother and his respect for his stepmother, Eliza, and his sisters kept him from actually breaking hearts.

Enjoying carpentry and developing a reputation for being good at it, James found construction work throughout Western Oklahoma Territory. He made friends easily wherever he went and helped one homesteader after another build a modest frame house, fences, perhaps a milk shed, a chicken house, outhouse, windmill tower, and storm cellar. By 1905, he was located in nearby Roger Mills County, building houses in and around Cheyenne, the county seat, and in Strong City, a new railroad town on the Washita River.

One summer day in 1906, James was sitting on a bench, munching on an apple while getting his horse shod at the Strong City Blacksmith Shop. He noticed a raven-haired teenage lass, pleasant face, high cheekbones, tiny feet, narrow ankles, barely sixteen, walking past. Something clicked. James's mouth watered, as though he were tasting tart, sweet wild strawberries. Their eyes locked, and both smiled simultaneously. James stood up and bowed.

"My, my, I've not seen you before! What's your name?"

"My name is Maudeen Swanfeather," she said with a blush. She had never seen such a dashing man. Her caution was swept away.

"I can't believe your boyfriend would let you come to town without him," James said.

"I don't have a boyfriend," she replied.

James bowed again and said, "Well, you do now! I am applying for that position!"

She laughed and took a half-step back. "You'd better be careful. Papa and Mama are in the general store, getting groceries. Papa is one-half Choctaw. If you try anything funny, he will run you off with his Bowie knife!"

"He'll have to catch me first. I'll dart and I'll bob and I'll run circles around him. There's one thing for sure, I'm never going to let you out of my sight!"

And he did not. After introducing himself to Maudeen's parents, Jenks and Theda Swanfeather, James Dalkens followed them home, five miles southeast of Strong City, openly professing that he needed to know where they lived because he intended to court Maudeen and win her for his wife. Mr. and Mrs. Swanfeather sat sternly in their wagon, staring straight ahead, contemplating the inevitable.

James and Maudeen sat in the back of the wagon, leading his horse by its reins and getting acquainted as fast as possible. He told her about his family, his childhood in Texas and Louisiana, his upbeat approach to life and his hunting skills, and his suddenly acquired desire to get married and have a farm of his own. She explained her family's Choctaw background. Her grandfather Swanfeather was a full-blooded "blanket Indian" fully engaged in Choctaw culture, but Maudeen and her three sisters, one-fourth Indian, did not wish to identify with their tribe. Their mother was an Anglo woman, and their paternal grandmother was Anglo. The Swanfeather sisters had gone to white schools, attended Methodist churches, and grew up with more white friends than Indian friends.

Their courtship lasted three weeks. Maudeen's parents did not like the fact that James was twenty-seven and she was barely sixteen. Nevertheless, their age gap was not all that unusual in those years, and he did fill out his clothes well, was pleasant, courteous, with a sense of humor, and was a hard worker, a good carpenter always with a modest sum of money in his pocket, and of good health. The Swanfeathers also had three other daughters at home old enough to marry.

On September 21, 1906, James arrived at the Swanfeather farm with a dozen Dalkens relatives, a Methodist Circuit preacher, an Oklahoma Territory marriage license, and an extra horse for his bride to ride. They got married in the Swanfeathers' backyard under the spreading branches of an old elm tree. During the ceremony, a horsefly landed on Maudeen's leg and drew blood, but she did not flinch. Her adult life was beginning. The wedding dinner consisted of three broiled roosters, corn bread and gravy, apple cobbler, and elderberry wine. Robert Dalkens played James's guitar as the wedding party danced a few rounds. Maudeen opened a basket of wedding gifts. The shivaree lasted three hours.

Toward evening, James and his bride rode off to the Washita River bottom, found a sheltered clearing in a persimmon thicket, spread a blanket on the ground, and began a lifelong honeymoon.

CHAPTER 2

James Begot and Begot

Through the fall and winter of 1906–1907, James made a living for his bride as a carpenter, building barns, houses, granaries, and corrals for homesteaders along the Western Oklahoma border. He and Maudeen set up housekeeping in a one-room sod house someone had built on an abandoned homestead near Strong City. James tried to file on the abandoned land, but the deed records were too entangled to provide a clear legal title. In 1907, concurrent with Oklahoma joining the Union as the forty-sixth state, Maudeen's father "proved up" the Swanfeather homestead. That is, Jenks Swanfeather received a legal transfer of deed to the 160 acres his family had subsisted on for five years. Weary of coping with the windstorms and droughts of Western Oklahoma, the Swanfeather family moved back near their Choctaw relatives in Southeastern Oklahoma and rented their farm to their son-in-law in time for James to raise a crop in 1908.

James and Maudeen settled into their new home just a few months after their first child, a hyperactive, rowdy son, Dexter Vernon Dalkens, was born, in August 1907. In January 1909, a daughter, Grace Elaine (Benjamin Bird's mother) arrived, and in September 1910, Maudeen gave birth to Russell, their second son. A third son, Wally, arrived in 1912. In 1914, Maudeen suffered a miscarriage when the coupling pole on their wagon broke and a load of firewood fell down on her. In addition to the miscarriage, the accident fractured her right collarbone.

During Maudeen's slow recuperation, five-year-old Grace dutifully tended to her mother's needs, and being the only daughter among a trio of brothers, and precocious, she tackled much of the housekeeping and cooking. Thereafter, the entire family—brothers and parents alike—came to rely on Grace to the point that her own needs and interests often were sacrificed for their sake. Willingly she assumed the role of responding to the needs of others and dreamed of one day becoming a nurse in a spotless white uniform. She was eager to go to school, and in September 1914, her parents enrolled her a year early after Dexter failed first grade because he would not pay attention to his teacher. They thought having Grace sit beside him at their desks would help him concentrate.

Dexter and Grace attended one-room Square Top School, about two miles from their home. Usually they rode old Bob, a one-eyed donkey, to school. Often becoming weary of being tied to the hitching post all day, old Bob learned to rub his halter off and return home without them, leaving them to walk all the way home.

Growing up with three boisterous brothers, Grace became a tomboy. She could climb a tree or throw a baseball as well as anyone. Russell, eighteen months younger, was an intense, athletic child, serious-minded, tall, thin, and handsome as a Greek statue. Wally, two years younger than Russell, was a chubby little cowboy with a thick Choctaw torso, always playing jokes on people as he rode about the place on a wild stick horse. One day, during the 1915 school term, he slipped away from home and rode his stick horse all the way to the schoolhouse and knocked on the school door, but the teacher concluded that the knocking sound was old Bob, the contrary one-eyed donkey rubbing against the building, which he often did. Unable to turn the knob, Wally turned his stick horse around and scampered home.

Dexter, a tall wiry lad with penetrating gray eyes, had a natural touch in handling horses and dogs but could not get along well with others. He was hyperactive, daring, reckless to the point of fearlessness, with a streak of cruelty. Often, when he became cross at someone over issues, real or imagined, he would go to the family outhouse and urinate all over the toilet seat. He loved to antagonize his siblings and did not care if he made them cry. Grace became a buffer between Dexter and her little brothers, often outwitting Dexter, deflecting them from threatening situations, showing the youngsters how to avoid him whenever possible, which fortunately was often, for Dexter was a loner. Dexter liked to wander about the countryside and often stayed gone for hours. He loved to hunt and fish and became adept at tracking, snaring, and killing small animals with a slingshot.

One day in the spring of 1916, nine-year-old Dexter jumped down into an old abandoned cistern half-filled with debris and could not climb out. His father, James, was on a two-day trip to acquire cottonseed for planting, which left Maudeen to pull her son out of the well with a rope. The strenuous exertion caused her lungs to hemorrhage. The family doctor tentatively diagnosed her with tuberculosis and advised James to travel with her and keep her out in the open air, away from the smoke of their wood cookstove, until her health improved. So James outfitted a covered wagon with chuck box, water barrel, and bedding, loaded the family into the wagon, and set out for the cool, dry climate of Southeastern Colorado.

The rain-swollen Canadian River held them up for two days until it could be crossed, then James drove his wagon team northwestward across the Texas and Oklahoma Panhandles into Southwestern Kansas. Hardly seven, Grace helped her father with cooking on the campfire and washing clothes in an iron pot of scalding water so that Maudeen would not need to breathe the campfire smoke into her fragile lungs. Despite the drudgery, Grace considered the wagon trip a great adventure. They made camp each day near sunset, the western skies often displaying spectacular colors as the sun descended below the horizon. They sat around the campfire at night, surrounded by the darkness, listening to screech owls and crickets and coyotes howling, and catching fireflies. They slept out on the wide-open prairie.

Each morning James arose before daybreak, stoked the fire, and brewed a pot of strong black coffee. When the coffee was ready, James poured a cup, took a sip, and started the day with a rousing "AmPolly!" His "AmPolly!" was the family alarm clock, and a code word that meant "Thank you, Lord, for the opportunities of the day. Let's all get up and make the best of it!"

The wagon drive sometimes covered more than ten miles a day, sending them past active prairie dog towns and forty-year-old buffalo wallows, small farmsteads, and large cattle operations. Russell and Wally picked up stray dogs along the way then lost track of them just as quickly as they appeared. The landscape was always changing. The family ate staples, such as fried potatoes and flour gravy, corn bread or biscuits baked in a dutch oven, red beans and rice, salt pork, and wild game that Dexter shot with their Winchester, which his father now allowed him to carry. They stayed for several weeks at Ford, Kansas, while James hauled grain during wheat harvest. By August they had traveled into Southeastern Colorado, past fields of sugar beets, alfalfa, and clover, and through undeveloped lands set aside for later development. They marveled at herds of wild mustangs roaming freely across the canyons and foothills. Dexter hoped to rope one and tame it but never came close. Snowcapped Pikes Peak rose majestically in the distance.

By September 1916, Maudeen's lungs had cleared and her health returned to her. The hardships of the journey had been worthwhile. James had earned enough wages in the harvest to buy a fresh team of horses that would pull their covered wagon back to Oklahoma in time for the children to enroll in school. The Swanfeather farm had been rented out in their absence, so James took his family to the Roosevelt community southeast of Hobart, in Kiowa County, Southwestern Oklahoma, where several of James's siblings and cousins had settled. His eldest brother, Thomas, then aged fifty-five and father of five, owned the Roosevelt Blacksmith Shop and the Roosevelt Hotel. Joseph Dalkens, aged forty-five, father of six sons, lived on a rented farm northwest of town. The town of Roosevelt was named after President Theodore Roosevelt, who had visited the area on one of his famous wolf-hunting expeditions.

James rented a farm one mile from Consolidated School Number 8, a four-room rural school, where all four of their children attended. Their first abode was a two-room frame house with an adjoining tent that served as the boys' room. James and Maudeen picked cotton to pay for school clothes and winter coats and boots for everyone. Waiting for spring to plant a cotton crop, James worked at carpentry and drove a canvas-topped school wagon (his regular wagon), on which students sat on two wooden benches running lengthwise. The sides were equipped with canvas covers that stayed rolled up in good weather.

James and Maudeen prospered at Roosevelt. The advent of World War I in 1917 meant high cotton prices for the duration. In 1918, with the boys old enough to do some of the fieldwork, they rented an additional farm nearby and moved their family into a large five-room house, which, for the first time in her life, provided Grace her own room. In 1919, after selling a good cotton harvest, James bought the family's first automobile, a special-model Ford touring car. James had hauled a bale of cotton to the gin that day; while he drove the empty wagon home, the salesman showed Maudeen how to drive the car and she drove it home alone. When she arrived, the chickens scattered and the dogs barked while she drove the Ford around in circles in the front yard until she figured out how to bring it to a stop. With a shiny, new black car in their front yard, James and Maudeen felt like millionaires.

The children were given a special ride out on the unpaved county road, and they bounced up and down, giggling in the back seat, as if it were a kiddie car ride in an amusement park.

Owning a car enhanced the family's social standing in those times, bringing prestige to Maudeen that she thoroughly enjoyed. With her strong, clear soprano voice, she was chosen to be lead soprano in the choir at Roosevelt Methodist Church. As an adolescent, she had learned to read shape notes at a three-day singing school. She was discovered to have perfect pitch, and having learned to play the piano by ear (no lessons), she often played the church's piano during Sunday services. Maudeen acquired an upright old piano at an estate sale in Hobart when Grace was ten years old, and soon Grace also was playing by ear, picking out many favorite ballads and most of the church hymns Grace had learned in church services.

In 1919, Maudeen also became president of the local Ladies' Helping Hands Club, a benevolent service to many ill and needy people, especially during the infamous influenza outbreak in 1919, when several souls in the community died in the epidemic.

John Jay Dalkens, the family patriarch, was among the victims that died in the influenza pandemic that swept the world at the end of World War I. John Dalkens's funeral and burial in Erath County, Texas, was the saddest reunion the Dalkens family had ever experienced. Other members of the extended family to die in the epidemic were Lucas Brown's ten-year-old daughter and Ethan Garfield, husband of Penny Dalkens, who became a widow at the age of thirty-seven. Thomas Dalkens brought Penny and her three children to Roosevelt and provided a home for them in his Roosevelt Hotel. There Penny eked out a living for her children as a saleslady next door in Jabour's Grocery and General Store.

In 1919, all of James's and Maudeen's children were inflicted with the influenza virus, but the youngster, Wally, was the only member of James Dalkens's immediate family whose life was endangered by the flu and the pneumonia that accompanied it. Wally was desperately ill for almost a month. Maudeen and Grace nursed him around the clock with poultices and prayers and rubbing lineament. In a rare moment of sympathy, Dexter carved his invalid brother a new stick horse and painted it with brown shoe polish. Grace leaned it against the wall beside the sickbed. While recuperating, Wally had visions of galloping across the prairie as soon as he was allowed to get out of bed.

With their father, John Dalkens, deceased, James and his brothers Thomas, Joseph, and Robert, all living in Southwestern Oklahoma, decided to hold the family clan together by conducting an annual family reunion the first weekend in June each year, beginning in 1920, after the school term ended and crops were planted. They selected a camping and picnic area at Camp Doris, about twenty miles east of Roosevelt, near the site of Lake Quanah Parker, in the Wichita Mountains Wildlife Refuge, a sixty-thousand-acre federal preserve that had been set aside by the McKinley administration in 1901. It was adjacent to Fort Sill US Military Reservation, a ninety-five-thousand-acre artillery training center, first established in 1869 by General Philip H. Sheridan as a cavalry post, an important base of operations in the military campaigns against the Plains Indians. Quanah Parker and his Quahadi Comanches surrendered there in

1875, and the Chiricahua Apache warrior Geronimo was brought there in 1894 and kept as a prisoner of war.

The Wichita Mountains contained many attractions that assured the promoters of the annual Dalkens reunion a good turn-out—camping, swimming, fishing, boating, mountain scenery, buffalo herds and other wildlife, and entertainment attractions at nearby Medicine Park, a resort community.

James, now forty-one, brother Joseph, forty-nine, arrived with their wives, Joseph's six sons, and James's four children, on the first Friday in June 1920 to reserve a camping area for the Dalkens clan, bringing iron kettles and wrought iron skillets, cans of lard, and three one-gallon cans of ground coffee. While Dexter, Russell, Wally, and Joseph's six sons laid out a baseball field and played "workup" until dark, Grace helped her parents scrub picnic tables, serve a supper of corn bread, salt pork, and beans, and prepare pallets for sleeping.

Next day, relatives arrived from all directions: From Roosevelt, Thomas brought his wife and four children, chairs, cots, tin plates, and cups from the storage room of his Roosevelt Hotel. At the age of fifty-nine, Thomas was to be the reunion's president, that designation going to the eldest male in the extended family. Accompanying Thomas's family was his widowed sister, Penny Dalkens Garfield, and her three children. Robert, aged fifty-four, came from Denim with his wife, six children, one grandchild, and a crate of live frying chickens that were to be the reunion's main course for Saturday evening meal and Sunday dinner. There was not a Dalkens woman, including eleven-year-old Grace, who—given a bucket of scalding water—could not wring a chicken's neck, scald and pick its feathers, gut and cut it up, and slap it battered into a frying pan in less than fifteen minutes.

Robert's twin sister, Izora Dalkens Tompkins, and her husband, Leslie Tompkins, a Durant, Oklahoma, attorney and newspaper publisher, brought four children and two grandchildren and a box camera with tripod for a group photograph of all those in attendance. Accompanying Izora was her stepsister, Hannah Brown Pierce, thirty-eight, whose husband farmed near Durant. Hannah brought the three youngest of her eight children, the five eldest staying home with their father to chop cotton. Mitchell, aged fifty-two, a ranch foreman from Erath County, Texas, brought his spouse, four children, and one grandchild and a huge chuck wagon keg of drinking water. Buford Brown, forty-four, who worked at an icehouse in Vernon, Texas, came with wife and son and a two-hundred-pound block of ice wrapped in a quilt, to keep the food fresh and the tea chilled.

Sister Jane Dalkens Oats, thirty-nine, and her husband, Sam Oats, a bricklayer from Gordon, Texas, brought their two daughters, five cakes (three chocolate, two angel food), and five apple pies, to be served with the clan's frequent coffee breaks. Having grown up mostly in Louisiana, the Dalkens family liked their coffee strong, black, and often.

Eliza Dalkens, widowed matriarch of the family, came with her son, Buford Brown, with whom she lived. Lucas, thirty-six, a Vernon, Texas, carpenter, and his wife brought their three surviving children. Lucas brought a trailer loaded with bedding and chairs, including Eliza's rocker, and firewood for the campfire. Eliza's son, Luger Dalkens, twenty-nine, brought his wife and four children from his acreage outside Oklahoma City, where he worked in Armour's meatpacking plant at the city's stockyards. Luger's family, who operated a roadside vegetable stand supplied by their large truck garden, brought baskets of ripe tomatoes, cucumbers, squash, and other vegetables for the reunion meals.

Unfortunately, the family circle was not complete. Hubert Brown, thirty-four, in the US Navy since 1907, was on active duty as a dry dock officer at San Diego, California. During World War I, Hubert had served in convoy duty in the North Atlantic, in the transport of US Expeditionary Forces to France. During the reunion weekend, Harold Dalkens, twenty-seven, a bricklayer working for a construction company in Oklahoma City, was in charge of a project to pour concrete for a large commercial building foundation. None of the four children of sibling Adesta Dalkens Campbell, who, in 1904, had died of complications with measles while pregnant, could be notified of the reunion, for after she died, their father turned them over to his relatives or to foster care, which resulted in their permanent loss of contact with the Dalkens family.

Nor was Callie Dalkens, twenty-five, the youngest sibling of the family, notified about the reunion, because no one in the family, including her mother, Eliza, knew where she was. Like many "babies" of the family, Callie could not wait to grow up. In 1909, at the age of fourteen, she married Jonah Rodgers, a nineteen-year-old friend of her brother Harold. Their marriage lasted just long enough for them to have two sons. Jonah kept the sons and soon remarried, while Callie moved away with new acquaintances. Her family lost touch with her for several years.

The 1920 Dalkens reunion established a pattern that was followed unbroken for the next ninety years. The eldest male served as president, made the arrangements, sent out the annual notices, and recruited individuals to bring certain items for the occasion. During the final meal of the reunion, they passed a hat for contributions to cover incidental expenses, such as postage for the president. Each family was responsible for bringing its own bedding. Usually, the first woman to arrive assumed the authority to set up preparations for the meals. In 1920, it was Maudeen; pleasantly and efficiently she took charge of preparing the Saturday evening meal.

"Robert, pull six fryers out of the crate. We are ready to scald them and cut them up."

"James, we are ready for you to brew a big pot of coffee."

"Jane, cut two of your cakes and two of your pies and set them on the picnic table next to the coffeepot, for dessert."

"Joseph, bring that pan of sliced potatoes over here to the fire. Penny and I are ready to get them fried."

"Hannah, lift the lid off that old black dutch oven to see if the corn bread is getting brown. Yes, my, my, that looks good!"

"Mama Eliza, watch those girls fill the tea pitcher. Don't let them make it too sweet."

"Izora, can you take that skillet that's got the fried chicken drippings in it and stir up a big skillet of flour gravy? There are folks here who have never sat down to a meal that did not have gravy."

"Luger, will you and your lovely wife slice up a big plate of tomatoes and cucumbers?"

"Buford, unwrap that big block of ice and bring us a jar of cold butter for the corn bread and the roasting ears."

The hardest part of preparing the meal was getting all the children to come in from playing long enough to wash up and settle down to fill their plates. The adolescent boys had broken in the baseball field, the grass in the base paths worn down to the ground. The girl cousins flitted from one activity to the next—hopscotching, ringing around the rosy, gossiping, hiding and seeking with the younger kids, playing school, polishing fingernails, styling hair, and watching the boys.

After cleaning up the pots and pans from supper, and as darkness crept in, the entire clan gathered around a bonfire and the oldsters took turns telling stories about the "good old days." Camping out under the stars reminded them of their childhood, when every two or three years John Dalkens moved his family with team and wagon in an overnight adventure from their old farmstead to new places to live. James's family recalled their wagon trip to Colorado in 1916. Dexter bragged that he had kept the family fed on wild game he took down with his old Winchester, and did anyone want him to go out early in the morning and take down a buffalo?

Thomas, who had taken singing lessons as a young man and had taught singing classes at the Roosevelt Methodist Church, capped off the evening by leading the family in several old favorites: "Home, Home on the Range," "God Bless America," "Oh, Suzanna," and "Shenandoah," then they turned to familiar hymns. "The Old Rugged Cross," "Amazing Grace," "In the Garden," "When We All Get to Heaven," and "What a Friend We Have in Jesus."

As the fire died down, the ladies all went out together slightly past the edge of darkness to the camp's outhouse to relieve themselves; individually the men stepped away from the light to relieve themselves. Then the group began to break up and take to their improvised beds: cots lined up together under a post oak tree, pallets on picnic tables, pallets on trailer beds, pallets on car hoods, sleepers stretched out uncomfortably in car seats. The older folks tended to fall asleep quickly, the children too stirred up to get drowsy. Too much caffeine in ice tea and coffee. Whispers here and there throughout the night. "Shhh! Shhh!" The Dalkens reunion weekend would never be a good place to get a good night's rest. Everyone swore next year to bring tents and their own mattresses. Or get rich and stay in nearby Lawton in a swanky hotel.

Sunday morning activities began at the crack of dawn with "AmPolly! AmPolly! Coffee's ready!" from James, always an early riser. Wally, who had learned to render a shrill, earsplitting whistle with two fingers to the mouth, awakened the entire camp. Hungrily the menfolk got a fire going and the ladies fried several pounds of slab bacon, cracked four dozen eggs, scrambled them in a large skillet seasoned with bacon grease, while leftover gravy was heating in a pot and biscuits were rising in dutch ovens heated at the edge of the flames. The Dalkens clan always observed a hearty breakfast, except perhaps certain young women affected by morning sickness.

Following breakfast, activities resumed where they left off the previous evening, the boys playing ball, the girls flitting from one activity to another, the ladies cleaning up from breakfast, and the menfolk telling tales while imbibing in their second or third cup of Louisiana coffee. Eliza, the matriarch, insisted that the family gather at ten thirty for a Sunday morning "devotional" service to worship their Lord. Joseph, the most devout of the Dalkens men, volunteered to lead the service, no matter that he was the only sibling to leave the Methodist faith to become a deacon in Roosevelt's First Baptist Church. He took his text from the parable of the prodigal son, thinking that some of his less-faithful siblings and their children should be reminded of God's forgiveness and appreciate from whence their true strength did come. At the end of his presentation, Joseph asked for a minute of silent reverence in memory of their loved ones who had passed on, then asked Maudeen to sing *a cappella* a hymn sung at all Dalkens funerals. Her strong, clear soprano voice cut to the heart:

There's a land that is fair-er than day
And by faith we can see it a-far;
For the Fa-ther waits o-ver the way,

31

To pre-pare us a dwell-ing place there.
In the sweet (in the sweet),
By and by (by and by),
We shall meet on that beau-ti-ful shore;
In the sweet (in the sweet),
By and by (by and by),
We shall meet on that beau-ti-ful shore.

Maudeen knew all the stanzas and sang them all. Among the siblings there was hardly a dry eye. Grace observed the pained expression of grief in her uncles and aunts and felt it herself. How she loved them all!

The Sunday dinner was just as good, and nearly identical to the Saturday evening meal, with every last fryer eaten and every cake and pie devoured before the families began to pack up and leave in an effort to reach their homes before dark. Eliza reminded everyone, "See you next year, if not before! If anyone hears from our little Callie, or from any of Adesta's children, let us all know. And pray for them every day!"

*   *   *

The 1921 reunion was equally as successful as the 1920 gathering, with additional attendees: Harold Dalkens, the construction foreman from Oklahoma City, and Hubert Brown, the career Navy officer, who was on leave. But no one had heard from sister Callie, and no one had learned of the whereabouts of any of Adesta's children.

Following the 1921 Dalkens family reunion, Eliza Dalkens came to spend a month with James and his family. Her jolly nature fit well with her stepson's happy disposition. She wore stiffly starched and ironed white dresses, with two starched petticoats that rustled as she sat rocking, tatting, knitting, embroidering, dipping snuff, sipping coffee, or reading her Bible. Wally and Russell competed in providing her snuff brushes made from elm twigs. Dipping snuff was a common habit for older ladies in that day. Eliza had been granted a Confederate Veteran Widow's Pension by the state of Texas, under a law that stipulated that she must reside in Texas at least six months out of the year to continue to qualify for the pension. Her legal residence was with her son Buford Brown in Vernon, Texas. Her retirement years developed into a pattern. She would visit children and stepchildren in Oklahoma for about six months then would return to Vernon to preserve her pension rights. She offered her children moral support in time of trouble, helped with new babies, shared recipes, and gave homespun advice, advocating practical sense and fundamental, Methodist-flavored Christian principles. Grace adored her.

Eliza's 1921 visit with James and his family coincided with a weeklong Protestant tent revival in Roosevelt. It was a well-attended, community-wide event. The high prices for farm products that had accompanied the World War I era had given way to an economic collapse on many American farms. Europe, now at peace, could feed itself. With vast surpluses in most farm commodities, prices plummeted. With hard times on hand, many folks turned to God for answers. The Nazarene revival team was renowned for providing rousing singing, emotional shouting, expounding on Biblical prophecies, preaching repentance of sins, or facing hellfire damnation. Eliza insisted that James take her and the entire family to services every evening. Despite being Methodist, not Nazarene, the family was swept up in the revival spirit the entire week. Maudeen participated in the music, the strongest, clearest soprano voice in the crowd.

Approaching adolescence, "the age of accountability," Grace was especially affected by the religious fervor. With the onset of puberty, with her breasts developing and with pleasurable sexual stirrings and urges coursing through her body, she was confused: what could she freely enjoyably self-express and what should she totally repress? At the conclusion of the first evening's revival service, she asked her grandmother about something that she had been pondering over and over to herself.

"Grandma, if a person was hiding and was up to secretly doing something that might be wrong, would God know about it?"

"Grace, honey, God knows everything we do. He wants us to do right but loves us even when we do wrong. That's why He sent His son Jesus to tell us how to live. Jesus Christ died on the cross for all our sins, and we can be saved from condemnation if only we accept Him as our Savior, whether we are always strong enough to resist temptation or not."

In the emotional heat of the revival, and in the clarity and assurance in Grandma Eliza's testimony, Grace was convinced unequivocally that she needed to accept Jesus as her Savior. On the final evening of the revival, when the evangelist issued the call for sinners to come up front to the prayer bench and "surrender to Jesus," Grace was among the first to respond. From that moment, her personal life and the moral and spiritual environment she would create for her future children would reflect her Christian principles.

By the age of fourteen, Grace had repressed much of her tomboyish mannerisms and was separating herself from the sometimes-crass and rough behavior of her brothers. She was going to be a lady, and there were certain boundaries that could not be crossed. She took her school studies more seriously than ever, finishing first in her class in 1923, when she completed tenth grade, the highest grade offered by Consolidated School Number 8. For her junior school year, Grace arranged to live with the elderly mother of their landlord, in Altus, about twenty-five miles west from the Dalkens home, and perform housework and cooking in exchange for room and board so that she could attend Altus High School.

Before many weeks had passed, however, Grace's father came and took her home. Her mother, Maudeen, was expecting a premenopause baby and was not doing well; they needed Grace at home.

Once more, she postponed her goals in response to the needs of others.

*   *   *

Olivia Dulce Dalkens was born on April 20, 1924. For several weeks, Maudeen adjusted poorly to the new arrival, suffering from what in later years would be diagnosed as postpartum depression.

Olivia was a beautiful child, whom James named and spoiled from the beginning. It did not improve Maudeen's emotional attitude to learn that her new baby was named after one of James's old girlfriends. Wally, who had enjoyed the advantage of being the youngest child for twelve years, had a hard time making a place for his little sister in his heart. Caring for the infant fell largely to Grace. She had wished for a sister most of her life, but as a playmate, not as a dependent sibling. Dutifully Grace cooked many of the meals, rocked and burped and bathed baby Olivia, slept with her through the night, kept clean diapers on hand—in essence, she served as a little mother, a role that for her seemed natural. Russell recognized Grace's self-sacrificing and pitched in to help with household chores more than most fourteen-year-old lads would do. Subconsciously Grace harbored a resentment that her chance to finish school was thrown aside for the benefit of others, but she loved her family, and her sense of loyalty in doing what was best for the family superseded her repressed private ambition.

Only marriage would release Grace from her sense of total responsibility to her parents and siblings, a marriage in which she soon would dedicate herself to a husband and children of her own.

CHAPTER 3

Horse and Surrey Days

B en's paternal family history had a Southwestern agrarian pattern, similar to the Dalkens history, with variations. His great-grandfather, Douglas Mortimer Bird, was an 1846 South Carolina medical school graduate who signed up to serve with Zachery Taylor's forces at the Battle of Monterrey in the Mexican War on September 24, 1846. In 1847, during General Taylor's advance to Buena Vista, Mexico, Dr. Bird contracted a chronic intestinal fever and was discharged to go back to civilian life. He opened a clinic in New Orleans and, by 1860, had married Floy Calhoun, daughter of a Louisiana sugarcane planter. Floy's dowry included five slave field hands and a personal body servant who was her mulatto half-sister, Dilsey, sired by Floy's father. In the Antebellum South, it was an unspoken common assumption that slave owners would behave as though they were entitled to copulate with their slaves.

During the Civil War, when the Union Navy invaded New Orleans in 1862, Dr. Bird and his wife evacuated to frontier Hill County, Texas, where he settled permanently. He practiced medicine in Hillsboro, the county seat, and started a family. There they lost possession of their small group of slaves on June 19, 1865—Juneteenth—when Texas slaves learned that the Civil War was over and their bondage had come to an end.

Practicing medicine in rural, unreconstructed Texas in the 1860s and 1870s was not a lucrative endeavor for Dr. Bird. There was little money. For delivering a baby, the fee was a heifer calf. To set a broken leg, a smoked ham. For a bottle of tonic, a dozen eggs. Treating a gunshot wound usually brought no fee but carried the threat of being drawn into a local feud or becoming a material witness to a crime.

Ben's paternal grandfather, Aaron Walker Bird, the second child of Dr. Bird, was born in Hill County, Texas, in 1867, about four months before his half-brother, Boudrow Bird, a quadroon, was born to Dilsey, who had remained in the Bird household following Emancipation because she did not have anywhere else to go.

Aaron and Boudrow were inseparable playmates who did not question the nature of their relationship or the difference in their skin color and did not care. Dilsey was too pretty and ambitious to remain with her former master indefinitely. In 1871, she attracted a young black suitor who took her and her child to Chicago, forever connected to the Bird family in undetected DNA and in the 1870 US Census, which listed Aaron and Boudrow Bird as children of Dr. Douglas Mortimer Bird, not listed as twins, but nevertheless born in the same year. Floy Bird and her half-sister, Dilsey, kept in touch through annual Christmas cards. Boudrow Bird grew up to marry a quadroon woman, and he fathered several children who were dark-skinned and proud of it, and several children who were light-skinned and proud of it.

According to family tradition, Aaron Bird grew up as rowdy and reckless as Texas itself in the 1870s and 1880s. As an adolescent, he became an ace at playing marbles and would wager on games of "keeps," for pennies, nickels, and dimes, winner take all. When he was fourteen, he signed up as a drover on cattle drives that passed through Hill County on their way to the railroad stockyards in Fort Worth. Aaron promised his mother he would go no farther north than the railroad's holding pens at the southern edge of Fort Worth, a wild cow town where the trail drivers were drawn into brawls and unhealthy liaisons in the barrooms and brothels of Fort Worth's notorious Hell's Half Acre.

Aaron Bird kept his promise to his mother at fourteen and fifteen, but at sixteen, his commitment wavered, and for the next ten years, he strayed dangerously close to becoming a derelict. His demon was whiskey, and it haunted him for the rest of his life. He worked on North Central Texas ranches for a year or two at a time, until he got fired for being drunk on the job; then he would work at day jobs here and there until he got hired on full-time again, only to repeat the behavior.

Aaron's salvation came in his late twenties, when he met Clara Williams, a pious, openhearted woman who found something good in everyone. She was the daughter of a shopkeeper in Hillsboro. They met at a brush arbor revival meeting, where Aaron had been drawn to the music. Clara turned and noticed the drunken cowboy on the back bench swaying to the uplifting hymns. As the congregation sang, "Amazing Grace, how sweet the sound that saved a wretch like me!" she heard Aaron sob, half-aloud, "A wretch like me!" During the invitational moment, when the evangelist called for all sinners to come forward, Clara approached Aaron and told him "God wants me to lead you to Christ. Won't you come forward with me to the front bench and kneel with me while we pray for God to save your soul?"

Aaron was taken aback—why did this beautiful stranger care so much about his soul? Reeking of liquor, Aaron admitted that his life was on the wrong track and agreed to go forward, confess his sins, ask God for forgiveness, and accept the Lord Jesus Christ as his personal Savior.

When the service ended, Clara started to walk away. "Come back!" Aaron cried. "You are my angel, my guardian angel. Without you, I don't know what to do!"

Clara returned to him, took him to a nearby hotel, checked him in to a room, and ordered him a hot bath. By the time he had finished bathing, she returned with a new suit of clothes for him and a hot meal. He was truly converted, and Aaron's change was miraculous. He turned to the Holy Bible for succor and to Clara for a purposeful direction in life. In his new commitment, he married her and pledged to help her establish a Christian family and to stay close to God by reading the entire Old and New Testaments page by page at least once each year. The more he craved whiskey, the more pages he read. He stayed dry.

*　　*　　*

Around the turn of the twentieth century, Aaron and Clara Bird moved to Munday, Texas, near relatives, and ran a livery service. In 1904, they had Leona, a lovely, blue-eyed, black-haired daughter.

With his mule team and wagon, Aaron hauled freight and commodities between the train depot and local stores. He also hired himself out to local farmers to haul their wheat to the grain elevator and their cotton to the town gin. When there was nothing to haul, Aaron worked as a day laborer and field hand, picking cotton, chopping weeds, digging graves for the local undertaker, and building new barbed wire fences for local ranchers whose pastures had been open range a generation earlier.

In early 1906, Aaron Bird and Clara, who was pregnant, moved with their two-year-old daughter to the Ioland community in Day County, Western Oklahoma Territory, to file a homestead claim on one of the few marginal, 160-acre homesteads remaining unclaimed in the Cheyenne-Arapahoe Reservation. Ioland was on the north side of the Canadian River, about twenty miles northeast of the Strong City community, where, incidentally, James Dalkens and the Swanfeather families were then located. Aaron Bird selected a tract that had no surface water but was located about a mile away from the river, from which he could haul barrels of water for family use and for their animals. Using a double-blade ax, Aaron cut slices of big bluestem sod and stacked them in a row six feet high and twenty feet long for the front wall of their new home. The ten-foot sides and twenty-foot back wall of their one-room dwelling was cut into the embankment of a sandy knoll. Aaron took lumber from his wagon bed to frame rafters for the bluestem thatch roof and to construct a door. The half-dugout, which was located near a county road that paralleled the east side of their tract, became the family abode.

Their neighbor on the east side of Aaron's homestead, Riley Foster, had fenced off his quarter section, but the county roadbed separated their land. The neighbor north of him, who did not introduce himself, had no boundary fences, but he had fenced off a small pasture in a secluded part of his land to hold a herd of cattle he created by stealthily gathering unbranded strays from the large herds that still grazed on unfenced land in the area, twelve to twenty head at a time, which he drove east to market. The quarter sections south of Aaron and west of him abutted the Canadian River and were unclaimed, because mostly they contained dunes of sand blown up from the river's floodplain, fringed with stands of sagebrush, cockleburs, and salt cedar, providing no land suitable for farming or grazing. Aaron's 160-acre tract was completely unfenced. Almost daily, a large herd of Texas longhorn cattle traipsed and browsed across the western half of his land on their way to water at the north bank of the river.

In early April 1906, a few weeks after beginning to live in their ten-foot-by-twenty-foot half-dugout, Clara gave birth to a healthy, black-haired son, Daniel Jefferson Bird (Ben's father), without assistance. It was a difficult delivery under harsh conditions: boiled water from the river, dirt floors, no windows, a dank and dusty dwelling, temporarily livable for healthy, ambitious people, but a health crisis waiting to happen for young children and a frail woman subsisting on an unbalanced diet of flour biscuits, fresh wild greens from nearby weed patches, salt pork, beans, and gravy.

The infant Daniel nursed at his mother's breast and stayed healthy. Leona drank a glass of fresh milk each meal, from the family's one milk cow. Aaron bought three hens for breakfast eggs, but within a month, skunks had broken into the chicken coop, bit into the hens' jugular veins, and sucked their life's blood out of them.

Having arrived at spring planting time, Aaron set about plowing the sod, first for a kitchen garden beside the dwelling, then a twenty-acre field for corn and cotton. Spring rains were sparse. The okra, green beans, sweet corn, squash, and cucumber seeds were planted according to the signs of the zodiac, but the nights were chilly and the seeds were slow to sprout.

The plowed furrows in the cotton field were nearly obliterated by the drifting sandy loam that was pushed into wavy dunes by Oklahoma Territory's incessant wind. Great invasions of drifting

Russian thistles—tumbleweeds—raced across the homestead and piled up along the county roadbed. Riley Foster's east-west boundary fence became completely covered by tumbleweeds and drifting sand. His livestock often stepped over the buried fences and wandered across Aaron's homestead, looking for sprigs of early spring grass.

Praying for rain and God's blessing, Aaron went to the river bottom to cut willow posts to use to build a fence to shut out the open-range cattle and to confine their mule team and their one milk cow once the spring rains came and crops were up and growing. He cut posts for half a day, went home for lunch, then spent the afternoon setting the posts in the ground around his plowed field. The day after he started setting the posts, he found a crude, intimidating note tacked to the last post he had set the day before: "If yu try to fence our cattle off from the river, yu will wish yu didn't!"

Aaron showed Clara the note, and they prayed about it. Aaron concluded that he could fence off his twenty-acre cotton patch without generating violence, and by the time he could afford to fence off the entire quarter section, the citizens of Day County would have voted to end the open range, anyway. So he returned to the river to cut more posts, but about midmorning, he suffered a slip of the ax and cut a gash in his left arm. He wrapped his handkerchief around the deep cut and went to the house, cleansed the wound with rubbing alcohol, then sewed it up with Clara's sewing needle and string from a flour sack. At supper, he revealed to his trusting wife that their milk cow had gone dry. That night, under the light of their flickering kerosene lantern, Aaron read the entire Old Testament book of Job, prayed for God's blessing, and went to bed.

An hour before morning, a skunk, smelling their food stash, dug through their thatched roof and dropped onto Leona's bed. Aaron scurried to open the door and chase the skunk out before it expelled its stench.

At first light, Clara declared quietly, "We cannot raise our children here." Then she began to gather all their belongings and bundled their possessions into their bedding.

Aaron pulled the lumber from the dugout roof and reassembled their wagon for a trip back to Munday, Texas, to supportive relatives, to a peaceful people, to a land of milk and store-bought bread, to day-labor wages sporadically offered and honestly earned. He was comforted in the belief that he understood the Old Testament book of Job.

"The Lord gave, and the Lord hath taken away; Blessed be the name of the Lord."

In 1907, when Oklahoma became a state, Day County south of the Canadian River was joined to Roger Mills County and Day County north of the river was added to Ellis County. The open range came to an end. For the next sixty-five years, Aaron's ill-fated homesteading venture would be the nearest anyone in the Bird family would come to actually owning land.

*   *   *

Back in Munday, Aaron rented a modest frame house for his family and resumed his livery business.

He did odd jobs when hauling was slow, read the Bible cover to cover each year, and became a deacon in the First Baptist Church. Clara maintained their household as a model of frugality, modeling her life after Christ's, canvassing the community to seek people who needed a helping hand.

While Aaron continued to read the Bible cover to cover each year, Clara concentrated on the gospels. "Blessed are the poor in spirit, for theirs is the kingdom of heaven… Blessed are they that mourn, for they shall be comforted. Blessed are the meek, for they shall inherit the earth."

Young Daniel and his sister Leona went to Munday public school and often attended the same class. Since the school was short on money and teachers, they combined two grades into the same room and taught the same subjects to both grades. Daniel excelled in mathematics. He was a respectful and obedient son who never caused his parents any worry. He embraced his father's faith and work ethic. Daniel enjoyed sandlot baseball and, with his sister and neighborhood playmates, played hide-and-seek and Annie Over, for hours, throwing a ball over the housetop to the rival player on the other side, who, upon catching the ball, would dart around the house, hoping to win the game by hitting the opposing player with the ball, if only the opponent were not running around to the other side of the house in the other direction. In the absence of expensive toys, it was fun and good exercise.

Daniel learned to appreciate what little they had, but his sister was ambitious for more. One day, Leona wanted to get married and move to a big city, where there was a lot to see and a lot to do. The next day, she was determined to become a schoolteacher. She read everything she could get her hands on. Their mother, Clara, encouraged her to seek God's will in her life, work on self-improvement, dress modestly, and not overdo the makeup.

When World War I broke out in 1917, an economic opportunity opened for Aaron to move his family to the town of Hobart, in Kiowa County in Southwestern Oklahoma, about ten miles northwest of the Roosevelt community, to work for a livestock dealer who was buying horses and mules to be trained and shipped to the American Expeditionary Forces in France.

When World War I ended, Aaron rented the livery stable that had been used for the procurement of the horses and mules for the army and operated it as the Filling Station, located just off the Hobart town square. In addition to livery services, it offered boarding for horses and had a taxi service featuring Aaron's four-door automobile. The taxi service also included a unique four-wheeled surrey, a novelty even then. Working part-time after school, Daniel enjoyed chauffeuring customers around in the surrey, mostly elderly folks wanting to go around town in a stylish, old-fashioned way, to the grocery store or to church or to visit the graves of loved ones in the cemetery.

The Filling Station also had a gasoline pump set up at the edge of the street for the growing number of automobile owners in the area, and it offered tire-repair services. Only a few of the town's streets had a hardtop surface, and all the county roads were rough, gravelly, or rutted, devastating to tires. Fixing flats was steady work. It provided much of the modest revenue of the establishment.

In 1924, Leona and Daniel graduated in the same high school class at Hobart and prepared to enroll in Southwestern Oklahoma Teacher's College at Weatherford, about fifty miles north. Leona was planning to earn a teaching certificate, and Daniel would major in mathematics. On registration day, Leona and Daniel walked up the steps into the Registrar's office side by side, but within five minutes, Daniel realized that he did not have a recognized goal that would motivate him to work his way through college. While Leona began to fill out her admission papers, Daniel turned and walked out the door, his life headed in a less-challenging direction. His proficiency in mathematics would be used as a sharecropper or as a wage earner.

* * *

Daniel Bird remained with his parents in Hobart and did not dwell on his future. He worked part-time at the Filling Station. Without a set goal, Daniel followed comfortably his father's lifestyle, working for wages and living humbly, doing odd jobs around town, trusting in the Lord that "things would work out," not expecting or wanting extraordinary experiences to come his way.

Nevertheless, for young men especially, fate often has a way to take one's measure, in war, in rancorous, aggressive peer relationships, or in community crises. It was on Christmas Eve 1924, in the neighboring community of Babbs Switch, that the one-room Babbs Switch Grade School was decorated for a Christmas program the teacher and students had prepared for the community. The room was freshly painted, and the odor of turpentine used for paint thinner permeated the air inside the building as a crowd filed into the room. In the rear corner of the room near the exit, a newly cut live cedar Christmas tree was festooned with cotton snow, tinsel icicles, and lighted red and green candles burning in silvery tin candleholders. Red and green crepe paper streamers were twisted together to form ropes that stretched from the top of the tree to each corner of the room.

Heavy wire netting was bolted over the windows to prevent storm damage and vandalism. The exit doors opened inward.

"Silent night, holy night," the program began. Children from each grade performed a skit, then a Santa began handing out sacks of Christmas candy, fresh apples, with mixed nuts and oranges, when suddenly a candle flame caught a branch of the cedar tree on fire, producing a sudden, explosive flash fire that engulfed the room, igniting the turpentine fumes, the incendiary tree, the cotton snow and the tinsel, the angels' wings on the children's costumes, the green and red crepe paper streamers, human hair and heavy winter clothing. In unison, a primordial shrieking scream pierced the night as parents clutched their children and rushed toward the door, now partially jammed shut by the bodies ramming and trampling one another and piling up like cordwood. Only those who leaped over or climbed over the pile of those being trampled survived the conflagration. They stood outside the burning building, beating their breasts and wailing for their loved ones being burned alive.

Thirty-six people perished in the 1924 Babbs Switch School fire. More than half the victims were children. Some entire families perished. Next day, as news of the tragedy spread throughout the country, young men gathered to recover the bodies, place the remains in body bags, and transport them to the funeral home in Hobart, where they were to be buried in Rose Cemetery, twenty of them in a mass grave. Daniel Bird volunteered to participate in one of the recovery crews, and he performed with a somber sense of duty, buoyed by his simple faith that in all things God's will is served, not ours to understand, but ours to accept in faith. He would never forget the odor of burnt human flesh, but neither would he let the experience snuff out his positive outlook on life.

The evening following the funerals of the Babbs Switch School fire victims, Daniel sat with his parents, Clara and Aaron, as his father read aloud from the book of Ecclesiastes:

To everything there is a season,
And a time to every purpose under the heaven;
A time to be born, and a time to die;
A time to plant, and a time to pluck up that which is planted;
A time to kill, and a time to heal;
A time to break down, and a time to build up;
A time to weep, and a time to laugh;
A time to mourn, and a time to dance.

* * *

Daniel's sister, Leona, stayed in college one year, covering her expenses by working in the school's janitorial department. She studied hard, took a full load of academic courses, swept and mopped floors, and cleaned ladies' restrooms. Because of a statewide shortage of teachers in 1925 and her need for an income, she received an emergency certificate to teach elementary grades and got a position at Consolidated School Number 8 for the 1925–1926 school term. She was to board at the home of the school board president, about a quarter mile from the school, close enough for her to walk yet stay fresh and dressed for the classroom. She was assigned grades 4 and 5.

Wally Dalkens was one of Leona's pupils, a fifth grader itching to be a sixth grader. He had graduated from stick horses long ago and now occasionally rode his small gelding, Domino, to school behind his father's school wagon. Domino then would be tied to the back of the school wagon and led back home, as James Dalkens returned to do a day's farm chores before school let out in the afternoon.

Leona found that Wally had difficulty concentrating on the lessons at hand; his mind wandered out the window and across the countryside. She offered to let him lead the Pledge of Allegiance each morning if he would behave himself all that day. He considered it a patriotic honor and tried to keep his part of the bargain.

Dexter Dalkens had dropped out of school in the ninth grade and was working part-time as a cowhand on the Bar C Ranch east of Roosevelt. Riding ranch horses and working with cattle and cow dogs suited him well. Now eighteen, he had grown to an impressive six feet, three inches in height. On his own initiative, he developed a natural talent for carving wooden figurines, animals, and people and weird, fantastic, monstrous creatures that might drive psychoanalysts crazy, wooden figurines about four to six inches tall that he placed on windowsills and shelves throughout the house and nailed to fence posts and barn walls. He had developed a bad reputation in the community among families with teenage girls, one of whom accused him of fathering her child. Dexter admitted having sex with the girl, but he denied fathering the child. His defense was, "She promised her mother that she would never lie down with a boy until she married, so we did it standing up." The teenager's child turned out to be somewhat slow-witted and closely resembled the teenage mother's brother. Dexter's peers began calling him Dexter the Sexter and Sexy Dex, nicknames to which he did not object.

One afternoon, after the school term had been under way for about a month, Dexter drove the school wagon for his father because James was in Altus, meeting with his landlord over a sharecropping matter. As Leona helped her smaller students climb into the wagon, she realized that Dexter was staring down at her, almost leering, it seemed. Their eyes met, his steel-gray eyes cold and piercing like a hawk, her soft blue eyes prim and cautious. He was eighteen and on the prowl, his aura emitting strong young unchecked virility. He liked her long thin, shapely body. She was twenty-one, alone, a career woman with supervisory responsibility.

"Goodbye, Miss Bird, goodbye, Miss Bird," her students began to say in cadence.

"Goodbye, children," she replied.

"Come fly, Miss Bird, come fly, Miss Bird, won't you fly away with me?" said Dexter with a suggestive grin.

Leona ignored him. The very idea!

Dexter stayed in the back of her mind for the rest of the day.

CHAPTER 4

Twisted Strands

There are many connections within the human population and swirls of interrelationships that are waiting to happen, like strands of hemp that form a rope. In the spring of 1926, a sandlot baseball league developed. The Roosevelt Roosters, the Hobart Hobos, the Altus Baptists, and the Altus Methodists scheduled Saturday afternoon games in a hay meadow behind Hobart's First Baptist Church. Daniel Bird helped build the backstop and lay out the base paths. He was first baseman for the Hobart Hobos. His father, Aaron, volunteered to be third-base coach. For the Roosevelt Roosters, Dexter Dalkens was pitcher and center fielder, Russell Dalkens first baseman and cleanup batter, Wally Dalkens unofficial bat boy, pinch base runner, and mascot.

While warming up for the first game between the Hobos and the visiting Roosters, Daniel stood on the first-base side, noticing that beyond the third-base line, a teenage girl was throwing high fly balls to the Rooster outfielders. *Who is that?* Daniel wondered. A teammate of Daniel's identified her as "Dexter Dalkens's kid sister." For a girl, she had an amazing arm. Daniel was not near enough to see her features clearly, but he was intrigued. When the game started, the Roosevelt girl dissolved into the crowd.

The following Friday, when school let out at Consolidated School Number 8, Daniel arrived in his surrey to pick up his sister, Leona, who was going to visit her family in Hobart. Grace was there with her father to accompany him on his school wagon route, delivering children to their homes along a four-mile route. Grace enjoyed the children and played word games and "I spy" with them to make the bumpy wagon ride more pleasant.

As Daniel's surrey sat parked beside the school wagon, he and Grace stared at each other. She was impressed with his straight, broad shoulders, his black hair neatly combed straight backward, his look of sincerity and honest face. He recognized that she was the girl with an amazing ball-throwing arm. Although neither of them was comfortable enough within their shyness to speak, each smiled tentatively, and something clicked. The sight of Grace's petite body and thin pretty face made Daniel almost hurt inside. She was seventeen and he was barely twenty, it was springtime and the sap was rising.

On the following Saturday evening, the school board sponsored a "box supper" to raise money to purchase a set of encyclopedias for the school library. The female students and ladies in the community were to prepare decorated boxes of delectable snack food to sell for the fund-raising. Gentlemen would bid on the boxes of their wives, sweethearts, or prospective girlfriends, hoping to buy the appropriate box and share the food and company of the lady who prepared it. A good time would be had by all, except perhaps unsuccessful bidders.

"Leona, may I borrow five dollars for the box supper?" Daniel asked his sister. "If Dexter Dalkens's sister fixes a box for the supper, I want to buy it. I have just bought a new baseball glove, and I am short on cash."

Leona laughed. "Five dollars! Nobody's box is going to bring five dollars in this little place."

"I want to be sure I have enough to buy it, anyhow," Daniel replied. "I'll pay you back next week, when Mr. Lacy pays me for some stovewood I delivered to him."

As the youngest member of the school staff, Leona was responsible for preparing the school auditorium for the box supper, yet she found time to prepare a box herself. She wondered if she was taking a risk. Perhaps no one would want to bid on her box; perhaps people were already considering her a dull, old-maid schoolteacher. She agreed to loan Daniel the five dollars if he helped her set up the tables and chairs and decorations.

When Grace Dalkens arrived at the box supper that Saturday evening, Daniel Bird was stationed at the door to see which box she brought so that he would know which one to bid on when the auction began. Grace glided past him through the doorway, carrying a shoebox decorated with green-and-gold wrapping paper pasted to the box and the lid. Grace held it up to her bosom, plainly visible, obviously wanting Daniel to see it. On the lid, there was a papier-mache bas-relief of Daniel's surrey, upon which a boy and girl were seated side by side. Daniel's heart leaped a beat.

Serving as auctioneer, the school superintendent began the sale by offering Leona's box first, and to her surprise, the bidding was brisk. "Two bits!" "Four bits!" "Six bits!" "A dollar!" "Two dollars!" "Three dollars!" "Three and a quarter!" "Three fifty!" "Three seventy-five!" and the bidding ended. She had not realized that several single young men in the community had noticed her tall statuesque figure, her long luscious raven hair, and her attractive face but they had lacked the courage to approach her, a teacher, whom they thought might hold herself above their humble class. Leona was doubly surprised and chagrined when the winning bidder turned out to be Dexter Dalkens.

Leona took her box of snacks from the auctioneer and carried it to a corner table and sat down, Dexter following close behind. She was surprised that Dexter was six inches taller than she was. "Thank you, Mr. Dalkens, for buying my snack box."

"Don't call me Mr. Dalkens," he said, "although I am a full-grown man with a man's intentions." He had a look on his face that implied he had a plan and the plan was working. "As soon as we get good and acquainted, I suspect we will have special names for each other."

"Well, I do not know about that, but thank you, anyway," she said, blushing. Leona began to wonder how she should try to handle his brash behavior. Some of the people in attendance began to watch them, smiling slyly. Embarrassment for Leona was inescapable.

Dexter sat down on the bench beside her, closer than necessary. "I was hoping your box wouldn't cost so much," he said, "so that I might have some money to take you out tomorrow. But some of your students' rotten parents were bidding on your box, trying to get on the good side of you. I guess I showed them."

Leona did not respond. She and Dexter sat silently as the bidding continued. They were to wait until all the boxes were sold before anyone started eating.

Daniel could have used some of Dexter's nerve. He wondered if he should start the bidding for Grace's box at one dollar or impress her by shooting the works with a five-dollar bid. Observers realized that Grace was hoping that Daniel would buy her box decorated with a surrey, for he was the only young man in the community who drove a surrey. As for the bidding part, Daniel handled it well. With token opposition, he won the bid at $2.50, one of the highest bids of the evening. When he and Grace sat down at the table beside Dexter and Leona, Grace said, "Thank you, Daniel, for buying my box."

Daniel was at a loss with what to say, but like her brother, Grace appeared to have a plan and the plan was working. The way to a man's heart is through his stomach. "I hope you like fried chicken," she told him.

"You bet I do," he replied, smiling.

The ice was broken.

While the bidding for the other boxes continued, Grace and her brother, Dexter, and Leona and her brother, Daniel, chatted casually about community activities, common acquaintances, and the sand-lot baseball season. The Hobart Hobos had lost their game to the Roosevelt Roosters, 4 to 2. They discussed the impressive athletic prowess of Russell Dalkens, who had hit two home runs, and the shenanigans of little Wally. During pregame batting practice, Wally had substituted an Irish potato for the baseball, resulting in the batter smashing the potato to smithereens. Then, twice during the game, after shagging foul balls, Wally threw potatoes instead of the retrieved balls back into the game.

When the auction was over and the dining began, Grace removed the lid from her box with a flourish, almost as though a drumroll was heralding her achievement. Daniel's eyes were as big as his stomach!

Grace's cooking experience since the age of five had reaped dividends: four pieces of golden fried chicken, one for her and three for him; two thick slices of sourdough bread, covered with butter and wild plum jam; two small triangle-shaped fried fruit pies made of dried apricots, vinegar, sugar, and cinnamon, cooked in butter and rolled in a crispy golden flour crust; two ripe, fresh tomatoes, sprigs of mint, two dill pickles, and two pieces of taffy candy. Daniel had never tasted such scrumptious chicken, crispy on the outside, moist and seasoned just right. He could eat chicken like that for the rest of his life!

As the evening's events drew to a close, Daniel made his move. "Grace, may I visit you tomorrow after church? We might go into town and get a scoop of ice cream at the Hobart drugstore…"

"Yes, that would be nice. I would enjoy that." She smiled, although she knew that the drugstore would not be open on Sunday. Emboldened by her acceptance of a date with him, Daniel groped under the table for her hand, found it, and took it in his. Grace let him keep it there, and she reassured him and set her claim to him with a subtle squeeze.

*   *   *

A few days after the box supper at Consolidated School Number 8, Wally Dalkens brought a package to school wrapped in an old newspaper. It was the box that Leona had used for her entry in the auction, which Dexter had insisted on keeping. "I paid for this box," he had declared. "I will find a use for it."

"Miss Bird, Dexter asked me to give you this," Wally said, handing her the box.

Apprehensive, Leona dared not open it in front of her students. From irresponsible Dexter, she expected something embarrassing.

That night, in the privacy of her boarding room, she removed the newspaper wrapping and opened the box, revealing a wooden figurine about six inches tall. Dexter had carved an image of himself, a tall slender, sinewy male, somewhat abstract and rough-hewed, but recognizably Dexter, standing proud and nude, except the figurine was holding a cowboy hat to conceal his genitals. Also inside the box was a note:

> *My dearest Leona,*
> *I love you. Please let me tip my hat to you soon.*
>
> *Yours truly,*
> *Dex*

Shocked and distressed that she had been unable to deflect his interest in her, yet doubting that he actually was serious about her, she sat down on her bed, laid the box beside her, and sighed. She could not acknowledge his gift or respond to his note. *Why is he doing this to me?* she wondered. *How does he know how lonely I am?* She wanted to hurl the dreadful thing across the room, but at the same time, she wanted to hold it to her bosom. What to do? What to do?

That night she brought the figurine beneath the covers with her and slept fitfully.

*   *   *

Daniel Bird and Grace Dalkens began to date as often as they could get together. If he could not borrow his father's car, he would drive his surrey to the Dalkens farm and spend the day, hoping to find time to be alone with his wonderful, new girlfriend. Sometimes they would go on long walks together, hopefully alone, but often babysitting Olivia, the toddler. Olivia loved Daniel and claimed him for herself. Realizing how much Daniel was beginning to mean to Grace, James and Maudeen found him totally acceptable as a suitor for their daughter and made him feel welcome, but they did wish he had a good, full-time job. Russell, Daniel, and Grace enjoyed donning baseball gloves and playing "catch" together. Wally loved to sneak around undetected and make a loud, smacking sound whenever Daniel and Grace stole a kiss. Dexter tried to pressure Daniel to convince Leona to go out with him, implying that if Daniel helped him get dates with Leona, Dexter could intervene on his behalf concerning his sister Grace, an illogical assumption because from the beginning Grace was completely devoted and receptive to her new boyfriend, while stating confidentially and emphatically to Daniel that she was a follower of Jesus; therefore, they could not become intimate with each other unless and until they got married.

Daniel knew he wanted her, could think of nothing else, and wanted her enough to propose marriage after dating only a month.

"Grace, I love you and want to marry you. What do you say?"

Grace's immediate nervous response to his proposal was to reveal to him the items she had already placed in her hope chest, sheets and blankets and towels that she had collected during the brief time she had been enrolled in the eleventh grade at Altus High School. Also hand-stitched lingerie, handwritten recipes she already knew by heart, sachets made from crushed roses and wildflower petals, tatted doilies and embroidered dresser scarves and pillow slips Grandma Eliza had made for her, a list of baby names, a hymnal, her baptism certificate issued by the Methodist Church.

"Well, how about it?"

Her next response to his proposal was to reach up and embrace him, her arms around his neck, her lips pressed against his right ear, whispering, "Yes, yes, I'll marry you, Daniel. My heart locked on you when I first met you. Just tell me where we are going to live and how you are going to support me and the children whom God will bless us with."

Suddenly whelmed by the potential responsibility he was offering to take upon himself, Daniel asked, "How many children do you think we ought to have?"

"At least a boy and a girl. Maybe three altogether."

Their plans took form in a herky-jerky fashion seen often among the young, impatient, underfunded, and unprepared. He was twenty, and she was just seventeen. Their age was not an issue, however. After all, Grace's mother had married when she was barely sixteen. Not wanting to lose Grace's help in tending to the toddler Olivia, Maudeen offered to let them stay in Grace's room with Olivia until they found a place of their own. Although Daniel liked the Dalkens family, he was not enthused about the possibility of living with his prospective in-laws, but if he went along with the suggestion, at least a date could be set for the wedding.

Their wedding took place on June 4, 1926, in the front room of the Dalkens home. Twenty friends and relatives were witnesses to the event. "Daniel Jefferson Bird, do you take Grace Elaine Dalkens to be your lawfully wedded wife, to love her, hold her, protect and support her, and keep her, in sickness and in health, for better or worse, till death do you part?" asked the pastor of Hobart's First Methodist Church.

"I do," said Daniel nervously.

"Grace Elaine Dalkens, do you take Daniel Jefferson Bird to be your lawfully wedded husband, to love him and support him, honor and obey him, and hold him, in sickness and in health, for better or worse, till death do you part?"

"I do," said Grace with a faint voice.

"By the powers vested in me by the throne of heaven, by the Methodist Church, and by the state of Oklahoma, I now pronounce you man and wife. Daniel, you may kiss the bride."

As the witnesses clapped and cheered, Daniel and Grace embraced and found each other's lips, just the way they had been practicing. There were no rings to exchange. First in line to congratulate the newlyweds were the parents of the groom and bride. Clara Bird had prayed during the ceremony that Daniel would soon find a good job or a farm to rent, prayed that theirs would be a Christian household, prayed that happiness would follow them all the days of their lives, and prayed that no one would introduce any alcoholic drink during the reception. James Dalkens hugged his new son-in-law and kissed his beautiful, dutiful daughter. Aaron Bird slipped his son a small roll of five dollar bills, and Maudeen Dalkens dashed into the kitchen to pull a cover cloth back, revealing a table loaded with wedding cakes, ice tea, and other refreshments. With her new husband at her side, Grace began to open wedding gifts, mostly inexpensive household items the guests knew she would need to set up housekeeping.

During the ceremony, Dexter Dalkens had stood beside Daniel's sister, Leona, brushed against her unobtrusively but often, and wondered when he and Leona would ever get to do what Daniel and Grace now could do as often as they wanted. Leona was constantly aware of Dexter's nearness—a magnetic current seemed to be pulling on them—but she refused to acknowledge anything of the sort.

"Someday soon, we should do this," he had whispered to her when the ceremony ended.

As the wedding party began to break up, Dexter helped Daniel carry a couple of cardboard boxes into Grace's room, one box filled with Daniel's clothes and the other box containing personal possessions: his baseball glove, his King James Version of the Bible, his school photographs, his high school diploma, a box of dominoes and a pack of cards, a melted tin candleholder from the Babbs Switch School fire, a stack of adventure books, a shaving kit, razor strap, toothbrush, fishing tackle, a whetstone, a bag of marbles, his one bow tie.

As evening approached, the Dalkens family settled into routine. All guests had gone. Maudeen and Grace prepared dinner, served it to their men, then washed the dishes. James and Dexter and Daniel sat on the porch and talked about James's spring crops and Dexter's new cattle-wrangling responsibilities and experiences at the Bar C Ranch. With Olivia curled up on his lap, Daniel revealed his plans to hire out for the summer, chopping cotton, hauling watermelons from nearby farms to town, and working part-time at his father's Filling Station in Hobart. Next year he wanted to rent a farm and try sharecropping, if an opportunity turned up. Casually the family was absorbing Daniel into their midst.

At bedtime, Grace carried Olivia into their room. Daniel followed close behind them and shut the door. The closed door would not provide them absolute privacy, but historically, millions upon millions of human mates have copulated in close proximity to others, even without walls and without closed doors. If there was no other way to do it, naturally, that was how it would be done. Patiently Grace rocked Olivia to sleep, laid her on a pallet near the bed, then got under the covers with her new husband, and like the two inexperienced virgins that they were, they let nature take its course to consummate their marriage.

Next morning, when James yelled from the kitchen, "AmPolly! Coffee's ready!" the newlyweds awoke to find Olivia sleeping under the covers, snuggled in between them, facing Daniel.

*   *   *

Leona had signed a contract to teach the fourth and fifth grades at Consolidated School Number 8 for another year and anticipated that the contract would be approved by the county school superintendent because she had received a good evaluation by the school principal. As summer came on, she retained her room-and-board arrangement in the school board president's home so that she could earn a modest income conducting morning tutoring sessions at the school for students who had failed their grades in the previous term. In the afternoon, she often walked the mile to the Dalkens farm to visit her new sister-in-law, Grace, but made a point to leave before Dexter would ride in from his daily ranching job.

Dexter sensed Leona's visits, although he never saw her there. "Leona was here today," he would say. "I can smell her."

Grace considered Dexter's interest in Leona a bad situation and cautioned Leona about it. "Dexter is rotten," she told Leona. "He cares only about himself and does not mind hurting others to get his way."

"I do wish he would leave me alone," Leona responded but did not reveal the conflict within her—the very characteristics she found in Dexter that disturbed her were the characteristics that, like Eve and the serpent, or like a moth to a flame, threatened to draw her into danger. An age-old human subplot: why a good woman who should know better succumbs to the wiles of a rake.

It happened in late June, when the signs were against her. It was a time of the new moon, and it was a time during Leona's monthly cycle whereby her mindless reproductive system had raised her body temperature, intensifying her yearning for God knows what.

She received a letter from the county school superintendent:

Dear Miss Bird,

Because of the significant reduction of farm income throughout Kiowa County these past two years, our county tax base cannot provide us enough revenue to extend your contract for the 1926–1927 school term. In addition, I must inform you that your temporary teaching certificate becomes invalid until you acquire more college hours. I have received good reports about your teaching ability and I encourage you to go back to college to complete your teaching degree. Public education will always need good teachers like you.

The letter left Leona feeling like a wilted flower pulled up by the roots. She realized she ought to go back to college, but the thought of sweeping and mopping floors and cleaning toilets again to pay for her tuition and expenses was hard to contemplate. She packed her things, paid up her rent to the school board president's wife, left her possessions on the porch to be picked up later, and began walking toward the Dalkens farm to see if Daniel was there to take her to their parents' home in Hobart. Usually, Leona had a distinctive walk, a long, deliberate stride in which she placed one foot directly in front of the other. But now she began to stumble, her eyes tearing up; she had a premonition she was walking into a trap. Suddenly from behind her came Dexter, who was through ranching for the day, trotting up on his large gray gelding. He sensed her distress.

"What's wrong?" he asked.

"I've lost my job," she said. "I don't know what I am going to do."

"Don't you worry, sweetheart. I will take care of you from now on. Give me your hand."

With no resistance and some assistance, he pulled her up behind him astraddle the horse, her skirt hiking up to expose her thighs. He turned the horse around and rode off in a new direction, to a secluded place he knew. Leona threw her arms tightly around his chest to keep from bouncing and sliding off. With a sigh of hopeless surrender she placed her cheek against his back. His virile musky odor wafted up from inside his shirt and filled her lungs, the sensual rhythm of the horse's gait stirred her secret places now splayed open by her straddling stance, her arms around Dexter embracing the flexed muscles of his chest as he handled the reins, her hands at his heart absorbing its rhythm. She was trapped inside a capsule of sensuality from which she would not escape. It was all she could do to keep from fainting.

CHAPTER 5

The Wind Comes Sweeping

A s if God's wrath suddenly was awakened, in early summer 1926, an ominous storm front rolled across the Great Plains into Southwestern Oklahoma, the heart of "tornado alley." A fifteen-year-old curly-haired neighbor, Dewey Hargrove, third baseman for the Roosevelt Roosters, was visiting his best friend Russell Dalkens, helping Russell and Wally chop weeds out of their cotton field so that next day they would be free to play ball with him. He wanted to improve his game so that he could make the Hobart High School baseball team now that he and Russell and the other "Con Eight" eleventh-grade kids would be transferring there.

In midafternoon, the Roosevelt community was hit with strong winds from a black cloud bank that rolled in from the northwest with frightening flashes of lightning and earsplitting claps of thunder. The three boys dropped their hoes and dashed directly to the Dalkens storm cellar, where the rest of the family was sheltered, just as the torrent began. The storm brought straight winds up to sixty miles per hour, golf-ball-size hail, heavy rain, incessant lightning and thunder, and a midsize tornado that cut a one-hundred-yard swath across the countryside. The Dalkens farm escaped wind damage, but James's cotton field suffered heavy hail damage; nearly half the green cotton bolls were knocked off onto the ground. Practically everyone in the community escaped the damaging winds in the shelter of their storm cellars, but Dewey's parents, Leon and Betsy Hargrove, two miles southeast of the Dalkens farm, were caught in the twister while trying to save seventy-five half-grown broiler chickens they were raising for food. Leon and Betsy had gathered most of the chicks inside the brooder house with them when the twister struck, a direct hit that instantaneously shattered the small wooden structure into a thousand exploding, splintered bits of debris.

After the storm passed, neighbors came to discover the damage the tornado had done. They found a bare spot where the brooder house had been, not a single chick alive or dead, but the crushed and crumpled, lifeless bodies of Leon and Betsy Hargrove were clutched together about a hundred feet away.

When the news of Dewey's parents' deaths reached the Dalkens place, Dewey was stunned and helpless. James and Maudeen took him under their care, notified authorities, and coordinated funeral arrangements. Dewey's next of kin was an elderly great-aunt in Houston, who, despite great infirmities, attended the funeral. She loved Dewey, but she knew she could not take care of him. She thanked James and Maudeen for their help and asked James to try to find a family who could move into the Hargrove home and help Dewey manage the farm on the shares until he was grown enough to do it himself.

Dewey, who had considered Grace almost like a big sister, immediately asked Grace and Daniel to move in with him. James drew up a sharecropping arrangement in which Dewey and Daniel would split the crop production. Grace would cook, keep house, do laundry, and help Dewey with his schoolwork. He would need to keep his grades up because he wanted to play varsity baseball, football, basketball, and track at Hobart High School with his best friend, Russell Dalkens.

And so Daniel and Grace moved to the Hargrove farmhouse with Dewey about a month after their wedding and provided the teenager a stable continuation of his life at the only home he had ever known. Dewey worked his way through his grief by playing catch with Daniel and Grace or Russell, who visited often. Daniel immediately took over the plowing, harvesting, fence-mending, milking, and other chores, while Dewey worked harder alongside Daniel than he had ever worked with his father. He realized he needed to learn how to perform all the farm work as fast and as well as he could, in the event that Daniel and Grace moved away.

Using the Hargroves' old model-A Ford roadster, which Dewey called the Jalopy, Daniel and Grace now had a means to haul produce to town, visit relatives, and go to church each Sunday.

Daniel determined that he and Grace would attend the Baptist church in Hobart, where his membership resided, and did not bother to discuss the matter with his loving wife. Silently Grace acquiesced in attending the Baptist church with him for the sake of family unity for their future children, although she would miss fellowship with her Dalkens relatives at the Methodist church. Daniel asked her to officially join his church, cajoled her and pleaded with her, but a major issue of conscience stood in the way: although the Baptist church asked Grace to play piano for their worship services when their regular pianist was absent, and Grace did so impressively, the Baptist church would not accept her Methodist baptism, which had not been full immersion. In good conscience Grace could not agree to be baptized again, for it would cast aspersion on her family's religious heritage.

*   *   *

Although Dewey's parents had not allowed him to drive, Daniel handed him the car keys on Saturday nights, on condition that Dewey be in by eleven. Out of gratitude for how Daniel and Grace were taking care of him, Dewey always complied.

During the night after he and Grace had boxed his mother's clothing for sale at a secondhand store in Altus, Dewey awoke screaming from a nightmare. He had dreamed that his parents' coffins were being swept away in a great flood and he was being drawn into the water with them. Grace and Daniel went to his bedside to calm him.

"Why did God take my Mom and Pa away in the tornado?" he sobbed. "They'd never done anything wrong. Is God going to come after me next?"

"Dewey, God did not take your parents away to punish them. He took them because it was time for them to be in glory," Grace said, hugging him.

Daniel said, "Don't worry, Dewey, your folks are in a better place." Then he paraphrased something his father Aaron had read following the Babbs Switch School fire, from the book of Ecclesiastes, the Old Testament book of wisdom: "And I declared that the dead, who had already died, are happier than the living, who are still alive." With his Bible in his hand, Daniel pointed out a nearby passage that seemed to be God's blessing upon their sharecropping partnership:

> *Two are better than one, because they have a good reward for their labour.*
>
> *For if they fall, the one will lift up his fellow; but woe to him that is alone when he falleth; for he hath not another to help him up.*
>
> *Again, if two lie together, then they have heat; but how can one be warm alone?*
>
> *And if one prevail against him, two shall withstand him,*
>
> *And a threefold cord is not quickly broken.*

Dewey did not come close to understanding the ecclesiastical message. "If two lie together, then they have heat" seemed sexual to him. "How can one be warm alone?" sounded to Dewey like a criticism of masturbation. He was going to be one of those souls who just could not comprehend the meaning of Scripture, and whose God would condemn him for his confusion. At least he was comforted to have Daniel and Grace there to care for him.

With a kitchen of her own and no alpha mother Maudeen constantly looking over her shoulder, Grace mastered one new recipe after another. The tornado had destroyed the Hargrove vegetable garden, but with staples of potatoes that grew safely underground, canned corn and tomatoes, dry beans, elbow macaroni, and salted pork, and a kitchen cabinet containing many spices, each meal was better than the last. Every meal featured either corn bread or biscuits, with butter and molasses and a big bowl of flour gravy flavored with bacon grease. "My boys can stand to gain some weight," Grace told herself. She did not know much about calories at that time, and in her world, cholesterol had not yet been discovered.

*   *   *

"Dexter Dalkens and I are getting married at the Kiowa County courthouse on the second day in August," Leona announced to her parents a week after she missed her menstrual period. "He now has a full-time job at the Bar C Ranch, and we are going to move into one of their granaries. Dexter and his boss, Richard Carter, are cutting a window in it today, and they are putting in a chimney flue for a wood cookstove."

"Leona, Dexter is still a teenager," Aaron responded, "and irresponsible at that. You have not given enough thought to this!"

"Yes, I have. It's something I've got to do. I have been going out with him. We have gone too far to turn back," she confessed without actually admitting that she believed she was pregnant. "I am trying to make the best of the situation."

Realizing the personal crisis with which Leona was now dealing, her father and mother acquiesced. Clara sat silently for a moment. She remembered the night she was moved to testify to a wild, restless, drunken cowboy named Aaron Bird and how Aaron had allowed Jesus to come into his life and turn him into a good and faithful husband. Clara, ever the trusting, faithful believer. Clara, who had never contemplated the concept of personality disorders. Clara, who was filled with Jesus power and could find something good in everyone. She had met Dexter only once, at Daniel and Grace's wedding.

"Leona, Dexter comes from a good Christian family," Clara pointed out. "Your father is right in pointing out that he is still immature. But I don't doubt you love him. I noticed how he followed you around at Daniel and Grace's wedding. My mercy, he surely must love you. My best advice is that you need to make sure you establish a Christian presence in your home. Do you know if Dexter has accepted Jesus as his personal Savior?"

"Everything has happened so fast we haven't talked about God."

"Embrace the thirty-first chapter of Proverbs, which describes what it takes to be a wife of noble character," suggested Aaron. "In First Corinthians, the apostle Saint Paul gives assurance that even if a husband is not a believer, the unbelieving husband will be sanctified through his Christian wife, and their children will be holy."

Leona promised her mother that she would try to bring Dexter to church with her the next Sunday. Clara invited them to Sunday dinner so that she might have an opportunity to get acquainted with Dexter.

"I'll go with you to church, Leona," promised Dexter, "and I'll go to Sunday dinner with your folks, but don't expect me to let anyone tell me what to believe about God."

Despite his bravado, Dexter was intimidated by Clara's spirituality, a good woman with a life's history of good deeds. Although Sunday dinner was somewhat overcooked, by Dalkens family standards, Dexter appreciated his future mother-in-law's pleasant hospitality and kept his tendency toward haughty indifference in check.

"Dexter, did you enjoy the church service this morning?"

"Yes, ma'am. I enjoyed the music. My family goes to the Methodist church. I think you Baptists outdo us in singing."

Clara chuckled. "Well, we do enjoy making a joyful noise unto the Lord. Dexter, do you love Jesus?"

"Yes, ma'am. Anyone who came up with Christmas has got to be all right."

"Leona has always gone to church. I do hope after you are married, you will take her to church."

"Yes, ma'am, when I can. Sometimes ranch work is seven days a week."

"Dexter, have you been baptized into the church?"

"Yes, ma'am, when I was a baby, I got sprinkled on the head. Of course, I don't remember it. But my mother has a certificate. It says I belong in the Kingdom."

Aaron broke into the conversation. "We Baptists believe that salvation comes from Jesus dying on the cross for our sins and that as soon as we are old enough to know right from wrong, we need to confess our sins and accept Him as our Savior. Then we get baptized like He did, fully immersed in a body of water, signifying that our sins are washed away."

Dexter responded, "I'm afraid that if I got baptized like that, my sins might kill all the fish downstream!"

Clara chuckled again. She liked the boy. Aaron only half-smiled and shook his head, thinking that his soon-to-be son-in-law had much to learn. Aaron and Clara helped Leona acquire the furniture and necessities to set up housekeeping in the Bar C Ranch's granary and served as witnesses at the marriage service in the Kiowa County judge's chamber at the courthouse. Daniel and Grace stood alongside them as best man and matron of honor.

Honeymooning in a remodeled granary is not to be found on any bride's list, but Leona and Dexter made the best of it. Dexter was an unbridled, uninhibited, experimental lover, and Leona became his willing carnal partner. She stayed excited by his verve and unpredictability. During the daytime, Dexter truly enjoyed his ranch work, and his boss, Richard Carter, appreciated his ability to handle the daily chores, taking care of the animals with efficiency and common sense. James Dalkens came for a week, tore down an old hay barn for lumber, and added on a kitchen and a porch to the live-in granary. Rachel Carter, the rancher's wife, enjoyed Leona's company and invited her to spend her afternoons at the ranch house to chat and pass the time together. Mrs. Carter loaned Leona her lifetime collection of romance novels, two or three at a time, which Leona enjoyed and appreciated. When it became obvious that Leona was pregnant, the ladies began sewing baby clothes and preparing nursery items for the coming event.

*   *   *

In September 1926, Russell Dalkens and his buddy, Dewey Hargrove, started their junior year at Hobart High School, where Russell made an early and significant impact in the school's athletic program. Tall, agile, alert, and fast, he lettered in football, basketball, baseball, glee club, wrestling, and track. Dewey tagged along and basked in his best friend's accomplishments. Russell's football coach described Russell as "the best end man on any high school in the state of Oklahoma" and predicted that he would receive a full scholarship at the college of his choice once his high school career was over. James and Maudeen were as proud as parents could be, and from the weekly *Hobart Record,* Maudeen started a scrapbook of sports articles highlighting Russell's achievements.

Back at Consolidated School Number 8, Wally plodded through the 1926–1927 school term, restless and impatient to join them.

* * *

"The Lord's will is at work in our lives" was Grace's way of informing Daniel that they were going to have a baby. Motherhood was her destiny, and she was eager to get on with it. The Dalkens family and the Bird family shared the excitement of anticipating the arrival of "double cousins," the result of full siblings marrying full siblings from another family.

Vernon Dale Dalkens was born on April 25, 1927, in the guest bedroom of the Carter ranch house. Leona was attended to by her mother, Clara, and Rachel Carter. Maudeen was on hand to cleanse and swaddle her first grandchild and identify family characteristics in the tiny new face.

Grandfathers Aaron Bird and James Dalkens sat in the front room during Leona's labor, James recalling all the times he was on hand waiting for a child to be born into the family, including nieces and nephews, several of his younger siblings, and five children of his own. In the secrecy of his mind, Aaron calculated the days between Leona's marriage and her delivery to discern how "early" the baby might have arrived. In constant silent prayer throughout the delivery and postpartum, Clara thought her first grandchild resembled her Williams side of the family, but she kept her own counsel about it. Maudeen ordered her son Dexter to sit down to hold his new son for the first time, and Dexter managed to do so while remarkably swaggering in a sitting position.

"It's a good thing he looks like me," Dexter remarked.

Three-year-old Olivia brought her favorite doll to give to the baby, but when she learned that the new arrival was a boy, she withdrew the gift and wondered why the baby had to be a boy.

Nursing her cherubic newborn for the first time, Leona thought her baby, Vernon, looked like her.

When Grace and Daniel arrived later in the day to welcome their infant nephew into the world, Grace's fetus stirred in her womb. "It's a good sign," Clara said. "The Lord intends them to be close, like brothers." Grace wondered how her mother-in-law could know that Grace was carrying a boy.

Grace's list of names for make-believe babies suddenly seemed counterfeit now that a real child was on the way. Daniel suggested they pick a name from the Bible, so Grace opened the Bible at a random page, and with his eyes closed, Daniel touched a verse with his finger. Grace read the verse, "Fill your horn with oil and be on your way; I am sending you to Jesse of Bethlehem. I have chosen one of his sons to be king."

Jesse Daniel Bird was born on July 10, 1927, in Grace's former room in her parents' house. Daniel was worried that his petite young wife would have a difficult delivery, so he went to Altus for a doctor. Although Grace was a small young woman, she had inherited from the Dalkens female lineage a wide pelvis. With Daniel sitting beside his wife and regretting that he had impregnated her because of the pain she was experiencing, Grace embraced the pangs of childbirth with courage and dignity. The delivery went smoothly. The doctor received the baby, announced it was a boy, clamped his navel cord, and gave him a good smack on his bottom to make him cry enough to generate good circulation and to clear his lungs. Then the doctor attended to postpartum matters, washed up, accepted a check from Daniel for $50, and left the new parents to carry on.

Instantly a full-fledged mother, Grace watched intently as Maudeen bathed and swaddled the newborn, showed the child to the menfolk, who were waiting at the door, then placed the newborn in his mother's arms for his first nourishment. Grace took her child to her breast and hummed a soft, sweet, reassuring lullaby. She knew, just knew, that her Jesse Daniel Bird was a special gift from God.

Silently Grace, the prairie Madonna, prayed a commitment to prepare her child for a God-filled life of significance.

*   *   *

Grace's conviction that her Jesse was a child of destiny led her to do something extravagant that generated the worst argument she and Daniel would ever have. On Jesse's first birthday, Grace and her baby accompanied her mother on a shopping trip to Lawton, which had more dry goods stores than all the other Southwestern Oklahoma towns combined. Maudeen was going to buy a new Sunday dress for Olivia and look for some school clothes for Russell and Wally, in bins of discounted clothes left over from the previous season. Grace's shopping project was to buy Jesse a new outfit and dress him in it for a birthday portrait at a local photography studio. Daniel had given her $15 to spend on a few drugstore necessities and a small bag of groceries.

Grace was somewhat a stranger to shopping. While she was growing up, the only money she ever spent was occasional change from her father's pockets when they were in town, for candy and other sundries, until she became old enough to hire out to neighbor farmers to chop cotton or, in harvesttime, to pick cotton or gather corn; and on rare occasions of babysitting, when she would actually get paid for it, perhaps a quarter or a half-dollar. Most of her earnings were spent on school clothes. With Jesse in her arms, she found a pale-blue Lord Fauntleroy romper, perfect for her handsome, blue-eyed boy. It cost nearly half of what she had to spend, but she had to have it. While Maudeen browsed for bargains, Grace went down the street to get Jesse's birthday portrait.

In the photography studio, Grace was no match for the saleslady. "My, what a perfectly beautiful baby! Are you entering him in a contest?"

"Oh, no. This is his first birthday, and I want to get a picture of him in his new outfit."

"Well, you certainly picked a good day! It just so happens that we are offering a huge discount today for a baby picture that we can display in this impressive oval frame with beveled glass, eighteen inches high and twelve inches wide. Your child will be perfect! The portrait will be color-tinted to capture the baby-blue colors of the outfit and the child's healthy, ruddy cheeks. For letting us display it in our front window for four months, we will ship it to you free of charge and let you pay it out in monthly payments, only $18.50 a month, starting in August. We will ship the portrait to you in time for Christmas!"

Grace couldn't believe her luck! So elegant a portrait, so handsome a child, such a wonderful surprise for Daniel! Grace anxiously signed the paperwork before the saleslady could change her mind. Jesse sat perfectly for the camera, donned a winsome smile, clasped his hands together, a pose for posterity and, possibly, future fame.

Once home, Grace could not wait to tell Daniel. "Honey, guess what? I got a special deal on Jesse's portrait. It is going to be displayed in their front window for four whole months, an oval picture with beveled glass, and it will be shipped to us for Christmas. It was a bargain at only $18.50 a month!"

Daniel winced. "Grace, let me see the paperwork." The tone of his voice took the joy out of Grace's shining moment. Daniel frowned and shook his head as he pored over the sales contract. "Grace, do you realize that $18.50 a month is a good chunk out of our grocery budget?"

"But they gave us a 40 percent discount!"

"Which will be eaten up by the 20 percent carrying charge. Jesse's precious baby picture is going to cost us over $100! Why couldn't you realize that?"

"I… I guess I'm not as good at math as you are," she said, her chin beginning to quiver.

"Well, all I can say is, you are really going to have to stretch our groceries for the next six months. I advise you to get my mother's bean soup recipe, because we are going to need to eat a lot of beans."

"Daniel, I'm sorry. I thought I was getting a good deal."

"Did you get coffee? Did you remember we are about out of coffee?"

"I forgot. Daniel, I said I was sorry," she sobbed.

"Grace, you must promise me that you will never spend money like this on anything else again without talking it over with me first," Daniel demanded. "There are a lot of things that you might want but we will never be able to afford."

"I promise," said Grace, wanting more than anything a reassuring hug.

Instead, Daniel walked out the door, needing fresh air and some space to contemplate for the first time that in reality, he was married to a gullible, inexperienced teenager.

For the next several minutes, Grace held her sleeping baby in the rocker and wept. She had lived without money for most of her life, but surrounded by loved ones, it had been no big deal.

For the first time in her life, she now felt what it was like to be poor.

CHAPTER 6

To Let Life Flow

Russell Dalkens did not receive an athletic scholarship to go to college. In December 1927, in the first quarter of his final football game in his senior year, while catching a long touchdown pass, he suffered a late hit that resulted in a concussion and a compound fracture of his right leg. He would fully recover from the leg injury, but not until after he graduated, after college athletic talent scouts disappeared. It would not have mattered, anyway, because his life took a totally new direction at the 1928 Fourth of July celebration at Roosevelt, where he met Donna Belle Lee, a native Alabaman whose widower father, Morrison Lee, was moving to Meers, Oklahoma, about thirty miles east of Roosevelt, to operate a small general store whose customers were families of workers at a gravel company that was converting nearby Porter Hill, a foothill of the Wichita Mountains, into concrete mix and road-building material. Donna Belle had taken the Greyhound bus from Alabama to Roosevelt to visit her cousin Betty Jeffreys, Russell's former classmate, for a week while Donna Belle's father moved the family's possessions to Meers.

Russell was smitten by Donna Belle's slow Southern drawl, her demure smile, her creamy, pale skin, her brown bobbed wavy hair, her dainty feet, her rapt attention to everything he said and did. Even before Donna Belle had met him, her cousin Betty had told her that Russell Dalkens was "the catch of the decade." Donna Belle was seventeen, impressionable, one more year of high school ahead of her, but mature enough to recognize his qualities. What a sincere, handsome heartthrob he was! When he talked to her and touched her, she was ready to melt.

Russell went to visit her every day she stayed with her cousin Betty, and Betty was clever at helping the lovestruck young couple find time to be alone. They realized they were tumbling pell-mell into everlasting love, so when they were planning their escapade, each vowed that they would not have sex together until they married, and at the time they said it, they meant it.

Betty and her parents were surprised to find the following note on Donna Belle's pillow on the day her father was due to come for her:

> *Dear folks,*
>
> *Thank you for my wonderful visit with you this week. When my father comes to get me, please tell him that Russell Dalkens is taking me to Meers on an exciting horseback ride through the Wichita Mountains Wildlife Refuge, to show me the buffalo herds, the lakes, the mountains, and the eagles. He is sure he knows the way because his family has their reunion there every summer. We will camp out two nights in the refuge and plan to arrive at Meers on the afternoon of the third day.*
>
> *Tell Daddy to take my things and not to worry. I will be safe with Russell.*
>
> *Love,*
> *Donna Belle*

Russell's note to his parents was much briefer:

> *I am taking Donna Belle to her father at Meers on old Ginger the mare through the refuge so she can see buffalo. I will be gone a few days.*
>
> *Russell*

They slipped away before daylight and were in ranch country by sunrise, traveling along creek valleys out of sight from public roads. Russell had rolled up a couple of blankets and mosquito netting, packed a knapsack with a box of crackers, a chunk of cheese, several strips of jerky, and a full box of Baby Ruth candy bars. A canvas water bag hung from the saddle. He aimed to get to the refuge, about fifteen miles away, well before dark.

When Morrison Lee arrived at Roosevelt around midmorning and found his daughter missing, he was hopping mad. He summoned the Kiowa County sheriff and insisted that the law recover his daughter and arrest the abductor. The sheriff read Donna Belle's note and chuckled.

"It sounds like a couple of young people are out to create a lasting memory," he said.

"Memory my foot!" Morrison replied. "You know what he's up to. Donna Belle is only seventeen. If this isn't outright kidnapping, at least it's statutory rape."

"Not in this state. I wouldn't worry about Russell Dalkens misusing your girl. He is as fine a young man as I have ever seen. I have seen his character displayed on the football field, and I have heard him give testimony at the Methodist church. I wouldn't mind if he took a liking to one of my girls. I guarantee you, your daughter is in safe hands."

"You're not going after them?"

"No. Right now they are halfway across the county, behind a hill in somebody's big pasture. It would take a pack of bloodhounds, which I haven't got. So why don't you just go home and wait to meet your probable, future son-in-law? In situations like this, it's best to **just let life flow**."

When Dexter heard the news that Russell was "gallivanting" across the prairie, he reached his own conclusion. "Well, well, my little brother has gone out to pick a cherry!"

James and Maudeen were reminded of their wedding night in 1906, blanketed down in a persimmon thicket on the Washita River. "I do hope they took enough food." Maudeen fretted.

"I reckon that if they are really in love, for three days they can live on air." James laughed.

Russell and Donna Belle's first day on old Ginger was a lark. Russell and his friends and brothers had gone fishing, coyote-chasing, and deer-hunting throughout the ranch country, and he knew where the back trails and gates and houses were. They made good time without seeing another soul. If they were being tracked, the only evidence they left behind were a couple of empty Baby Ruth wrappers every two or three miles.

Riding old Ginger was a cozy matter. Donna Belle was in the saddle, and Russell sat behind her, his arms around her, handling the reins, her head up under his chin. Their togetherness was magical, their lives falling perfectly into place. By midmorning, they had decided that they would get married on the first Saturday in June 1929, following her May graduation from high school. By noon, the July heat was stifling, but they hardly noticed, shielded from the sun by Russell's hat and bolstered by the joy of knowing their relationship was set for life.

They created a kissing game: for every meadowlark they saw, Russell would nibble or kiss Donna Belle on her neck or ear; for every red-tailed hawk, she would turn her head and kiss him on the lips.

"I don't know what a red-tailed hawk looks like," she confessed as the game began.

"Don't worry, I will spot them for you," he said. It was great habitat for red-tailed hawks, and old Ginger detected a slight shift of her load quite often as the couple leaned together to kiss. Russell had keen eyes that could spot a hawk half a mile away.

About 1:00 p.m., they stopped for cheese, jerky, and crackers under a big cedar tree on the north bank of a natural lake fed by Boggy Hollow Creek. Russell tethered Ginger and let her graze while they ate, found a spring where he refilled their water bag, then after watering the horse, they resumed their eastern trek, arriving at an unattended, unlocked service road gate through the west fence of the refuge, about two hours before sunset. Russell was not sure that horseback travel was allowed inside the refuge, so he went down a draw on the south side of Black Bear Mountain, out of sight from any road, and headed to the east side of Granite Lake, to a grove of willows in a sheltered cove hidden away from the campground area administered by park personnel.

"We are about halfway to Meers," he told Donna Belle. "We will camp here tonight, let old Ginger rest and graze, and tomorrow morning we will go find the buffalo herd." He watered the horse, let Ginger wallow in the sand on the beach, then tethered her with a long rope that allowed her to graze.

"Before we make our camp, I want to go swimming, cool off, and freshen up," said Donna Belle. "Can we swim here?"

"Sure," said Russell, "but we have no swimsuits." He did not tell her that he had seen a big black snake in the water several yards away.

"I've gone skinny-dipping all my life," she replied. Then she added naively, "Don't worry, we will be covered by the water. I know you will behave yourself. You go in first while I turn my head away. Then you turn your head while I come into the water."

Indeed, each had gone skinny-dipping before, with both boys and girls, but not since puberty.

Russell stripped off quickly, although he had misgivings about stripping off and maintaining self-control after holding and kissing his sweetheart all day. "Here I go, turn your head," he said as he walked into the water, his tight-muscled buttocks exposed to the breeze.

Donna Belle sneaked a glimpse just before he splashed down into the lake. *What a sturdy, handsome man,* she thought. She hoped all their sons would look exactly like him.

"Keep your head turned," she cautioned as she began to unbutton her blouse.

Russell waited patiently for a minute then stole a glance just as she was lifting her right leg to shake her panties off her foot, revealing her utmost privacy and her smooth white inner thigh. He turned away, upset with himself for daring to see her naked, realizing now that his desire for her would be even more intense. To complicate the situation, he had expected his genitals to become somewhat diminished in the cold water, but just the opposite occurred. Immediately he became erect and stayed that way.

"Brr!" she cried as she waded out toward him. "This cold water is just what I need. I'm afraid I have sunburned today." She kept her arms folded to conceal her breasts as she bobbed toward him. He crouched down neck-deep, cupped his right hand over his crotch, and wondered how in the world, with her so desirable, could he maintain his moral resolve until June 1929. When she reached him, she also lowered herself neck-deep in the water and held on his left arm for balance. He tried to stay sideways to her, to conceal his erection.

"Oh, this cold water feels so good," she said. "What a beautiful lake, what a beautiful place to be! Russell, let's try to always be this happy!"

He was at a loss for a reply. He hoped she would not detect his aroused condition, but after bobbing in the water for a few minutes, she rubbed her left forearm against him and gasped, "What is happening!" She was confused, frightened, betrayed. She searched his eyes, looking at him as if she did not really know him. They had been beaus for only a week.

He tried to explain. "Don't worry," he said, "I can control myself, my brain and my actions, but you are so luscious I just can't keep my body from reacting. This skinny-dipping was not a good idea, and I am so sorry."

Realizing he had already won his struggle for self-control, she put her hands on his shoulder and said, "We are going to wait until we are married before we go all the way, aren't we, darling?" He nodded. Sensing the need to concentrate on something else, she asked, "So do you think it will be all right if I get my hair wet in this lake water?" Russell dipped his head under the surface to show her the lake water was safe.

Suddenly Donna Belle screamed, "A snake!"

A large black snake was slithering on the surface just a few feet away. She threw her arms around Russell's neck as she screamed, and the snake disappeared under the water.

"Get me out of here! Please! Please!"

He gathered her in his arms and carried her out of the water, fully composed and in control, Russell the protector. When he put her down she continued to cling to him, trembling. As they stood together, her breasts and his crotch pressed against the other's bare flesh, the warm breeze began to dry them off. Exhausted from the swim and the brush with the snake, slowly they began to relax. Again she trusted him completely. She was so precious to him, he could never be so selfish as to draw her into risky premarital sex, with unnecessary complications and possibly unwanted pregnancy.

Slowly they dressed, without talking. Donna Belle used Russell's comb to put the wave back in her dampened hair. He spread one of the blankets out on the ground and rolled up the other blanket for a pillow. He walked down the lakeshore a short distance and found two willow stakes that beavers had gnawed. Taking a heavy rock, he pounded the stakes into the ground at the head and foot of their pallet and stretched the mosquito netting over the stakes like a pup tent. Russell moved Ginger's tether so that she could reach fresh grass. They ate a snack of cheese, jerky, and crackers and finished their evening meal off with Baby Ruth dessert. The sunset faded, and dusk crept in upon them. "Tomorrow we will go look for buffalo," Russell announced as they crawled onto the pallet, adjusted the netting above them, and stretched out on their bed, fully clothed. It had been an important day, a tiring day. They soon fell asleep nestled beside each other.

Just before sunrise the next morning, they were awakened by a chorus of deep grunts, followed by Ginger snorting with surprise. A herd of seventy to eighty buffalo had grazed down to the lakeshore, and some of them were watering just a few yards away. "Don't make a sound," Russell whispered. "These prehistoric brutes have poor eyesight and poor hearing, and with us downwind from them, they will not know we are here."

The refuge's bison herd descended from six bulls and nine cows that had been imported from the New York Zoo in 1905 when President Theodore Roosevelt officially designated the Wichita Mountains a game preserve in an effort to save the bison species from extinction. In the ancient Wichitas, they were thriving.

Cautiously Russell led Donna Belle to a nearby granite boulder that jutted about four feet off the ground, where they could sit safely and watch the herd. The shaggy bulls and cows snorted to mark their space. Buff-colored babies followed their mothers like shadows, some of them nursing to start their day with a belly full of milk. Russell and Donna Belle watched intently as some of the larger bulls wallowed in the damp sand, while others sparred with their stubby horns, banging their huge heads together, a clash of shaggy titans. For about an hour, the herd grazed and watered before drifting over the horizon, out of sight.

About midmorning, Russell and Donna Belle snacked and broke camp. Their travel eastward took on a more tentative aspect, because they were paralleling a service road and they did not want to be detected. They skirted the back side of Geronimo Ridge, Moko Mountain, and Cedar Mountain and stopped at noon on an isolated tributary of West Cache Creek. They counted their remaining Baby Ruth bars and began to ration them.

The afternoon leg of their journey took them through rough terrain at the foot of Mount Lauramac, where Russell dismounted and led Ginger past jagged rocks and along narrow paths, watching for rattlesnakes. They were thrilled to hear the trumpeting call of bull elks on the slopes of the mountain.

Late in the afternoon, Russell detected a cougar picking up their scent and trailing them, until he hurled a rock at it and it disappeared.

Just before sunset, they reached a grove of post oaks on Custer Creek. Old Ginger got a well-deserved drink of water, while Donna Belle dismounted and stretched. "Sweetheart, look up there," said Russell, pointing to three wooden crosses silhouetted on the crest of the hill above them. It was a site called the Holy City, where in 1926 a Congregational Church from Lawton began to conduct an annual Easter Passion Play.

"Can we go there?" she asked.

"Yes," he replied. "This part of the refuge is closed for the day. Nobody else will be around."

Silently they led Ginger up the hill and stopped at the foot of the central cross, located at the edge of a natural amphitheater.

"Let's camp right here at the foot of the cross," Donna Belle suggested.

"I can't think of a safer place," said Russell.

They fixed their pallet and sat down to watch the shadow of the cross stretch across the hillside to the east. It seemed to them they were witnessing a profound extension of the power within the symbol, until the sunset disappeared. Night came quickly.

"This is a good place and a good time for us to say a prayer," said Donna Belle. "You go first."

"Dear God, we thank You for making these old mountains 650 million years ago," Russell uttered.

"Dear Lord of all, thank You for the buffalo babies, the eagles, faithful old Ginger, the sunshine, and the streams. Thank You for protecting us from the big old black snake and from the cougar," she prayed.

"Thank You for bringing Donna Belle to me," said Russell. "Please be with us as we make plans for our marriage."

"Dear God, please don't let Daddy shoot Russell tomorrow. Please don't let us get caught before we get out of the refuge. Forgive us if we've broken the law."

"Amen," Russell said.

"Amen," said Donna Belle.

Next morning, at first light, they broke camp and returned to the grove of post oaks on Custer Creek, where they rested until early afternoon. From the canopy of their oak sanctuary, they could hear highway traffic entering and exiting the refuge on State Route 115. Russell speculated that the exit was only about a mile distant, with Meers less than three miles away. At noon, they finished their cheese and crackers and ate their last two candy bars.

Mounting old Ginger, they skirted around Mount Sheridan, an impressive barrier, and in a brisk trot they used the highway right-of-way to leave the refuge quickly.

"Don't worry about Daddy," Donna Belle said as they cantered into the village of Meers. "He'll be all right when he sees that I'm all right."

They found Morrison Lee on a stepladder, trying to install a sign on the facade of his general store, as they pulled up and dismounted. "Daddy, we're here!" said Donna Belle. "We have had a wonderful time. This is Russell. You will really like him. I'm going to marry him next June!"

Morrison stepped down from the ladder, relieved, but angry. "Young man, I ought to take a whip to you!" he said to Russell. "Or a shotgun, if you have wronged my daughter!"

"Oh, Daddy, I'm the same as I was, except my nose and arms are sunburned. I can't wait to tell you all about our trip through the refuge!"

"Here, let me help you with that sign," offered Russell. He lifted the sign, LEE GROCERIES & GENERAL STORE, and positioned it where Morrison had been trying to bolt it, stretching his arms high over his head, leaving the stepladder for Morrison.

The next day, Russell mailed a postcard to his parents:

> *Hello, ya'll!*
>
> *We had a good trip and got to Donna Belle's father's place okay. He was mad, but only for a little while.*
>
> *I am helping him open his store. Then I am going to try to get a job with the gravel company at Porter Hill. I plan to marry Donna Belle next June, so I need to make some money and stay around here to keep the other fellers away. I will bring old Ginger home next weekend and get my things.*
>
> *Love,*
> *Russell*

James and Maudeen were not surprised at the news. When a young Dalkens man finds the love of his life, he stays with it.

Wally was not so understanding. "My stupid brother! He is going to shovel gravel all day, day after day, just to stay near a girl!"

With his best friend not around any longer, Dewey Hargrove changed plans. No more sandlot baseball for him, and no more farming. "I am going to join the Navy and see the world," he told Daniel and Grace. "I hope you will keep living here and farm this place until I'm twenty-one, when I can sell it. Put the money from my share of the crop in my bank account for me, and when I sell the farm, I will invest it all so that when I retire from the Navy, I will have a nest egg to live on."

Grace had come to feel like a surrogate mother to Dewey; to see him leaving brought her tears. On the day he left for his induction, he was carrying a brown paper bag holding two dozen peanut butter cookies.

*   *   *

Russell and Donna Belle got married on the first Saturday in June 1929. The ceremony took place at the foot of the central cross at the Holy City. It was to be a private service only for the family, but since it occurred on the same weekend that the Dalkens clan was congregating for their annual family reunion encampment nearby in the Wichita Mountains Wildlife Refuge, the family affair included nearly a hundred relatives.

Those present at the wedding were led to believe that the newlyweds would spend their wedding night in a bridal suite in a Lawton hotel; instead, Russell and Donna Belle drove to the parking area on the western shore of Granite Lake, from which they backpacked bedding, mosquito netting, cheese, jerky, crackers, Baby Ruth candy bars, and a bottle of wine to the east side of the lake, to a grove of willows in a sheltered cove hidden away from the campground area.

CHAPTER 7

Dust to Dust

B abies are going to be born when they are due to be born, no matter what the economic situation may be with their families or
their nation. Leona and Dexter's second child, Kirby John Dalkens,
was born on January 22, 1929, on the verge of the greatest economic
depression in American history. Kirby was a miniature image of his
father: gray eyes, sharp chin, brown hair, long body, demanding. He
cried fiercely for his nourishment, and he could not tolerate a wet
diaper. When he was awake, he flailed his arms almost constantly,
indicating another hyperactive, athletic Dalkens had joined the
family.

Farm commodity prices, including cattle prices, plummeted,
along with everything else, when the stock market collapsed in 1929,
except wheat prices, which remained high because of grain production problems worldwide. In 1930, farmers in the northern plains
plowed up thousands of sections of native grassland to plant wheat,
and they produced a bumper crop. Then a severe drought engulfed
the Great Plains beginning in 1931, and it would last until 1939.
The seasonal northern cold fronts, with high winds sweeping down
the eastern slope of the Rockies, or from the Arctic, blasted across the
dried-out, plowed-up plains, creating vast dust storms that blew the
topsoil away. There were fourteen dust storms in 1932, thirty-eight
in 1933; the first one occurring in early 1933 killed the winter wheat.
The great dust storms of 1934 destroyed thirty-five million acres of

topsoil. In May 1934, a great cloud of dust reached all the way from the Great Plains to New York City and Washington, DC, influencing the national press and the federal Congress to strengthen their support for New Deal emergency measures of President F. D. Roosevelt, particularly his farm policies. American farmers had lost their foreign markets because of the worldwide depression, but despite the persistent drought across the plains, they overproduced for the home market. With such a surplus, prices were too low for them to show a profit. The New Deal tried to bolster farm prices by buying up vast amounts of grain and cotton. In 1933, six million pigs were slaughtered.

James Dalkens, a lifelong Democrat, was an enthusiastic supporter of FDR and took pleasure in the many comments friends, acquaintances, and strangers made concerning how much he looked like the president. But Dexter was skeptical about a president who would slaughter and bury six million pigs while food lines of hungry people were found in most American cities.

"The New Deal is crazy," Dexter proclaimed. "On one hand, they are telling farmers to cut back on production, to create shortages that will raise prices, and at the same time, they are building fertilizer plants to provide fertilizer to increase production!"

"At least they are trying to do something instead of just claiming everything is hunky-dory, like Hoover did," James responded. "And by the way, a lot of the pork from those six million slaughtered hogs was used to feed poor people. In a crisis, try something, try anything. If it doesn't work, throw it out and try something else."

The Dalkens family, descendants of subsistence farmers, knew that hard times were the best time to concentrate on producing food crops like potatoes, watermelons, garden vegetables, fryers, eggs, turkeys, butcher hogs, fresh milk, butter, clabber, cottage cheese. Even when there was no money to be made, the family with food on the table was not poor.

Nothing seemed to bring relief against the recurring dust storms. Daniel would plant a crop, only to have the seeds blown out of the ground or covered with sand dunes. In 1930 and again in 1931, he produced only five bales of cotton on a twenty-acre patch, providing barely enough income to pay the interest on his bank loan and get an extension to buy seed for the next season. The old Hargrove jalopy that he had been using broke down for weeks at a time, sitting in the front yard until Daniel could scrounge repair parts.

Housewives either learned to cope with the wind and dust or give up the struggle. They could not hang a wet wash on the clotheslines for three days after a dust storm had passed, because enough of the electrified dust particles were still in the air to turn the whitest clothes a dingy gray. Grace kept a supply of dish towels on hand to dampen and place over the windows during the storms, to try to keep out the sifting dust particles, and to have the kerosene lamps ready to burn in the daytime, when the sunshine was blotted out. The chickens would go to their roost in the daytime, when the storms darkened the sky. Egg production declined.

*   *   *

The stresses of the Depression permanently altered the extended Dalkens family. Thomas Dalkens, eldest of the clan and president of the reunion, lost his life's savings when the People's Bank of Altus collapsed following the stock market crash in 1929. He died of a heart attack in 1930. His widow sold the blacksmith shop and the hotel in Roosevelt and moved to be near a married daughter in Oklahoma City. Oklahoma City became a beacon for Dalkens relatives who were weary of the farm, who were ambitious for the opportunities and pleasures of city life. All of Izora's grown children had moved to Oklahoma City in the 1920s, one son an electrician, another a Linotype operator—a profession learned at his father's Duncan newspaper. One daughter married an Oklahoma City electrician, another married an attorney who became a state Supreme Court judge, another married a fire department officer who became fire chief. Robert Dalkens's eldest son, Marshall, became chief accountant for an Oklahoma City motor company and helped all four of his sisters find work there as secretaries or bookkeepers.

"Come to the City, come to the City" was a siren call for other relatives to become urban Oklahomans. Citizens all over the state, except in and around Tulsa, began to champion the state capital city, which they called the City. The City, the City, the City.

In the late 1920s, three of Thomas Dalkens's children married and moved permanently to California, near Mitchell Dalkens and his married children, all of whom had fled hard times in Erath County, Texas, back in 1926. Continuing his career in the US Navy at San Diego, Hubert Brown arranged for his widowed stepsister, Penny Garfield, to work for one of his fellow officers as a housekeeper, nanny, and cook. All of Penny's children accompanied her to California. Four of Joseph's sons, now married, with young families of their own, also migrated to California. They had had enough of farming; they would apply themselves to new opportunities that California seemed to have in abundance.

Statistically, the Dalkens migration to the West Coast was part of an enormous demographic shift brought on by the Depression. "Okies" went to California from a dozen hard-hit states. Not one of the Dalkens family members was ever called an Okie, at least not to his face. Each held his head high and defied the image of scruffy, down-and-out, undereducated farm migrants. Unlike the stereotypical Joad family in John Steinbeck's *The Grapes of Wrath*, Dalkens family members were articulate, thanks to the lasting influence of the family's historical matriarch, the schoolteacher Lydia Godby Dalkens. Seeking good-paying jobs and careers, they stayed away from agricultural work altogether. In the early 1930s, newly arriving cousins were taken in by California relatives, who helped them relocate and find permanent work.

Regularly, James received letters from nephews and nieces urging their Oklahoma kinfolk to pack up and come to California. California, California, California.

In the face of one crop failure after another, James and his children stayed put. City life and West Coast adventures did not appeal to them. James did not see how he could keep his identity and feel close to God if he did not stay rooted to the land.

* * *

Daniel and Grace's second child, Jane Eliza Bird, arrived on March 18, 1930, on a blustery, snowy day. Janie was a blonde, the only one in the family. She shared several of her aunt Leona's features—long and lithe, with soft-blue eyes, peaches-and-cream complexion, and fatefully, Aunt Leona's vulnerability. Grace believed that her prayers had been answered: she had a healthy, handsome son and a healthy, beautiful daughter. The family circle was complete. Yes, additional babies would be nice, but hard times discouraged creating more mouths to feed. So she and Daniel practiced the rhythm method of birth control, enjoyed their intimacy, and shared parenthood with joy and gratitude to God.

In May 1932, after Daniel had planted the cornfields and the cotton patches and prayed for rain, he and Grace received a letter from their young landlord, Dewey Hargrove, stationed in San Diego:

Dear Daniel and Grace,

I need to tell you that I have sold my farm to Bankers' Land and Realty Company of Wichita Falls. I did not get as much for the place as it is worth, but in this economy I could not expect much. I thought a long time about this, because I know how much work Mom and Pa put into the farm, but what did it get them?

I know that I will never want to come back there, because the Navy is my family now. It is a good life, a girlfriend in every port. Ha ha! You both were so good to help me out when I was left alone, and I will always be grateful. I just want you to know that I insisted that a clause in the sales contract guarantees you sharecroppers' rights through the year 1935. The buyer has agreed to that.

When you move out and go somewhere else, take as much of Ma and Pa's furniture as you can use and tell the secondhand store in Hobart to come and get what's left.

Sell the cows at the Altus sale barn but keep the best heifer for yourself, to start your own herd. If the old jalopy is still running, you can have her.

Tell my friend Russell hello for me, and I am wondering if he is changing baby diapers yet.

I am being transferred to Galveston, Texas, in a few weeks. I hope you can come and see me there. I will show you a good time.

Love,
Dewey

Daniel was sad to receive the news that Dewey had sold out. "It is just foolish for someone who owns a farm to give it up for a few hundred dollars," he told Grace. "Anyone who owns land owns the future. At least I do appreciate him guaranteeing that we can live here and farm this place for three more years."

"Yes, by then the weather and the crops should be doing better," replied Grace. She was too happy with her babies and her marriage to dwell on negative realities.

* * *

Russell and Donna Belle Dalkens welcomed their first child, a son, on October 14, 1932. They named him James Morrison Dalkens, after their respective fathers, and called him Jimmy. Jimmy was a husky, swarthy baby whose arrival caused Russell to give serious thought to a job promotion offer at the Porter Hill gravel company that promised increased wages but carried great risk from handling dynamite and blasting caps. Donna Belle beseeched him not to take it. "It's not worth it, darling. Jimmy and I could not live without you. Money is not important. Being together to share our lives and cherish our time together, that's all that matters."

Russell took her words to heart and kept his hands on a scoop, working around the railroad yard, where gravel cars were loaded under huge bins and conveyer belts, around tons of gravel moving briskly, with occasional mishaps that could bury workers alive.

*   *   *

Wally Dalkens's role as a tagalong kid brother ended in 1929, when Russell Dalkens had moved to be near his sweetheart, Donna Belle Lee. Wally struggled through high school; he found nothing in his schoolbooks that he believed he could apply to his life. Team sports kept him in school, but he was not fast enough to be an outstanding athlete. He seemed more at home on horseback, and as soon as he graduated from Hobart High School in 1931, he went to work for the Bartley Brothers Rodeo Company near Elk City, Oklahoma, thirty miles from his parents. His new job required him to travel with rodeo stock from town to town across the West. He enjoyed feeding, grooming, loading, and unloading the rodeo stock, the bucking horses and bulls, and the roping calves, traveling via cattle car from one rodeo to the next. But he stayed homesick for the folks back home. Had it not been for the opportunity the rodeo circuit gave him to compete in the roping events, he would not have lasted. Wally was a good-enough roper to compete, but rarely to win the calf-roping competition. Only ropers who could afford the finest, most talented horses won consistently.

At the Guymon, Oklahoma, rodeo in 1933, Wally introduced himself to a lovely, raven-haired seventeen-year-old ticket booth attendant named Valdetta Weaver, one of nine children of an old-time cowboy from the XIT Ranch in the Panhandle. Each day at the Guymon rodeo, Wally and Valdetta shared a table at the hamburger stand, teased each other in an innocent, flirtatious way, and exchanged mailing addresses. In the following months, Wally made quick trips to Guymon whenever he could, his intentions open and direct: he wanted to marry Valdetta. After his fourth visit, their plans materialized. Wally met Valdetta and her family at the county courthouse, where they exchanged vows. Valdetta Weaver Dalkens then packed her belongings in a new cardboard suitcase and accompanied her new husband on the rodeo circuit.

*   *   *

Aaron Bird's Filling Station closed down in 1932 for lack of customers. He had to sell the surrey, an item of growing curiosity, but he kept his car and a mule team and wagon to continue a livery service operating from his home. Customers were few and far between. Attaining the age of sixty-five, Aaron began to receive a monthly old-age pension check from the state government, hardly enough to keep food on the table and pay the rent, but appreciated.

The more conditions worsened in the community, the more Clara Bird tried to do for others. She considered the Depression as a call for Christians to do unto others as they would wish others would do unto them. Aaron was lucky to earn ten dollars a week and took on any temporary, odd jobs available.

Thank the Lord beans were cheap and Clara had a four-star bean soup recipe. She kept a kettle of beans on the stove almost continuously, sometimes flavored with a ham bone and sometimes with salt pork, sometimes flavored with pepper sauce and garlic. When she learned of destitute families in and around Hobart, Clara called upon them, bearing good wishes and jars of beans or chicken soup that she gifted to them with a request: "Let me know what you think of my recipe," as though they were doing her a favor.

The recurring dust storms planted the spirit of hopelessness into depressed individuals who expected life to be difficult anyway. The death rate increased among the elderly, the asthmatic, and those with frail dispositions. Clara developed a reputation for being helpful to distraught families who could not afford to have their deceased loved ones handled by a mortuary. Clara was not afraid to work with the corpses; with loving care, she cleansed them, laid them out, pressed their eyelids shut, closed their mouths, folded their arms on their chests before rigor mortis set in, helped the menfolk lay the deceased in their pine coffins, and reassured the mourners that God's will was being done, they would understand it all by and by, life here on earth was just temporary for us anyway, and God's promise was that He was preparing for us all a better place. If the families were Catholic, Clara knew where to place the candles. Now nearing her midsixties, she stayed tired and driven.

On days when he had no other tasks to do, Aaron drove his wagon to woodlands on the Elk Creek floodplain west of town to gather stovewood along the public right-of-way to sell or to distribute freely to Clara's needy people. In the timber he came upon a group of Kiowa Indian families living in tents and teepees, following the "old way." Their campsite was one they had used for generations. Although the Indian families had been granted 160-acre landholdings and the government had built them comfortable small wooden frame houses, many Plains Indians throughout Western Oklahoma arranged through their Indian agent to lease their lands to white farmers for a modest amount of rent. During the warmer months, the Indian clan clustered their teepees on an Indian tract in timber near a stream. Suffering from all the same deprived conditions the economy imposed on poor white families, Indian families faced an additional deadly menace during the dust storms: their susceptibility to communicable pulmonary diseases, especially whooping cough, influenza, diphtheria, and tuberculosis.

Aaron worked out an arrangement with Jacob Pahtwah, the elder spokesman for the Kiowa encampment, whereby he could cut wood on their land for a share of the wood. Soon he learned that the encampment was struggling with several cases of tuberculosis. Aaron offered to notify the Kiowa Indian Agency to send a medical team, but Jacob Pahtwah said, "No, they will only haul us to the government hospital to die. It is better that we stay here on our land and try our old ways to heal and pray to the spirits of our fathers to help us find the way to travel through this part of our life's journey. If we die, we die our way." Many of the inflicted tribal members who earlier had been sent away to tuberculosis sanitariums had returned in coffins.

Aaron dreaded Clara learning about the situation at the Kiowa village; he feared she would risk her own health by devoting herself to a hopeless cause. Sure enough, when she learned of the Kiowas' plight, Clara cut two white muslin bedsheets into pieces and sewed them into white uniforms, a knee-length white duster with a gold cross stitched upon it, and a nurse's cap. On days when Aaron went to the woods to cut firewood, he dropped Clara off at the Indian village with a pot of chicken soup. The Kiowas found disfavor with her bean soup. They received plenty of beans in their monthly allotment of staples from the agency, and they used the gaseous "thunder beans" only when nothing else was on hand.

The Kiowa women accepted Clara's help with gratitude and dignity. In the 1870s, Quaker missionaries had brought the Christian faith to the Plains Indians, and Methodist and Baptist missionary groups had ministered to them in more recent times. Some of the Kiowa women were devout Christians, but the Kiowa men tended to be lukewarm about "church ways." Their self-image and their status in the tribe required them to at least pay homage to their ancient culture. They believed in the sun and the forces of nature, storms, and buffalo herds and facing their enemies. Their way to wisdom, status, and maturity was through their success in acquiring visions. Smoking peyote had become a common way to hallucinate, but the Plains Indians also learned to use liquor to achieve a similar stupor and visions. Alcoholism was rampant among the Kiowas. Many of their men and some of their women spent their allotments on whiskey or beer when they could get it. Oklahoma was a dry state, and the federal government prohibited selling liquor to Indians, but people of all cultures who craved liquor usually were able to find it. In many Oklahoma counties, bootleggers operated under the aegis of the county sheriffs, and often the bootlegger and the sheriff were one and the same.

Clara assisted the tubercular victims, trying to help them find comfort and recovery however she could, washing their bedding, feeding them soup, brushing their hair, laying her hands upon them, and praying openly for their recovery. She conducted devotional services for those who wanted to participate and read many of her favorite Bible verses to provide hope, faith, and relief to all who were suffering. The Kiowas' major treatment for disease was to sweat the disease out of their bodies, and although Clara wondered if the procedure only aggravated the condition of the afflicted, she honored their practice and helped prepare boiling water and blankets to cover their heads and induce the steam treatment they desired. One by one, as the tubercular victims wasted away and died, Clara stepped aside and honored the Indian way of mourning and burying their dead.

During the midst of the seventh dust storm of the 1933 season, Clara's days of devoting herself to the needs of others came to an end. She began to cough up blood, and her doctor ordered immediate and extended bed rest. Tuberculosis had taken over her frail body and it broke her down quickly.

Within three weeks, she could not get out of bed. One day in early April, she coughed incessantly and passed out for lack of oxygen. Her lungs rattled with the blood and fluid she no longer was able to expel. Aaron stayed awake through the night, wiping her brow. In the middle of the night, she roused and asked him to read a passage from the Gospel of Matthew:

> *Come, ye blessed of my Father; inherit the kingdom prepared for you from the foundation of the world:*
> *For I was an hungred, and ye gave me meat: I was thirsty and ye gave me drink;*
> *I was a stranger, and ye invited me in;*
> *Naked, and ye clothed me; I was sick, and ye visited me;*
> *I was in prison and ye came into me.*
> *Then shall the righteous answer him, saying, Lord, when saw we thee an hungred and fed thee? or thirsty and gave thee drink?*
> *When saw we thee a stranger and took thee in?*
> *Or naked, and clothed thee? Or when saw we thee sick, or in prison, and came unto thee?*
> *And the King shall answer and say unto them,*
> *Verily I say unto you, Inasmuch as ye have done it unto one of the least of these my brethren, ye have done it unto me.*

Next morning, Clara could not raise her head, and she passed in and out of consciousness. Aaron asked a next-door neighbor, a fellow church deacon, to summon Daniel and Leona to their mother's bedside. Through the morning and into the afternoon, Aaron and Daniel sat on Clara's right side, Dexter and Leona sitting on her left. Her four grandchildren were not brought into the sickroom, for fear of contamination, but Grace held up Jesse and Janie and Leona's Vernon and Kirby, one at a time, to Clara's outside bedroom window for Clara to see them and bless them, and Grace watched the children play all day with a rope and a puppy and sticks and a ball in the front yard.

Near sunset, Clara roused briefly and asked Dexter to hold her hand. "Dexter, I have prayed for your soul more than anything else in my entire life," she said in a faint voice.

"I appreciate that, Mother Bird."

"I hope to meet you in heaven someday, when you have lived a good, full life."

"Yes, ma'am, I'll see you there."

"I'll be with Jesus soon. What do you want me to tell Him?"

"Tell Him thanks for our babies. And we could use a good rain."

Clara smiled her last smile. "I know you'll take care of Leona and your sons and my precious Aaron when he gets old. See to it that he doesn't go without."

"Yes, ma'am."

"I need to close my eyes now."

"Yes, ma'am. You take it easy."

She then turned to her husband. "Aaron, my precious, I will be waiting for you."

"Yes, my angel."

Clara's eyes were closed. Her every breath was a struggled gasp. "I see a bright light... shining through a door," she whispered. "I see loved ones... waiting for me. I know them..."

Her funeral was simple and well attended by people whom she had helped and befriended. Pallbearers were Daniel and Dexter, Russell and Wally Dalkens, and two young men she had taught in

Sunday school years earlier. The minister declared that Clara Williams Bird had laid up enough treasures in heaven to last a billion years.

*   *   *

Clara Bird's remains were placed in a double-burial plot in Altus City Cemetery. Aaron divided his modest home furnishings between Leona and Daniel, except for a bed, his cedar rocker, a small wooden table, two straight-backed chairs, and a few kitchen items. To be near Clara's grave, he moved his remaining possessions into a one-room apartment over a retail store in downtown Altus, paying his monthly rent from his Oklahoma Old-Age Pension check. There he would live for many of his remaining thirty years. Hour after hour he read the Bible using the light from a naked light bulb that hung over a gas cooking range, his source of heat as well as his kitchen stove. He shared a community bathroom down the hall with four other residents, who, without planning a formal schedule, nevertheless developed a symbiotic time whereby each of them had sole use of the bathroom at precise intervals each day.

For a few hours each day, Aaron ventured down to the street near a busy corner, leaned against a store facade, and like similar solitary elderly men throughout the world, looked at nothing in particular and saw everything in general, daydreaming about the past as the present passed by.

On Sunday mornings, Sunday evenings, and Wednesday evenings, he walked two blocks to Altus First Baptist Church for worship services there. He especially appreciated the church music and sat as near to the choir as possible. He often attended choir practice on Thursday evenings, just for the uplifting pleasure of listening. He was invited to join the choir as a tenor, but he could not carry a tune in a basket, and he knew it. He just simply wanted to absorb what he believed were the sounds of the soul.

Occasionally he worked in and around Altus at whatever day labor he could find. Once a month, he carried a hoe to the Altus Cemetery a mile outside of downtown and cleared the weeds off Clara's grave.

In autumn, he paid the monthly rent on his upstairs one-room downtown apartment for three months in advance then hitchhiked to the cotton harvest under way in South Texas to pick cotton from there across Southwest Texas into New Mexico and Arizona, returning just before Thanksgiving. In the spring, he again paid his rent three months in advance, packed his cardboard suitcase, and hitchhiked to the cotton patch country to chop cotton. He lived in migrant farm workers' camps, where the other farm workers came to know him and respect him as Old Man Bird, the Bible reader. He prayed for their health and souls and laid hands on them whenever they asked. He lived on canned pork and beans, fried potatoes, sardines and crackers, boiled eggs, bologna sandwiches, coffee, and soda pop. His children did not hear from him regularly, except in brief monthly notes when he sent his earnings to Leona to put in the bank in her name should Dexter abandon her (which Aaron expected), in which case, if in dire need, she could use Aaron's earnings for herself and her children. His personal financial goal was to make a monthly contribution to missionary work and to save enough money to pay for his burial someday, with a granite monument to mark his and Clara's graves.

Each December between Thanksgiving and Christmas, Aaron visited Daniel and his family for a week or two, and inevitably, during the visit, he would go to bed with a hacking dry cough, weakness in his chest, cold chills, and shortness of breath. "Daniel, I think you had better call a doctor," he would say on the second or third day of being bedridden. "I think my heart is about to fail."

The doctor would come and examine him and find his heart to be strong and his lungs to be clear, but Aaron would let the physician know, "When I get down and have pain like this, a hot toddy with milk, raw egg, and rye whiskey always gets my circulation going again."

And so it was that Aaron Bird, lifelong alcoholic, found a way in his later years to acquire a fifth of whiskey legally in dry Oklahoma, where retail liquor was illegal, ingest it safely and legally as prescribed medicine in the bosom of his family, and temporarily quench his craving for whiskey without committing a sin, unless imagining illness or feigning illness is a sin. His symptoms disappeared as the whiskey ran out.

*   *   *

Dexter Dalkens was affected by his mother-in-law's death in an especially negative way. He had always been in awe of her, for Clara Bird had walked so close to God. Nevertheless, she had been a source of stability to him; her compassion for him and her positive expectations of him had brought out his best efforts. The values she had hoped to find developing in him had made him seek or at least pretend to have those values, but now that she was gone, he was bitter. She had sacrificed herself for a dirty camp of Indians, and for what? Tuberculosis and a grave. This at a time when he needed hope, because his desire for Leona had waned, diluted by regularity and familiarity. He loved his sons, Vernon and Kirby, but they were not enough like him to please him, and had they been, he would have resented that too.

Dexter enjoyed his work on the Bar C Ranch, and an enjoyable, new development was keeping him there. From a fishing and hunting magazine, his boss, Richard Carter, had the idea to build a hunting lodge on a lake in the center of his 1,200-acre ranch, taking advantage of Dexter's hunting and fishing skills, his bravado, and his mastery in handling hunting dogs. Advertisements in the *Daily Oklahoman* were bringing wealthy Oklahoma City professional men to the hunting camp for weekend outings, for which they paid well. Dexter earned extra pay as a guide when the Bar C Ranch hosted a hunting group, and he got to do what he enjoyed most—hunting, fishing, working with dogs, drinking, and gambling half the night. Often the men in the hunting parties brought along their girlfriends, not their wives, and Dexter was sly enough to enjoy some of them also.

Leona dreaded the aftermath of the weekend hunting groups. While her homemaking energies were confined to a remodeled granary, a husband who took her for granted, and two constantly demanding children, Dexter came home overstimulated and impatient. He had not said an endearing word to her for months.

One Saturday night, he did not come home to her at all; instead, he was in bed at the lodge with a call girl who had been brought there by an older man Dexter described as "a squat, rich, drunk, under-endowed, no-neck sugar daddy banker" who had passed out before 9:00 p.m.

"Dexter, your sons have been missing you," Leona told him the next day. "Would you like to take them out with you for a while today?"

"Impossible. Leona, do not bore me with such foolishness."

PART II

The Formative Years

CHAPTER 8

Against All Odds

A person's line of existence has many strands and coincidences upon coincidences. Or else, everything is predetermined. In either case, miracles abound. If Abel had slain Cain, or if Cain had slain Abel then killed himself, or if early man had not migrated out of Africa, if the Angles and the Saxons and the Vikings and the French had not crossed the English Channel, if the Pilgrims had not crossed the Atlantic in the 1600s, if the Scots Irish had not crossed the Appalachians in the 1700s, if the Dalkens and Bird and Williams families and the Swanfeather Choctaws had not crossed the Mississippi River in the 1800s, if Dr. Mortimer Douglas Bird had been killed at the Battle of Buena Vista in 1846 or died of dysentery in Mexico in 1847, if John Dalkens had not survived gangrene at Vicksburg in 1863, if James Dalkens had been swept away in the 1900 Galveston hurricane or not had his horse shod in Strong City, Indian Territory, on a certain day in 1906, if Maudeen Swanfeather or her father or grandfather Swanfeather had taken Choctaw spouses, if Aaron Bird had been trampled to death in a longhorn stampede during the cattle drives or died of alcoholism in his twenties, if Clara Williams had not seen the face of Jesus in an alcoholic derelict and fallen in love with him, if Grace Dalkens had not been pulled out of school in 1923, if Daniel Bird had been burned to death in the Babbs Switch School fire in 1924, if a particular spermatozoon had not injected a certain ovum

101

in 1933, Benjamin Ray Bird would not exist as others came to know him.

*   *   *

In May 1933, after Daniel Bird had planted a corn crop and a cotton patch and repeatedly prayed for rain, he signed up to participate in a federal temporary-work program to build a new bridge across the Washita River, about thirty miles from his farm home near Roosevelt. The New Deal program that funded the construction project allowed farmers and other men with families from that area to work for two weeks then rotate off the project to allow others to work for two weeks, spreading the funds to benefit as many families as possible. The government provided tents, cots, and three meals a day.

It was stressful for Daniel to be away from his family for two weeks, but the money he earned at the bridge project paid for staples that lasted for several weeks—sacks of flour, cornmeal, potatoes, beans, a ham and a slab of salt pork, a bucket of lard. Grace and other homemakers of that era learned how to stretch commodities to keep food on their families' tables. While Daniel was away, Grace kept the cows milked and the cream separated, the garden hoed and the fresh vegetables gathered. Young Jesse, their serious-minded first child, tried to help as much as possible. Not quite six years old, he could tell which vegetables were ready to be gathered and he had enough grip in his fists to milk Sadie, a docile old cow who often turned her head around and tried to lick his head, as though he were her baby.

The temporary, two-week job seemed longer than that for Daniel and for his wife. In this, their first separation Grace came to realize how significant her regular conjugal relations with her husband had become to her sense of well-being. As Daniel drove the Hargrove jalopy home to rejoin his wife after fourteen days apart, he was edgy and primed for romance, as libidinous as he had been before their marriage. There developed in his testicles a certain new spermatozoon, among a legion of new spermatozoa. One among thousands, tens of thousands, tens of hundreds of thousands, one in multiple millions that would gush forth that evening into Grace's vagina. The average healthy young adult male produces from twenty million to over one hundred million sperm cells each day. What were the odds that a certain spermatozoon that would contribute one-half of the chromosomes to form a living being that would become Benjamin Bird would successfully weave and wobble through a maze of tubes and rivals and survive to impregnate a contemporary egg that, on that very day, was being released by one of Grace's ovaries, an ovum that would contain chromosomes that would comprise one-half of the characteristics of the living being that would become her beloved, unexpected, unplanned little Benjamin? The odds: infinitesimal.

For the first half-hour after he reached home, Daniel sat in a chair with a child on each knee. Jesse showed him some drawings he had done and a wooden toy he had made for Janie, while Janie was hugging her daddy, bouncing up and down, giggling, pulling on his overalls suspender, playing with his esophagus. Grace planted her hand on Daniel's shoulder, rubbed his neck affectionately, then went to the cookstove to prepare a dinner feast of fried chicken, corn bread and gravy, and a tray of fresh radishes, onions, cucumbers, and English peas from the garden. For dessert, she opened a can of cling peaches.

That evening, the children were put to bed early. Daniel and Grace went to bed without delay and melded together. Until that evening, they had steadfastly followed the rhythm method of birth control since Janie had been born to avoid an unwanted pregnancy. It was not a "safe" day for intercourse, but safe-smafe, they had been apart too long!

In the creation of a pregnancy, timing is crucial. For fertilization to occur, Daniel's sperm had to be thrust into Grace's vagina within a few days before or on the day of her ovulation, for sperm cannot remain fertile more than forty-eight to seventy-two hours after ejaculation.

Bingo!

Once ejaculation occurred, the race was on. Over one hundred million spermatozoa swam toward a common destination, their journey fraught with heavy mortality. Some rambled aimlessly, while most scrambled headlong toward an instinctive goal. Which one, if any, would prevail? Possibilities seemed endless. Alongside a sperma-tozoon that could become a world-champion sprinter was a pigeon-toed klutz; a dentist, a baker, a banker, a mortician, a matchmaker, a mystic, a researcher who might find a cure for a disease not yet dis-covered; a thousand teachers, brain surgeons, carpenters, barmaids, chefs, nurses, gardeners, miners, farmers, murderers, lawyers, thieves, ministers, rapists, judges, idlers, fiddlers, overeaters, underachievers, disbelievers, spies, nuns, nudists, whores, bores, firemen, plagiarists, mechanics, masochists, technocrats, Democrats, conservatives, pres-ervationists, humanitarians, hoarders, intellectuals, heterosexuals, bisexuals, homosexuals, transsexuals, asexuals, vegetarians, parlia-mentarians, evolutionists, predestinarians. Dashing forward head to head in a dead heat were a potential Mensa genius and a village idiot.

A vast percentage of the sperm failed to find Grace's cervical opening into her uterus. Many of the millions that entered her uterus through her cervix swam several millimeters in seconds, lashing their sperm tails into strands of cervical mucus, propelled by uterine con-tractions and by chemical attraction into her fallopian tube.

Within fifteen minutes after ejaculation, a few dozen sperm approached the egg. Several of them began to try to attach their sperm heads to the outer coating of the egg, the sperm heads releas-ing enzymes that digested a path through the coating in an effort to bind to the plasma membrane of the egg. Although about three thousand sperm ultimately reached the egg, the egg accepted only one (our little pre-Benjamin), then the egg released enzymes that made it impermeable to all other sperm.

When Daniel and Grace awoke the next morning, they again indulged in conjugal union, but for the new ejaculates, it was too late. The specific sperm that was to determine one-half of what the new creature Benjamin Bird was to be, and the ovum that was to determine the other one-half, had conjoined, enlarged, mixed their chromosomes, and now, in the form of a zygote, were drifting down Grace's fallopian tube in a weeklong journey toward her uterus.

In the mixing of the chromosomes, the variety of gene com-binations was very great. Would Benjamin be right-handed or left-handed? Blue-eyed, brown-eyed, green-eyed, cockeyed? Would he have hair like his father or like his great-great-great-great-grand-mother whozis? Which chromosomes ended up in designing the new baby was entirely a matter of chance. Or as his deceased grandmother Clara Bird would have believed, it was by God's grace.

With her husband home, Grace basked in an overwhelming sense of well-being, joyous in how simple and happy their life together was, still unaware that she was going to have another baby. As the fertilized egg—now a zygote—drifted down her fallopian tube, it became a solid ball of cells, then after about six or seven days, it converted itself into a hollow ball of layered cells as it imbedded itself in the thickened wall of her uterus. The inner layered mass of cells became the embryo, the remaining cells became the placenta, attached to Grace's uterine wall so that the embryo could receive nourishment from an umbilical cord fed by Grace's bloodstream. Still unaware of what was happening within her womb, Grace began to be affected by hormonal changes that prepared her body for the pregnancy. Inexplicably she had persistent thoughts about how pleasurable it had been to nurse her babies at her breast, at least until the little tykes sprouted baby teeth.

*   *   *

In early June 1933, at the annual Dalkens family reunion, Grace became somewhat tense and prayerful as she realized that she had missed her menstrual period. Janie, barely three years old, clung to her constantly, while Jesse followed the older boys around the camp and tried to participate in whatever they fancied to do. Janie was not accustomed to be around a crowd of people. With Janie in her arms or tugging at her hem, Grace tried to help in preparing the reunion meals despite a slight case of nausea. She wanted to turn Janie over to Daniel while she helped with the food preparation, and she became uncharacteristically annoyed when Daniel and several of the men organized a domino tournament. A domino table was no place for a toddler who liked to put small items into her mouth. Nimble with numbers and skilled in math, Daniel progressed quickly to the championship round and remained there, oblivious that his wife was not having a good day.

Grace detected a subtle sociological trend among her cousins at the 1933 reunion that also distressed her, a drifting-away from the cohesive, harmonious unity within the extended Dalkens family. While James and all his remaining first-generation siblings would hold one another dear to their bosoms until they died, their children—all first cousins—were growing apart. The California cousins were beginning to talk differently, dress differently, lose touch with their agrarian heritage, and take on cosmopolitan ways.

Likewise, the Oklahoma City group comprised a clique, more urban than agrarian, but not quite as sophisticated as the Californians. After the Saturday evening reunion meal was served and before all the dishes were washed, the cousins split into their special groups, the Californians driving off to Lawton to go night-club dancing, the Oklahoma City group taking a case of beer to the lake to go swimming, the rural Southwestern Oklahomans and their North Texas cousins, in farm overalls and denim jeans, sitting around the campfire, talking about the domino tournament (Daniel won second place), the weather and the crops, the New Deal, Dizzy Dean and the St. Louis Cardinals, the rise of Adolf Hitler in Germany, and reminiscing about how nice and slow their lives had been before the Great War disrupted the world and the automobile came along.

Next morning, Eliza Dalkens's Sunday morning devotional service was not very well attended.

*   *   *

Before revealing to Daniel (who did not closely keep track of such things) that she had missed her menstrual period, Grace wanted to see if her monthly cycle might have been merely naturally disrupted by something other than pregnancy. The day after returning home from the Dalkens reunion, Grace conducted a secret inventory of baby things in her cedar chest. How many usable cloth diapers and baby clothing articles were left over from Jesse and Janie's infancy? If she was pregnant, her third child would be born in February 1934, in the dead of winter. How many baby blankets? Flannel gowns? Booties? If she was carrying a boy, could Leona hand down any of Vernon's and Kirby's little boy rompers?

Meanwhile, the embryo's cells had begun to take on specific functions. By week 3 of gestation, its brain, heart, spinal cord, and intestinal tract began to develop. In weeks 4 and 5, arm and leg buds, eyes and ear structures, vertebra, and other bones began to form. The heart was beating at a regular rhythm, sending a bloodlike fluid into rudimentary vessels.

For Grace, cooking breakfast had become a challenge; the aroma and taste of food at that time of day made her nauseous. One morning during the fifth week of pregnancy, she dashed from the kitchen table through the back door and vomited in the yard. Daniel followed her outside and asked worriedly, "Honey, what's wrong?"

"I think I'm pregnant," she said and began to cry.

She and Daniel had agreed not to have another baby at least until the economic depression was over; he had declared that they could not afford another mouth to feed. She was apprehensive about how he would react to the news. Daniel's response was predictable: a mixture of prideful masculinity that news of impending fatherhood brings even to the humblest or most calloused male specimen, concern about the added responsibility that providing for another child would place upon him, and solicitation for the welfare of his beloved wife.

"If we are going to be blessed with another child, so be it. It's God's will," he said, hugging her. "Why don't you go back to bed and rest a while? I will finish feeding the kids and clean up the table."

From that time forth, Grace became preoccupied with eating the right food and resting sufficiently, for the sake of her unborn, while devoting herself to the full-time responsibility of mothering the two angels she already had. She wanted to stay well so that costly doctor's visits could be kept to a minimum. Daniel helped her with the children and the household chores when he was not out in the fields, and on Sunday afternoons, after they returned from church, he took on the Monday washday task by tackling his heavy overalls and work shirts and their bedding with scalding water, a scrubbing washboard, and homemade lye soap in a big black kettle in the backyard.

In week 6 of the gestation, the embryo's arms and legs had lengthened and had formed fingers and toes, and its lungs began to form. In week 7, elbows, nipples, and hair follicles were developing, and the brain continued to grow. By week 8, the embryo's eyelids, external ears, and other facial features were developing. Grace was brimming with a healthy pregnancy, and her heart swelled with love for her husband and children. She was still seeking perspective on just how this third child developing within her would fit into the family. Jesse, her firstborn son, had his sixth birthday on July 10, and as she baked him a cake and wrapped his birthday present—a new lunch box for him to carry when he started school in the autumn— she could not alter her conviction that although each of her children would be special and loved equally, Jesse the firstborn was destined for greatness. Jesse and Janie had yet to learn that they were going to have a little brother or sister. Janie remained a little emotional, clinging vine. Grace encouraged her to do "mother" things with her dolly, hoping that Janie would soon outgrow her toddler stage, else Grace would be dealing with two babes in arms simultaneously.

*　　*　　*

As one of the hottest, driest summers on record began, Daniel kept the water trough clean of debris in the cow lot so that Grace and the children could splash in fresh, cool water being pumped into the cow trough by the windmill each afternoon, when the heat inside the house became stifling. The water level reached Janie's neck; Grace watched diligently in event that Janie stumbled and went under. Jesse held on the side of the trough and splashed his feet as though he were in a long-distance race. To avoid the stifling heat, they stayed in the water each day until their skin wrinkled.

By the ninth week of pregnancy, the embryo's face was well-formed, with eyelids that remained closed; its limbs were long and thin. By week 10, all organs had begun to form; red blood cells were being produced in the liver. By week 11, the embryo had become a fetus, its basic structure laid down. Male genitalia had formed. By week 12, its fingers could make a fist. Its head made up nearly half of its body size.

By week 13 of the gestation, teeth buds were being formed. By week 14, fine hair was growing on its head. By week 15, the fetus's bones became harder, and it developed more muscle tissue. Grace could feel a fluttering in her lower abdomen as the baby began to make active movements. There was a visible bulge in Grace's abdomen, and everyone in the community could tell she was pregnant. Maudeen explained the situation with her friends in the Ladies Helping Hands Club and at church by saying, "My daughter Grace is about to go into confinement," an archaic term that implied that a woman who showed pregnancy was expected to hide it, at least as long as possible, because to some people, pregnancy implied wrongdoing, and to other, more superstitious people, there was a fear that a pregnant woman was highly susceptible to have a spell cast upon her by evil, medieval spirits who wanted to harm or mark the baby.

In week 16, the unborn baby's ears could hear the muffled sounds of Labor Day activities at Roosevelt's town square, as the community met for its annual Summer Festival, featuring barbecue, watermelon, hot dogs, and homemade ice cream. Grace and her sister-in-law Leona sat on a park bench in the shade of a giant pecan tree and watched their children play as festivities transpired.

Jesse and Vernon were starting their first grade of school the very next Monday, a new generation of Dalkens descendants at Consolidated Number 8. Jesse and Vernon joined two new classmates they had met at enrollment earlier in the week, and the boys were off to see the activities, four-year-old Kirby tagging along. Grace noticed that Jesse had assumed leadership of the small group, and she was pleased, but not surprised.

There were sack races for the kids, barbershop quartet competition, Kiowa round dances performed by Native Americans, and a horseshoe-pitching contest, in which Daniel won second place. Maudeen won a husband-calling contest, hands down. "Happy! Happy Dalkens!" Folks could hear her easily from a mile away. Maudeen's prize was a cowbell. James laughingly pointed out, "My wife does not need a cowbell when she yells 'Dinner!' I can hear her from the back of the pasture! I have never missed a meal!"

Grace was pleased to see Janie make friends with other children her age and drift away to a sandpile to play with them.

In week 18, the fetus's eyebrows and lashes were formed, and by week 19, it had fingernails and toenails. Grace often could feel the baby moving as it became more active with increased muscle development. During week 20, a visit to the doctor's office confirmed that Grace was carrying a healthy child; the fetus's heartbeat was heard clearly with a stethoscope. By week 22, the baby began to store fat from its mother's bloodstream and its bone marrow was producing blood cells.

In a normal pregnancy, the mother's blood cells do not leak into the fetus; the placenta blocks the transference of elements potentially harmful to the unborn. Nevertheless, there are researchers who believe there are instances wherein a woman—especially one who has already produced a male child—will react to the testosterone being produced by her new, unborn male child by developing antibodies against the testosterone, and the antibodies may intrude into the male fetus at a time when the child's future sexual preference is being determined.

In October, Jesse brought his first report card home from school, all As and Bs. His teacher noted, "Jesse is so serious—needs to relax and enjoy his work." Jesse told his mother, "Mrs. Thraxton is asking me to learn letters that aren't even in my name. What a waste!"

Grace decided it was time to inform Jesse that the bulge in her tummy was a little brother or sister for him and Janie and that when the baby was born after Christmas, Jesse would need to be a big boy and help her take care of Janie and the baby.

"It ought to be a girl," said Jesse, "so that Janie will have someone to play with and not follow me around all day. I am already filling up the boy spot, anyway!"

During week 24 of Grace's pregnancy, the family attended a Halloween party that Maudeen was hosting for nine-year-old Olivia and several of her school chums. Olivia was dressed as a princess; her schoolmates wore scary or funny masks. Grace cut a cat's face out of cardboard and covered it with black linen for Jesse to wear. Vernon and Kirby each had one of their mother Leona's worn-out stockings pulled over their heads. Dressed in black, Maudeen flitted about the house, cackling like a witch, offering sweets, lemonade, and sour candy, her face smeared with lipstick and soot. From time to time, Grace noticed that her unborn baby seemed to jerk in startled reaction to the loud noises the children were making. For tiny Janie, the costumes, masks, laughing, and screaming were too much to absorb. She cried intermittently throughout the evening and would not leave her mother's lap until Daniel carried her outside so she could escape the impact of the weird sounds and spooky behavior. Soon she was playing mother to a litter of young kittens that had been born under the front porch.

*   *   *

During the next three weeks, the fetus's brain development progressed rapidly and its nervous system developed enough to control some body functions. It could open and close its eyelids, its mouth could make sucking motions, it could simulate rhythmic breathing movements, and its fingernails, footprints, and fingerprints were well-formed. Its bones were fully developed, but still soft and pliable, as it nestled safely in the sac of amniotic fluid.

Thanksgiving occurred on Thursday of the twenty-seventh week of Grace's pregnancy, and as usual, James and Maudeen had all their children and grandchildren over for the special day. It had not been a good crop year, as the drought had persisted and dust storms had resumed with each autumn cold front that blew in from the northern plains. Nevertheless, there was much for which to be thankful. James's glass was always at least half-full, never half-empty. Back in the summer, James and Daniel each had signed up for a new federal program offered by the Agricultural Adjustment Act that provided benefit payments in exchange for plowing up a portion of their cotton crop. The payments were appreciated but had to be shared with their landlords, and the money had not lasted long.

As each of his children arrived for Thanksgiving dinner, James's heart swelled. On that day, at least, they all seemed happy. Russell and Donna Belle were there from Meers, with Jimmy, their handsome year-old firstborn son. Dexter and Leona were still living austerely in the granary on the Carter Ranch, where Dexter kept a steady job. Daniel and James each had suffered an almost total 1933 corn crop loss, and their pastures were parched, but their milk cows were freshening; they would have cream to sell through the winter. All the Dalkens families had cultivated bountiful vegetable gardens that they had kept watered from cisterns and windmills, and their storm cellar shelves were filled with glass jars full of canned goods that would last until spring.

Maudeen had hatched out over thirty turkeys in 1933, and the biggest and fattest tom was the centerpiece entrée for their Thanksgiving meal. Grace's swollen abdomen stuck out so far that she found it more comfortable to sit sideways at the table. Eating for two, she was ravenous. James blessed the food and gave thanks for the hands that prepared it and asked the Lord to watch over them and bring Grace to a safe delivery in the forthcoming year.

Everyone stayed over Thanksgiving night because next morning was the annual hog-butchering day. James had raised a litter of spotted Poland China pigs and had fattened them enough to fill everyone's meat boxes, which were always kept on the north side of buildings, out of reach of the sun's warmth and in exposure to northern winter winds. All the pork was covered with seasoned salt and maple sugar to preserve it, and although it would sometimes become rancid before it was all eaten, usually it lasted through the winter.

During the weeks leading up to Christmas, Grace's unborn baby's body fat increased, and it began storing calcium, iron, and phosphorus. Grace waddled around the house in constant discomfort, and the discomfort kept her from sleeping soundly, day or night. She was already larger than she had become with each of her two earlier pregnancies, and it made her wonder if she had miscalculated when the baby was due. She felt ready to deliver it already. Preparations for Christmas challenged her, not only because she lacked energy, but also because there was little money. She managed to stitch together a new Christmas dress for Janie and a new blue shirt for Jesse. Monday before Christmas Day, Daniel took a ten-gallon can of cream to town to sell at the creamery, and he used the money to buy Janie a new infant dolly, Jesse a Tom Mix gun and holster set, and for Grace, a soft lavender-colored sweater.

Two days before Christmas, Daniel and Jesse took a bow saw out to the creek bottom in the back of the cow pasture and cut a small cedar tree to decorate. Cedar trees in Western Oklahoma always had sparse limbs on their south side, shaped by Oklahoma's predominate southern wind. Daniel nailed the small cedar tree onto a stand and helped Grace position it in a corner of the living room, where its bare side was hidden in the corner. Decorating the tree became a family tradition: strings of popcorn, red and green crepe paper streamers, peppermint candy canes instead of candles, and papier-mache angels, Santas, reindeer, and snowmen, handmade by Grace and crayon-colored by the children. Stockings were stuffed with apples, oranges, and candy, pinned high on the tree, out of Janie's reach.

The extended family again gathered at James's and Maudeen's on Christmas Day to exchange presents, although each family, like Daniel and Grace, had just enough money to buy a few gifts for their own children. Maudeen bought Olivia a new dress and a comb-and-brush set for her lavish head of chestnut-colored hair. Wally and his bride, Valdetta, home for the holidays from their rodeo circuit, received brightly colored matching Western shirts and a new lasso. Maudeen bought her husband a new, pearl-handled pocketknife, and James gave Maudeen a lacy pink nightgown. When Janie opened her present and found a new infant doll, her first reaction was to pick up her scuffed-up first doll and throw the dingy thing away.

Grace used the situation as a teachable moment. "Janie, honey, mommies can have two babies, or even more. We don't throw babies away when a new one comes along. We hug and love and care for them all. See, you can carry one in each arm."

"Yes!" Janie exclaimed, in the longest sentence she had ever uttered until then. "Like Pretty Kitty Pussy Purr-Mew's kitties under the porch!"

*   *   *

Most of the 1934 New Year's celebrations were canceled in Western Oklahoma by an enormous dust storm that darkened the day on New Year's Eve, dust so thick that cars had to pull off to the side of the road for three hours or more—their lights could not penetrate the dust. Olivia was brokenhearted that the New Year's Eve party at Roosevelt First Methodist Church was canceled. She lived for parties, planned for them, and sought reasons for additional parties. What a depressing way to start a new year, letting an old dust storm shut down their lives. She asked her father why God was so mad at them that He would make them live in a dirty, dusty old world month after month. "It seems like God wants us all to die and He is already beginning to cover us up!"

"No, honey, that's not true," James replied. "God didn't cause these dust storms. Foolish, greedy men who plowed up the prairie have caused the dust clouds. God wants us to be good stewards and take care of the land. Be patient. God will bring the rain again and the grass will grow back and cover the land, and the dirty, dusty things will go away. God wants us to prosper and be happy. Why, He has put a new life into your sister Grace's tummy because He wants us to go on and on!"

In late January 1934, James and Daniel again signed up with the New Deal's AAA program that provided cash payments to farmers who would agree to limit their acreage for planting cotton.

Daniel also worked part-time in a federal forest service program that planted shelter belts of trees along fence rows and roadways perpendicular to the prevailing wind: locust trees, Chinese elms, tamarack, catalpa, spruce, red cedar, mulberry, green ash, yellow pine, and other fast-growing species of trees that were designed to grow into a windbreak so that the soil could be protected from future wind erosion.

The tree-planting project would be expanded into an eight-year program to plant shelter belts from Canada into Texas.

* * *

Toward the end of the second week in February 1934, Grace's pregnancy was nearing full term. Her uterus, cradling a fetus totally ready for birth, drooped down into her lower abdomen. Her vulva was swollen, and her pelvis felt like it was ready to pull apart. She walked with constant discomfort and spent most of her time reclining or sitting down, her uterine muscles twitching from time to time with slight prelabor contractions. Daniel began to take Grace and Janie to Maudeen's every day while he went to work on the shelter-belt tree project, in case she went into labor while he was gone. Jesse sat beside Olivia on the school bus and got off the bus when she did; after school, Olivia entertained Janie and Jesse in a playhouse she had created down in the storm cellar.

On the late afternoon of February 24, as Daniel arrived to pick up his family and take them home for the evening, Grace suddenly doubled up in pain. Immediately, Maudeen shifted into midwife mode. "Daniel, carry your wife into Olivia's room. James, stoke the potbelly stove. We've got to get the house hot enough to keep Olivia's room warm, then go out and fill up the laundry kettle and get some water to boiling. Wally, take Olivia, Jesse, and Janie to Dexter's and Leona's to spend the night. Be sure to take school clothes for Olivia and Jesse to wear tomorrow. If Olivia stays here and hears what is going on, she may never want to get married and have children. Daniel, why don't you run into town and notify Dr. Bellish that Grace is in labor? And while I don't think there is any need for him to be here for the delivery—Grace has done this twice before in fine fettle—see if the doctor can come and check on things early in the morning."

"No, I want Daniel to stay here beside me," Grace protested. "Wally can notify the doctor after he comes back from taking the kids to Leona's."

Maudeen was correct. Grace's third delivery was routine, although it took almost all night. The labor contractions came slowly. Daniel sat beside Grace and held her hand, mopping her brow with a damp rag. He had not been enthused about having a third child, but he had tried to hide his feelings from Grace; the die was cast, they were having three children, and that was that. *Dear Lord,* he prayed silently, *please help me accept this new child as a gift, not a burden. Thank you for our boy Jesse. He is already helpful with the chores, and I guess another boy eventually would come in handy. It might be easier for Grace to have another girl, to help around the house and be a playmate to Janie, so I will just leave this up to You, leave this in Your hands, and I pray that You will help Grace through this delivery and that the baby will be all right. I just promise You I will try to be a good daddy."*

It was way past midnight before Grace's cervix had dilated enough for Grace's uterine contractions to begin to position the baby toward the pelvic ring so that its head could approach the birth canal.

The contractions now came quickly, the spiraling uterine muscles from the upper segment of the uterus pushing against the baby, the lower muscles that now incorporated the expanded cervix drawing the baby forward in an expelling motion that would gradually draw the widened cervix up over the baby's head. In the earlier stages, Grace had been encouraged by Maudeen to breathe hard, take long deep breaths, and when it hurt too much, hit Daniel on the shoulder or just yell!

"Oh, Lordie! Oh, Lordie!" wailed Grace when the spasms came. "Oh, flitter! Ooh, flitter! Oooh, God gas a goose!"

Now that the baby was inching into the birth canal, Grace's screams were full-fledged screams, and the stress on the baby—whose world was changing shape drastically—caused its little heart to beat like a powwow drum. "Easy, girl, easy! You're doing fine," said Daniel, who—once the amniotic membrane broke and fluid gushed forth—stifled an impulse to bolt away and run out into the night.

"Quickly, Daniel, hand me an armful of those ripped-up sheets!" urged Maudeen. "It won't be long now!" To James, waiting in the living room, she shouted, "Honey, bring me a washbasin of scalding-hot water!"

The contractions were now pushing the baby's head through the pelvic brim, its head turned parallel to its tiny shoulders and tilted backward so that its forehead would lead its way through the vagina, its head temporarily changing shape or "molding," elongating as it moved like a corkscrew through the birth canal.

"Push! Pussshh!" Maudeen now urged. "I can see its little crown!"

The next contraction was excruciating—it brought Grace a sharp, burning, and stinging sensation. It also brought out the baby's head, which turned in a countercorkscrew fashion to restore its normal relationship to its shoulders. In the next series of contractions, the baby's shoulders emerged in a corkscrew movement as the head had done. "One more push," ordered Maudeen, and the baby slithered out onto her opened palms.

Suddenly, Maudeen lifted the baby by its heels and gave it a sharp slap on its buttocks to induce breathing. "Ee-wah! Eh-wah!" the newborn cried.

"My God, it cries like a donkey!" James shouted from the living room, laughing and giving thanks that the birthing was done.

"It's a boy!" Maudeen announced. "And it is going to have good fortune, because it was born with a membrane cap over its little head. That's a Choctaw sign that he will have psychic gifts, or gifts of prophecy, or power to bring peace amongst enemies!" Deftly she tied a string knot an inch around the still-attached umbilical cord, about four inches from the baby's navel, and a second string knot an inch away from the first, then took a pair of scissors from the basin of scalding water, poured alcohol over the scissors, and snipped the cord in two. The baby continued to wail, "E-wah, Ee-wah, Ee-wah!"

"My stars!" Maudeen exclaimed as she continued to wipe the mucus away. "This little baby boy is almost redheaded! Where on earth did this sandy hair come from? Grace, you did well, a large baby, and you've had only a little bleeding." Quickly she swabbed the infant clean with steamy strips of ripped-up sheeting, dried him off, wrapped him in a blanket, and handed him to his mother. "Grace, you need to nurse this little boy right now to calm him down, and the nursing process should help the afterbirth turn loose as well."

Grace nestled her newborn on her left forearm and positioned her left nipple to the baby's lips. Immediately the crying stopped as the baby clamped down on the breast and sucked mightily, an instinctive miracle. Instinctively, Grace began to hum a lullaby. The birthing room was suddenly gratefully quiet.

Daniel slumped in his chair, sighed with relief, and began to relax for the first time in hours. Suddenly he realized with a sense of guilt that he and Grace had not even considered what to name the baby, an indication that neither of them truthfully had wanted the child. But now that he was here, of course they loved him. After a moment, Daniel asked, "Grace, what should we name this little fellow?"

"Go get Dad's Bible and open a page," she replied.

James brought his Bible from the living room and handed it to Daniel then leaned over the bed to see his new grandson. "He's got my daddy's hair," he declared. "John Jay Dalkens had fine, mousy golden, light-reddish-brown hair."

Daniel opened the Bible randomly to a page and pointed his finger to a verse and read, "Lest Satan should get an advantage of us; for we are not ignorant of his devices."

"Good God, no! Try another page."

Daniel turned to the book of Joshua, pointed his finger at random, and read, "This was the inheritance of the children of Benjamin."

Dawn was breaking. Benjamin Ray Bird first saw the light of day at first light of day, February 25, 1934. He would always be an early riser.

CHAPTER 9

The Fourth Stage of Labor

D r. Bellish arrived at the James Dalkens homestead shortly after 7:00 a.m. on February 25, 1934, and found Grace resting and her baby sleeping at her breast. Maudeen was bustling about in the birthing room, wadding the soiled rags and Grace's detached placenta into a bundle that would be burned in a trash barrel in the back-yard. "Doctor, everything has gone well, and we have a healthy, new grandchild," announced Maudeen with pride and a hint of boasting. She had assisted the physician in numerous births in the community throughout the years. "There was only a minimum of bleeding."

"Mother Maudeen, with you in charge, I had no worry," replied the doctor, opening his bag.

He took Grace's hand and checked her pulse then used a stetho-scope to check her heart. Then he pulled the covers back and looked under Grace's gown to confirm that she had gone through the three stages of labor in good form. The dilation was receding, the passage of the baby had caused no serious tearing, and the placenta had dis-charged without substantial bleeding.

"Grace, has your milk come down?" he asked.

Grace nodded. "Yes, and the baby has a full tummy."

"Good." Dr. Bellish then used the stethoscope to check the baby's heartbeat and lungs. "Sounds good," he murmured. He placed eye drops in the baby's eyes, bringing on a short series of "Ee-wahs," and inspected Benjamin's navel cord. He took a half-dollar coin from his pocket, sterilized it in alcohol, placed it on the infant's navel, and wrapped a tight band around the baby's abdomen. "Keep this coin pressed against his navel for two or three weeks so that he will have an 'innie' and not an 'outie,'" he instructed. "Then put the coin in the bank to start a college fund. Ha ha."

From his medical valise, Dr. Bellish took a set of scales and weighed the newborn. "Eight pounds, ten ounces. Twenty-one inches long. This young man will be as tall as his daddy and his uncles."

"The radio weatherman predicts a bad dust storm is rolling in tonight," the doctor continued. "Grace, your baby's lungs are fragile. You need to keep him in an inside room of the house, with the doors closed, and don't expose him to the wind at all. Keep a damp towel over his crib during the storm and for as long as the dust particles are floating around in the air."

Dr. Bellish then went into the kitchen, where James, Daniel, and Wally were eating a breakfast of scrambled eggs, fried bacon, and hot biscuits soaked in red-eye gravy, a syrupy concoction made from a mixture of water, bacon grease, and maple sugar. "Daniel, spell out your new baby's name for the birth certificate."

"B-e-n-j-a-m-i-n R-a-y B-i-r-d," spelled Daniel. "Doctor, I regret I am not able to pay you today, but I'm working on the shelter-belt tree project over by Mangum, so I will take care of the bill when I get paid next week."

"Fine."

"Doc, sit down and have a bite of breakfast," invited James.

"No, thanks. I had a bowl of oatmeal before I left town," the doctor answered. "James Dalkens, I caution you to stop eating that greasy red-eye gravy. It will clog your bloodstream and kill your heart!"

"But I was weaned on red-eye gravy and other Cajun stuff that made a man out of me," said James, laughing. "Doc, you are sure getting crabby in your old age. Ha ha!"

"James, I am just telling you the truth," replied Dr. Bellish. "You men need to prepare yourselves for a bad dust storm that is rolling in tonight. I need to go to my office now and treat some folks with lung and throat problems caused by the last norther. Mrs. Sumpter from over on Cobb Road is coming in today. She got caught out in the January 1 storm, and the grit damaged her eyes so bad she is now legally blind. You can't be too careful in these awful storms!"

"Wally, carry the doctor's bag out to his car for him," said James as he sopped his plate clean.

Daniel returned to the bedroom to check on Grace and their new son just as Maudeen was taking Benjamin's wet diaper off. The baby's sudden exposure to cold air on his damp skin caused him to emit a urinary stream, upward. Suddenly Maudeen gasped and turned her head, muttering sharply, "That little squirt just peed in my face!" The tone of her voice brought on a new outburst of "Ee-wah, ee-wah, ee-wah!" from baby Benjamin and initiated an awkward, almost-strained lifelong relationship with his grandmother that neither of them would ever understand.

Grace snickered, "He's just getting back at you for spanking his bottom."

Grace and Daniel then made plans to gather their children and return home before the dust clouds arrived. Daniel picked Janie up at Leona's and told her that she had a little newborn baby brother.

"My baby! My baby brover!" Janie cried gleefully as she wrapped her two dolls face-to-face in a single blanket.

On the route back to the Dalkens farm, Daniel stopped at Con 8 School to pick up Jesse; school was let out early so that all the children could be delivered to their homes before the storm hit. As soon as Jesse joined Daniel and Janie in the Hargrove jalopy, his father told him about his new brother.

"Daddy, you should have gone to work to plant trees today," said Jesse the responsible. "Now that you have another mouth to feed, we will need more money!"

"But I was up all night helping your mother," he explained. What a predicament, explaining one's behavior to a critical six-year-old son!

When they arrived at the Dalkens home, Jesse and Janie rushed in to see their new brother. Grace was sitting in a rocker in the living room, holding the infant in her arms. "Shh! The baby is napping," she whispered.

"But he needs to see us," said Janie. "He's ours too!"

Gently Grace unwrapped the blanket to reveal Benjamin's sandy-red hair. Janie patted gently on the blanket and smiled in wonder. "Why, he's a carrottop!" exclaimed Jesse, creator of instant nicknames. "Grace, if you're up to it, we need to get home before the duster rolls in," urged Daniel. Gratefully he hugged Maudeen, thanked her for ushering Benjamin into the world, and handed James an imaginary cigar. "I hope you are pleased with your new grandson," he said.

"You bet!" said James.

On their way home, Jesse declared his protective role concerning his new brother. "It's a good thing he has me to look out for him. I will teach him to swim and throw a ball and fight off bullies!"

When Daniel drove up the lane to the Hargrove house, he could already see the billowing black cloud churning in from the north. The cows were heading toward their shed, the chickens taking to roost.

"Jesse, run out and lock the chickens in for the night. Be sure to count them, twelve hens and a rooster. Gather the eggs and hurry back to the house, because the storm is about to hit us here. Janie, hold Daddy's hand. Grace, are you able to carry the baby into the house?"

"I certainly can. I have been carrying him around for nine months already. He's a darling, he has me floating on air."

They had hardly got settled in and bolted the door shut when the wind shifted sharply and the dry cloud of rolling dust slammed against the house, bringing an electrified crackling sound and driving minute wafting particles of dust in through the crevices in the windowsills and around the door. Heeding Dr. Bellish's advice, Grace asked Daniel to place an orange crate on a chair in their bedroom closet, which she lined with a downy blanket. She was going to use it as a crib, with a damp cloth over it to protect her newborn from the dust particles that inevitably found their way into the room.

* * *

At the age of one month, Benjamin's world was a flannel gown, a swaddling blanket, a stocking cap, an orange crate crib in a bedroom closet, diaper after diaper, and sweet, warm, nourishing breasts. Slumber. Blurry vision, light, darkness, rocking, crying "Ee-wah, ee-wah," nursing, burping, lullabies. Slumber.

Wet diaper, dry diaper, wet diaper, dry diaper, dirty diaper, "Ee-wah, ee-wah," dry diaper. Slumber. Baby lotion and talcum powder. Smells, sounds, comfort, discomfort, "Ee-wah, ee-wah," slumber.

Sounds and noises that were becoming recognizable: Grace's reassuring voice and her lilting lullabies, Daniel's deep bass, Jesse's tenor, Janie's cooing and whining, wind whistling outside, a creaky rocking chair.

Slumber.

Grace seemed to always be washing or changing or drying diapers. "This baby wets more diapers than both my other babies combined," she declared. "I hear that rich people don't have to wash diapers, they just throw the dirty ones away and buy new ones whenever they run out."

Jesse the inventor put his mind to work and soon thought of a better way. "I will fix a hose and fit it onto Benjamin's little boy-thing and hook the hose to a bag and tie the bag to Benjamin's leg. That will work for boy babies. For girl babies, I don't think they have anything to work with," concluded Jesse the anatomist.

At three months, Benjamin was a bundle of smiles. He watched his parents and siblings, listened to them, recognized their individual voices, laughed and gurgled, and repeated sounds. He explored his hands and feet and tried to grasp objects and draw them to his mouth. A few weeks later, he could roll over from his belly to his back, sit up when propped, grasp objects, and try to toss them, drop objects, and cry to get them back.

At six months, Benjamin had a smile that was instant, especially for Janie, who loved him and treated him like an animated doll. Ben's reaction to Jesse was more tentative. Sometimes Jesse's heart was open to his baby brother, and sometimes there seemed to be a barrier that hinted that the lives of the two brothers would drift far apart. Jesse liked to prop Benjamin up against a pillow, watching him roll over and try to scoot toward a toy with which Jesse tantalized him.

At seven months, Ben easily recognized his own name and other common words, say "Mama" and "Dada," creep or push-crawl across the room to explore, find objects, shake them, and bang them and chew on them, drooling and imitating sounds. At nine months, he was pulling up, taking steps while holding on to something or someone, moving toward individuals he recognized and loved, but remained shy and upset with strangers. His grandmother Maudeen fit halfway between family and stranger: sometimes he would let her hold him and do things for him, but often in her presence he fussed unless Grace was holding him or he was at least within his mother's reach.

In the evenings, in the security of his father's lap, he could sit forever, safe and contented.

On Benjamin's first birthday, his parents were so absorbed in coping with a hard winter with little money that no special observance occurred, no baby picture taken. Grace noted the developmental progress of her year-old child and was well pleased, except that his baby teeth were coming in and she was beginning to look forward to the day that he no longer needed to suckle.

*　　*　　*

The year 1935 was a year of substantial and drastic change. Not just from the weather, which remained as dry and dusty as 1934, but also partly because of people giving up or giving out, their means of livelihood crippled from the sustained national economic depression. For example, Russell and Donna Belle Dalkens had their second child, Donald Joe, "Donny," in February, just as the gravel company where Russell worked announced a 20 percent wage cut. Morrison Lee's general store went broke, and he moved back to Alabama to live near a sister. Russell began to look for a farm to rent so that at least he could try to grow crops and feed his family.

In 1935, Wally Dalkens's bosses and sponsors on the rodeo circuit went bankrupt, ending Wally's rodeo career, so he and his pregnant teenage wife, Valdetta, moved in with his parents near Roosevelt, their married life unfolding in his old bedroom. Wally helped his father farm for the rest of the year.

The fact was that James, in his late fifties, was slowing down. He had bouts of arthritis or rheumatism or gout, and many mornings he simply could not function very well. He appreciated Wally's help and paid Wally small amounts of cash. Valdetta might have found her life under the roof of alpha-mother Maudeen a bit stifling, but with her having come from a family of nine children, the peace and privacy in Wally's room was more than she had ever experienced. Maudeen loved her beautiful young daughter-in-law and tried to make her feel welcome in their home. Under Maudeen's mentoring, Valdetta became a good cook, an adequate but not overachieving housekeeper, and a devoted wife. She and Wally were expecting their first child in November. She adored Wally and constantly lavished affection on him. Wally thrived under her attention and returned her love in kind.

Eleven-year-old Olivia, on the other hand, considered Valdetta an interloper, intruding upon Olivia's role as the most beautiful girl in the family. Olivia was not openly hostile toward her sister-in-law— her parents would not have allowed that—but there was a respectful coolness between her and Valdetta that did not go away. The fact was that Wally himself had never quite accepted Olivia openheartedly because she had taken his place as the baby of the family. Had Olivia not been absorbed in her own interests, the interrelationships might have boiled over from time to time. She loved magazines and monthly journals, especially movie magazines, and she knew how to pry subscription costs from her father. She copied hairstyles from the movie stars, and she sent off for their autographed photos. She clipped out coupons and lied about her age to order free samples of everything from vials of perfume to free tubes of lipstick, to recipes that she intended never to use, to phony requests for lovelorn advice from columnists.

Using three-cent postage stamps or penny postcards, Olivia flooded the mail with orders for free stuff, to send for something every day and receive something in the mail every day; in that way, she connected to the rest of the world and psychologically escaped the constraints of growing up on a dry Western Oklahoma sand hill farm. She spent a lot of time in the privacy of her bedroom, standing in front of the mirror, styling her hair, improving her posture, practicing the art of enticement, monitoring the slow, certain growth of her bosom.

*   *   *

In 1935, Daniel's and Grace's lease on the old Hargrove place was expiring, so Daniel planted their last crop in the dry and dusty soil and wondered what their next move would mean. Would Jesse need to change schools? Would they wind up in another county, in another church, near relatives, or far away?

In 1935, Dexter and Leona Dalkens's life took a most drastic turn. The Bar C Ranch, where they had lived from the beginning of their marriage, received a double blow. Because of the extended drought, the pastures were barren, the cattle herd became unproductive, and the cows that had survived the 1934–1935 winter were too poor to breed and produce a calf crop, but even if they had, cattle prices were too low for Richard Carter to break even. His major source of income had been the hunting lodge that Dexter had artfully managed, but the hunters and their girlfriends had become more and more wild and licentious, until one night during a drunken orgy, the lodge caught fire from a carelessly tossed cigarette and burned to the ground.

"I am going to have to let you go," Richard Carter told Dexter the morning after the fire. "While I don't blame you for the fire, Dexter, I do believe that during the past months, you have let the goings-on at the lodge get way out of hand. In addition, I am going to use the New Deal Drought Relief Service project to sell what remains of my cattle herd to the government for $14 a head, not much money, but at least more than I can get for their skin and bones at the sale barn. So I am going to let my ranch lie fallow until the drought breaks, if ever it happens. With no cattle, there is nothing here for you to do. You and Leona can live here as long as you need to while finding another place. Dexter, here is a week's severance pay, and $50 for your gray gelding, if you need to sell him. That's the best I can offer."

Dexter took the payment and wasted no time changing the course of his life; he had been contemplating making a break for some time. He went to the live-in granary and started packing.

"Leona, my job here has played out. Tomorrow I am moving you and the boys to Altus to be near your daddy, then I am going to Oklahoma City to find a better job. I have a lot of contacts there now, and that's where the money is. Kiowa County is a dead place. We should have left it to the Indians a long time ago."

Leona stood silently and watched Dexter begin to pack. Nothing he had said to her surprised her. "I will come back and get you and the boys as soon as I get situated," he said.

Leona did not believe him. "Why don't you take Vernon and Kirby to your folks for tonight?" she said. "So they won't have to see us breaking up the only home they have ever known."

By bedtime, everything in the granary was packed but the bed itself; the boys were at their grandparents. A fateful moment arrived as Dexter and Leona lay together. He was tired and sleepy, worn-out from packing their possessions and from the previous night's hunting lodge orgy, in which he had participated full force. She realized that this was the last time they would ever sleep together. Her nerves were wound tightly like an alarm clock spring ready to go off. She needed to purge herself from the last iota of her desire for him, she needed to exorcise his heartless hold on her, she needed to throw a fit, she needed to explode, she needed to bring a complete and final climax to her life with him. Yes, climax, Climax. *Climax!*

Suddenly Leona gouged Dexter in the ribs and grabbed his genitals, turned her face to him, and bit his ear. "I'm burning up!" she snarled. "I need to burn to the ground like your awful, evil sex pit of a hunting lodge! Service me, you devil, if there's anything left of you!"

Startled, he turned and lifted himself up on his knees. Immediately she slithered beneath him and began to thrust against him. This was not what he wanted or ever expected from her—suddenly she was a stranger, and he felt as though he were being raped, in an episode that was dreadful and exciting.

He achieved an erection and their sexual encounter was frantic, not under his control but under hers.

He was soon spent, but she went on, clamping down on him and using her legs to hold him in a vise, pounding against him like a dervish, bumping and moaning, "Out! Out! Out!" Soon he was in pain and she was in agony, but still she went on, "Out! Out! Out!"

Dexter tried to end the encounter by turning on his back, but she stayed clamped onto him, riding him, and continued thrusting, moaning "Out! Out! Out!" As he lay limp and raw, she continued on her wild, raw solitary journey toward a mental-physical state of sexual emptiness, until finally she said, "It's over! It's over! Thank God it's over!" She collapsed in a subconscious heap, her back turned to him, permanently bereft of all desire.

*   *   *

The next day, Dexter rented a modest bungalow about three blocks from Altus's downtown area and moved his family there. It was a shotgun house consisting of a front living room, a middle bedroom, a kitchen in the back of the house, and a screened-in back porch, where Vernon and Kirby, aged eight and five, would sleep. In the backyard there was a tree swing, a sandpile, and a water hydrant, a fun place for the boys. As soon as he got the furniture moved in and the beds made up, Dexter wrote Leona's new address on a piece of paper and unceremoniously left for the City.

In Oklahoma City, Dexter immediately went to work for Larney Medford, one of the occasional hunters who had frequented the Carter ranch. Medford was an Oklahoma City bootlegger, part owner of a taxi company, and shady dealer. Dexter chauffeured his boss and drove a taxi part-time, delivering whiskey to clients from the trunk of his cab and delivering call girls to hotel liaisons with spurious and prominent men of the city. Within a week, he had moved in with Sally Roe, a buxom blond prostitute he had enjoyed keeping company with on weekends back at the Carter lodge. He lost the piece of paper with Leona's address, but it did not matter. He was not going back, he was not sending for them, and he was not sending them anything.

Leona faced the sole responsibility of raising her sons with somber resolve. Her father, Aaron, was nearby to help as much as he could, but he was gone to harvest or cotton-chopping for months at a time. Besides, he could not help her administer physical discipline, even if he wanted to: Vernon and Kirby were too fast for him. Aaron helped Leona get the boys to Sunday school and church at Altus First Baptist Church each week and stayed with them when Leona began to work part-time cleaning downtown offices after work hours, janitorial work similar to what she had done during her year at college. Sometimes, when Grandfather Aaron was off in the cotton fields, her boys went to the offices with her and helped by emptying wastebaskets; sometimes they stayed home alone, eating cheese and crackers and peanut-butter-and-jelly sandwiches, protected only by Leona's prayers to keep them from harm. Gradually she acquired enough income to pay the monthly rent and buy staple groceries, and she visited the church's benevolent clothes bin regularly to select shirts and pants and shoes for her sons.

Out of adversity comes strength. Leona faced years of poverty, and her life swirled in and out of economic and emotional whirlpools, trying to keep a steady hand in raising two boisterous, often unruly children. Her anchor to sanity was that she had a goal beyond getting her sons raised: she intended eventually to go back to college and complete her teaching degree. She would do it quietly, a grinding stepping stone at a time. She began to wear her lush raven hair in a bun. She wore long loose skirts, long sleeves, drab colors, no makeup, her body language saying that she did not have a man in her life and she did not want one. She took in ironing in the daytime and expanded her janitorial work in the evenings. She read uplifting Bible stories to her children when she found time, made sure they were learning their numbers and the alphabet, taught them to tie their shoes, talked to them about morals and maxims, made them brush their teeth, prayed with them, and taught them to give thanks for their daily bread.

In the solitude of the night Leona found rest, wearily drifting off to sleep imagining that she was preparing lesson plans for the next day for an imaginary classroom of students in an imaginary school.

*   *   *

It was not an AmPolly morning. At dawn, a week after Thanksgiving 1935, James Dalkens sat at his kitchen table, alone, with a freshly brewed cup of coffee. The entire household had been up until midnight packing and loading household goods and furniture onto Uncle Joe Dalkens's borrowed farm truck with its high sideboards, and everyone needed to cap off a good night of rest in order to face the rigor of their imminent move to the Denim community in Roger Mills County—especially Maudeen, who was not taking the change very well.

So much had happened in the last ten days. News of James's beloved brother Robert's death of a stroke, a trip to Roger Mills County for the funeral, meeting with Robert's children following the burial when they asked him and Maudeen to move to Robert's farm and operate it for the next three or four years until Robert's son Rayford could resolve his financial obligations in Greeley, Colorado, where he and his family operated an auto-repair shop. The remaining five of Robert's six grown children lived in Oklahoma City and had no interest in returning to the farm.

It was an easy decision for James. As a single young man, he had spent several years at Robert's homestead on the Canadian River northwest of Denim. Back in 1901, he had helped Robert build his six-room, two-story frame house, his barns and fences, and rode for the doctor when three of Robert's four daughters were born. Robert's farm was "the old homestead" to James, his favorite place on earth. Robert had prospered there, and the farm had grown to 320 acres, now reaching clear to the Canadian River bottom.

For Maudeen, the move was going to be difficult. They had lived in the Roosevelt community for nearly twenty years. They had thrived there; they had roots. Maudeen had a good reputation as the guiding leader of the local Ladies' Helping Hands Club, lead singer at the Methodist church, and a recognized, accomplished midwife. She did not want to move, and she expressed this to James as she began to cry on their drive back from Robert's funeral. She had not cried at the funeral; she rarely cried at all.

"Why, sweetheart, you will be just as appreciated in Denim as you are now in Roosevelt, once we get established," said James, trying to console her. "There is a Methodist church in Denim. We will join it our very first Sunday. And if there is no Ladies' Helping Hands Club, why, you can start one. What better way to wind up in charge?"

"But we will be moving farther away from Grace and her family and Russell and his family and Dexter's sons," she complained, a complaint that was greatly alleviated a few days later, when they learned of a New Deal program in which non-landowning family men could move onto abandoned, federally held, foreclosed farms that had been mortgaged to banks that had failed. Applicants could obtain a long-term, low-interest federal loan to purchase up to six milk cows, a team of draft animals, farm implements, and seed. Both Daniel and Russell had signed up for the program, had qualified, and had already gone to Roger Mills County to pick out an available farm.

Russell had selected a 160-acre farm northeast of Denim, halfway between Denim and the Antelope Hills, a picturesque, historic site where, in 1858, in an inconclusive Indian battle called the Battle of Buffalo Robe Creek, Texas rangers had confronted an encampment of Comanches who had been making raids into North and Central Texas. Russell and Donna Belle and her toddlers, Jimmy and Donny, had already moved. Russell had acquired his cows and a team of brown mules and had broken ground for a big vegetable garden. Donna Belle had ordered twenty-five white Leghorn pullets from the Montgomery Ward catalog and had a big cardboard box waiting for them beside her kitchen stove as soon as the mailman delivered them. She hoped Jimmy and Donny would keep their hands off the fragile, fluffy babies when they arrived. Donna Belle had gotten acquainted with one of their close neighbors, a pioneer woman named Augusta Metcalfe, who was becoming recognized as a renowned primitive artist of Southwestern Oklahoma pioneer culture.

Daniel had signed up for a 160-acre farm northwest of Denim, sight unseen—it was the only available farm near the Robert Dalkens homestead. It was about halfway between town and Robert's old homestead, a strategic location. Should his old jalopy break down, James and Maudeen could come by on their way to town and offer transportation to the grocery store and to church. And whenever James or Daniel went to the general store in Denim, they could bring back two one-hundred-pound blocks of ice for their respective wooden iceboxes, which in cool weather might last a week.

"Thank God for the New Deal," James muttered as he freshened his cup of coffee. "God bless F. D. Roosevelt!"

He heard a stirring in their bedroom. Maudeen was rousing. Then he heard an infant cry: Wally and Valdetta's two-month-old son, Gary, was bawling for his mother's breast. At Denim, Wally and Valdetta were going to live in the two upstairs rooms of Robert's farmhouse; Wally was going to farm with James on the halves and hire out to neighbors on occasion. Daniel and Grace were moving nearby in a week or two. Thank the Lord, everything was falling in place.

*   *   *

Grace shared her mother's apprehension about pulling up roots and moving to Roger Mills County, although she realized that Daniel's lease of the Hargrove farm was expiring. "Daniel, let's wait until Jesse's six-week period is over at school so that he can start a new six-week period at his new school at Denim. Then, too, your father comes and spends a few days with us at this time of year. Let's not move until just before Christmas." Her heart was connected to the warm, comfortable home wherein she had conceived her children, loved and served her husband, and reverenced her Lord. She wanted to cherish the place as long as possible.

Grandpa Aaron came for his post-Thanksgiving visit and had a jolly time bouncing and romping with his toddler grandson. Ben was intrigued by Grandpa Aaron's mouth: he had no teeth! Ben would ease his index finger up to Aaron's lips, giggling, waiting for Grandpa to—snap!—like a turtle, at which point Ben squealed with delight. "Benjamin, you are quite a little puppy!" his grandpa said repeatedly and blessed him. "May God smile on you, Benjamin Bird, until your dying day." Ben respected Grandpa Aaron's need for quiet time, when Aaron sat in the rocker and read his Bible, dozing sporadically, snoring, as old men tend to do. Ben stood beside the rocker, listened to the snores, and respectfully mimicked them, eyes closed. "Konkphew, konk-phew, konk-phew…"

On the third day of his visit, Aaron began to cough and sniffle. He wore his denim jacket all day, shivering, and went to bed early. Daniel recognized his father's symptoms as a prelude to a bout of psychosomatic illness that could be cured only with a hot whiskey toddy. Aaron had come to his son's home not only to visit but also to acquire his annual dose of medicinal whiskey. He had to come to Daniel's because his daughter, Leona, would not humor him his game to get liquor. Daniel decided to spare the doctor a house call and cut the course of the illness short by going straightway next morning to Dr. Bellish's office for a prescription.

Daniel's strategy worked: Aaron was bedridden for only two days. Benjamin sat in a chair at his bedside and listened to his grandpa, half-tipsy, humming gospel hymns and uttering prayers of supplication and thankfulness. Aaron held his Bible over his heart, showing Ben and Janie a lock of Clara's gray hair from a packet taped inside the Bible's back cover. The Bible and Clara's hair lock gave him the strength to fight off the craving and stay away from the demons another year. The lock at the back of the Bible spurred Aaron each year to read on and on in order to get to the end of the book, as though he were coming closer and closer to the love of his life.

"Whose hair?" asked Janie.

"Your grandma Bird's hair. She is our guardian angel."

"Where is she?" Janie asked.

"She is in heaven with Jesus, waiting for us there."

"Do you need to die to be an angel?" asked Janie.

"No. She was an angel before she died."

"What was her name?"

"Clara. She was your daddy's mama."

"Mama Clara," said Janie. "I will tell my babies about her."

"Cara Mama," Benjamin said as he stretched his arm across his grandpa's chest and stuck his index finger to his grandpa's lips.

Snap!

Giggles all around.

*　　*　　*

On the Sunday morning before Christmas, Daniel and Grace dressed their children in church clothes and drove Aaron home to Altus, where they all attended services at Altus First Baptist Church with Leona and her sons. Leona sat between Vernon and Kirby to keep them from poking each other in the ribs. Janie sat beside her mother and fidgeted with the buttons on her Sunday dress. Benjamin moved from Grace's lap to Aaron's lap to Daniel's lap, where he stayed because it was a firm, safe place to be, sitting in a strange place among a crowd of strangers. The timbre of the congregational singing and piano banging captivated Ben and made his tummy tremble. He wondered why the big man on the stage talked so loud without stopping. Jesse sat beside his father and listened to the sermon intently.

"Daddy, why did the preacher talk so much about hell?" asked Jesse as soon as the service was over and they were walking to their car.

"Jesse, preachers are called by God to tell the story of Jesus, how He died so that we can live forever if only we believe in Him and trust Him to save our souls," Daniel explained. "The preachers have got to tell us about hell because that's where people who don't trust Jesus go."

Confused, Jesse shook his head. "What about the people in the jungle and the faraway mountains and China people who have never heard of Jesus? And what about people who were born before Jesus? And what about little babies like Benjamin who don't understand much of anything?"

"Son, all I know is that God is a just and loving God and He will do the right thing, and those who know about Jesus and don't follow Him are in trouble."

Daniel wanted to visit his mother's grave before they moved farther away, so they drove to a store that was open on Sunday and bought soda pop and fixings for bologna sandwiches, then the extended family drove to the Altus City Cemetery and picnicked on benches beside an open tabernacle. It was rather chilly, but the sun was out and the air was calm. Initially, the children were subdued by the somber rows of gravestones, although Janie and Benjamin had no idea what they were.

Jesse, Vernon, and Kirby soon became preoccupied by Vernon's new, pearl-handled pocketknife—no one knew where it came from. "I found it on the street in front of our house," Vernon claimed. While waiting for the sandwiches to be served, the boys began to play a game of mumblety-peg.

"You boys be careful with that knife," cautioned Daniel.

"I will get it and hide it at my first opportunity," Leona vowed as she assisted Grace in preparing the sandwiches. Although Grace was afraid it might upset Leona to talk about Dexter, Grace tried to sound casual as she asked Leona if she had heard from him; was there a possibility that he might be coming home for Christmas?

"I have not heard from Dexter since he went to Oklahoma City," Leona said as a matter of simple fact. "I don't expect him to come back." The matter was dropped.

"Leona, I regret that we're moving farther away from you and the boys," Daniel said. "I wish we could be helping you more, you with your hands full. I know Papa tries to help you, but there is just so much he can do. Why don't you let the boys come and spend some time with us this summer when Vernon's school is out? You can put them on the MKT bus and we can pick them up at the Cheyenne bus station."

"I would like to do that," said Leona, "not this summer, but in another summer or two, after I have saved up enough money to go to summer school at Southwestern Teachers College. I still plan to get a teaching degree, God willing, and get a teaching job."

As soon as the bologna sandwiches were ready, they paused and bowed their heads while Aaron gave a blessing over the food. The church service had made them all hungry. Only Janie and Benjamin could not eat an entire sandwich; Grace finished Janie's and Jesse finished Ben's. Daniel and Aaron each had two.

As soon as the meal was finished, Aaron, Daniel, and Jesse walked several yards to Clara's grave, where they knelt and bowed their heads. Daniel prayed to thank the Lord for the life and memory of his mother. Aaron prayed mostly to Clara, while Jesse stayed silent and wondered, *Just what do I need to do to be saved? What really happens to people when they die? If they believe in Jesus, are they guaranteed to go to heaven, but if they have doubts, will they go to hell to be tormented forever? How can I be sure that when I die I will keep existing? Or will I vanish when my body rots in the ground?*

With Benjamin underfoot, Grace began clearing away the scraps from the meal, while Vernon, Kirby, and Janie went running up and down the rows of tombstones, the boys hiding behind the large ones and jumping out to spook their sissy cousin Janie.

Only Leona, whose life had already smacked her in the mouth, sensed the irony in their juxtaposition: they had just absorbed a sermon on hell, this family bent on reaching heaven, while their children were running up and down row upon row of lifeless, buried human remains.

*　　*　　*

On the evening of the same Sunday when Leona and her sons were with Daniel's family at the church and the cemetery, Dexter Dalkens was sitting at the bar in Cherry's Scarlet Kitty Kat Lounge on an isolated stretch of highway in rural Western Nebraska, drinking a beer and eating a salty, greasy hamburger heavy with mustard, pickles, and onions, while his boss, Larney Medford, was upstairs, trying to overcome erectile dysfunction in bed with a pathetic, drug-addicted teenage prostitute from Omaha.

Dexter's Christmas season was revolving around a weeklong trip in his yellow cab to Nebraska and South Dakota, driving his boss on a pheasant-hunting expedition that included nightly visits to the area's brothels. Dexter was bored with chauffeuring Larney around, and pheasants were scarce because of the persistent drought, but Larney's money was good.

Just as Dexter was finishing his hamburger, a truck driver entered and sat down beside him. "Who in the hell has driven a yellow cab with an Oklahoma license tag all the way up here?" he asked.

Dexter bristled. "I did, if it's any of your damned business!"

"No offense, buddy," replied the trucker. "I was just trying to make conversation. I have been on the road for over a day and a half, and in my damned truck I have nearly gone crazy talking to myself. Here, let me buy you a beer. Bartender, another beer for me and my friend."

Dexter toned down. "Thanks for the beer," he said. "That yellow cab outside is privately owned. I drove my boss up here to go pheasant-hunting. He's upstairs now, trying to get some mileage out of a limp dipstick."

"My name is Harry Worley," offered the trucker. "I'm on a haul between San Francisco, Seattle, and my home in Chicago."

"I'm Dexter Dalkens." They shook hands.

"Dalkens. I know an old gal named Dalkens," Worley responded. "Callie Dalkens. She's a waitress at a truck stop on the south side of Chicago. I do business there all the time. She's a sharp-tongued old girl whose hair is as red as a strawberry, and she don't take no lip from nobody. As I recall, I remember her talking about being from Oklahoma City."

"My God, she's probably my missing aunt," said Dexter. "Small world, after all. If she is my aunt Callie, next time you see her, tell her that her old mama is doing poorly. Grandma Eliza is living with her son Harold in Oklahoma City now so she can be near heart specialists. Her old ticker is wearing out. I don't see her much, but I run into Harold sometimes."

"I'll tell Callie, but she's not likely to go see her. She is raising a redheaded, freckle-faced Negro daughter, and I doubt she'd expose her to Southern segregation."

"Is Callie married?"

"No. Callie don't take up with anyone for very long at a time," said Worley, "but she'll kill a tiger blindfolded to protect her girl. It's funny how being a parent will affect your behavior. Right now, I'm as tired as a turd, but I'm about to drive straight through to Chicago just so I can spend as much Christmas time as I can with my two boys. I told my boss not to send me out on another run until after Christmas. I have bought my boys a Lionel train set with an eighteen-foot track, and I can't wait to see the look on their faces when we get set up. The track is going to take up all of our living room!"

"I don't have no kids," said Dexter, dodging behind the false security of a double negative. "You're lucky to have enough money these days to buy anything for Christmas," he continued, steering the conversation away from parenthood. He and Worley got into a discussion of the Depression, New Deal highway construction, the drought—anything but children—until Worley hit the road again.

Dexter had not intended to go upstairs at all, except perhaps to see if Larney had given up or passed out, but he now had an urge to take himself up into a private room and lay down a little money for the privilege of losing himself inside someone's willing, faceless body.

*   *   *

Leona made a mistake in asking her sons what they wanted for Christmas; likely, she would lack the means to fulfill their requests. "New shoes," said Kirby, five. His hand-me-downs had holes in their soles, and handmade cardboard insoles hardly lasted a day.

"I want a new daddy," said Vernon, eight. "I've been playin' like Jesse is my brother and Uncle Daniel is my daddy, but they are movin' away, so it won't work for me anymore."

Leona sighed. "I will make you a plate of fudge," she said.

Moving On

At sunrise, December 20, 1935, moving day for Daniel's and Grace's family, James arrived in Uncle Joe's truck in time for breakfast. Before sunrise, Daniel and Jesse had gone out to the chicken house to gather the hens and their old red rooster off the roost and stuff them into a crate that was to be tied on the back of the jalopy for the trip to Denim. Grace had a pot of coffee ready for them all and a skillet of scrambled eggs, bacon, a pan of hot biscuits, the last bowl of butter from the Hargrove cows, and a jar of peach preserves. Janie was still sleeping, but Benjamin had been up, wide-awake, following his mother around the kitchen, recognizing that something different was about to take place. A stack of small cardboard boxes and all their clothes, still on hangers, were gathered near the front door, ready to be put into the jalopy.

"You won't need to move this kitchen table," James announced as Grace began to ladle eggs and bacon onto everyone's plates. "I have made you a new table and benches out of some pine boards I found up in the loft of Robert's main barn. Wally and I have already set it up in your new home, along with a potbelly woodstove stoked with kindling, just waiting for you. We cleaned out the flue and checked the chimney too and swept the cobwebs out of the corners. You have a good well of water there. Although the windmill is broke down—it needs a new rod—the hand pump works easy enough for the kids to pump and carry water to the house."

"Thanks for everything," Daniel said, "and thanks to Uncle Joe for letting us use his truck again. He is very generous."

"Joe feels obligated for all the harvest work we did for him last fall, when the last of his boys packed up and went to California," James said. "In this family, what you give, you get back."

"I don't know what we can give you for our new table," Grace said. "I can't wait to see it."

"You can pay me for it by taking that bacon grease on the stove and turning it into a bowl of red-eye gravy so that Daniel and Jesse and I can sop it up with the last of these great biscuits!"

With her father involved, Grace was beginning to feel better about the move. She had many good memories from her childhood days in Roger Mills County and believed her children would do well there. The list of furniture and other items from the Hargrove household that she and Daniel agreed to take, based on Dewey's suggestion, also brought her comfort. Within an hour, the truck was packed with furniture and the jalopy was filled with clothes and small boxes, washpots tied to the doorknobs, a mattress tied on top of the car roof, with the chicken crate bringing up the rear.

"My stars, from the looks of this old car, people will be thinking we are on our way to California!" said Daniel. "Well, let's climb in and be on our way. Don't look back, look ahead."

Jesse climbed into the truck with his granddad. Grace carried Janie, who was still drowsy, to the car and propped her in a corner of the back seat, against a pile of clothing. Benjamin was going to ride on his mother's lap. Daniel checked the tires and started the motor. "We'll follow you, in case anything falls off the truck!" he yelled to James.

"Daddy, don't lose the chickens!" Jesse yelled back as the vehicles began trundling down the lane.

When the little caravan reached the mailbox at the county road, Daniel stopped the jalopy so that Grace could leave the following letter for the mailman to send on its way:

December 20, 1935

Dear Dewey, our jolly sailor,

The purpose of this letter is to let you know that we are moving to Roger Mills County.

My dad is going to be farming his late brother Robert's place on the Canadian River, and both Daniel and Russell have received federal loans to rent 160-acre farms nearby in the Denim community. Russell and Donna Belle have a second son, Donny, who is now about ten months old. Their oldest, Jimmy, is now three. They have already moved.

In response to your generous offer to let us take some of your parents' furniture, we are taking your mother's foot-pedal Singer sewing machine, the cream separator, the kitchen cupboard, the wooden icebox, the kerosene cookstove, the old cedar rocker, two straight-backed chairs, some of the pots and pans, etc. Also the wrought-iron double bed, the dresser, the cedar chest, and the big steamer trunk. And the jalopy, of course, if it will get us there. We want to pay you for these things, and we will try to send you some money from time to time as our situation allows. Daniel has arranged to have all your cattle sold at the Altus sale barn; they will be sending you a check. We did not keep a heifer as you suggested because we were afraid it would have disqualified us from receiving the government loan, which will provide us six milk cows from a common pool that has been gathered from abandoned and foreclosed herds, as well as a team of plow horses, a two-row planter-cultivator, and a turning plow. The secondhand store at Hobart is coming for your remaining possessions, and they, too, will send you a check.

We do not like the tone of the news about Hitler threatening a war in Europe. I wish you would get out of the military and come back to God's country. I wish you could see our little family. Jesse is eight years old and wants to be grown. His sister, Janie, is nearly as tall as he is and looks a lot like her aunt Leona. Little Benjamin is a happy bundle of giggles and snot. He has already learned a lot of words and makes up a few jabbery, new ones of his own invention.

We love you and pray for you. Pray for us.

Love,
Grace and Daniel

When they pulled out onto the county road and turned toward Denim, Grace could not help it.

She looked back.

*   *   *

Benjamin Bird's earliest memory was of a dusky late–December 1935 evening when his family moved into an unfamiliar, weathered two-room frame house on the farm his father had rented northwest of Denim, Oklahoma. He was in and out of his mother's arms as they watched Granddad James Dalkens back Uncle Joe's truck, loaded down with their household possessions, to the covered open porch that spanned the entire southern side of the dwelling, a scene that became etched in his memory. Each of the structure's two rooms was twenty-four feet wide and twenty feet long, and each room had an outside door opening onto the splintery porch. At the west end of the porch, near the kitchen door, Daniel had parked the old jalopy, packed down with clothing, bedding, and small stuffed cardboard boxes. Janie sat in the back seat, holding both her dolls, refusing to get out of the car at least until someone lit a lamp in their new home.

To her, the house seemed foreboding, cold, dark, haunted. Janie was near to whimpers.

Daniel removed a small kerosene lamp from a box, filled it with fuel from a three-gallon can that had been tied to the car's running board, carried it into the kitchen table, and lit the wick. Soon a warm, subdued yellow glow began to illuminate the room, revealing the size and warm character of the pine dining table and benches James had made for his daughter. Daniel then went into the front room, where James and Jesse were entering with a lit kerosene lantern, and together they lit the potbellied woodstove. "Come in, Janie, and show us where you want us to put your bed," called Grace from the kitchen door. "Daddy has got the fire started. It's soon going to be nice and warm." Then she turned to James. "Dad, I really like the table and benches you made for us. The table is large and smooth and strong. It should serve our needs for years and years. I will cherish it, you know I will."

"The cedar chest is the first thing off the truck," said James. "Grace, where do you want it put?"

"Put it in front of the north window in the front room," she suggested, "so that when the kids use the top of it as a table or desk, they will have good light." Holding Benjamin, she directed the establishment of the order of things in her new home. "Set up the double bed with its headboard against the east wall, but leave room between it and the northeast corner of the room for Benjamin's cot so that I can reach over from my side of the bed and check through the night to see that he keeps his covers on. Janie's cot can go into the northwest corner. Jesse's cot can go in the southwest corner. Put the rocker in the middle of the room beside the stove, place the steamer trunk along the south wall next to Jesse's cot, and put the dresser along the south wall between the trunk and the front door. The sewing machine needs to be set up in front of the east window so that I will have good, natural light when I sew."

The children's cots were surplus military equipment that had been allocated to the men on the bridge-building project Daniel had worked on in 1933. James and Wally had used the sides of a strong cardboard box, two white pine stud two-by-fours, and a one-inch pipe four feet long to improvise a clothes closet in the southeast corner behind the front door.

Jesse took it upon himself to begin unloading the clothes and the small boxes from the jalopy.

"Janie is not getting out of the car," he announced, carrying an armful of clothes to the closet.

"Benjamin, be a big boy and sit here on the trunk while I go out to the car and bring your sister into her new home," said Grace, who realized while walking out into the deepening darkness that in the bustle of packing and moving, she had not given her sweet five-year-old daughter much attention. She found Janie huddled in a corner on the back seat.

"Sweetheart, step out of the car and Mama will carry you into our new house," Grace said comfortingly.

"No," Janie whined. "I want to go home."

"This is your new home, honey. Come in and see where we are putting your things."

"I don't want to. This is a bad place. Something bad will happen here."

"Oh, no. We will be happy here. You'll see."

"God can't find us here. We left Him back there."

"No, I promise you, God is here. He is always with us. I have already prayed to Him to watch over us."

"Did He hear you?"

"I am sure He did."

"All right, then," Janie replied as she stepped out of the car, "if you promise to tell Him what we need every day."

As Grace carried her middle child into the strange little house, she said reassuringly, "Janie, you can talk to God yourself. You can tell Him we need Him to watch over us. He loves to hear from children."

"All right, then. Can I ask Him for a kitty?"

"You surely can. We are going to need one. I noticed a mousehole in the kitchen baseboard."

Grace sat Janie down on one of the benches at the kitchen table and said, "Janie, sit here with your babies and help me decide where the kitchen things should go. Daniel, you all put the kerosene cookstove against the inside wall, away from the drafty windows and door. Put the icebox against the north wall and the cupboard against the south wall near the stove. Place the washstand in the southeast corner near the back door so we won't have so far to carry the buckets of well water. Daniel, can you keep the cream separator on the back porch during good weather? Meanwhile, we'll leave a place for it just inside the door."

Once Uncle Joe's truck was unloaded, James headed for the old homestead two miles down the road, where Maudeen, Olivia, Wally, Valdetta, and their infant, Gary, were waiting. Grace began unpacking the boxes that Jesse had placed on the kitchen table. "Jesse, did you bring everything in from the car?"

"All except this little old blue stick horse," Jesse replied, handing Benjamin a homemade toy made from a broken blue broom handle with an attached horse head Grace had made from one of Daniel's stuffed heavy wool socks, with the outline of a mouth and nose stitched in with heavy brown yarn, eyes made of large coat buttons, and stubby ears pinched and stitched in the corners of the sock's heel.

"Ole Blue!" Benjamin squealed and began to stride through the house in a slow, toddling trot.

"Benny, don't make such a racket," said Janie. "You'll wake up my babies!"

With their life's possessions safely tucked inside their cozy, new abode and the children beginning to feel safe and comfortable in their new surroundings, Daniel filled the cookstove's kerosene tank, sat down in one of the straight-backed chairs, and sighed. It had been a long busy day.

"Daddy, the chicken crate is still tied on the back of the jalopy! We ought to take the lantern and go out and find the chicken house and put old Red and his hens on the roost," said Jesse, "so that when they wake up in the morning, they will be right at home."

"Check in the crate to see if they laid any eggs today, if you want eggs for breakfast," suggested Grace as Daniel and Jesse went out to take care of one final chore. In their absence, Grace went to the trunk, removed Jesse's large oval first birthday portrait from a blanket in which it was wrapped, and hung it on a nail on the east wall above the headboard of their bed. She and Daniel never discussed the portrait, but she saw to it that it was always there above their heads.

Grace put covers on their beds then lit the kitchen stove, found her canister of cornmeal, and cooked a pot of cinnamon-flavored cornmeal mush for their evening meal. The light of the kerosene lamp flickered and danced on the kitchen's walls, which were covered with newspapers a previous tenant had pasted on the walls of both rooms in 1932, front pages and comic pages and sports pages of the *Kansas City Star*, the *Sayre Sentinel,* and the *Cheyenne Star*, old news events and pictures and funny papers that perpetually whetted Benjamin's curiosity to the point that he would ask someone to read them to him, the comic strips first, then the old news. He would ask, "What's that word?" followed by "What's that word?" until he recognized and remembered many of the words. By the age of three, he would be reading several of them himself, especially the pages that were pasted on the wall beside his cot.

*   *   *

The next morning, after breakfast, Daniel and Jesse went out to do the morning chores. First, they went to the broken windmill to use the hand pump to fill two buckets of fresh water, which they carried into the kitchen's washstand, providing for the family's drinking water, handwashing, dishwashing, and cooking. Then they fed and watered the chickens and put fresh straw in the nests but did not allow the hens out of their house until they became accustomed to their new home, for fear that they would wander off and be lost. Then they inspected the storm cellar, located about ten feet west of the kitchen door. The previous tenant had left the cellar door open; consequently, sand from a series of dust storms had blown into the cellar, burying the steps and forming a large deposit of sand on the cellar floor. "Jesse, you and Janie need to take buckets and scoop up all the sand out of the cellar and pile it up in a nice mound on the shady side of the house for Janie and Benny to play on. But right now, son, let's go find a little cedar Christmas tree."

Daniel and his firstborn then took a bow saw and walked north from the house to explore the farm along the edge of a sixty-acre field paralleling the county road. In the field were strips of thirty-two rows of bare cotton stalks, interspersed to combat the impact of wind erosion with strips of sixteen rows of corn stubble that farm animals had eaten down almost to the ground. To Daniel, the cotton stalks and the corn stubble appeared to be at least two years old. Apparently, the farm had been abandoned for a year.

At the half-mile point, Daniel and Jesse reached the northeast corner of the field then walked westward along the farm's north fence line, adjacent to a neighbor's badly eroded cotton patch. Dunes of sand and tumbleweeds were piled along the fence row, in places covering all but the top barbed wire strand and the tops of the cedar fence posts. Daniel realized that the entire fence line would need to be pulled out of the sand and be rebuilt before livestock could graze the field.

"Daddy, I don't see even one tree," Jesse declared as they reached the northwest corner of the farm. They turned south and walked down a gentle slope along the west fence line, soon coming to a gate on the east-west fence line of their hundred-acre cow pasture, which spanned the south boundary of the farm, from the house and barn to the western boundary. The pasture appeared to have been heavily grazed in the past years of drought, since it was devoid of bluestem, gramma, and other desirable grasses that cattle favored and had crabgrass, sagebrush, grass burrs, and acres of thick stands of stunted oak shinnery, a useless, invasive ground-cover oak plant that spread from its lateral roots and rarely reached waist-high. When hungry, under-fed cattle developed a taste of the shinnery's oak leaves or tiny acorns, it wrecked their liver and kidneys, Daniel later would learn through experience.

As they walked eastward back toward the house and barn, Daniel and Jesse came upon a deep narrow ravine that paralleled then crossed the farm's southern boundary line, eroded down to a stratum of sandstone. The canyon stretched eastward toward the southeast corner of the farm, past the barn and a large garden site below the well, then to the county road, where a rickety wooden bridge spanned the gorge. Jesse recalled the rumbling echoes that Uncle Joe's truck and their jalopy had reverberated as they crossed the bridge the night before. Embedded in the canyon's sandy clay walls were remnants of bison skulls—porous, decimated remains of their thick horns—indicating that generations of Indian hunters had used the ravine to stampede bison into the chasm for slaughter.

When they returned to the house, they learned that Grace had already discovered the ravine when she and Janie and Ben had gone out to feed breakfast scraps to the chickens and to use the outhouse, which was located several yards beyond the chicken house. She had then taken the children to inspect the cowshed, where she noticed that there was no fence at the south end of the cow lot: their animals would be confined in a corral whose south line was a gaping ravine!

"Daniel, we cannot allow the children to play outside this house until you have built a good, secure fence to keep them away from that dreadful, dangerous canyon!" she declared.

"I know," he replied. "There's an old pigpen beyond the cow lot that is made of woven wire, which I will take up and use to stretch a barrier from the bridge past the cow lot westward as far as the hog wire will reach. We won't need a pigpen until I can raise a corn crop to feed them, anyway. Meanwhile, before I can put seed in the ground, I have a lot of work to do. Jesse and I are going to Elk City today to buy six milk cows and a team of horses, a planter, a plow, and a wagon. Because there are no trees on this place, I will need to haul firewood from the river bottom right away since we still have a long stretch of winter weather ahead of us."

"Bad news, Mama, about a Christmas tree," said Jesse. "Our new farm does not have one tree!"

"Well, we will just make do with what we have," Grace responded. "Son, go find me a large tumbleweed, a middle-size tumbleweed, and a baby-size tumbleweed. Daniel, please fill one of my washtubs with water and stir a quart of white lime into the water. Our Christmas tumbleweed tree is going to be white as snow."

And so it was. Jesse scurried along the fence row and found three well-formed tumbleweeds, which Grace dipped into the white-wash in the tub and placed on the porch to dry. When Daniel and

Jesse left for Elk City in the jalopy, she put Benjamin, who cried to go with them, down for a nap.

Then, with all their menfolk out of the way, she placed the large whitewashed tumbleweed in the northwest corner of the kitchen, placed the medium-size thistle on top of it, and topped them off with the small tumbleweed. She and Janie tied them together with red and green paper streamers and tinfoil icicles, saved from past Christmases, along with strings of freshly cooked popcorn, old homemade papier-mache ornaments, old pine cones, and colorful, curly seedpods gathered years ago from the Wichita Mountains. When the last item was in place, including a tinfoil star on top of the improvised tree, Grace stepped back and surveyed their creation. The tree was beautiful. Only one thing was missing: there were no wrapped presents for her children.

"Janie, thank you for helping me decorate our beautiful Christmas tree. Now it is time for you to lie down with your doll babies and give them a nap." Grace needed a quiet time to gather her thoughts.

While her children napped, she sat at her wonderful, new table and contemplated their new home. And their blessings. The two-room shack was the humblest house in which she had ever lived, yet everything they owned fit snugly into place. Her parents and her sister, two of her brothers, and their families lived nearby. All her loved ones were healthy. Her husband appreciated her and worked hard for them and loved her totally. They would soon have new milk cows, precious milk, cream, butter, clabber, cottage cheese, whey. Their little flock of hens provided enough eggs for breakfast and recipes every day. Their well water was clean and sweet and soft enough to help their weekly wash turn out fresh and clean.

Christmas would not be a dud. She had enough remnants in her rag box to make matching nightgowns for Janie and her dolls; a red bandana for Jesse, with embroidered arrowheads and holsters and stirrups and lassos; enough yarn to put a decent tail on Benjamin's blue stick horse; and enough yarn to knit each of her children a pair of brown mittens. She had enough ingredients to make gingerbread men for everyone; and for her lover, a plate of fudge and a guarantee of mutual rewards.

* * *

Benjamin was thrilled when the trucks arrived from Elk City, first the cattle truck with six cows and two plow horses—a matched team of silver-gray geldings. A second truck arrived, with a four-wheeled wagon, a two-row planter, and a plow.

"My cows! My cows!" Ben shouted gleefully as the animals were unloaded into the corral.

"What are their names?" Janie asked Jesse, who had ridden back from Elk City in the cab of the cattle truck.

"The roan one is called old Roan, the red one is old Red, the little yellow Jersey is old Yellow, the black-and-white-spotted one is old Spot, the brown one is old Brownie, and the red-and-white one with the white heart in her forehead is old Heart," said Jesse, the unimaginative pragmatist. "Daddy says old Brownie is going to have a baby right away!"

"Jesse, which cow do you pick as yours?" asked Janie.

"I pick old Spot," he replied.

"I pick old Heart," said Janie.

Jesse began to pump water into the cow trough while Janie watched her father unload the team. "What are their names?" she asked.

"Bill and Hector," Daniel replied. "Bill goes on the gee side, and Hector goes on the haw side." His experience working with horse teams at his father's livery stable and teamster business back in the 1920s had served him well. He had picked from over a dozen teams. Bill and Hector would prove to be the best most manageable team he would ever have.

Benjamin's interest remained unwavering at the cow pen. He stood just outside the fence and could not keep his eyes off the small yellow Jersey, her dark eyes large as saucers. Apparently, she had been someone's pet back when she was a calf, because she came to the fence, stuck her nose through the panel, and smelled Ben's hand. He patted her on her head and fell in love. "Ole 'Lellow picks me!" he beamed.

"Jesse, now that we have a regular, occupied barnyard, I think it would be safe for you to go let the chickens out," said Daniel. As Grace watched the barnyard activities from the porch, she noticed a heavily pregnant calico cat slip out from under the porch to watch what was happening.

Hmnn. Janie's simple little prayer has been answered, she mused. *Janie will soon have a whole batch of kittens to mother.*

She went inside to the icebox and retrieved a strip of leftover bacon, went out, and tossed it to the cautious cat, who seized the morsel and darted into the cellar to eat it. A few more morsels and a few saucers of milk, and Grace would have her mouser. A few more days and Janie would own a litter of kittens.

*   *   *

Daniel was grateful that the December weather had been milder than normal, the winds lighter than usual during their move to Denim and their settling in, but he knew it would not last. On his first day of working with his new team of horses, he and Jesse hitched them to the wagon and went to the river bottom on Robert's old homestead for firewood, gathering enough in two days to last over a month, should the weather turn bad, which at that time of year in that latitude was inevitable. Daniel was pleased and grateful that Jesse was working so hard and effectively helping him with chores since they had moved. As fast as Daniel found driftwood and dead tree limbs and cut them into stovewood, eight-year-old Jesse stacked the load neatly on the wagon and fed tufts of dry grass to the horses. Old Bill and Hector seemed to enjoy pulling the wagon.

On the third day, Daniel and Jesse, who carried a bucket with hammer, pliers, and staples for his father, dismantled the old pig-pen, saved and reused the staples, and used the woven hog wire to build a barrier fence along the ravine, from the bridge on the county road past their garden site, through the south end of their corral, and beyond to the west as far as the roll of hog wire would reach, almost to a point where the rim of the canyon wall was dented slightly by a rarely used whitetail deer crossing, used by deer migrating out of the Canadian River bottom to the isolated, wooded creeks in ranch country a few miles away. The deer crossing was a steep slide down the canyon wall and up the other side, manageable only by nimble-footed whitetails who could leap halfway up the wall and scamper to the top before gravity could pull them backward.

In bed that evening, after the children fell asleep, Grace told Daniel in sweet whispers how much she appreciated his work in keeping their home warm and their children as safe as possible. "One good deed deserves another," he responded as he cuddled her in his arms.

*   *   *

The next day was Christmas Eve. Daniel hitched Bill and Hector to the turning plow and prepared the garden for spring planting. Potatoes, onions, radishes, leaf lettuce, and turnip greens could be planted in about six weeks. The plowed soil, meanwhile, could hold moisture from late winter snow and rains, lessening the need to pump water onto the garden from the nearby well.

That afternoon, James, Maudeen, and Olivia came for a visit and brought a sewing project for Grace. James had volunteered to be Santa Claus at a Christmas program at the Denim Methodist Church that evening. He and Maudeen had become new members of the church. His Santa Claus suit needed a bit of adjusting at the waist. While Olivia entertained Jesse, Janie, and Ben outside on the front porch, playing with some string and a ball and the Calico cat, which had taken up with the children, Daniel and James were adjusting Bill's and Hector's harness out in the cowshed. Grace and Maudeen sat at the Singer sewing machine and worked on the red Santa Claus suit, which featured a ruddy, garish, red-cheeked mask made of oil-cloth, pasted stiff and shaped with a round face colored with gaudy, clownish paint; the mask's openings for its eyes and mouth seemed almost ghoulish.

Benjamin soon wandered in and stood beside his mother's chair, watching the stitching apparatus go up and down, up and down, clickity, clickity, click, and the foot pedal whir, whir, whir. Suddenly, impulsively, Maudeen pulled the mask over her face, held it at a slant, turned to Benjamin, cried "Boo!" and laughed.

Caught by surprise, Benjamin was shocked, paralyzed with fear. His whole body jerked, and he screamed soundlessly, traumatized beyond voice. For a few seconds, he stopped breathing, then gasped, and moaned faintly. Grace turned to him and swept him into her arms, thumped him on his back firmly, and rocked him back and forth until he could cry. "Mother! How could you frighten this baby so!"

Maudeen stopped laughing. She had expected a different response from her grandson. Kids love to do scary things and have scary things done to them, else there would be no Halloween. "Why, I never expected Benjamin to be such a fraidy cat," she said. "Where's his Indian blood? Back in native times, Indian babies were never allowed to cry out loud, for it would allow enemies to find their village. Indian mothers taught their babies not to cry by pinching their nostrils shut and cupping their hands over their mouths."

Grace had never been so upset at her mother. She carried Benjamin to the rocker and began to calm him down. "Well, Mother, you can just finish the alteration to the Santa Claus suit yourself. I am going to take care of my baby."

"I swear, Grace, you smother your children. Give them a chance to toughen up!"

The incident was not mentioned again. Grace had too much innate respect for her mother to dwell on it.

Christmas celebration was on the way. That evening, Daniel and Grace and their children, Russell and Wally and their families, James and Maudeen and Olivia together attended the Christmas Eve services at Denim Methodist Church. Olivia sat near the back of the sanctuary with three junior high school boys she had gotten acquainted with in Sunday school class the previous Sunday. She told the teenagers that she was fourteen, just a year younger than they were, and she wore her hair in an upsweep, which made her look older than her actual age of nearly twelve. The tissue paper she had stuffed into her bosom also contributed to the deception.

The Yule program featured congregational singing of Christmas hymns and a nativity skit performed by several nervous children who required constant prompting, interspersed with a devotional message delivered by the chairman of the deacons, who took his text from the Gospel of Luke:

> *And she brought forth her firstborn son, and wrapped him in swaddling clothes, and laid him in a manger, because there was no room for them in the inn.*
>
> *And there were in the same country shepherds abiding in the field, keeping watch over their flock by night,*
>
> *And lo, the angel of the Lord came upon them, and the glory of the Lord shone round about them; and they were sore afraid.*
>
> *And the angel said unto them, Fear not: for, behold,*
>
> *I bring you good tidings of great joy, which shall be to all people.*
>
> *For unto you is born this day in the city of David, a Savior, which is Christ the Lord.*

Special music was then performed by a men's quartet. James slipped outside into the dark to change into the Santa Claus suit. Maudeen, who had been impressive in two choir rehearsals she had attended since moving to Denim, was asked to sing a solo. She sat at the piano and accompanied herself, selecting a short hymn that reverberated with her rich soprano voice:

> O love sur-pass-ing knowl-edge! O grace so full and free!
> I know that Je-sus saves me, And that's e-nough for me.
> O won-der-ful sal-va-tion! From sin He makes me free!
> I feel the sweet as-sur-ance, And that's e-nough for me.

O blood of Christ, so pre-cious, poured out on Cal-va-ry!
I feel the cleans-ing pow-er, and that's e-nough for me.
And that's e-nough for me, O that's e-nough for me:
I know that Je-sus loves me, and that's e-nough for me.

The congregation applauded. Maudeen had won their hearts. The chairman of the deacons asked her to sing it again, since Santa had not yet arrived. She sang it again and trilled the chorus. Henceforth, she would dominate the music program at Denim Methodist Church.

Suddenly, the church door swung open and Santa entered with a bag of goodies and a jolly "Ho! Ho! Ho! Merry Christmas!" The congregation squealed. Santa's mask was all askew. Dressing in the darkness, James had mistaken the mouth hole for one of the eye-holes, which made Santa appear to have had his neck broken, his white beard flowing from his right shoulder. The adults roared with laughter. The children stared, bewildered. Santa had had an accident! His reindeer must have crashed the sleigh!

Maudeen rushed to the rescue, pulling the mask into proper fit, and—since James could not see well because the eyeholes did not fit his large face—she helped hand out small brown paper sacks, each containing an apple, an orange, Brazil nuts, peanuts, walnuts, taffy, peppermints, red-and-black licorice, and rainbow ribbon candy, given first to all the children, then to the adults, many of whom were still laughing at Santa's ludicrous arrival.

"Santa sounds like Granddad," Janie observed.

Frightened, Benjamin hid his face in his mother's chest when the masked man first arrived, and trembled throughout the remainder of Santa's visit. Ben would not show his face, even when Santa's helpers brought him his own sack of goodies. Grace wrapped him snugly in her arms and rocked back and forth protectively. She suspected that Benjamin would never believe in Santa Claus, thanks to Maudeen's thoughtless practical joke. Grace concluded that for Benjamin not to believe in Santa Claus was an acceptable forfeiture, so long as he would learn the true story of Christmas and grow up to believe in Jesus.

CHAPTER 11

Winter Worryland

Christmas morning was crisp and cloudy, following a cold night. Had there been any moisture in the air, there would have been a heavy frost. Daniel arose at daybreak and stoked the woodstove to life. His family would be arising one by one, in warmth, while he went out to the cow pen and checked on old Brownie.

When Daniel returned to the house, no one had stirred, but when he announced, "Old Brownie has had a Christmas baby!" the children popped up simultaneously to see and celebrate an important occurrence. Grace bundled them up and sent them out with their father.

"Is it a heifer or a bull?" asked Jesse.

"What color is it?" asked Janie.

"It's a little red heifer," Daniel reported.

"What's its name?" asked Janie.

"Little Red," suggested Jesse.

"Why not Christmas?" asked Janie.

"Let's call her Merry," said Daniel, carrying Benjamin.

They entered the cowshed and saw the new, wobbly calf, still wet, nursing its mother. "Baby cow!" Benjamin squealed with delight. He had a new playmate.

It was too cold for the children to stay and watch the new baby for more than a minute. When they returned to the house, they found that Grace had placed three gifts under the thistle Christmas tree: First, Janie opened her gift and found her new nightgown, and she squealed when she found her two dolls dressed in gowns identical to hers. Jesse opened his present and unfurled a bright-red bandana. Proudly he put it around his neck and tied the corners so that his initials, JDB, would show. Although he would not tell his sweet mother so, Jesse did not care for his mittens. "These dad-gum things make me feel like a dad-burned craw-dad," he whispered to his father. Daniel pulled Benjamin's blue stick horse from behind the thistle tree and displayed its new, bushy tail of yarn. Ben laughed and stuck the stick horse between his legs, tail in front, head on the floor. "Benny has made a joke!" said Janie.

The family sat down for breakfast at their new table: potato pancakes, bacon and maple syrup, and scrambled eggs. "Next week from old Brownie we'll have butter for our pancakes," Daniel announced.

"And milk for our teeth and bones," added Grace.

When the children were not watching, she handed Daniel a full plate of rich chocolate fudge. "Merry Christmas," she said. "Hide this in the cupboard. With the goodies the kids got last night at church, they don't need any of it."

"Merry Christmas, sweetheart," he responded and handed her a small vial of perfume he had purchased at Elk City when he and Jesse had gone to buy cows.

Around midmorning, the family piled into the jalopy and drove to the old homestead, for Christmas dinner with the extended family. James, the patriarch, was beaming. All his family was there except for Dexter and his family. Everyone had a good laugh remembering the slant-headed Santa the night before but they were cautious in the way they discussed the incident in front of the children. Old toys and a few new toys occupied the toddlers, Jimmy, three; Benjamin, nearly two; Donny, nearly one; and Gary, two months, he on a pallet, already trying to grasp and shake a baby rattle. The young cousins played well together without actually playing together, each absorbed in his own toy until he wanted someone else's, a situation requiring occasional adult intervention. Jesse sat quietly and listened to the men, to learn grown-up things. Olivia and Janie stayed in Olivia's room, playing dress-up. Olivia had cajoled her parents into buying her a cosmetics kit for Christmas if she promised not to wear any of the makeup in public until she was at least sixteen, a promise she planned not to keep and they suspected they could not effectively enforce. Janie watched Olivia apply mascara to her lashes and brows, although she did not need to; her lashes and brows already were naturally beautiful.

Wally had gone hunting in the river bottom the previous two days, successfully. Maudeen, Grace, Donna Belle, and Valdetta chit-chatted in the kitchen, catching up on news and gossip as they prepared a Christmas feast of quail, mallard, wild turkey, sweet potato pie, home-canned green beans and tomatoes, plum pudding from canned wild plums, dressing, and gravy. James had caught an opossum lurking about the chicken house three evenings earlier and kept it alive in a barrel until Christmas morning so that Maudeen could roast it for him and anyone else adventurous enough to eat it. She agreed to serve it. "Only if you don't expect me to taste it!" James had a Cajun recipe from his Louisiana days. "The trick is to cook all the grease out of it and roast it smothered with plenty of spices," he advised. "Then soak it in gravy. And don't let it grin at you," he added, laughing.

Christmas at his grandparents' house was an intensive learning experience for Benjamin, in an unfamiliar place among unfamiliar people. Russell and Donna Belle had been unable to make many visits between their previous home in Meers to Roosevelt, because Russell had been working at the gravel company six days a week, and on Sundays he had been too tired to drive to visit relatives. Benjamin wondered who they were and studied them closely. He liked them. He liked Jimmy and Donny. He especially studied his uncle Russell—tall, handsome, chiseled features, a deep, kind voice. Russell noticed Benjamin's intensity.

"Tuff Nut," Benjamin said to his uncle Russell, pointing to the trade name label on Russell's denim pants, a label identical to the brand he had learned to recognize on his father's overalls bib.

"Sister," Russell said to Grace, "you have a very smart child. Benjamin is trying to absorb everything that is happening. I think he understands beyond his age. He is going to make a career with his mind. He will be brighter than most of the rest of us. He must have inherited characteristics that we Dalkens people do not usually have. It must have arrived with his sandy red hair."

Uncle Russell motioned to Benjamin, inviting him to come sit on his lap. Ben went to his uncle and presented him with a wide smile. Russell picked him up and began to bounce Ben on his knee. "Trot a little horsey, go to town, get some candy, and don't fall down!" Donny noticed that his father was holding another child and promptly crawled across the floor, fussing with jealousy. Russell picked them both up, one on each knee, and bounced them together. "Trot a little horsey, go to town, get some candy, and don't fall down!" He dropped his legs to make them slide off each time he said "Fall down!" It was a fun game for them all, and Benjamin hugged his uncle Russell with gratitude and devotion when the game ended. A bond was established between them that had value—Benjamin now had a big strong friend, a mentor, a hero, someone outside his immediate family to trust and love.

*   *   *

Janie's premonition that bad things were going to happen to them at Denim became validated in mid-January 1936 when a fast-moving blizzard swept across the Great Plains, catching off guard the rural people who had no radios, no daily news, no weather bureau forecasts. It was a school day. All seemed normal when the yellow school bus came by on its route from the river road, where it picked up Olivia and a dozen other children, then stopped to pick up Jesse at their mailbox. For the first week, Olivia saved him a seat beside her, but then she began to sit near the back of the bus with her new junior high friends. Every day from their east window, Grace watched Jesse climb the steps onto the bus; she watched the bus cross the rickety bridge and, in low gear, pull up the steep hill beyond the bridge and disappear over the hill with her firstborn on board. A subtle anxiety would possess her until he returned home at the end of the school day. She had no time to watch for the bus, but she could hear the rumbling sound when it crossed the bridge and stopped at their mailbox to let Jesse off.

Jesse had not been enthused about attending Denim Public School after the New Year's holiday. He had been so helpful to Daniel in getting the farm chores done and their new operation under way. "Why can't I just stay home and help you do the farming, like Uncle Wally works with Granddad?" he asked. "I can do a lot of things to help you."

"Jesse, you are a good help, and I'm so proud of you," his father stated, "but you are only eight years old. Wally is a grown man who finished high school. You need to finish school, learn good English, and learn about good health and biology, how to grow plants, and learn to add and subtract, multiply and divide, so that you'll know how to keep others from cheating you."

Jesse acquiesced. "Well, I'm willing to go to school until I am big enough to throw the harness over the horses' back," he said. "By then I'll know enough to quit school and start living. Work makes me strong, school makes me weak!"

The fact was, Jesse liked school, liked making friends and playing sports with them at recess and competing with them for grades; he liked to learn, and he liked his teacher, but he did not think Mrs. Fustus was as smart as his father.

On this particular day, there soon developed ominous signs at home and at school. There had been three solid days of strong, dry south wind. The air crackled with electricity. In the classroom, the girls' hair stood out from their scalps and their dresses sparked as they fidgeted uneasily at their desks. Mrs. Fustus's rayon dress clung to her legs and revealed the shape of her thighs and buttocks, so she started the day sitting down at her desk, only getting up to raise the window shades when dark clouds rolled in soon after school began.

At home, Grace felt heaviness in the air (the barometric pressure was falling rapidly, but she could not know that). Daniel came in from the barn, having finished milking, separating the cream, and feeding Merry a half-gallon of skim milk. "A bad duster is rolling in," he told Grace, "probably with some real cold air. It will hit here in about ten minutes. I noticed it when the cows decided to stay in the barn. The chickens are smart too—they are out scratching, but they are staying very close to their coop."

Grace was making up their beds. At Jesse's cot she found his brown mittens stuffed in his pillowcase. "That little rascal! Why won't Jesse wear his mittens? Let's hope he doesn't need them." Janie and Benjamin were dawdling at the table, slowly finishing their oatmeal and buttered biscuits.

"I think I'll stay indoors this morning until I see what the weather is going to do," said Daniel. "What can I help you with?"

"Why don't you bring a couple of extra buckets of water to the house, in case the well pump freezes during this storm? Then put some damp towels in the north and west windows, to keep some of the dust out." Grace heard the calico cat scratching at the door, wanting to get in. "And fix Calico a box in the corner by the icebox. She is wanting to come in out of the storm, and I am wanting her to thin out the mice in this house. I found mouse droppings along the baseboards yesterday, and that is something I simply will not tolerate!"

Quickly Daniel fetched the water then found a small cardboard box in the cellar, placed a burlap sack in the bottom of it, and let Calico slip into the house. He placed her box in the northeast corner of the kitchen. Janie sat on the floor beside Calico's box and petted her. "This is your bed, Calico," she said. "When you find your babies, you can bring them here."

Suddenly, the house was shaken with a blast of sustained, strong north wind as the storm struck. Grit pounded against the windowpanes, and the wind whistled around the corners of the house and down into the chimney. Daniel looked out the window of the kitchen door and noticed dirty flecks of dust-laden snowdrops whipping past. "At least it looks like we will get some moisture out of this," he commented.

Benjamin was uneasy about the changes taking place outside and reached up for Daniel to take him in his arms. Daniel held him at the window, and they watched the snowflakes become whiter and larger speeding by. Daniel was grateful to have had the opportunity to pile a good supply of stovewood against the porch wall just outside the front-room door. To keep the house warm, they would likely need to burn a good portion of it in the next few days.

"Do you think that school will let out early today so the bus can run and get the kids home before the roads become bad?" asked Grace. She tried to sound casual, but Daniel detected her anxiety.

"There is a regular whiteout taking place outside already," Daniel reported. "We should soon know what the school is going to do, because at the speed this storm is rolling through, it must have already hit at school."

The volume of snowfall and the velocity of the wind disturbed him; at this pace, snowdrifts would pile up quickly and block the east-west roads. This was becoming a regular blizzard. He looked toward the barn and noticed snow already piling up against it. He pulled the damp towels from the north windows and was surprised to see that a drift of dirty snow blowing from out of the sixty-acre field north of the house was already piled halfway up to the windowsill. A dusting of snow was blowing inside onto the sill from around the window's frame.

If motherhood is a collective, animate entity and it possesses a compartment of anxiety embedded between compartments of fear and grief, Grace's psyche hovered there for the next several hours. "If school let out when the storm struck, shouldn't the bus be here already? Daniel, why don't you bundle up and drive the jalopy down to the mailbox and wait for Jesse, in case he can't see the way to the house?"

"I've drained the car's radiator so the block won't freeze and burst," he replied. "Besides, there's a snowdrift across the driveway already. It isn't passable. None of the roads are passable. Surely, they've kept everybody at the schoolhouse, nice and warm, until this storm blows past."

"But what if they didn't?"

"Grace, honey, responsible adults are in charge of our kids at school, and responsible adults are in charge of the school buses, and they have kids of their own. They're not going to make decisions that jeopardize the kids."

"But the storm moved in so fast they might not have realized what was happening until it was already too late!"

There was nothing Daniel could say that would assuage Grace from worrying. He was worried himself, more than he wanted her to know. He got a pack of playing cards out of the dresser drawer and began playing solitaire at the kitchen table, because he did not know what else to do. Grace flung herself from one household task to another to make the time pass until something could occur. Every few minutes, she went to the east window and looked for the school bus, looked for the storm to break, looked for the sky, looked for the guidance of the Holy Spirit. But there was nothing for her to see but blowing snow, nothing to hear but the howling wind, although from time to time she imagined she heard Jesse's frantic cries, wailing in the wind.

Janie and Benjamin were aware of their parents' anxiety, and it made them nervous. They drifted to the security of the closet, took a chair and a blanket, and turned the closet into a hideout, where they played with Calico and Janie's dolls and talked in subdued tones for the rest of the day. When the time came for the bus normally to arrive and the bus did not come, Grace sat down in the rocker beside the potbelly woodstove and began to rock slowly and dab at tears that began to blur her eyes. Daniel shuffled the playing cards over and over, laying them out on the table for another game of solitaire, and another, and another. And another. At dinnertime, Grace arose from the rocker, fried several strips of cornmeal-battered salt pork, and made biscuits and gravy, while Daniel set the table, five plates— one for him at the end of the table, one for Grace on Daniel's right, one for Benjamin beside Grace, one for Janie at Daniel's left, and one for Jesse beside Janie's place.

"Come to dinner." Grace called her children and began to distribute a strip of crispy salt pork and a biscuit in each plate, then she ladled gravy beside each pork strip. She poured a glass of skim milk for each of them. Then she sat down quietly as Daniel blessed the food: "God, we thank Thee for this food. We thank Thee for the moisture in the snow. Please take care of our creatures out in this storm, and especially watch over Jesse tonight as we pray for him, and for Olivia, and for all the kids at school. Amen."

"Amen," echoed Janie.

"Amen," whispered Ben. "And amen for Jesse. Daddy, where's Jesse?"

"Jesse and Olivia are staying at school tonight, until the storm goes away," said Daniel, with slightly broken voice.

Grace looked across the table at Jesse's plate, which she had filled. She tried to take a bite from her plate, but she had no taste for anything. She arose quietly and went into the other room, sat down in the rocker, and wept softly so that Janie and Benjamin could not hear. Beneath the table, Calico affectionately rubbed against Janie's leg and begged for food.

"Don't feed the cat at the table, Janie," Daniel said.

"I won't," Janie promised as she began to pass morsels across the table to Ben, who promptly dropped them under the table beside the calico cat, outside his father's sight.

In the face of the blizzard, Daniel canceled all outside evening chores, except to bring in enough stovewood to last through the night. Then he cleared the table and washed the dishes while Grace sat quietly beside the woodstove, her eyes closed in prayer, slowly rocking to and fro. Daniel placed Jesse's untouched plate of food on a shelf in the wooden icebox then lit the kerosene lamp and placed it in the center of the table.

"Janie and Benny, go put on your nightclothes then come sit at the table beside Daddy while I read you some stories out of your *Children's Illustrated Bible Stories.*"

They loved to listen to Daniel read. Dressed for bed, Ben stretched out on the bench beside his father, his head on Daniel's leg for a pillow. Wearing her new Christmas gown, Janie stretched out on top of the table several inches away from the flickering lamp, her head pillowed on her doubled-up right arm, her dolls lying beside her. The first story was about the Good Shepherd going out into the storm to rescue the lamb that was lost. The second story was about the Good Samaritan, who saved a wounded traveler. The third story was about the little gray donkey that carried Mary into Bethlehem on the night that Jesus was born. The fourth story was unnecessary, for Janie and Benjamin had fallen asleep. Gently Daniel carried each of them to their cots. Grace brought each of them extra covers for this, the coldest night of the winter, then she sat back down in the rocker and resumed her watch.

Daniel came and knelt beside her, took her right hand in his, and recited by heart Psalm 23:

The Lord is my shepherd; I shall not want.

He maketh me to lie down in green pastures: he leadeth me beside the still waters.

He restoreth my soul: he leadeth me in the paths of righteousness for his name's sake.

Yea, though I walk through the valley of the shadow of death, I will fear no evil:

For thou art with me; thy rod and thy staff they comfort me.

Thou preparest a table before me in the presence of mine enemies:

Thou anointest my head with oil; my cup runneth over.

Surely goodness and mercy shall follow me all the days of my life: and I will dwell in the house of the Lord for ever.

Grace squeezed his hand, then together they recited the Lord's Prayer:

Our Father which art in heaven, Hallowed by thy name.

Thy kingdom come. Thy will be done on earth, as it is in heaven.

Give us this day our daily bread.

And forgive us our debts, as we forgive our debtors.

*And lead us not into temptation, but deliver us
from evil: for thine is the kingdom, and the power,
and the glory, for ever.
Amen.*

This was followed by Daniel uttering a short entreaty: "Dear God, our hearts are heavy tonight because our son Jesse is separated from us during this terrible storm, along with Olivia and the other children. We do not question the storm—we know it is part of Your divine design. We just ask that You provide Jesse the comfort and protection and love that we would provide him if he were here. Amen."

"Amen," echoed Grace. Then she resumed her slow, anxiety-driven rocking.

Daniel turned out the kerosene lamp and went to bed. The rocker moved her forward, brought her back, forward, back, forward, back, ticking off the seconds, minutes, hours through her mother's anguish, confirming her kinship with all mothers whose children were missing, some of them never to return, some of them lifted to glory, some of them reunited following uncertainty and acute distress. Once this her ordeal ended she would wonder how they possibly endured it, those mothers who were stationed at sickbeds and mothers who stood beside small fresh graves, worldwide millions of mothers of starving children, historically millions of Southern slave mothers whose children for hundreds of years were sold away in chains and never heard of again, mothers of sailors lost at sea, mothers whose sons went off to war to be blown to bits, mothers of runaways and mothers of prisoners, mothers of stillborn babies and crib deaths and suicides, and Holy Mother Mary grieving at the foot of the cross.

* * *

The storm broke about an hour before sunrise. The wind continued pushing bitter, cold air around the corners of the house, the chimney still whistling, the receding weather front sending the snow clouds southeastward toward Northern Louisiana. Daniel, who had slept but little, got up at dawn and found Grace sleeping in the rocker, her head tilting forward. He stoked the fire, dressed and bundled himself in an overcoat, and took an empty bucket to the barn to milk old Brownie. When he returned, he found Grace stirring about in the kitchen. Calico had accepted her bed, and from there she watched Daniel crank the cream separator. Grace caught a cupful of warm skim milk and set it down at Calico's box. Daniel returned to the barn to feed Merry, then poured a pan of warm skim milk for the chickens, whose water pan was frozen solid. He scattered a quart of grain for the hens and gathered yesterday's eggs, which had frozen and cracked open. He took them to Grace, who would thaw them out in a pan and scramble them for tomorrow's breakfast.

When he returned to the house, he found Grace, Janie, and Benjamin sitting at the table, eating cornmeal mush and jellied, buttered biscuits. Grace had Daniel's plate set with bacon, biscuits, and gravy, with a steaming cup of coffee. "I am going to walk the school bus route and bring Jesse home," he said. "I am afraid that if they try to keep him at school until the buses can run, he just might try to slip away and come home on his own."

"Take his mittens to him," said Grace, "and a scarf and a stocking cap. I'll put them in your overcoat pocket."

After the stressful night without Jesse, they sat in silence and ate their meal, then as they were about to rise to clear the table and carry their plates to the washstand, the ceiling above the table suddenly collapsed under a burden of snow that had drifted in through cracked shingles and from layers of dust that had sifted in layer by layer from years of dust storms. Wide-eyed, shrieking, Benjamin and Janie dived under the table, out of harm's way, in case more of the ceiling fell in. Daniel and Grace cleared the debris, and then, to hold in the warm air, they tacked a sheet over the gaping hole in the ceiling.

"What can happen next?" asked Grace.

"Something bad," said Janie, "something bad to Jesse."

"Be careful not to slide off the bridge," Grace cautioned Daniel as he set out to find their firstborn.

167

She watched from the east window as he slogged through two-foot snowdrifts out to the road, past their mailbox, and onto the bridge, then up the steep hill and out of sight.

"We'll make a big pot of cocoa when Daddy brings Jesse back," she told Janie and Benjamin. "We'll make some snow ice cream. We'll have popcorn, and I'll make some taffy candy!"

On the road, heading south, with the brisk northern wind behind him, Daniel made good time for about a mile then slowed down as he ran short of breath. His feet and his face were getting numb from the frigid air. The bright sun shining on the snow nearly blinded him. He plowed on, eyes nearly shut, finding on the left side of the road drifts three or four feet high, filling the bar ditch and covering the fence line that paralleled the road. He kept to the right side of the roadway, which was nearly swept clear by the wind except in places where tumbleweeds, plum thickets, or shinnery had caught the drifting snow and piled it in great, swirling snow dunes four or five feet high. At the two-mile mark, the bus route turned left onto an east-west road, and immediately Daniel ran into an impassable solid bank of snow ranging from two to four feet high, spanning the entire roadway. His only recourse was to leave the roadbed and walk eastward along a fence line, in places pulling himself along by hanging on to the top strand of barbed wire, snagging his gloves from time to time, but moving on.

As Daniel reached the crest of a small ridge, what he did not want to find was a stranded bus, but there it was, a half-mile away, its left front wheel in the bar ditch, a snowbank reaching almost up to the level of the school bus windows. Daniel wanted to shout at the bus, to see if someone would answer, but he was too out of breath to yell. He wanted to race to find life there, but he could only plod and pull himself along the fence line, sometimes bogging into two feet of snow, sometimes three or more. When finally he reached the bus, he wanted to find angels hovering over a dozen warm and blanketed lively children, and he audibly prayed, "God be with us," when he bent down to peer into the windows. He saw nothing. The bus was empty. That was wonderful! They had not frozen to death in the stranded bus. That was terrible! They had deserted the bus and wandered somewhere out into the storm. Where? *Where?*

Looking eastward, the direction from which the bus had come, Daniel saw a waft of gray woodsmoke curling into the air from a farmhouse beyond the next ridge, about a quarter mile away. The children had to be there, he figured. Yes! When the bus became stranded, the driver must have led the children to safety. Daniel looked for their tracks but found none. They must have left the bus early in the storm. He returned to the fence line, and the smoke beckoned him to strive on. His progress seemed so slow, although actually he was nearly running through spaces where the snow was hardly more than a foot deep. As he approached the house, he heard—yes!—children's voices. *Several children.* He recognized Olivia's laughter. He pounded on the front door.

The door opened. "Come in!" said Ethan Olin, the homeowner. "I am guessing you are somebody's daddy."

Daniel looked across the room and found Olivia sitting on the floor, in a circle with three older boys, playing Chinese checkers. From the next room he heard Jesse officiating in a game of Guess What?

"Yes, thank God they're all right!" said Daniel. His son was safe. Life was going to go on.

*   *   *

Waiting for Daniel and ("Please, dear God!") Jesse's return, with nervous anxiety, Grace stayed busy, keeping the woodstove blaring hot. On the cupboard she placed a box of cocoa mix, five cups and saucers, a large pan for scooping snow for ice cream, a bottle of vanilla extract, a cup for cream, and the sugar bowl. Then she began to stir and heat a mix of brown sugar and molasses for taffy candy.

About forty-five minutes after Daniel began his trek to find Jesse, Grace was startled by her brother Wally's shrill whistle right outside the kitchen door. Wally was riding his roping horse and leading a second horse with folded blankets tied to its saddle, himself tracing the school bus route to find Olivia. His mother, Maudeen, was nearly distraught worrying about Olivia.

"How about a warm cup of coffee beside the fire to warm up my old bones?" he asked, dismounting and tramping into the house. "I saw Daniel's tracks down by the mailbox, heading south. How long ago did he leave?"

"Hardly an hour ago," said Grace. "He's gone to find Jesse." She poured Wally a cup of leftover coffee from the pot she had brewed on the wood heater for breakfast.

"Good Lord, Sister!" Wally exclaimed. "You have got this wood-stove red-hot! You're in danger of burning this old house down!"

"But I've just got to stay busy doing something," she replied. "I know that Daniel and Jesse will need a good thawing-out when they get home."

The house was so warm and stuffy that Wally hardly stayed long enough to finish his cup of coffee.

"Wally, if you can bring my men home safely, I'll bake you a cherry pie," Grace vowed.

"Don't worry, Sis, these horses can plow right through all the snowdrifts between here and Canada!"

Janie and Benjamin rushed to the east window to watch Uncle Wally ride back out onto the county road, cross the bridge, and go over the hill. Janie asked her mother where so much of the snow came from, and did God intend to dump it all at once? Benjamin wanted to play with Calico, but Calico was being cranky and aloof, out of reach under the bed. Grace stepped out onto the porch and scooped up a pan of clean, fluffy white snow, brought it inside to the cupboard, and stirred several drops of vanilla extract, a cup of sugar, and two cups of cream into the pan full of snow.

"What's that?" asked Janie.

"It's snow ice cream," said her mother. "I am putting it into the icebox, and we are going to eat it and celebrate when your brother and your father come home."

"A party! A party!" said Janie.

The party was late. It was late afternoon when finally Grace noticed Wally's and Daniel's heads bobbing into sight at the crest of the hill, then the horses and their four riders came clearly into view. Olivia was wrapped in a blanket, riding behind her brother Wally on his roping horse, then Daniel and her son Jesse—her beloved son Jesse!—riding the other horse, Jesse in the saddle, handling the reins, wearing his mittens. By the time the riders had arrived and tied their horses to the porch's wooden posts, Grace had steaming cups of hot chocolate on the table for everyone, with a plate full of taffy candy. When Jesse entered, Grace threw her arms around him and hugged him so hard his feet left the floor.

"I was worried to death about you, big boy!" she said.

"Aw, we were all right," Jesse shrugged.

"Jesse is a big hero," Olivia announced. "Mr. Rogers, the bus driver, ran into the ditch because he could not see the road—the snow was blowing into his windshield so hard. So he said we all had to line up and go out into the storm and go back down the road to Olin's mailbox and go to Mr. Olin's house and stay there until the storm was over. So we got out and Mr. Rogers broke through the snowdrifts and led the way and we all took hold of the person in front of us and followed Mr. Rogers to the Olin house, stepping into the tracks of the person ahead of us. But nobody noticed that Mary Kinnard, the little first grader, did not get out of her seat—she was too afraid, so she stayed on the bus—but Jesse told us he looked up and saw her looking out the window at him, so he went back into the bus to get her. But we didn't know they weren't following us. So Jesse led her down the steps and she climbed on his back, and he carried her all the way to Mr. Olin's mailbox and followed our tracks to Mr. Olin's house and knocked on the door, and we let them in before we even knew they were missing!" "Why, Jesse, you were so wonderful!" Grace beamed, and teared up, and gave him a hard hug.

"How did you find the strength to carry her all the way?"

"Well, I... I don't really know. She wasn't very heavy, and I didn't think about whether I could do it or not. I just did it. And doesn't the preacher say that when we try to do the right thing, God will always give us the strength to do it?" He seemed embarrassed. "So where is the ice cream?"

And so Grace's belief that her firstborn was a child of destiny was confirmed, and she served a big pan of vanilla snow ice cream, and the little two-room sharecropper's house was warm and cozy, the family circle intact. When Wally and Olivia resumed their trek to the old homestead, Olivia was riding behind Wally on his roping horse, her arms around her brother's waist, his sturdy body protecting her from the sharp north wind. This was the closest they had ever been to each other, and closer than they would ever be again.

Benjamin absorbed a lifetime of memories from the 1936 blizzard. He would never forget the blowing snowstorm, his mother's anxiety, the ceiling falling in on their breakfast table, the snow ice cream, and Jesse's new dimension, which Ben would accept but never fully understand. He simply recognized that Jesse had a special strength and always would be worthy of respect.

The ice cream party ended with a slight, squeaky sound emanating from Calico's box.

"Calico has caught a mouse!" cried Janie.

The children ran to Calico's box and found three tiny new, wet kittens seeking their way to the milk ducts on Calico's puffed-up tummy as Calico purred and licked her babies dry.

"New baby kittens!" Janie squealed. "One is white, one is black, and one is dressed like its mommy!" Janie reported. "Jesse, what will be their names?"

"One is Snow Whitey, one is Stove Blacky, and the speckled, squeaky one is Squeaky," said Jesse, decider of names.

CHAPTER 12

From the Bridge

On balance, great good came from the snowstorm: it brought enough moisture for Daniel to plow his sixty-acre field to prepare it for spring planting. It took several days for him to drive Bill and Hector up and down the old rows, turning two new rows at a time, across the entire field. Benjamin sauntered at the end of the rows, picking up worms and bugs to feed the chickens, and watched everything for at least an hour each morning. To Ben, the new rows of fresh, damp dirt smelled of a hopeful, mysterious anticipation he sensed from his father. Ben liked the smell and texture of newly turned soil. To Daniel, the anticipation was for forty acres of a bumper crop of cotton, ten acres of bountiful corn for feed for horses and butcher hogs, and ten acres of lush sorghum for fodder to feed their cows and grain for their chickens through the next winter. If he could make thirty or more bales of cotton, he could pay off the government loan and begin payments to buy the farm for himself. If only the rains came. No matter what, he would trust in God, who controlled the rain, and accept God's will.

Meanwhile, Daniel guaranteed his family a level of security by making certain that their vegetable garden would yield in abundance. The sandy loam soil was perfect for a garden, the barnyard nearby would provide a bounty of fertilizer, and the well beside it would allow him to overcome another droughty summer. He replowed the one-acre garden in rows running east and west, which sloped slightly toward the east, perfect for a subirrigation system that he constructed from old tin cans cut open in each end, cans that he found in various area trash dumps along the road. He cut out both ends of the tin cans and laid them end to end to create a leaky, sieve-like pipe system, which he placed in the bottom of every third row, connected to a lateral line extending out from an open bucket half-buried beneath the well faucet, where water pumped from the well would run into the bucket then drain out into the lateral line that fed the submerged tin-can assembly running down every third row.

In early February, Russell and Donna Belle and their young sons spent a Sunday afternoon visiting at Grace and Daniel's home. It was a warm day, which allowed Janie and Ben to play with Jimmy and Donny outside on the pile of windblown dirt that Jesse had carried from the cellar. They dug holes into the mound and tunneled all the way through, where Janie placed Calico's kittens in the tunnels to watch them stalk and pounce and hide from one another. Jimmy brought toy cars, and the boys rolled the cars up and down the mountain roads they built and channeled the roads into the tunnels.

Grace and Donna Belle visited at the sewing machine while Grace sewed seams and hems into a new dress and apron Donna Belle had stitched together. Grace told her lovely sister-in-law about their ordeal during the blizzard, and Donna Belle related how she and Russell and their boys had fared during the storm. Their mail-order chicks had arrived, and they had to keep their box right beside the stove to keep them from chilling to death. Jimmy and Donny had sat for hours watching the chicks scratch their litter and eat and cheep and sleep. Their water well had frozen during the storm, so they had to melt pans of snow on their stove for water. As soon as the storm ended, their neighbor Augusta Metcalfe rode a paint mare over to their house to check on them and stayed for a nice visit. Augusta cautioned them that in their community the coyotes, skunks, and chicken hawks would be a constant menace to their free-ranging chickens, and she expressed an interest in posing Russell and his mule team in a landscape she wanted to paint someday out in his cornfield, with the nearby historic Antelope Hills as background.

Daniel and Russell replaced the broken rod on the windmill and—with Jesse watching everything they did-tested Daniel's underground irrigation system and concluded that with sufficient wind power to move the blades, the entire one-acre garden could be watered in just a few hours. Then Jesse and the men went out to inspect the little cow herd. For the past few mornings, both old Red and old Roan appeared ready to deliver calves. They found old Red lying down in a shinnery patch, with a new, dried-off dark roan bull calf beside her, and old Roan was against the west fence, licking off a newborn whiteface heifer.

"We'll call Roan's new baby Whiteface," said Jesse.

"Don't bother to name old Red's bull calf," Daniel said. "We'll sell him as soon as he's old enough to wean. But soon now, with two fresh cows and the spotted cow likely to calve in a month or two, we'll be selling enough cream to afford to put some good vittles on the table!"

Back at the house, Grace brewed a fresh pot of coffee and served a freshly baked plate of peanut butter cookies to celebrate their visitors.

"Can I have coffee today?" asked Jesse.

"No, but I'm making cocoa for all you kids," replied Grace. "Jesse, go out to the sandpile and tell everyone to come in for cookies and cocoa."

When Benjamin learned that two new baby calves had been found in the pasture, he was torn between excitement and disappointment—why hadn't he been on hand to help find them?

"What are their names?" asked Janie.

"Roanie's baby is Whiteface," Jesse informed her, "but we can't name the other one because we can't keep it."

Jimmy and Donny began to bicker over the same cookie. "Here's mine," offered Ben. He did not like to see fussing. His uncle Russell shot a secret wink to Benjamin, and Benjamin screwed up the left side of his face and tried to shoot it back. "Tuff Nut," Uncle Russell said to Ben.

"Tuff Nut," Ben answered.

*   *   *

Benjamin's second birthday on February 25 went without fanfare. The general store in Denim had just stocked seed potatoes, onion sets, and vegetable seed packets; therefore, on Benjamin' second birthday, the family planted potatoes, onions, greens, radishes, beets, and other early root crops, according to the signs of the zodiac, and piled stacks of straw from the barnyard throughout the garden to cover emerging early plants in case they were threatened by a late frost. When the tilling of the garden soil exposed worms, bugs, or larva, Ben swept them up in a tin can and raced between the garden and the chicken pen to offer the morsels to old Red and his favorite hens.

"This one for you, this one for you, and this one for you," he said as he made them share the good stuff like his mother did with morsels and desserts at the kitchen table.

The day was half-gone before Grace or Daniel even realized their baby was two full years old. In celebration, she served rice pudding for dinner that evening. Ben's precocious development made him seem older, but his simple sweetness and his birth order cemented his life's role as the baby of the family.

If only he didn't awaken so early. Every morning, when Grace awakened, she automatically reached across to Benjamin's cot to see if he was properly covered, half-expecting him not to be there, because half the time he was not. Ben always awakened before anyone else did, and if it was still dark, he would either lie quietly thinking of the stories of the people in the newspapers pasted to the wall, or hum faintly, so as not to awaken anyone, or if the room was chilly, he'd get out of bed and pull his blanket to another bed, to find warmth. He learned that it would not work with his mother, because as soon as he slipped in beside her, she would put him back on his cot and weigh him down with more covers.

He learned that he could not slip into bed on his daddy's side either, because Daniel always had the covers tucked under his body, to counteract his sweetheart's tendency to pull covers and roll up in them. He learned that Janie's cot was not acceptable because it was cluttered with dolls and other girl things.

Ben's favorite place was Jesse's cot, where he would seek Jesse's rock-solid warmth, his back turned to Jesse and his cold feet tucked against Jesse's thigh, if he crawled in bed with Jesse carefully without waking him. The problem was that Ben's cold feet usually caused Jesse unceremoniously to push him off the cot, leaving Ben his last option, to go to the place where he often took his daytime naps—the closet floor—where he would burrow into the middle of the pile of clothes waiting to be washed, curl up in a fetal position, and breathe in the melded odors of their lives together, including his father's sweaty work shirts and overalls, smelling of farm chores, and Jesse's acrid shirts. His favorite piece was one of his mother's silky pink slips or nightgowns, held against his face, from which he breathed her essence into his subconscious as he sometimes drifted back to sleep again, relaxed and comforted by the physiological connection to the safe, comfortable time of his recent development in her womb.

When the weather grew warm and the days lengthened into springtime, Ben would get out of bed at the first sign of daylight, dress himself (the right shoe on the right foot about 60 percent of the time), and go outside to wait for the day. The first time he did so, Grace found him on the porch, sitting beside the box, holding Calico and her kittens, petting them and talking to them. "Ole Calico hums to me!"

Another morning, she found that he had ventured out to the chicken house, peeking through a knothole and talking to old Red, the friendly rooster. Benjamin reported, "Ole Red crows and crows!"

One morning in late April, Grace went out to look for Benjamin and he was nowhere to be seen.

Nervously she rushed to the barn, where lately Benjamin had tended to go, into a stall in the corner, where Merry and the other baby calves were kept, and she found Ben in the stall, lying down with the calves, who were waiting patiently for their morning pail of skim milk. Ben's head was propped against Merry's stomach. "Ole Merry's tummy growls," he snickered.

At breakfast that morning, Grace asked Daniel to relocate the latch on their kitchen screen door up above the level for Ben to reach. "We can't have him wandering around all over the place while we are still asleep," she cautioned. "There are snakes and scorpions in that old barn!"

So the latch on the screen door was raised, and Grace's strategy worked for two days, until Ben noticed that Jesse used the end of his mother's broom handle to punch the hook out of the latch just before bedtime so that he could go outside to pee. The next morning, Ben was still in bed when he heard a sound of distress: a lost, abandoned puppy was wailing in the ravine beyond the barn.

Benjamin did not know exactly what was making such a sad, forlorn sound, but he knew he had to go find it. He dressed quickly, the right shoe on the right foot, grabbed his blanket, tiptoed to the kitchen door, pushed the latch open, and rushed out into the early predawn toward the canyon.

Grace and Daniel soon were awakened by the sound of thunder—a much-prayed-for rainstorm was approaching. "Hopefully, we'll catch enough moisture to get our cotton planted," said Daniel as he finished dressing. Grace reached across to Ben's cot to check on him—and found nothing. She sat up, stepped into her house slippers and searched the house for Benjamin. When she noticed the latch was unhooked, she said, "That little scamp is too smart for his own britches!" She stepped out onto the porch, surveyed the outbuildings, and quickly noticed Benjamin's blanket snagged on a tall weed—right at the edge of the ravine!

"Daniel, come quick! Ben's blanket is down at the edge of the canyon! Our baby has fallen into the canyon!"

Together they raced to the ravine, Daniel holding Grace's hand, pulling her along; he praying silently, "Please, God, don't take our baby, please don't take our little boy!" she in her nightgown and slippers, wailing, "O God, no! O God, no!"

Aroused by the commotion, Jesse and Janie stood on the porch, still in their nightclothes, Janie jumping up and down, screaming, "Benny's dead! He fell in the ditch and now he's dead! I just know he is! I told you something bad would happen here!"

"Shut up, Janie!" Jesse retorted. "Benny's not dead. He's just probably all skinned up, maybe with a busted nose, if he landed on his head. You'll see!"

When Daniel and Grace reached the ravine, Grace grasped the blanket and dropped to her knees, distraught. "I can't stand to look," she cried. "I am supposed to die before any of my children do!"

Daniel peered down into deep morning shadow, focused, and found him. Benjamin was sitting with his legs folded under him, holding something in his lap. Daniel could not make out what it was. Ben looked up at his father and waved. "Daddy, a baby dog!"

When Grace heard Benjamin's voice, she cried for joy. "Thank God!"

"Benjamin, are you hurt?" asked Daniel as Grace crawled to the edge and looked down at her child.

"No. But baby dog is hungry." When he saw his mother, Benjamin smiled and held up a little brown puppy.

"Sweetheart, do you hurt anywhere?" asked Grace.

"No."

"Your brother is okay!" Daniel shouted to Jesse and Janie on the porch.

"See, I told you he was all right," said Jesse, authoritatively. "I guess you will learn to listen to me."

Daniel turned to Grace. "I've got to slide down the deer slide and get him out of there before a rainstorm washes him away."

"Here, take his blanket. He's probably chilled."

"I'll carry him down past the bridge and climb up at a cattle crossing on our neighbor's place. I know there is one, because I have seen his cattle grazing on both sides of the canyon."

"Hurry, then," Grace begged him, "before you both get washed away! I'll go share the good news with the kids and get dressed. Be careful sliding down the deer slide—don't mash Benjamin!"

Daniel splayed his legs out as he commenced his descent, to slow his momentum, and landed at the bottom of the ravine on his rump with a thump, which caused Benjamin to laugh. "Wheee!"

Daniel picked up his son carefully and asked, "How did you get down here without breaking your neck?"

"Cara Mama," Ben replied. "We slide."

Daniel did not hear what Benjamin said because the puppy, still in Ben's arms, whined as it was being mashed between them.

"What did you say?"

Benjamin would not say it again. He patted the puppy on its head. "It cried. I found it," he explained.

Daniel placed Ben on his right hip and began the walk down to the cattle crossing. As they passed beneath the bridge, Daniel noticed a busted cardboard box containing several dead puppies. He turned his body sideways so that Benjamin could not see them. Apparently, Ben's new puppy had been packed on top of its littermates, its fall cushioned by them when callously someone tossed the box out of a moving vehicle. Ben's puppy was the sole survivor.

Grace hurried to the house and hugged Jesse and Janie and shared with them the good news. Then she dressed, and they all walked down to the mailbox at the road to wait for Daniel and Benjamin. The thunder drew closer, the wind shifted, and sprinkles began to fall as Daniel and Ben appeared walking toward them from out of the neighbor's pasture. Grace ran across the road to the neighbor's fence and took Benjamin in her arms so that Daniel could vault across the fence. "Child, whatever are we going to do with you, you little adventurer!"

"Our new baby dog!" said Ben as he handed the puppy to Jesse.

"It's a boy," reported Jesse.

"What's his name?" asked Janie.

"He's the color of the feed we give to our cows," said Jesse. "His name is Bran."

Grace did not wait until breakfast was cooked and eaten to feed little Bran a saucer of skim milk. She realized that fate had found a way, startling and hair-raising as it was, to provide Benjamin a new and constant companion.

The rain provided Daniel sufficient moisture to risk planting his valuable cottonseed, so next day he and Jesse worked in the field all day, Daniel guiding Bill and Hector up and down the rows, Jesse pulling the cottonseed sack along the fence row at the edge of the field so that Daniel could keep the planter boxes filled. Grace tried to catch up on ironing and mending clothes while Benjamin and Janie spent hours playing on the porch with Bran and Calico's kittens. The kittens were grown enough not to be intimidated by the new puppy, while Calico watched the new arrival with a mother's caution.

Bran accepted the kittens as new littermates to play with, romping and chasing tails. Crawling around like a puppy himself, Benjamin strayed too close to the edge of the porch and tumbled off backwards, almost knocking his breath out of him. As he picked himself up, whimpering for a moment, Janie asked him, "Benny, how did you fall into the canyon without breaking yourself?"

"Cara Mama," he replied. "We slide."

"Oh," said Janie. To her, at her age, it was a logical explanation acceptable enough to allay any doubt and normal enough to forget.

CHAPTER 13

No Brakes, No Breaks

The year 1936 saw the number of dust storms increasing, and the temperature soared. Daniel's cotton, corn, and sorghum plantings came up to a good stand but struggled to grow in the dry heat. To cope with the heat, as soon as the school term ended, with Jesse home all day, Grace and the children—and sometimes Daniel—spent an hour or two each afternoon in the livestock water trough, over which Daniel stretched a muslin tarpaulin. He cultivated the row crops following each shower, which was seldom, to create a dusty mulch to retain the soil's moisture. He and Jesse controlled weeds that grew among the rows with their finely honed chopping hoes. Pumpkins, watermelons, cantaloupe, and squash were planted in gaps in the cornrows where corn seeds had not sprouted.

Fortunately, the pasture held up for the family's small group of milk cows, and the weekly sale of cream at the general store kept the family supplied with staples to supplement their vegetable garden. Old Spot delivered a spotted bull calf in early March, with old Heart following in May with a roan heifer. In late May, old Yellow, the Jersey, became sick and aborted a calf and continued to pass dark, watery feces. Unfortunately, she had become addicted to shinnery oak leaves, which poisoned her kidneys and liver. She lay down and died in the middle of the shinnery patch, and Daniel left her carcass there for the buzzards and coyotes. He did not intend to tell the family about their loss until the carcass was eaten and the bones began to bleach. He saw no reason to impose the sadness of death, even of an animal, upon his beloved children until circumstances made it inevitable. But Benjamin, who claimed the Jersey as his special cow, missed her right away.

"Daddy, where's Ole Lellow?"

"She's gone to heaven," said Daniel, "and that's all I can say about it for now. We have a busy day ahead of us, so let's get going!"

Benjamin could not comprehend how a cow could get to heaven. She couldn't fly. She couldn't drive a truck. Did cow angels carry her away? Anyway, "Ole Lellow" was his best friend, and he would miss her. He wanted to ask his daddy more questions, but he knew his father did not want to talk, and Benjamin respected that.

During the cooler hours of the mornings, the entire family devoted themselves to their garden. To have a reliable water supply to grow bountiful vegetables in the deep, sandy soil was a godsend. The crops were "laid by" early in June, and with their garden flourishing, Daniel and Jesse packed a bushel basket of fresh produce to take to the 1936 annual Dalkens reunion in the Wichita Mountains.

All Dalkens descendants from Roger Mills County attended the reunion, traveling there in a two-car caravan in which Grace and her two youngest children rode with Russell and family, while Daniel and Jesse rode in James's roadster with everyone else. Olivia insisted on riding beside Daniel, with whom she had always had a deep affection. Someday, she said, she wanted to find a husband like him. In Russell's car, Donna Belle sat quietly beside her husband. They had not attended the reunion since their wedding day, and she was going to have to pretend that she remembered everyone who was there, although she hardly remembered any of them. Janie sat beside her aunt and rattled on about how she took care of her two doll babies. In the back seat, Grace entertained Jimmy, Ben, and Donny with make-believe stories and guessing games. Ben enjoyed playing with his cousins, sandwiched between them in age, and during several recent visits back and forth, a camaraderie had developed with them, although Jimmy and Donny preoccupied themselves with physical activity—they loved to wrestle and kick balls—while Ben shied away from physical competition and managed the relationship with his cousins by cerebrally staying a half-step ahead of them.

The 1936 Dalkens reunion was not very well attended because of the extended drought and depression and the gradual erosion of interest from the California cousins. Grandma Eliza was not there, being too weak to travel, and her absence put a damper on the whole affair. Nevertheless, there were happy moments, true affection, kinsman to kinsman, and fun, because the family contained individuals like James, who insisted on it. Romping and kicking inflated rubber balls and otherwise showing off, Russell's and Donna Belle's impressive young sons became the center of attention, epitomizing a hope for the best in the future for Dalkens men: muscular, handsome faces, naturally tan, athletic.

"Keep them coming, Russ," said Uncle Joseph, whittling on a weed stem. "Your sons will do a fine job of carrying forth the Dalkens banner!"

"Hear! Hear!" agreed Uncle Harold.

"What strong, handsome boys!" said Aunt Jane. "And what about Wally's son Gary, who is already beginning to crawl!"

Maudeen sat quietly and soaked in the compliments about her Dalkens grandsons, but James couldn't help boasting that perhaps, as the family patriarch, he had had something to do with passing on the high quality of the family's handsomeness and physical standards.

"Posh!" Maudeen retorted. "The best explanation of the perpetuation of the best qualities of the Dalkens family comes from the quality of the long-suffering women that Dalkens men have married!"

Everyone then laughed and agreed.

Benjamin's freckled skin, sandy red hair, and frail-looking arms and torso paled in comparison to his husky cousins. He remained quiet beside his mother and tried to understand everything that was happening. He sensed that the people there were very special to his mother, so that meant they were also special to him. Janie joined a group of girls to play jacks and paper dolls, while Jesse drifted off with a group of boys who wanted to play make-up, a game of baseball. Daniel unloaded his garden produce then set out to best everyone in a game of dominoes. Too shy to circulate, Ben clung to Grace and presented a wide smile to anyone who noticed him.

"My, what a sweet boy!" said Aunt Jane, who bent down to hug him. Benjamin hugged back.

Maudeen overheard Aunt Jane's compliment and grimaced inside. To her, *sweet boy* were code words meaning, "What a little sissy, whom Grace is likely to smother to death."

*   *   *

On their return trip from the 1936 Dalkens reunion, Daniel observed fruit and vegetable stands at strategic crossroads near several Southwest Oklahoma towns, and it came to him that because of the abundance of his garden, as soon as Grace, Maudeen, Valdetta, and Donna Belle had canned and dried all the vegetables that they could store, he and Jesse could set up a small vegetable stand at the intersection of US Highway 66 and US Highway 283 near Sayre, thirty miles south of Denim. Route 66 was the major highway to the West Coast, and throughout the Depression, there had been a steady stream of migrants—potential customers—passing through on their way to California.

So Daniel started accumulating cardboard boxes and grocery sacks from the extended family, and on Jesse's ninth birthday, he took Jesse and Benjamin with him to the intersection of Route 66 and US 283 near Sayre and set up a fruit-and-vegetable stand on the northwest corner, where westbound traffic, slowing down to traverse the intersection, would have an opportunity to see the impressive collection of vine-ripened tomatoes, cantaloupe, squash, okra, green beans, roasting ears, onions, new potatoes, black-eyed peas, and fruit: peaches, pears, apples, plums, and cherries from the old homestead, fruit trees from an orchard that Robert and James had planted before Oklahoma became a state.

With her men out of the way, Grace used the day to cut and sew new skirts, blouses, and dresses for Janie to wear to her first year in school, beginning in September.

Daniel had unhinged their cellar door and brought it with them for use as a display table, resting it atop two orange crates. Their first customer was a widow from Elk City who was going to Sayre to visit her ailing sister. She bought six lush red vine-ripened tomatoes, a sack of green beans, and a sack of mixed fruit. The venture seemed to be getting off to a good start. "We have already made enough money to pay for our gasoline," Daniel told his sons. Benjamin hopped and skipped around the stand, excited to be meeting new people under circumstances controlled by his father. He was eager to see how the strangers talked, hear what they said, see what they wore, and see what they bought. Jesse, in his first project to actually make money, was a deeply serious merchant. Constantly he rearranged the produce to display it in its best possible appearance.

Their next customer set the tone for what the day was going to bring. A middle-aged couple from Southern Illinois, on their way to California, stopped in front of the stand and, motor running, looked at the produce. Then the man turned off his motor and slowly approached Daniel. "Mister, my wife and I would like some of your stuff, but I'm afraid we'll need to do some dickering because we just don't have any extra money. We're from near East St. Louis. Our dairy cows banged out last month, and we had to sell them all, but the bank had a big note on the cows and wound up with all the money. I hid a steer and sold it to a neighbor for cash for gasoline to get us to the West Coast. We started out with a package of sandwich meat and bread, but the meat went bad yesterday, so we're just, uh, kinda out of food."

Daniel extended his hand.

"My name is Walter Voorhees," said the customer as they shook hands.

"My name is Daniel Bird. What do you have to dicker with?"

Walter pulled a pearl-handled pocketknife from his pocket. "This was Papa's genuine Barlow knife. We had to bury Papa last month. He just got tired of all the bad times and just sort of gave up. I offer to trade you his knife for a sack full of foodstuff—tomatoes and squash and apples and stuff that won't spoil in the next few days. We plan to drive straight through…"

186

Jesse's eyes lit up at the sight of the pocketknife. It was something he would really like to own. He tugged at his father's overalls and whispered, "Yes."

Daniel accepted the knife and handed Walter a grocery sack. Walter motioned to his wife to come from their car and pick out the items. She was a small stooped woman whose fate was in the hands of a husband who no longer seemed sure he could adequately manage their affairs. They circled the stand and picked a variety of produce that could be eaten without being cooked. Walter presented the sack, full to the brim, to Daniel for approval. Daniel leaned over the sack and looked in, as if to seal the deal.

"Much obliged," said Walter.

"Godspeed on your trip," Daniel responded.

Walter carried the filled sack to his car, and his wife waved to Benjamin, a fresh tomato in her hand, as they pulled out onto Route 66 and headed west to an uncertain future.

Jesse could not wait to get his hands on the knife. "Let me see the knife, Daddy. Can I have it? I have always wanted a knife like that. Where is it?"

"Son, the knife is in the bottom of their sack. I dropped it in their sack just before they left."

"But why? I needed that knife!"

"You didn't need it as bad as he did. It was his papa's knife. He cared about it, he kept it in his pocket."

"So they just cheated us out of a whole sack of produce!"

"They didn't cheat us, son. They were really needy. It was the Christian thing to do."

Jesse could not understand why it was Christian—Christlike—to let someone get the best of you. About thirty minutes later, Jesse got another insight into the matter. A small flatbed truck stopped. Inside was Delton Willard, a farmer who had been evicted from his farm near Joplin, Missouri. Sitting beside him was his wife, Daisy, and their year-old son. Piles of clothing and bedding were stuffed on the floorboard and behind the seat. On the flatbed of the truck were two frayed and flattened mattresses, upon which sat three sisters, aged eleven, nine, and seven. Their wind-whipped hair hung down in their faces, their dresses rumpled, their bare feet grimy. That night, they would be sleeping on the dusty mattresses, under the truck. A hemp rope was tied across their laps to keep them from bouncing off the truck. As soon as they saw the vegetable stand, they untied themselves and slid to the ground. As the three sisters approached the stand, Jesse saw three dirty, shifty-eyed, delinquent beggars plotting to grab something and run. Benjamin, on the other hand, saw three frightened, lost puppies that had fallen into a hole. The girls were too embarrassed to make eye contact. Ben sensed their empty rumbling stomachs.

Delton Willard asked Daniel if he would let them have some fruit and vegetables on credit—when they got to California, he would find work and mail Daniel a check as soon as he was paid his wages. "Life has taken us to a bad turn," said Delton Willard. "The bank foreclosed on us, and day before yesterday, they sent a bulldozer to tear our house down. We had about ten minutes to get out while the dozer man was fueling. We grabbed our clothes and our mattresses. We didn't have any food to pack, just a sack of old seed corn that we parched to munch on until we reach the West Coast. I hope it don't tear up our kids' stomachs. Last night the sheriff let us sleep in the Sapulpa jail, and they fed us a good pot of beans, but they made us leave early this morning because they don't want vagrants hanging around for handouts."

"Well, I guess we can let you fill a box," Daniel responded, "but don't mail us back any money. Next time you take your kids to church, just put the money in the collection plate."

Jesse was speechless. At the far end of the stand, Benjamin was busy. "One for you, one for you, and one for you," he said as he handed each sister a plump, ripe tomato. Next, he handed each of them a peach, then an apple, then a pear, dropping the items one by one into the girls' pouches, which they had formed by holding up the hems of their dresses in front of them. "One for you, one for you, and one for you."

Shaking his head in disappointment, Jesse watched the old flatbed truck pull out onto Route 66 with a box of vegetables that he had helped grow, a part of their work and their property simply rolling off down the road. "Daddy, we shouldn't be giving any of our stuff to a bunch of beggars!"

"They aren't beggars, son," said Daniel. "They are people a lot like us but who have had a turn of bad luck. But for the grace of God, and a federal loan, we might be roaming about the country on the highway ourselves, in Dewey's old jalopy, which we don't even own. The Bible says Jesus wants us to be kind to strangers, and when we can, we ought to feed the hungry and care for the poor."

"If being a Christian means we have to let ourselves get cheated, I don't think I want to be a Christian."

Daniel frowned. "Son, you don't really mean that. Today you seem to be letting your thoughts come from the back part of your brain, where greed and selfishness and resentfulness and anger are found. Try to let your thoughts come from the front part of your brain, like Benjamin does, near your eyes, where you can see what your heart feels, love and patience and caring for others more than yourself."

That evening, they returned home with not much money made, not much produce left, and the lad Jesse wrestling with his conscience and life's contradictions. How could it be that while life demands that individually we are responsible for ourselves, we are also responsible for others? He who had carried little Mary Kinnard on his back through a blizzard could not discern why he should be responsible for people whose problems were in part due to their own mistakes.

That night after supper, Daniel announced that he would reinstall the cellar door tomorrow. Instead of trying to sell produce on Route 66 each week, he would take a load of produce to the churches in Elk City that maintained emergency relief kitchens. Then he gathered his children at the kitchen table, and for their daily Bible reading, he selected a passage in which Jesus told his followers to do unto others as we would have them do unto us.

That night, as he lay on his cot, Jesse wrestled with his soul. He truly wanted to be a Christian, to be Christlike, and go to heaven. But he also wanted to be Jesse, to have personal ambition and possess things for himself and not share things with people who did not deserve it.

Janie lay on her cot, pumped up with joy for her new school clothes. Soon she was to be a big schoolgirl, no longer a baby. One of her dresses had yellow daisies!

On his cot, Benjamin's cup was running over. So much happened that day! People were so interesting! A parade of incidents, a mishmash of events, like the 1932 newspapers on the walls that surrounded him. That so much could happen in 1932 and so much could happen on Jesse's ninth birthday meant that his life would be full, full, full! He felt secure. When he tossed and turned on his cot and his heel bumped against the wall of the shack that was his home, he liked the strength of the solid sound of the thump. He liked his hard narrow cot. He liked his skin.

*   *   *

It is impossible to know how protective Grace would have remained toward her youngest child had not a freakish, avoidable accident occurred in the autumn of 1936. Compared to Russell's husky super-sons, Jimmy and Donny, Benjamin did seem thin and frail, but basically he was a healthy child, happy as a lamb in clover, with a good appetite and good digestion. As a nursling, Ben never quite emptied her breasts, and this led Grace to believe he had a sensitive, finicky disposition. She was always urging him to eat more. "Finish your food, empty your bowl, one more bite." Although for his size, he ate enough. She found that she could always stuff him with scrambled eggs, which he loved, salted and peppered and softened with butter or ketchup, easy to swallow even when he was sated. He ate so many scrambled eggs his baby teeth came in yellowish, and that also caused Grace to be concerned about his health. Then, too, he was such a light sleeper, rousing at every little sound, and always early to rise. To her, who valued sleep, that was not healthy.

The tipping point came late one Saturday afternoon, when Grace was driving the jalopy home from Denim, with Benjamin her one passenger. Daniel had taken his two-row planter to the blacksmith shop a day earlier to get a broken piece welded and left his team, Bill and Hector, there overnight to get their hooves trimmed and to pull the mended implement home again the following day. Jesse and Janie were away, visiting their Dalkens grandparents for the day. Grace and Ben were to go home in the jalopy while Daniel followed them, driving the team home, pulling the planter. Grace had little experience driving a car, having had to compete with three brothers for driving time while growing up, yet on occasion, after she married, she had driven the Hargrove jalopy without incident to the grocery store in Roosevelt, on straight flat roads she knew well.

"You should have no trouble," Daniel reassured her as she slipped behind the wheel. "Just remember, if you have to use the brakes, sometimes you need to pump the brake pedal a time or two to get it to take hold." Benjamin was surprised to see his mother put the car into gear and start driving, for the first time in his memory, and he muttered a tentative "Whee" as he settled down in the front seat beside her. "Benjamin, you will need to keep still and not take hold of mother's arm until we get home," she cautioned as she left town. There were no seat belts in those days, no child car seat.

Once outside Denim, the road made a ninety-degree left turn, which Grace negotiated smoothly. With growing confidence, she continued westward two miles, then took a right turn toward home, but misjudging her speed, she fishtailed slightly and the steering wheel wobbled as the car turned north. She overcompensated for the wobbling wheel and the car began to swerve, so she removed her right foot from the gas pedal and pushed the clutch down with her left foot, letting the car gradually coast to a stop. Somewhat unnerved by the incident, she sat still for a moment before resuming the drive.

After driving another mile or two, her confidence not fully restored, she became apprehensive about guiding the car down the approaching long hill sloping steeply to the creaky narrow bridge near their home. That the bridge had no side rails was to her a most-worrisome matter. Daniel had told her about finding Bran's dead littermates under the bridge in a busted box—to fall from the bridge most likely meant certain death! At the crest of the hill, with the bridge in sight, Grace decided to put the jalopy in low gear, to slow it down, but as she moved the gearshift into neutral, one of the front tires hit a rut; this made the car veer and caused her foot to slip off the clutch. Its gear now disengaged, quickly the car picked up downhill speed. Grace rammed both feet onto the brake pedal, but in absolute panic she failed to pump the brake pedal. The brakes failed to take hold and the car gained forward momentum and Grace's eyes locked on the dreaded bridge. Benjamin yelled "Whee!" and suddenly, Grace decided it would be better to crash the jalopy into the left embankment than risk flying off the bridge to their death, so she jerked the steering wheel to the left and the car bounced across the drainage ditch and came to a jolting stop against the road's left embankment. Benjamin's body was hurled against the dashboard, and his face flew into the shattered windshield. The percussion knocked him unconscious.

"Oh, dear Lord, what have I done!" Grace screamed. She reached for Benjamin and noticed a large lump on his forehead, several small cuts at his hairline, and a sharp sliver of glass stuck through his lower lip. "God help me!" she cried as she lifted him out of the car and laid him down gently on the embankment. Benjamin moaned faintly as he began to regain consciousness, but as she pulled the glass sliver from his lip, Grace could not tell if he was even breathing. "God, please save my baby! I'll do anything you want if only you will save my baby!" She tore a six-inch strip from her petticoat and began swabbing at the blood that now covered Ben's face. His eyes opened, and he reached for her and began to whimper: he hurt inside too much to cry. He suffered bruised ribs from the impact, no broken bones, but Grace could not know that. His back was sprained, and his bruised ribs and a bruised vertebra would bother him for weeks. Grace was afraid she had crippled him for life.

Cradling Ben in her arms, Grace hurriedly carried him to their house. With each step she took, her emotions ricocheted from gratitude that he was still alive, to self-loathing that she had driven so poorly, to anxiety that Benjamin was permanently crippled, to wrath that nature had created the dreadful ravine, to resolve to give Benjamin special care should he always need it, to resentment that Daniel had put her in such a risky situation, to wondering if she had been injured herself and was too preoccupied with Benjamin to notice, to anger that the community had allowed such a dangerous bridge to exist, to a commitment that she would never try to drive again. As she crossed the bridge, she strode across it in the exact center, as far away from the edges as she could get. When she turned into their driveway, half-grown Bran bounded out to meet them.

"Tell Bran I hurt," whispered Ben.

Bran tried to jump up to lick Ben on the hand, but Grace gently pushed him away. Once inside, Grace laid Benjamin on the bed and undressed him. She looked for contusions and found bruises on his right side. She noted his short breaths—he could not take deep breaths because his ribs hurt when he did. "We need to get him to the hospital," she told herself. "I wish Daniel would hurry home."

When Daniel reached the crest of the hill and saw the jalopy smashed into the embankment, then approached near enough to see the bloodstained strip from Grace's petticoat lying on the embankment, he whipped the team into a fast trot, rattled across the bridge, and rushed into the house.

"What happened?" he asked as he noticed Benjamin stretched out on the bed, whimpering.

"I couldn't get the brakes to work, so I stopped the car by turning it into the bank. Benjamin hit the windshield and bruised his side. Daniel, we need to get him to a doctor right away. He probably has a bad concussion, and he may be bleeding inside!"

"Our car's broke down. We don't have the means to take him anywhere," Daniel answered. "Ben, are you hurting bad?"

The thought of going to a doctor frightened Ben. "No, just almost bad."

Grace was determined to provide her baby the care he would need. "I'll ask my mother and father when they bring Jesse and Janie home," Grace said. "They can drive us to that little hospital in Sayre."

When James and Maudeen brought Jesse and Janie home from their all-day visit, Benjamin stopped whimpering. He did not want his grandmother to see him cry. Jesse and Janie leaned over their wounded brother, who closed his eyes so that he would not have to talk to them.

I knew that something bad would happen here, thought Janie.

Grace showed Maudeen the cuts at Ben's hairline, the cut under his lip, and the bruises on his right side. Maudeen drew upon her experience as a mother who had tended to cuts and scrapes of her five reckless, active children; her active leadership in the Ladies' Helping Hands Club, in which she had studied first aid manuals; and her assumption that she always knew what to do.

"Shouldn't we take him to the hospital?" asked Grace.

"Does he have any broken bones?"

"No, apparently not."

"Has he spit up blood?"

"No."

"He'll be okay. Bring me your roll of adhesive tape and your scissors, and I will cut a little patch to close the cut on his lip, so he won't have a scar when it heals. And do not let him take a nap until late bedtime, because if he has a concussion, it is risky to let him sleep too soon—he might lapse into a coma."

"What's a *coma*?" asked Janie.

"It's when you go to sleep and you don't die yet but you can't wake up," explained Jesse.

"I'll keep him awake," offered Janie. She brought their *Children's Illustrated Bible Stories* to the bed, sat at Benjamin's feet, and began to make up one-line stories from the illustrations as she thumbed through the book randomly. Jesse accompanied Daniel and Grandfather James, who towed their jalopy to the mechanic at the blacksmith shop in Denim. Daniel would sell old Red's bull calf to pay for the parts and repairs. Maudeen accompanied them to town to buy some items at the Denim General Store.

Grace wanted to take Benjamin in her arms and rock him, but he seemed to hurt too much to be touched, so she let Janie continue her one-line illustrated Bible stories. "Zaccheus, come out of that tree and feed me some soup!" "Noah said, 'Don't have a big flood unless you've got a bird to fly out and find dry land.'" "Don't let your lambs get lost in a snowstorm, 'cause Jesus doesn't have any mittens." "The widow gave her little mite away, but she still had a flea." "Daniel was lucky the lions did not like his flavor." "Mother Mary was glad

Jesus was perfect, so she didn't have to wash diapers." "Samson loved Delilah, and Delilah loved hair."

Grace was relieved that Benjamin was breathing somewhat easier, and she was amused by Janie's interpretations of biblical illustrations. She went into the kitchen and set about to prepare dinner, returning into the sickroom a few minutes later to find Janie continuing her one-line stories. "Jesus told the people to say the Lord's Prayer so they would not forget God." "God gave us the rainbow, but He hired little gypsies to hide the gold." "Don't plant your seeds on rocks, or the birds will eat them up!"

Grace noticed that Janie had shifted her position on the bed; her left foot was nestled between Benjamin's legs, her toes wiggling against Ben's crotch. "Janie, move your foot! What on earth are you thinking!"

"But I am paxifying Benny. He likes it. See? He has stopped whining."

It was true—Benjamin was more relaxed than he had been since the collision.

"You can't touch anyone else's private area that way! Move your foot!"

Janie slowly withdrew her foot. "But I wasn't touching him with my fingers. Aunt Olivia says that toes don't count."

"What does Olivia have to do with this?"

"She showed me today how to paxify. She was babysitting Aunt Valdetta's little Gary. She had him on a pallet on the floor and was tickling his little sack of balls with her toes while she read her new movie magazine. She said the big girls at school told her how they paxified their boyfriends when they got them mad. Boys like to have their sack of balls jiggled and tickled."

"Well, you just forget everything that Olivia said. It is so... so disgusting! And don't you ever do such a naughty thing again."

Janie returned to her *Children's Illustrated Bible Stories* and knew that her mother was right. But she thought that Olivia was also right. Wiggling-jiggling-tickling works.

Gradually Benjamin recovered from his injuries. Within ten days the bruises on his side had disappeared. For the rest of his life, there would be a tiny unnoticeable scar on his lower lip.

Sometimes he would complain of a backache, and this caused Grace to fear that he had suffered a moderate, permanent spinal injury; she would need to guide him through childhood—and perhaps beyond—with a certain level of protective caution.

Ben would remember the collision, the shattered glass, the blood, his mother's hysteria, but he would not remember his sister's pleasant, innocent incursion into his crotch, or his mother scolding her for it. Subconsciously, though, he might have been made to associate pleasantly sexual feelings with behaviors forbidden for him to do.

On his own Ben had already begun to learn where the pleasurable places were, and pleasing ways to touch them. Would it take his family's subtle guidance, especially his mother's, to keep Ben within the boundaries of proper, acceptable sexual behavior?

CHAPTER 14

As the Twig Is Bent

Despite her innate shyness, when Janie started school in September 1936, she loved it. Jesse let her sit beside him on the bus on her first day, but not after that; Jesse belonged in the back of the bus, where the big boys were. For her first day, she wore her yellow daisy dress, and she looked like a sunny garden angel. She would have worn it every day if Grace had let her. Grace had cropped Janie's hair just below her ears, and her thick bangs covered the top part of her forehead, drawing attention to her winsome light-blue eyes. One could see that she was destined to grow into a wholesome, beautiful young lady, the type that Norman Rockwell would have wanted to paint. She looked forward to the school bus ride. She sat beside Olivia on the second day, but Olivia also drifted to the back of the bus, where the big boys were. On the third day, Janie sat beside her new classmate, Joseph Kinnard, a timid little lad, and his sister, Mary Kinnard, whom Jesse had saved from the blizzard.

"I am going to marry Jesse," Mary told Janie matter-of-factly. "He won't talk to me now, but when we grow up, I am going to marry him."

At school, Janie liked to line up in two rows to learn the Pledge of Allegiance at the flagpole, then march into class, her teacher in charge. She also liked recess time, and reading time, but not numbers, and not nap time. Why nap when there was so much to do? She wanted to get on with it. She loved her books, especially her first reader, *Dick and Jane*. She was the first in class to learn to spell her name, and she read "See Dick run. See Jane run. See Dick and Jane run" with enthusiasm. "See Dick jump. See Jane jump. See Dick and Jane jump" also enthused her, but she wished they would get on to wherever they were running and jumping.

Janie brought her books home every night and asked her father to listen to her read. Benjamin stood faithfully, patiently behind her chair and looked over her shoulder and learned every word as fast as Janie did. He also thought Dick and Jane were a funny pair, always running and jumping; didn't they ever hear of just walking?

For Benjamin, the hours Jesse and Janie were at school seemed endless. He asked Grace to play school with him, so she sat him in a chair facing the kitchen wall and asked him to read the wallpaper while she went about her chores. He actually picked out several words he knew, and from the 1932 articles he had cajoled others to read to him over and over, he related those news stories from memory or ad-libbed them. When Janie learned the ABC song, Benjamin learned it equally as well, and throughout the school day, when he was alone with his mother, he often broke out loudly into the lyrics:

A, B, C, D, E, F, G,
H, I, J, K, L, M, N, O, P,
Q, R, S, T, U, V,
W, X, Y, and Z.
Now I know my ABCs,
Won't you come and play with me?

Over and over and over and over, until Grace wanted to run out of the house, screaming, and jump into the cellar and shut the door. But she didn't. If the weather was pleasant, she sent Benjamin outdoors instead, where Bran was waiting. Bran had gotten too big to play with the kittens, and they avoided him by skittering up the posts to the porch roof, to lean over and watch what the silly pup would do next. Ben liked to throw sticks and balls and watch Bran fetch, and Bran thought it was a great game, but only for a while. Both of them preferred to explore within the boundaries Grace dictated: "Don't go past the outhouse and don't go out to the road." Sometimes, excited with the sheer joy of being, Benny and Bran would go racing around the house as fast as they could go, Bran disappearing around the corner before Benjamin could hardly get started, then Bran would reverse direction and come back around the corner, slamming into Benjamin. Ben would scream and giggle and chase Bran in the other direction, until *slam*! Here came Bran again, again, and again.

When the days were warm, Benny played on the sandpile in the shade of the house, and Bran napped beside him or sniffed and dug at the holes that penetrated the mountain of sand, searching for mice or bugs, which he warred against constantly. Disturbing moments occurred on occasion when Bran heard a certain rattletrap pickup approaching out on the county road. He would snarl, jump up barking, and run toward the road before Benjamin could hear anyone approaching. The pickup, which belonged to Mel McGreggor, a reclusive farmer who lived where the road dead-ended against the Canadian River bottom, rattled past the mailbox and rumbled across the bridge before Bran could reach the road. Nevertheless, Bran barked fiercely until the vehicle had climbed the hill and slipped out of sight. A similar scenario occurred when McGreggor returned from town. No other passing motorist bothered Bran at all; only the old rattletrap from the dead-end river road held his grudge and roused his anger.

Benjamin not only had Bran to play with, he also had a whole barnyard of friends. When the calves were first born and for several weeks until they were weaned from wanting to nurse their mothers, Daniel kept them in a pen beside the barn. *Bucket-fed* was the term farmers used to describe the practice of separating the baby calves from their mothers and feeding them a small ration of skim milk from a pail while selling as much milk or cream as possible. Ben liked to walk among the calves and rub their heads and talk to them in an endearing jargon that made sense to no one, although the tone was gentle. "Bah bah, baby boo boo, coo coo, lopey dopey ropey mopey soapy, lee lie lee lie lee lie lo."

Ben's relationship with the chickens was a more complex matter. When he was around the chicken yard, most of the hens expected something edible from his hands, but he could not always deliver. They became accustomed to him appearing among them throughout the day, along with Bran, who clung to Ben like a shadow because old Red, the rooster, did not tolerate Bran strolling through the flock on his own. On occasions, when Grace went out to the chicken yard to catch a fryer for dinner, Bran learned that when Grace singled out a fryer, Bran could gain favor by leaping on the fryer and holding it down with his paws without injuring it until Grace could seize it. Grace would pat Bran on the head and exclaim, "Good boy! Good boy!" Bran lived to please, and his tail went wild at every praise.

Jesse had shown Ben how to carry water from the cow trough to keep the chicken's water pan filled, and Ben took on the task as a legitimate, responsible chore that he enjoyed because it made him feel important to the whole farm operation. He also took on the task of carrying fresh eggs from the nests to a bowl in the wooden icebox, one or two or three at a time. He learned not to put eggs in his pockets—the fragile things broke so easily and oozed down his britches leg.

Grace used all the broody hens that wanted to set and hatch their eggs to do so, each separated and protected in brooder coops. Hatching chicks throughout the spring and summer meant that the family could have fried chicken on a regular schedule, with various sizes of chicks coming along throughout the season.

Hatching day was always a thrill for Ben. He was forbidden from disturbing the brooder hens, but he could sit behind the brooder coops and listen for the *peep peep peep* of baby chicks emerging from their shells. At hatching time, Grace checked the mother hens in their nests every few hours to make certain that eggshells from newly hatched chicks did not encapsulate the eggs of chicks yet to be hatched. She showed Ben the newly dried, fluffy chicks, most of them the color of old Red, the master of the flock.

One day, Ben was shuttling back and forth from the house to the chicken yard, making an egg run, when one of the laying hens squatted in front of him, in a natural reflexive breeding stance that hens assume when they anticipate that a rooster is about to mount them. With the squatting hen at his feet, Ben bent down to pet her when suddenly, from nearby, old Red came flapping his wings in a rage to attack the interloper about to mount one of his hens. Wings flapping and legs slashing, old Red buried his beak in Benjamin's scalp, whacked Ben's cheek with the brunt of his wing, and scraped his spurs into Ben's forearms, drawing blood in three different places. Screaming in terror, Ben raced to the house while Bran gathered the courage to chase old Red back toward the chicken house. Grace, who had seen everything from her kitchen window, rushed out to rescue her child. "Oh, my poor baby! That mean old rooster! I will kill him and boil him for dinner!"

"No!" Benjamin cried. "Ole Red my friend! He crows for me!"

"Benjamin, don't you realize what just happened to you? That sorry rooster flogged you! He has you bleeding all over!"

"He thought I was a *woof!* Please don't hurt him!"

Grace carried Ben into the washstand to wash off the blood. "Child, you are the most forgiving person I have ever seen. I just pray your big heart doesn't come back to hurt you. For now, it is back to the bandages for you, my poor child. Maybe you will have a scar to remind you that even friends can turn on you."

*   *   *

Swirling in the mist of Benjamin's early memories was a motor trip he and his mother took with Granddad and Grandmother Dalkens in James's Ford touring car on Route 66 to Oklahoma City in October 1936, when he was not yet three. They were in the city to be on hand at the rape trial of his uncle Dexter Dalkens, a taxi driver who was facing charges that he had forced himself on his call girl girlfriend, Sally Roe, trumped-up charges stemming from Dexter's effort to blackmail certain prominent city leaders whom he had delivered to illicit liaisons with Sally's call girl acquaintances.

The Oklahoma City trip expanded the horizon of Ben's life permanently. The sweep across more than a hundred miles of country new to him exposed him to the realization of just how large the world might be. During the midday court recess, the family bought the fixings for bologna-and-cheese sandwiches, and they picnicked at the

Oklahoma City Zoo. There were elephants and tigers, giraffes and lions, bears and monkeys, which, to Benjamin, ever more would be too large and real to fit neatly into storybooks.

Ben was much too young to understand the trial and its ramifications. Grandmother and Granddad Dalkens wept openly at the jury verdict that sent their eldest son to prison for five to fifteen years. They did not get an opportunity even to talk to Dexter. Grace awkwardly accepted a gift, a new cut-glass stemmed cake platter, from a contrite Sally, who claimed that she was required to testify against Dexter because she was under a death threat from powerful men who feared the blackmailer Dexter and arranged the trial in order to get him out of circulation.

"Justice is not blind, but cross-eyed," shrugged Dexter's court-appointed attorney, "so that rich and powerful people can evade the legal focus between right and wrong."

There would be no appeal.

In the wake of the trial, Ben noticed the profound humiliation and sadness of the family, but it did not dampen his excitement in the trip back home across Southwestern Oklahoma. So much to see, a world so big, miles of hills and valleys and trees and cows, farms, and birds and other cars sweeping past at the breathtaking rate of thirty or forty or fifty miles an hour!

"Mama, look! A baby deer!"

"That's just a clump of dead grass, Ben," his mother answered. "Settle down, child, you'll wear yourself out. Why don't you put your head on my lap and take a nap?"

Benjamin was afraid he would miss something and never have a chance to see it again. Soon darkness pulled the curtain on Ben's panorama, and weariness set in. He was sound asleep on his mother's lap when they came to a stop in front of their old farmhouse, only to be awakened sharply when the car door opened and his mother's new cut-glass cake platter fell out on the gravel and broke to pieces.

"It's just as well," said Grace, sighing. "It would always remind me of my poor, foolish brother locked away in prison."

* * *

February 13, 1937

Dear Leona,
*   The warden has brought me a copy of your divorce papers. I must say I am pleased about it because it is a good feeling to feel free. I am glad you had the good sense not to try to get child support, because I would not pay it if I could. I never wanted those kids in the first place. Vernon is too much like you, and Kirby is too much like me. Grace always said I was mean because I enjoyed hurting people, and she might be right. I guess I am the devil's own. So you will not be surprised when I tell you that if you ever take up with another man, I will kill him.*

Love,
Dexter

*   *   *

A person's psyche may become affected and one's conscience can be shaped permanently by moments of stress the impact of which remains in one's subconscious long after the details of the stressful incidents are forgotten. For Benjamin, certain incidents affected him so keenly that he developed a supersensitive conscience. For instance, in late spring of 1937, when Ben was three, he and his cousin Jimmy were playing with toy cars on the floor of Grandmother Maudeen's kitchen on a day when the extended family had gathered to harvest and can garden produce. Grace and Valdetta were in Maudeen's garden, picking the last row of green beans, while the toddlers, Donny and Gary, threw clods at fence posts, laughing loudly when their dirt clods hit a post and exploded. Inside, Maudeen and Donna Belle were washing jars, snapping pods, and blanching them for the pressure cooker for canning. When one of Jimmy's toy cars veered off course, Ben crawled across the floor to retrieve it alongside a table where Maudeen was working. The toy had come to rest between

Maudeen's legs, and as Ben reached for it, he glanced upward in fear of being stepped upon. Suddenly Jimmy cried, "Grandmother, Benny is looking up your dress at your panties!"

"My stars!" Maudeen reacted angrily. "Benjamin, you bad little boy, invading a woman's privacy is about the worst thing a boy can do!" She jerked him off the floor and sat him down roughly in a chair in the corner behind her large cast iron cookstove. "You stay there in that chair and don't say a word! When your mother comes in from the garden, I will see to it that she punishes you!"

Grace was shocked when she came in from the garden and Maudeen told her that she had caught Benjamin looking up her dress. Grace carried her errant child into the living room and sat him down roughly on a wooden bench. In her haste to placate her mother, Grace overreacted. What prurient interest could a three-year-old boy have in peeking up his grandmother's dress to see her panties? After all, he had already seen them out on the clothesline, big floppy old pink things flapping in the wind.

Nevertheless, her mother, Maudeen, had been offended, her privacy invaded by Benjamin, and the child must be punished. Without a word, Grace bent him over the bench and spanked him. "I hope this will teach you to respect the privacy of others!" she said sternly.

"But I didn't do it, Mama," he sobbed. "I did not look at Grandmother's panties."

"Then why would she say you did?"

"Grandmother does not like me."

"Of course she does. Now you go in there and tell her you're sorry."

"I don't want to."

"It's what a good boy would do."

"All right, then." Head bowed, Benjamin returned to the kitchen. Without looking up, confused, he apologized. "Grandmother, I am sorry about your panties."

Benjamin was realizing that a child can be punished not only for what he does wrong but also for what only appears to be wrong.

* * *

In late May 1937, the family matriarch, Eliza Brown Dalkens, passed away at her son Harold's home in Oklahoma City and was buried in Oklahoma City's Memorial Park Cemetery. James was not aware of his beloved stepmother's passing for several days because there were no telephone lines in that part of Roger Mills County. Death messages had to be sent by telegram to the nearest train station then mailed to their destination. Word of her death had gotten around by the time of the 1937 Dalkens reunion, and when the family gathered and sang their favorite old hymns, Maudeen brought forth a heart-stopping rendition of "Sweet By and By." The family gathering became more of a requiem than a happy homecoming.

Eliza had received a letter from her long-lost daughter, Callie, just two days before her passing, and there were those who said that Callie's letter brought on her death. Harold brought the letter to the reunion so that those who wanted to read it could do so and react as each saw fit.

May 23, 1937
Chicago, Illinois

Dear Mama,
I pray you are in improving health, and if not, I know you will have a nice place waiting for you in heaven. I love you and miss you so much, but I cannot come to see you, and this is the reason: I have a beautiful, intelligent, redheaded, freckle-faced thirteen-year-old mulatto daughter named Loretta, who is the joy of my life. I would not dare bring her South and expose her to all the prejudices down there, and I could not come without her. I remember all the "nigger" jokes my brothers used to tell, and I know how unfair black people have been treated in Louisiana and Texas, where I grew up. As for Oklahoma, the abuse is just as bad.
I know it broke your heart when I left Jonah and left our two sons, but at that time, I felt I had

no choice. Jonah often beat me and accused me of cheating on him if I so much as looked at another man. When our sons scorned me and started treating me the same way, I could not take it anymore.

Loretta's father was a wonderful cook at a café on the south side of Chicago, where I worked, the kindest, sweetest, most handsome Christian man, who was there for me when no one else was. He died of sickle cell disease five years ago.

Now, about Loretta: Sure, there is prejudice and abuse here in Chicago too, but not everywhere. We live in a neighborhood that is accepting of diversity, and she is in a good public school and is doing well. I take her to a colored church, where she sings like an angel. She wants to go to college and become a physician, and she is smart enough and determined enough to do it. So I am staying here and putting her through medical school, and someday, when I join you up in heaven, we can both look down on her and be proud.

Love,
Callie

All the older folks at the reunion took turns reading Callie's letter, and it evoked a variety of responses, from snide remarks to measured compassion. "A redheaded darky is still a darky." "I wish I had known about Jonah. I would have taken care of him." "Poor Callie! One bad decision after another!" "So, a redheaded jigaboo cousin! Ain't we proud!" "It's about time this family produced a doctor! Ha! Ha!"

When James read the letter, he wrote down Callie's address, intending to write her. He had fond memories of his youngest sister. She loved to ride behind him on horseback, with his steed going as fast as possible. "Faster! Faster!" Emulating all her older siblings, she grew up too fast. James was one of Callie's older brothers who had

206

enjoyed telling "nigger" stories, and every time James came across a black street urchin in town, he thought it was good sport to offer him a nickel to "dance a jig." It was a calloused, bigoted expression of the segregated culture into which he had been born. He admitted to himself that black folks ought to be treated more fairly, but social equality? He was not ready for that. It would take a later generation.

James never mailed Callie a letter. He never wrote one.

*   *   *

In the year 1937, the dust storms increased during spring and early summer, and the drought continued, with months of torrid summer heat that scorched the fields. Daniel cut his stunted cornstalks down with a hoe and used a pitchfork to stack the fodder for hay for the cows and horses when winter came. The sorghum field was harvested in the same manner. The cotton crop was promising up until late June, when the heat and dryness caused the cotton stalks to shed most of their green bolls. Only the irrigated garden fulfilled its promise of bounty, and the family was comforted by cellar shelves filled with canned fruit and vegetables and dried root crops.

By the middle of June, the days were so hot that during the nights, hardly anything in the house cooled down, so Daniel moved their beds outside, the double bed onto the porch and the three children's cots to the slab roof of the cellar. The children found it to be fun, like camping out, and comforting, because the night breeze from the south had them reaching for covers before morning. The first night they slept outside, lying on their backs, looking up into the heavens, they were awestruck by the vastness of the universe, the countless stars. Jesse could identify only the Big Dipper, the moon, and the Milky Way.

Stricken by the enormity of it, Janie began to cry. "What's wrong?" asked Jesse.

"We're so tiny, everything else is so big, God can't find us here," Janie sobbed.

"Of course He can. God is all-knowing. The preacher says God counts every hair on our heads," stated Jesse.

"Mama says my old hair keeps coming out and more new hair comes in, so how can God keep track of that?"

"With God, all things are possible."

"But how do we even know if there is a God?" asked Janie. "Where is He? Is He on one of those stars?"

"God is everywhere," Jesse said.

"Prove it," challenged Janie.

"Well, just look at those stars. He keeps everything in working order. If there was no God, everything up there would start crashing and burning and falling down on top of us."

Janie squealed as she saw a shooting star. "Look, there's one now, moving across the sky and burning up! Someday we're all going to just burn up!"

"Naw, that's just a shooting star. Ever once in a while, God likes to light a firecracker."

"Oh," sighed Janie, and she yawned. "I'm going to close my eyes now and go to sleep. I will see you silly brothers in the morning, if the sky doesn't fall down on us."

Benjamin's cot was nestled between Jesse's and Janie's, and he soaked in everything that they had been talking about. He could not understand the immensity of the universe, and the mystery of it all created an uneasy feeling in the pit of his stomach. But there it was, spread clear across the sky, and despite his uneasiness, he accepted it and appreciated it. It was a good show. To him, Jesse sounded like he knew what he was talking about. Jesse knew everything.

Meanwhile, Ben could sleep in safety, because Bran was curled up at his feet.

CHAPTER 15

So Grows the Twig

W hen Jesse and Janie returned to school in September 1937, Benjamin again found himself without a regular playmate, so he found other ways to turn everyday life into adventure. Grace now felt it was safe enough for him to go out on his own all about the farmstead, with the exhortation, "Stay away from the canyon!" so he was off and running. Bran was always at his side, or racing ahead, sniffing out snakes and other potential dangers. One hour, Ben was catching grasshoppers, putting them in a jar to take to the chicken pen to feed the hens. How they scrapped and clucked and competed for the delicacies, threshing insects to pieces with their beaks then gobbling them down! Many of the hens had acquired special names— Frances, Marcy, Margean, Penelope—that Janie had concocted for them because their combs and wattles and beaks reminded her of the hairstyles, eyes, and noses of neighbor ladies. Ben tried to get them to take turns for their delicacies—"One for you, one for you, and one for you"—but old Red and the more-aggressive hens could not be controlled.

Benjamin spent hours playing "cow-and-calf bottles," a special make-believe game he created in which discarded, empty medicine bottles, ketchup bottles, Tabasco bottles, pepper sauce bottles, soda pop bottles, empty bottles of all shapes and sizes became a growing herd of cattle; the smaller bottles, such as fingernail polish bottles and aspirin bottles, were the baby calves, while the largest bottles became his horses as he drove the herd from pasture to pasture, in enclosed portions of his sandy play area on the shady side of the house, where fences made from string for wire and sticks for posts created a big make-believe ranch having several pastures. Grace had shown him how to build the fences, and Grace used her kitchen butcher knife to cut the flaps off a sturdy cardboard box and cut off one side of the box that, turned upside down, became an excellent barn. A matchbox became Ben's ranch wagon. Bran had to be taught to leave things alone, for if he so much as pulled on the string fence, it was like a tornado had swept through the whole operation.

When Jesse visited one of his friends, Ben requested that Jesse bring him two or three new cow bottles from their trash pile. "Baby calf bottles would be nice too," he said. He was in a constant state of anticipation to increase his herd, but of course, Jesse was too proud to rustle through trash dumps for throwaway bottles. "Carrottop, you are a silly mess," said Jesse.

Ben's favorite pastime was hiking out to the pasture, where the real cows were grazing. He loved the cows and saw in each of them a distinctive personality, a living fellow creature worth knowing. He watched them compete for the feed in the trough, he watched them chew their cuds, and he watched them lick a salt block with tongues that seemed as long as his arm. He watched them drop great piles of rich, steamy manure. When they got accustomed to him in their midst, often two or three of them at a time would approach him to be scratched on their ears or on the underside of their chins.

Ben learned to tell when it was time to drive the small herd in for milking, and he learned that an authoritative stick in his hand respectfully changed their regard for his presence. In turn, the cows realized that a trip to the barn lot meant a bucket of sweet feed and relief for their strutted, milk-filled udders.

One evening, after milking chores were done, Ben noticed something unusual about one of the cows.

Old Heart, one of the dry cows, seemed restless.

"Daddy, look! Ole Heart is walking funny. She's got something sticking out from under her tail!"

The cow had been experiencing labor pains for several minutes, and her amniotic sac was protruding like a water balloon. She lay down as a series of contractions squeezed her abdominal muscles, then when the pain momentarily subsided, she got up and walked around the cow pen as the unborn calf was being pressed inside the cow's uterus into the proper position to enter the birth canal.

"Benny, Heart's getting ready to have a baby. We mustn't disturb her. You need to go into the house now and help Mother and Janie set the table for supper. Jesse and I are going to oil the cultivator and the wagon wheels. You can come and get us when dinner is ready."

"But I want to watch Heart find her baby. Where is the baby now?"

"Heart doesn't want you and Bran to watch. It makes her nervous. Now go on to the house like I told you."

Ben walked away, but as soon as Daniel and Jesse left to adjust plowshares on the cultivator and oil its wheels, Ben dashed around the barn out of sight, crawled under a feed trough about twenty feet from Heart, pulled Bran down beside him, and watched intently. Heart was now lying on her side, fully engaged in delivering her calf. The amniotic sac had broken, spilling fluid on the ground and revealing the calf's left front hoof. The contractions came sporadically every minute or two, pushing the right front hoof out a few inches behind and above the left hoof, soon to be followed by the emergence of the unborn calf's muzzle, which Ben could not yet recognize.

Within five minutes, the contractions had pushed out the calf's front legs and its entire head, its ears pinned back and its tongue lolling out the side of its mouth due to the pressure from having its body fully lodged in the birth canal. Ben was amazed! The calf's head was covered with a portion of the punctured amniotic sac, its nostrils visible, but it was not yet breathing. Its blood flow continued to depend on its mother's heartbeat through the umbilical cord, still attached.

Heart continued to strain mightily, facing the most difficult part of the delivery. Her contracting abdominal muscles must quickly push the calf's shoulder through the birth canal, or the limited blood flow to the calf's heart and lungs through the umbilical cord, now squeezed tightly in the birth canal, would be insufficient to keep it from suffocating. With one final contraction, the slick wet calf, now gasping for breath, was sent slithering out on the ground. Ben was astonished! There it was, its hind legs still partly embedded in its mother's body, a newborn calf shaking its head, gasping for breath, its legs beginning to flail themselves feebly into an instinctive urgent effort to get its lungs filled with air, stumble to its feet, find food, survive.

The calf bleated faintly, whereupon Heart struggled to her feet, breaking the umbilical cord. Then she turned to clean the amniotic mucus from her new baby, starting at its head, licking along its neck and shoulders and all over, stimulating blood flow as mother and baby established their bond.

Ben noticed Heart's punctured sac, much of it still attached inside her uterus; it was cascading out of her vulva as a thick strand of fleshy, bloody mucus. The act of parturition from her calf began to stimulate hormonal changes in the cow's body that would promote milk flow and cause the afterbirth to gradually detach itself and be expelled on the ground. The bloody sight shocked Ben, who concluded that the cow's insides were all coming out, and she would die!

Quickly Ben crawled out from under the feed trough and dashed around the barn. "Daddy! Daddy! Come quick! Ole Heart has a baby calf, and now her insides are coming out!" Bran barked with excitement.

"Bennie, you little sneak, you are supposed to be in the house, helping your mother."

"But come and see the new baby, come and see what's wrong with Heart!"

Daniel and Jesse walked to the cow lot fence and looked at Heart. "Ben, she's doing just fine," said Daniel. "We need to leave her alone. Let's go eat dinner, and afterward, we'll all come out and see how the baby is doing."

During the meal, Ben stayed excited and awestruck by what he had witnessed in the birth of Heart's calf, and he described to Janie in limited vocabulary but in great, messy detail about the birth, some of the details a bit hard to digest at the supper table. Afterward, Daniel told all the children to help with clearing the table and washing the dishes before they went out to see the newborn, which was wobbling on its feet but successfully attaching itself to its first dinner.

"What's its name?" asked Janie.

"It's a girl," said Jesse. "We'll call her Lottie, because she was born in the lot."

"She's mine," claimed Janie. "Daddy, please, can I have her?"

"She's mine," said Ben, "because I saw her first!"

It would not be the last time Ben would be first to find a newborn calf, because as time went on, he practically lived with the herd. They were his friends, and he was interested in everything they did.

*　　*　　*

For Thanksgiving 1937, Leona and her father, Aaron, and her sons Vernon, ten, and Kirby, eight, bought round-trip bus tickets to Cheyenne, Oklahoma, to spend the weekend with her brother Daniel and his family, and the extended Dalkens family at the old homestead. Leona had just completed a correspondence course that she would apply to her future teaching degree, and she wanted to cap off the achievement by discussing with Daniel and James her tentative plans to send her sons to Roger Mills County for six weeks in the summer of 1938 so she could attend summer school. She and her sons were returning to Altus on Sunday to get the boys back in school and for her to resume her evening janitorial work in downtown establishments, while Aaron would stay for his annual week's visit with his son Daniel. Aaron had just returned from cotton harvest in West Texas. He was weary, and he was craving his yearly tonic.

Daniel picked them up at the bus station in Cheyenne, where Jesse and his cousins began incessant chattering. They had always been close, boisterous playmates before Jesse had moved away; they wanted to make up for lost time. Jesse, Vernon, and Kirby would spend the weekend at the old homestead with their grandparents so that Aaron could sleep on Jesse's cot and Leona could sleep on Janie's cot; Janie would sleep on Benjamin's cot, and Benjamin would have a pallet on the closet floor, where he often napped anyway.

At James's and Maudeen's Thanksgiving dinner table, with all the extended family present, Leona announced that she had divorced Dexter following his conviction to prison, not because she ever planned to remarry, but because as a single mother, she might become eligible for future public assistance, if necessary. Because of her Dalkens sons, she hoped she would still be accepted in the family.

"Of course you are one of us," said James. "We all love you." This was the first divorce he could recall to occur in the entire extended Dalkens family since Callie had moved away. "We're just so proud you and your boys and Aaron can be with us today. Aaron, will you honor us by giving thanks to God for our blessings?"

Embarrassed and somewhat caught by surprise, Aaron reverted to his standard blessing: "Gracious Lord, for all these and other favors, we thank Thee very much. Amen." Benjamin had heard the same prayer several times before, but with no teeth, Grandpa often did not speak clearly, and Ben thought Grandpa Aaron said, "Radishes, slaw, for olives and other flavors, we thank thee berry munch. Amen."

After dinner was served and then cleared away, the entire family drifted outside. It was a balmy day for late November. Maudeen wanted to take several group photographs with a new box camera Olivia had acquired through her coupon-clipping activities. First, Leona, Aaron, Vernon, and Kirby, their guests of honor, were photographed. Then family groups—Russell's family of four; Wally and Valdetta and little Gary, who was wearing a cowboy outfit, including boots and spurs and bandana and a Roy Rogers gun and holster set that he had received on his second birthday just a few days earlier; then Grace's family of five; and then Maudeen, James, and Olivia.

Maudeen then lined up select groups of grandchildren. "First, Jesse, Vernon, and Kirby, the Three Musketeers! Where are they?" The boys had disappeared.

"They have run down to the woods, toward the river," reported Janie. "They are going to climb trees and play outlaws and sheriffs."

"Well, then, we'll photograph them later," said Maudeen. "Now, for the three young Dalkens musketeers, Jimmy, Donny, and Gary. Line them up right here in front of the garden gate."

"Wait!" said Russell. "There are four in this group. Here's Benjamin! Ben, you little Tuff Nut, stand here between Jimmy and Donny."

"But Benjamin is not a Dalkens, he's a Bird," said Maudeen.

"He's half-Dalkens, just as Jimmy and Donny are half-Lee and Gary is half-Weaver," Russell replied. "We will take pictures of these four fine fellows every Thanksgiving until they are grown." And so Uncle Russell made certain that Benny was not left out. Ben did not understand that he had almost been discriminated against, but he knew that his champion hero, Uncle Russell, had stood up for him, and his smile for the camera was wider than the others', his head tilted slightly toward the left.

Next, Maudeen wanted a photo of her only granddaughter, Janie, standing alone, but Janie was too shy to stand by herself, so her aunt Olivia stood beside her. Olivia never refused to allow her picture taken. "I wish there were such a thing as color photography," said Maudeen. "It would be wonderful to contrast the olive complexion and dark, chocolate-brown hair of Olivia with Janie's blond peaches-and-cream."

Because the weather was so nice and James wanted to celebrate the presence of all his grandchildren, he organized an outing, a hayride to the river bottom, so that the children could play in the sand and the ladies could gather pecans and persimmons and the men could gather firewood. For the next two days, the men would be cutting and hauling firewood for the winter. Benches were placed in a horse-drawn wagon, outfitted similar to James's school wagon back when they lived near Consolidated Number 8. They all piled on, and James drove the family down a trail into the woods and onto a sandbar along the south bank of the Canadian River.

While the men gathered driftwood, Maudeen led an expedition of her daughters into the edge of the woods. First, they gathered a three-gallon bucket of persimmons, edible now that there had been at least one hard freeze, necessary for releasing the sugars in the otherwise-bitter, puckery persimmon fruit. Their main objective was to find enough native pecans to make several pecan pies for Christmas season, as well as pralines and divinity candy. The native pecans were tiny—hardly larger than one's thumbnail—but contained an oil that made them oh so rich and tasty. It took great patience to crack and shell enough pecan meat for even one pie. Daniel had more patience and determination than anyone else to stay with such a menial chore, and it was because he ate a generous portion of the meat as he cracked and shelled them. The ladies needed to gather at least two gallons in order to make the project worthwhile.

Aaron, who likened gathering pecans to picking cotton—stoop labor—helped gather driftwood for a time, but soon he wandered off a few hundred yards down along the riverbank to reflect on the spring of 1906, when he and Clara attempted to homestead on the north bank of the Canadian about thirty miles east from where the Dalkens outing was now taking place. Those were hard times, Aaron recalled vividly, when Daniel was born in a half-dugout. He now regretted that they had not endured, for if they had, Aaron and Daniel might now be stable landowners, picking cultivated pecans under patented, thin-shelled thirty-year-old pecan trees that he could have planted, trees that would outlive his grandchildren and great-grandchildren. Unfortunately, it was not God's will for the Bird family to be land-owners, he concluded in 1906, and he now concluded again.

Meanwhile, James rested at the hay wagon, watching his small covey of grandchildren playing in the damp sand. James had offered to watch the children because he was in considerable pain from gout in his left foot and from arthritis in his hands and shoulders, although he did not divulge his misery to anyone. There was no rea-son anyone should know; it might put a damper on their happy time together. He watched Janie make a collection of mud pies, muffins, and cookies, while Jimmy, Donny, and Gary were molding the sand into balls and throwing them out toward the center of the sandbar that covered most of the river. It had been so droughty for so long that on warm days, there was no river flow at all except for seepage underneath the sandbar, where carelessly one could become bogged down in quicksand. James noticed that Benjamin was acting as a sort of supplier, using a small stick to scratch and loosen the sand, which he offered to the other children for their games. All the chil-dren were getting damp sand all over them, but the sand was clean, and when dried, it would brush off with hardly a trace remaining. Or so he hoped, not wanting to be in trouble with their mothers. James regretted that he had not homesteaded near his brother Robert back in 1900, when land was still available, for if he had, he might now be in a position to leave a small farm to each of his children, who were now struggling on marginal, rented farms. He hoped that at least he could occupy Robert's land for a few more years, until Robert's son Rayford moved back from Colorado. James had been wrestling with whether it would be wrong for him to pray that God would find a way to keep Rayford in Colorado indefinitely, to postpone James's moving off the old homestead for several years.

After about two hours, Daniel, Russell, and Wally had gathered a pile of driftwood large enough to occupy their saws for the next two days, and the womenfolk had strolled back to the wagon with their collection of persimmons and pecans. "My stars!" exclaimed Maudeen. "James, why did you let these kids get so dirty?"

"That's not dirt, dear. That's play sand, clean enough to eat. Do you want to try one of Janie's pies?"

Jesse, Vernon, and Kirby had remained in the river bottom woods all afternoon, switching from one fun activity to another, climbing, running, hiding, hunting. As the outing was coming to an end, Wally was preparing to summons the trio with one of his shrill, bone-rattling whistles when the youngsters sauntered in with their bounty. Their pockets were crammed with pecans, and Vernon was holding up a fat young swamp rabbit, already skinned and gutted, ready for the skillet.

"Vernon saw this big swamp rabbit run into a hole," Jesse reported, "and so he took his pocketknife and cut a long stick with a sharp, forked end on it, and he stuck the stick into the hole and twisted it until he rolled up the rabbit's fur into a knot, then he pulled the rabbit out, squealing, and bashed its head in with a stick, and cut its stomach open and pulled its guts out, and pulled its fur off, and cut its head off, and now it's ready for the frying pan!"

"Grandmother, will you cook this rabbit for us big hunters tonight?" asked Kirby. "Vernon said he would share it with you if you cooked it for us."

"I certainly will," offered Maudeen. "Vernon, I'm so proud of you! Rabbits and squirrels are edible game during the months whose names contain an *R*."

"Vernon, your daddy must have done a good job teaching you how to hunt and dress game," offered James.

"No. Daddy never took me hunting," said Vernon.

"He likely didn't have enough patience to do it," Wally speculated.

"Then Vernon must be a natural-born hunter," said Maudeen. "It's his Choctaw blood!"

"Am I really part Indian?" asked Vernon.

"One-sixteenth," Russell said, chuckling. "Our Indian blood must be heap-strong medicine! Or else Vernon is just a natural-born hunter, with an instinctive ability found in descendants of the survival of the fittest."

They all climbed onto the wagon and headed back to the old homeplace. Sitting in the back of the wagon, his thin legs dangling from the wagon bed, Aaron Bird kept silent. This was a Dalkens day. But as he watched the wagon wheels unroll their ruts back on the sandy trail, his memory rolled back beyond when he became a toothless old cotton picker, back beyond recent seasons, when Vernon and Kirby occasionally actually listened to his early-day stories, way back to the inside edge of the nineteenth century, when as a wild and restless Texas cowboy, after riding a fence line all day, or looking for strays, he hunkered down out of the wind in a sandy wash, squatted beside a small campfire of dried cow chips and twists of bluestem, and manufactured a meal of roasted prairie dog, or jackrabbit, or rattlesnake chunks, or cottontail twisted out of a hole with a strip of barbed wire.

CHAPTER 16

Family Matters

Returning home on the MKT bus with her sons, Leona was uplifted by the weekend trip to Denim. She had made plans to have Vernon spend next summer with his grandparents, and Kirby would stay with Daniel's family while she went to summer school and resumed studying for her teaching degree. Her sons had enjoyed spending wholesome time in the country with their relatives, and she was glad to get them away from Altus for a few days. While she was at work, her sons had started going downtown on their own, with a shoeshine kit that they had put together, and no amount of discipline from her seemed to deter them. Vernon and Kirby had started making money and spending it on junk food and candy and hiding it from her. The chairman of the deacons at First Baptist Church told her that her sons were seen spending time in the Rack-It-Up Pool Hall and that he had notified the sheriff's constable to arrest the proprietor if he caught the boys in the pool hall. But the problem was, the pool hall had a back door, and whenever the constable came in the front door, Vernon and Kirby dashed out the back door and were on the next street before they let the constable catch them, whereupon they would ask him if he needed a shine, which he usually did. They only charged a dime per shoe but had no change for those who paid with a quarter.

Aaron stayed at Daniel's for a week before returning to Altus and planned to help with the woodcutting, but by the time Daniel returned from taking Leona to the bus station at Cheyenne, Aaron was already abed with the chills, in his heavy blue denim jumper, hacking and softly moaning. "Daniel, do you have a doctor here at Denim?" he asked. "I think I am going to need some medicine."

"I'll see about it first thing in the morning," said Daniel.

He had learned that the closest place to get whiskey was at a service station on Highway 33 just across the Oklahoma-Texas boundary a few miles west of Denim. Aaron started on his hot toddy treatment by noon on Monday, and by Tuesday, he was sitting in the rocker, holding Benjamin, reading the Bible aloud to his grandson, who asked him, "Grandpa, tell me about the people in the Bible who had cows." Aaron seemed to become revitalized when he was around Benjamin; the child's enthusiasm, mixed with whiskey toddy, perked him up. Ben observed Grandpa's yearly hot-toddy occurrence with a certain anticipation: soon a new whiskey bottle would be added to his herd.

Aaron did not know if he could explain the Old Testament stories about herdsmen at a level that Benjamin could understand, but he would give it a try. "Well, Benjamin, I can tell you that Adam's second son, Abel, kept flocks, and the Lord looked with favor on him. Then Abraham and his nephew Lot had flocks of sheep and herds of cattle, and God smiled upon them, but they had to compete with others for the grazing lands, and they fought their neighbors, so it was a violent country, and always has been. Then there was Abraham's grandson Jacob, one of the greatest of all herdsmen, who worked as a herdsman for his father-in-law, Laban, for seven years to get permission to marry Laban's beautiful daughter, Rachel. But after the seven years were up, Laban insisted that Jacob marry Leah, his eldest daughter, first then work another seven years to marry Rachel, so Laban cheated his son-in-law out of seven years of work. In turn, Jacob cheated Laban, because Jacob's wages were to be paid by receiving all of Laban's spotted, speckled, and brindled livestock, and so Jacob used only spotted, speckled, or brindled males to breed Laban's females, resulting in most of the offspring being spotted, speckled, or brindled. Benjamin, I suspect this story is too complicated for you to understand, but if you grow up to be a cowman, just remember this: people who raise cattle tend to cheat one another. When I was a young man, I worked over a dozen years in Texas cattle country, where I concluded that the only people who are more crooked than cowmen are bankers, lawyers, and horse traders."

"Did God smile on Laban or on Jacob?" asked Benjamin.

"Well, Jacob was a good manager, and the Bible says he grew exceedingly prosperous, so I suppose you can say that God smiled on Jacob, although he must have had a hard time pleasing two wives."

"Were Jacob's children spotted, speckled, or brindled?" asked Ben.

Aaron chuckled and took a sip of his toddy. "Child, you've asked a question that I can't answer," said Grandpa Aaron, "and it probably won't be the last."

*　　*　　*

In December 1937, Daniel went to Elk City to confer with Walter Williams, the bank official who was administering the federal program that had provided Daniel his opportunity to farm on foreclosed land. Daniel sought help in purchasing seed corn, cottonseed, and sorghum seed for 1938 spring planting. Waiting in the outer office for the interview, Daniel noticed a shelf of golf trophies that Walter Williams had won in weekend tournaments at area country clubs.

Meeting with Daniel, Walter Williams, with wide girth, in suit and tie, was all business. "Tell me, Mr. Bird, how did your 1937 crop turn out?"

Daniel shook his head. "As you know, rainfall was very sparse again this year, but after every little shower, I cultivated my crops to leave a cover of dust on the ground to hold in the moisture, and the corn and sorghum held on until late July, when I had to cut it down for fodder before all the grain could develop. At least I have enough fodder to get my cows through this winter. As for the forty-acre cotton crop, it was stunted by the drought, but I kept it plowed and hoed clean, and somehow there were some damp, low places where the cotton roots reached down far enough to stay alive, and so I harvested a total of three bales."

"Three bales off of forty acres," said Walter Williams. "Hmmn. That is a bale for every thirteen acres. I don't know many men industrious enough to pull a cotton sack over thirteen acres for just one bale. Mr. Bird, that is commendable."

"I didn't have an option to do anything else," Daniel replied. "My wife and kids pitched in and helped. It meant the difference between going into the winter without new coats and shoes for the kids, and the money from the three bales plus money from selling a steer allowed me to pay off our feed bill at the Denim General Store and make an annual payment on a line of credit that we ran up at Jabour's Grocery and General Store back in Roosevelt before we moved. We owe our landlord back there also and try to send him a token payment every Christmas. We always try to keep our expenses down. We have a subirrigated garden that produces all the fresh vegetables we can eat and preserve, and our milk cows have produced a ten-gallon can of cream about every week, which provides us the money for staples and everyday expenses."

"Tell me, Mr. Bird, what about your calves? From your six cows, can't you sell calves and come up with a down payment on the land? After all, the program you are signed up for is supposed to allow you to make a modest down payment on the land. At ten dollars per acre, the purchase price for 160 acres is only $1,600, and the farm is yours. The 10 percent down payment is only $160."

Daniel tried to explain how difficult it was to come up with extra money. "First of all, one of our cows died of shinnery poisoning last year before she ever had a calf, and from the other five cows, we kept three heifers, which are now bred to calve in the spring, and we kept one of the bull calves for a herd sire; and we sold a steer to pay repair costs on our car. This year, we had four heifers and plan to keep them all to increase the herd, because they would bring only about $20 each at the sale barn, and we have more pasture than acres for cultivation anyway."

Walter Williams frowned and said, "Well, I advise you to come up with a down payment to purchase the farm, Mr. Bird, because next year is the last year you are guaranteed first option before it is offered on the market. Outside money is now coming into Western

Oklahoma to buy up available land for the mineral rights, because of the activity in the oil fields near Elk City. The oil speculation is moving in your direction. Next year is also the final year for us to help you with seed purchase. We'll send you a check in a few weeks, the same as last spring, for the same amount of seed, then the program will have only one more year to run, so be advised."

Daniel left Walter Williams's office with mixed feelings. He resented that a pencil pusher with a wide girth was in a position to tell him how to map his future, he who labored in nature's way to provide for his family, when the only connection that Walter Williams had to nature was a synthetic connection while using a variety of clubs to knock a tiny white ball over mowed grass into a sequence of eighteen little holes. Daniel was grateful that he would have seed money for another year, but he was uneasy about the prospect of having the land sold out from under him in a year or two, for he did not see how he could ever scrape $160 together for a down payment. With the likelihood that James and Maudeen would also lose their occupation of the old homestead, a family upheaval seemed to be on the way.

*   *   *

The weather patterns through the winter and spring of 1938 duplicated the drought of past years, with the addition of a grasshopper plague that erupted in June. The dry, hot weather served as an incubator for hatching trillions of grasshoppers across the entire Southwest, and they hatched and passed through Roger Mills County in great swarm clouds, stripping the leaves off the corn and sorghum and cotton plants. Thank goodness the garden produced early, and the canning and the harvesting of root crops were completed before grasshopper damage became so bad. Grace knew how to cut off damaged, chewed-over sections of squash, tomatoes, cucumbers, and okra and salvage the good parts so the table was well provided every day.

Again, for the third straight year, Daniel had to cut down his corn and sorghum for fodder before the grain fully developed, and again the family moved their beds outside for the summer because of the incessant heat. Daniel bought a thirty-gallon pickle barrel with a spigot in the bottom of it and built a seven-foot scaffold beside the windmill to hold the barrel and a ladder for Jesse to use to lift buckets of water to fill the barrel every day so that the sun-warmed water would be available each evening for the family to take refreshing showers. Grace ripped the seams out of a cotton sack and tacked the muslin to the frame of the scaffold to serve as a modesty screen. The children considered the pickle barrel shower a profound luxury and hardly noticed the pickle smell that permeated for several weeks.

In early June, Kirby came to live with them for six weeks, and Vernon stayed with his grandparents on the old homestead while their mother, Leona, went to summer school. Kirby's presence in his uncle Daniel's household caused an unexpected strain because, at the age of nine, Kirby was openly preoccupied with sex. The hours he and Vernon had spent loitering on the streets of downtown Altus and the time they had roamed in and out of the Rack-It-Up Pool Hall exposed them to men who thrived on telling dirty jokes and talking disrespectfully about sex with women, and men who had no compunction from abusing others for their own gratification, and although eleven-year-old Vernon seemed to have escaped damage, it was obvious that Kirby had been affected. He peppered his conversation with scatological references, and on the second day of his stay with his uncle Daniel's family, while he and Janie and Benjamin were playing Chinese checkers on the porch, Kirby tried to pull Janie's panties down and grope her. Janie ran crying into the house to her mother. Grace tried to admonish Kirby, but she had difficulty even talking to him, for he merely sulked. That night, and for the rest of Kirby's stay, Janie slept on a pallet on the porch beside her parents' bed.

Regularly Daniel took Kirby for long private walks and tried to impress upon him the need for decency and respect for the feelings of others and warned him that if he did not behave and clean up his language, Kirby would have to go home and stay with Grandpa Aaron in his downtown one-room apartment. Kirby did not seem contrite, and when Daniel looked into Kirby's eyes, he saw Dexter's self-centered, hedonistic personality. To Kirby's credit, he did restrain himself from outright rebellion, but his prevalent preoccupation with sex emerged often. In an environment without a bathroom, he openly exposed himself when he emptied his bladder, and when he sat inactive and restful, he invariably fondled himself through his pants pocket. "Pocket pool," he called it. Benjamin noticed Kirby's behavior and wondered about it, especially at night, on the cellar slab roof, where their cots lay side by side.

One evening, when Jesse was spending the night with Vernon over at the old homestead, leaving Kirby and Benjamin alone together in their cots on the cellar slab roof, Kirby paused from fondling himself, turned to Benjamin's cot, and asked him for a "blow job." Ben had no idea what Kirby was talking about and would not have responded anyway. Ben did not feel comfortable toward Kirby. His double-cousin made him nervous, and while he found Kirby interesting, he did not find him pleasant.

As Kirby's summer visit transpired, Jesse became Kirby's anchor, his role model. Kirby admired Jesse, who became eleven years old in July. Kirby tried to emulate Jesse's confidence, respectfulness, and wholesomeness. Jesse created activities that he and his cousin could enjoy doing together. He and Kirby built tiny kites out of oiled paper and molted chicken tail feathers and used Grace's spools of thread to sail them out of sight. Despite Grace's misgivings, the boys modified the deer crossing into a steep path down into the floor of the canyon and played in the shade of the canyon walls for hours.

When Kirby slipped and muttered an epithet, Jesse emphatically kicked him hard in the seat of his pants and told him, "Hush that dirty talk, or I will black your eye!"

Once or twice a week, Grace allowed Jesse and Kirby to walk the two miles to the old homestead to spend the day with Vernon, who was thriving from the six weeks with his grandparents. He ate everything in sight, gained nearly eight pounds, and grew an inch taller. Vernon relished the role of being recognized as the eldest grandchild, and it seemed that Maudeen especially went out of her way to give Vernon a good experience, as though she must compensate for Dexter's neglect of his children.

Recalling her own childhood grappling or doodling for fish along the banks of flowing streams in South Central Oklahoma,

Maudeen donned a pair of James's blue denim overalls and one of his oversize work shirts and took Vernon doodling for catfish in water holes along the banks of the Canadian River where the fish had laid their eggs. Vernon was astonished at his grandmother's Choctaw bravery, as she ignored the possibility of stirring up angry, poisonous, aggressive water moccasins, and marveled at her skill in feeling along the riverbank for catfish holes, trapping the quarry in the billows of her shirt and tossing them out upon the embankment, for dinner.

At the old homestead, Jesse found a pile of used lumber and selected six strong straight narrow poles, onto which he attached pegs and harness strips to convert the poles into stilts, upon which he, Vernon, and Kirby spent hours strutting about stiffly, standing six feet tall. Along the roadbed they found hundreds of small round hard yellow gourds that became perfect missiles with which they played "king of the hill," knocking one another off their stilts in a battle to the finish, creating lots of bruises on their shoulders, backs, arms, and legs and a black eye now and then, a painful but character-shaping experience, preparing them for future conflicts, fistfights, football tussles, and possibly, military war. Youngest and smallest of the trio of combatants, Kirby fought most fiercely, angrily, and riskily, and rarely won.

On the last Friday in July, Leona completed her summer term at Southwestern Oklahoma Teachers College and took a bus to Roger Mills County to reclaim her children. They had become very homesick to be with her, but they did not look forward to returning to the streets of Altus. On the next day, the extended Dalkens family traveled across the Packsaddle Bridge to picnic at a privately owned, spring-fed, gravel-bottomed swimming pool at Grand, the ghost town site of the old Day County Courthouse. Under the shade of massive elm trees, Maudeen and her daughters served a lunch of fried chicken, potato salad, sliced tomatoes, cucumbers, wilted vinegary greens, butterscotch cookies, chocolate cake, and chilled cantaloupe. Grace cautioned everyone not to go swimming until their stuffed stomachs settled, for fear of cramps, but every man there became a self-appointed life guard; they threw caution to the wind and made a big splash jumping into the shallow end of the pool, where the youngsters who could not swim bobbed around in knee-deep to waist-deep water.

Only Valdetta, Olivia, and Donna Belle had swimsuits, single-piece, with short sleeves. Everyone else had cutoff pants, including Maudeen, Grace, and Leona, with blouses. Benjamin's swimwear was one of Jesse's outgrown old cutoff school pants, with a drawstring for a belt, awkward with pockets full of water. Jimmy, Ben, Donny, and Gary got into a game of splash and dash, splashing and running in circles, until Ben fell and went underwater, coming up nearly strangling, swallowing a mouthful of water and drawing water into his windpipe. Grace rushed to him, swooped him into her arms, and carried him to a shady spot. Coughing, he asked, "Mama, did I almost drown?"

"No, honey, but why don't you stay here in the shade and play in the sand, because I can't have you swallowing any more of this murky water or breathing any more of it into your windpipe. I can't have you getting a bout of pneumonia on top of getting sunburned. You'll be all right playing here in the shade while I go back into the pool and teach Janie to swim."

Russell, one of the self-appointed lifeguards, observed Benjamin's situation and decided to approach him and engage the lad. "Hey, Tuff Nut, come with me and help me patrol the pool to guarantee that everyone is having fun. Okay?"

"Okay," Ben responded. He would never turn down an opportunity to do something with Uncle Russell.

"Here, jump on my back and put your arms around my neck, and we'll wade out amongst the masses."

Benjamin complied, jumping onto Russell's back, his arms locked around Russell's neck, his head peering over Russell's right shoulder. As they waded into the pool, Russell asked Ben to describe what he was seeing.

"I see Mama trying to show Janie how to swim," said Ben.

"Are they having fun?"

"I don't think so. Janie is stiff and whining and holding her head up like a duck, and Mama is working hard to keep her patience."

"Do you know what *patience* means?"

227

"Sure. Mama says I am always trying hers."

"Russell, be careful with Benjamin," said Grace. "He has already swallowed some of this dirty water!"

Russell pretended he didn't hear her. "What else do you see?" he asked Ben. "What are my boys doing?"

"Jimmy is on Vernon's back and Donny is on Jesse's back and Gary is on Kirby's back, and they're going around in circles, trying to pull one another down in the water."

"Are they having fun?"

"Well, they're laughing a lot and screaming and acting rough with one another, so if they're laughing, they must think it is fun," offered Benjamin.

"What do you think?" asked Uncle Russell.

"They should be helping one another enjoy the water instead of bothering one another, I think," said Ben.

"Do you see the ladies? What are they doing?"

"All the ladies but Mama are standing in a circle, bobbing up and down, but not very much, because they don't want to get their hair wet. They're talking about somebody, so they must be having fun."

Russell chuckled. "What are the men doing, Benny?"

"Granddad is watching the boys wrestle in the water to see that they don't get too rough. Daddy is floating on his back, pretending to be asleep, and Uncle Wally is paddling around in a big old lazy circle."

"What about me?" asked Russell. "What am I doing?"

"You are showing me how not to be afraid in the water."

"So do you want to go all the way across the pool and back, or are you afraid, Benny?"

"With you, I'm not afraid of anything!"

With Benjamin locked around his neck, Russell stretched out across the surface and glided over the water, Russell the mentor, the embodiment of simple, reliable, gracious, comely, powerful masculinity; Benjamin the eager, dedicated wannabe.

CHAPTER 17

Strong Vines, Tender Grapes

In late summer 1938, just before Jesse and Janie were to begin a new school year, two misbehaving neighbor boys, Jacob Jiggs, who was twelve, and his brother, Jethro Jiggs, who was eight, burned their father's haystack down while lighting hand-rolled cigarettes they made after stealing their father's pouch of Bull Durham tobacco. Four-year-old Ben and Janie and Jesse watched the flames and smoke, about one-half mile south of their front yard, as Mr. Jiggs's entire winter supply of hay burned to the ground. As the fire burned, Janie used red, yellow, gray, and black crayons to draw a picture of the fire on a piece of cardboard. Benjamin watched intently as the flames surged and the hay disappeared gradually in a cloudy drift of smoke that crossed the ravine below their barn and passed overhead.

Next day, Mr. Jiggs came to ask Daniel if he would trade some of his corn shocks and sorghum fodder for one of Mr. Jiggs's butcher hogs. If not, the Jiggs family would have to sell their small herd of milk cows because they had nothing to feed them through the winter. Daniel allowed that he did not have much fodder to spare, but he appreciated Mr. Jiggs's plight, and certainly, the Bird family would benefit from acquiring a butcher hog. Jesse stood beside his father and listened intently as the deal was being made. Benjamin was in awe of "the haystack-burning boys," Jacob and Jethro, who had accompanied their father. Ben was fascinated by their haughtiness and handsome, roguish features. Almost mesmerized, he wandered off with them into the nearby cowshed. Jacob had been suspended and held behind a grade in school after threatening his teacher. He seemed older than twelve, because he was imbued with a recklessness that led him to say naughty things and engage in indecent conduct with abandon, a prime candidate to drop out of school altogether.

"Hey, little boy, go stand back there in the corner of the shed while I take a leak," Jacob ordered.

Benjamin complied with shock and embarrassment. Jacob then unbuttoned his fly and exposed himself. "Here, watch me and see how far I can piss," he ordered, having cornered Benjamin with his forceful stream of urine. "Don't you like the looks of my pecker? Don't you want to touch it?" he asked with a devilish grin.

Speechless, Benjamin was trapped. He was compelled to watch, to avoid being urinated upon, and he was stunned that anyone could dare behave so wildly, could emit a stream of urine with such force and volume! Jacob chuckled as he emptied his bladder.

Ben remained cornered, red-faced with embarrassment. Nearby, Jethro, the eight-year-old, seemed annoyed that his brother was finding such sport and he was being left out. "Hey, little boy," Jethro asked, "what's your name?"

"Benjamin Ray Bird."

"How old are you?" asked Jethro.

"Four and a half," Ben replied.

"Well, little Bird, you sure have got a lot of ugly little freckles on your nose. Let me show you how to take them off. Here, smear some of this fresh cow shit on your nose, let it dry there, and then all your ugly little freckles will bleach away." Jethro picked up a small dab of manure in his hand and attempted to smear it on Benjamin's nose, but Benjamin slapped his hand away and the dab of manure splattered on Jethro's shirt.

"Why, you little son of a bitch!" Jethro swore through clenched teeth as Ben ran from the shed and sought safety beside his father. Benjamin had never heard curse words before, and he was struck with their impact, how dramatically the curse words made Jethro's anger seem more menacing.

For the rest of the day, the traumatic urination episode with Jacob stayed fresh in Benjamin's mind. He was afraid to tell his parents about it for fear they would punish him for going into the shed with the bad Jiggs brothers. Jethro's curse words, *son of a bitch*, kept resonating in his ears and popped out spontaneously that evening after dinner while Ben and Janie were stretched out on the floor, drawing and coloring with crayons. Needing a green crayon to draw an apple tree, Janie deftly plucked a green Crayola out of Benjamin's hand. In a sudden flash of anger, Ben responded, "Hey, give me back my green, you little son of a bitch!"

Shocked, Grace dropped what she was doing, swept Benjamin off the floor, dragged him to the washstand, and forcefully washed his mouth out with a bar of hand soap. "Benjamin, we don't use such filthy words! I'm going to wash them out of your mouth and out of your mind. Don't you ever say such a terrible, ugly, evil thing again!"

Bursting into tears, Ben sputtered and gagged on the nauseating taste of soap.

"Where on earth did you ever hear such words?" she asked. "It wasn't your daddy, was it?"

"No."

"Jesse?"

"No."

"Granddad?"

"No."

"Grandpa Aaron?"

"No."

"Uncle Russell?"

"No."

"Uncle Wally?"

"No."

"Then who was it?"

"One of the haystack-burning boys got mad at me for getting cow poop on his shirt and called me that," Ben said.

"Well, from now on, you just stay away from those dreadful boys. They're nothing but trouble! And don't let me hear of you playing with cow manure again!"

That night, as Ben lay on his cot, the day's unforgettable events gripped his thoughts. He knew he would never use curse words again, for if he did, his tongue might lather. The image of Jacob's forceful stream of urine trapped him again, forced him in his mind to envision Jacob's impressive organ in action. To Ben, it was an awesome thing. If Jacob ever asked him again if he wanted to touch it, Ben might actually touch it, if it did not break any rules of proper male behavior, because a pleasant, new stirring in Ben came just from thinking about it.

*　　*　　*

Appropriately, it was his father, Daniel, who—mostly through example—provided Benjamin guidance on proper male behavior concerning bodily functions in their world with no indoor plumbing: When you go to the outdoor privy, never wet on the toilet seat; if you can't hit the hole, pee behind the outhouse. Always turn your back to those who are outdoors with you when you need to relieve yourself. Pee behind a tree. Wet behind the barn or the chicken house. Do not make eye contact with anyone when you do it.

From Cousin Kirby, during his summer visit: Never shake it more than two or three times when you are finished peeing, for if you do, you are playing with it.

From Jesse: When you are wrestling with your cousins or your friends, never grab or feel their crotches, because under all circumstances, one's private parts are untouchable. Always. Untouchable. Never look at another boy's private parts. Look away, look away.

Ben had never witnessed his father's privacy, or even Jesse's. Jesse the modest hovered in the far back corner when he changed his underclothes. On Saturday-night bath time, after the evenings had become too cool for the family to shower outside beside the well, Grace heated buckets of bathwater on the kitchen stove and poured it into one of her washtubs and pinned a blanket on a rope strung alongside the stove to screen off the bath area. One by one, in privacy, everyone in the family bathed in the same water—unless one of the kids had been playing too much in the dirt, in which case Grace heated fresh buckets of water for those at the end of the order: first, Jesse the fastidious, then Janie, then Ben, then probably with a fresh supply of clean bathwater, Grace and then Daniel. Everyone's privacy was respected by all, except by Grace, who, in her capacity as mother, needed to be in and out of the bath area to make sure the kids were washing behind their ears. Then, too, Daniel enjoyed having his wife scrub his back.

*   *   *

On a warm October 1938 afternoon, while Jesse and Janie were at school, Daniel replaced a strip of his tin can subirrigation line that had rusted out in a low part of the garden closest to the county road, digging a shallow trench for a replacement section. Benjamin was alongside, playing in the fresh dirt and looking for worms and tumbling with Bran. Suddenly, Mel McCregger's rattletrap pickup was returning from town, coming over the hill south of the bridge. Bran raised his hackles, barked, and bounded through the garden fence onto the road. At last, he had reached the bridge in time to confront the terrible menace that had thrown him and his littermates away.

"Come back, Bran! Bran, come back!" Benjamin shouted. "Don't get run over!"

Bran's focus was on not allowing the rattletrap to pass. As soon as McGreggor rolled onto the bridge, Bran flung himself against the sharp edge of the front bumper, which cut an open gash in his throat; Bran's body tumbled through the air and rolled to the very edge of the bridge. McGreggor did not even slow down—he just drove on. In a death throe, Bran's legs twitched and caused his body to slip over the edge.

Benjamin screamed, "Bran, my friend! Bran, my friend! Daddy, that old man killed Bran!"

Daniel gathered Benjamin into his arms and carried him to the house, Benjamin crying uncontrollably. "It's okay to cry, Ben. It's okay. It's okay. Thank God Bran didn't suffer very much. It's okay."

Grace had heard Bran's barking and the rattletrap's passage and Benjamin's screams, and she knew what had happened even before

Daniel told her and placed Benjamin in her arms. She sat in the rocker and patted her child's back softly, suffering for him and sharing Ben's heartbreak. "There, there," she said softly. "There, there…"

Daniel took a shovel and descended into the canyon at the steep deer crossing that Jesse and Kirby had modified, and walked under the bridge. Flies and ants were already swarming over Bran's eyes, mouth, and the gash in his throat. Daniel dug a hole beside Bran's body two feet deep, nudged the body into the shallow grave, and before covering it, retrieved several scattered bones from Bran's littermates and lay them in the grave beside him. Then he filled in the grave and smoothed it over. "Dust to dust," he muttered as he completed the task.

When Daniel returned to the house, Benjamin had cried himself out and was now quiet and pensive.

"Daddy, are any animals in heaven?"

"Yes, son. I am sure there are."

"How do you know?"

"Well, the Bible says that Jesus is coming back from heaven on a great white horse and He will be leading an army of men on great white horses. So there must be a lot of animals in Heaven."

Ben accepted that and nodded. "If there is room for bunches and bunches of great white horses, then there must be extra room for a good little happy brown puppy dog, right, Daddy?"

"Right, Benjamin. You can believe that."

Benjamin seldom mentioned Bran again. He knew that death was real: the body dies and rots. He saw it in baby chicks that got smashed and snakes that Daddy or Jesse killed in the cellar and hung on the fence to make it rain and Granddad's baby calves that got the scours too bad to survive. He knew that Bran's body was buried and already rotting under the bridge. But that was not really Bran. The real Bran was in heaven. Ben had to believe that. Or else he might as well just jump off the bridge. Weary from his long bout of crying, Ben laid his head on his pillow and descended into a nap.

"Daniel, this child is so sensitive. I am afraid he will live a life of pain and sadness," said Grace.

"I don't foresee it that way," Daniel responded. "His smile is too wide. He's always trying to help others feel better. I think that puts him mostly on the front side of happy."

When Ben awoke, Jesse and Janie were home from school. When they were told of Bran's death, they wanted to run down to the bridge and see the grave. Grace would not let them. "Don't either of you ever set foot near that dreadful bridge!"

Janie then took her turn to cry about Bran. "I just knew something bad would happen here!" she sobbed.

"Don't cry, Janie," Ben consoled her. "Jesus needs Bran up there with Him, to lick the angels' fingers, and to bark if the old devil tries to slip in."

*   *   *

Because of the extended 1938 grasshopper plague, Daniel harvested only three bales of cotton, hauling the last one by wagon to the gin in Denim just a week before Thanksgiving. Since it was the last wagon trip to town for the year, Benjamin was allowed to accompany his father, sitting on top of the load of cotton alongside Daniel, a nickel in his pocket for a jawbreaker at the general store, his head covered with Janie's bright-pink stocking cap because Grace could not find Ben's brown cap and she would not let him go to town in an open wagon in damp, cold air with his head uncovered.

To accompany his father was a major treat for Ben, rarely experienced because Daniel did not like to deal with extra parental responsibility when he had regular work to do. "Benny, sit back and don't lean over to watch the wheels turning, or you will fall off and break your neck," Daniel cautioned. Ben occupied himself watching Bill and Hector pull the wagon in tandem, their hooves striking the dirt roadbed in cadence with the jingling and squeaking of their harness as the pair matched each other stride for stride. They defecated whenever nature dictated without missing a beat. Benjamin openly enjoyed watching old Hector lifting his tail to empty his bowels of a large quantity of perfectly shaped "horse biscuits," dark green, steamy, and aromatic, plopping to the ground and disappearing under the rolling wagon.

"I like to smell horse do-do," Ben confessed innocently to his father. "I wish all do-do smelled like that."

He continued to watch Hector as the last of the manure biscuits were expelled cleanly, followed by the involuntary flexing and relaxing of Hector's sphincter muscle, like a camera shutter, resulting in a full view of the inner wall of Hector's anus, at Ben's eye level a pink and wrinkled sight to behold. Hector's bowel movement ended with the horse flicking his tail, a seemingly haughty commentary that while humans might harness them and drive them and even ride them, humans should not be considered superior to horses if they could not defecate with such flair.

When Daniel and Benjamin entered the town of Denim, they passed by the schoolhouse on their route to the gin. Janie's teacher happened to be standing at the window and saw Benjamin in the bright-pink cap. "Janie, I did not know you had a little sister. What is your little sister's name? I just saw her on your father's wagon as they passed by."

Janie could not wait to tell the family that Benny had been mistaken for a girl, a good joke for the family, but for Benjamin an embarrassment so sensitive that he would never wear anything resembling pink again.

Daniel's reluctance to allow Benjamin to accompany him at work led to a memorable fifth birthday in 1939. February 25 was cold and windy, with dust heavy in the air. Since it was his special day, Ben anticipated that he might be allowed to do anything he wanted to do, such as going with his father to Granddad's place to cut and haul firewood. But no. Said Daniel, "Cutting and hauling wood is hard work, and I can't have you underfoot." So for Benjamin, it was no go, except that he knew the way to Granddad's place, and although he might not be able to keep up trotting unnoticed behind the wagon, he knew how to get there anyway. Ben followed the wagon for almost a quarter mile before Daniel noticed his head bobbing up and down behind him, whereupon Daniel picked up the child, turned the wagon around, and took him home, carrying Ben to the porch steps, where he gave him a hard spanking.

"Benjamin, what's wrong with you! Do you want to get lost in a dust storm? If you want to stay in this family, you have got to mind your daddy!"

What a birthday, what a way to learn that there is a limit to one's birthday rights, thought Benjamin tearfully. One's birthday may not be so special, after all. Ben would always remember the spanking and his father's threat of rejection, and not even the bowl of tapioca pudding Grace fixed him for lunch seemed to matter.

CHAPTER 18

Shunned

In the spring of 1939, in Benjamin's fifth year, with Jesse and Janie away at school all day, Ben's unbounded imagination created a playmate to fill the void left by the death of his dog, Bran. Brody was his imaginary friend's name, and he was exactly the same age, size, and intelligence as Benjamin, and he looked like Jacob Jiggs would have looked like at the age of five. Brody virtually appeared one day when Ben was playing cow and calf bottles. His imaginary pasture was full of newly acquired bottles from Granddad and Grandmother Dalkens's trash dump behind their barn. Ben had discovered them after last Sunday's family dinner. He gathered a feed sack full of bottles of all sizes, including many small aspirin bottles that Granddad Dalkens had used in his bout against arthritis in his shoulder and tiny nail polish bottles and perfume bottles that Aunt Olivia had used. The aspirin bottles were baby bulls, the perfume and nail polish bottles were heifers. Many of Ben's large cow bottles now had small calf bottles beside them, and his sandy, string-lined pasture was overstocked.

"Brody, let's play like you have bought the ranch next to mine, so we are going to build you a new fence around it with this string, like this, and we are going to move some of my cow and calf bottles to your new pasture. You can't have my cows for keeps, but you can have half their calves to build your herd, and I will keep half their calves and we can help each other with branding and feeding and doctoring them when they get sick, and we can build a trench silo, and put green feed in it, and cover it over with dirt, and then this winter we can push the dirt back and the trench will be full of silo stuff and our cows can have something to eat after their pasture is dried up and eaten away. See, that's how you raise cattle…"

So while Jesse and Janie were at school, Benjamin worked very hard helping his imaginary playmate, Brody, get set up on his new ranch. The fences were built quickly, and some of the cow and calf bottles were moved to Brody's ranch, and Ben enjoyed playing with Brody because Brody always did what Ben wanted.

And so Ben had a playmate, a secret way to fill his day, and nighttime too, when he was on his cot, unable to fall asleep right away. Brody would slip under the covers beside him. "I won't ever tell anybody about you," Ben vowed in a whisper, "or they will make you go away." Brody was a confidant and a pal, and when he was around, Ben was never afraid of the dark. And sometimes, when Ben was restless in bed and needed to be touched, Brody would touch him there, on the pleasurable, untouchable place, touching the untouched.

*   *   *

Benjamin learned to tell time by looking at the kitchen clock to identify specific times on the family's daily schedule: The children were to be in bed by the time the little hand was on nine and the big hand was straight up. Daddy and Jesse got up to do the milking and other morning chores after the alarm rattled off when the little hand reached six. The school bus arrived on weekday mornings for Jesse and Janie when the little hand was on seven and the big hand was on three. When the little hand was on four and the big hand was on six, it was 4:30 p.m., time for the school bus to appear over the hill south of the bridge, bringing Jesse and Janie home. Grace allowed Ben to run down the lane to the county road to wait for the bus but would warn, "Don't cross the road, Benjamin, or a car might run over you. And don't go near the bridge!"

"Yes, Mama, I won't," he promised.

Never mind that on average, fewer than six vehicles drove by each day, including the school bus and the mail carrier.

On this particular day, when Benjamin got to the road and stood beside the mailbox, waiting for the bus to arrive, he noticed a cardboard box on the other side of the road. Apparently, it had blown off someone's truck. It was exactly the right size for Ben to convert into a pretend barn for Brody's new ranch so that the cow and calf bottles could be protected from a pretend storm.

"Janie, will you go across the road and get me that cardboard box?" Ben requested as soon as his sister stepped off the bus.

"I don't have time, Benny," Janie replied. "Mama is going to make me a new dress tonight, and she wants me to hurry to the house so she can do the fittings and cut the pieces before she has to cook dinner."

Ben turned to Jesse, who always walked too fast for Ben to keep up without skipping. "Jesse, can you go back across the road and get me that cardboard box?"

"Go get it yourself," said Jesse. "I need to hurry and change my school clothes. Mama has promised to cook me a fried chicken dinner tonight if I go out to the back of the pasture and help Daddy fix a big hole in the fence where Mr. Autrey's roan bull busted through and bred one of our cows."

Ben's curiosity was stirred. "How did Mr. Autrey's bull bread one of our cows?" he asked, skipping faster to keep up. "Did the bull light-bread her or corn-bread her or biscuit-bread her?"

"You silly little carrottop," Jesse said, chuckling, "you really are a dope!"

When they reached the house, Benjamin rushed to his mother and asked, "Mama, can I go get a cardboard box and make a new barn out of it for my new cow and calf bottles?"

"Slim chance you will find a cardboard box around this place," Grace said dismissively. "Janie, stand right here in front of me and be absolutely still so I can pin this pattern to fit you. It looks like I am going to have to add an inch all around—you have grown so much lately!"

Grace had created a pattern out of sheets of old newspaper and had washed and ironed three large pieces of paisley-printed muslin that had once been flour sacks, a cloth material commonly used in those years when money for clothes was hard to come by. Janie loved the paisley pattern and cooperated fully with her mother because she wanted to wear her new dress to school the very next day.

Since his mother was preoccupied with Janie and the sewing project, Ben decided that he should rush back to the road and retrieve the cardboard box before the wind blew it away or someone else got it. Never mind that he was disobeying his mother by crossing the road; he looked both ways—twice—scooped up the box, and carried it triumphantly to Brody's pretend ranch land. It was going to be a perfect barn for Brody, and he was glad he could give it to him, because it was better to give than to receive. The box only needed to have its flaps cut off and one of its sides cut out for a door, and Ben knew just how to do it: get his mother's butcher knife in the kitchen and use it to remodel the box.

Benjamin was forbidden to play with Grace's kitchen utensils— especially her only butcher knife—but since Grace was busy with Janie, Ben decided that he could sneak the knife outside, cut off the flaps, and put the knife back where it belonged before anyone could know. It was just too important not to risk it, and even if he got caught, he could handle a paddling for the sake of his friend Brody.

Unless something went terribly wrong.

Cautiously, silently Ben took the knife from the cupboard drawer; carried it outside, walking slowly, blade down; and sawed off the cardboard flaps just the way he had seen his mother do it, then the next step was to cut out one side of the box for a wide barn door. The project was going well until suddenly—*snap!* The blade hit a large metal staple and, old and heavily corroded at the edge of the wooden handle, broke off completely.

Immediately Benjamin knew he was in big trouble and there was no escape from being punished severely. His mother's only butcher knife! Smothered with remorse, silently he placed the knife pieces back in the cupboard drawer then went outside and crept down into the storm cellar, not to hide, but to find strength within its walls, because Brody was there to help him steel himself for the painful punishment he deserved.

Ben's punishment would not be what he expected.

A model of efficiency, Grace soon completed the fitting for Janie's new dress, cut the pieces, then laid them aside until after dinner. She would sew the dress together after dinner dishes were put away and the children were in bed. "Now, for our fried chicken dinner," she announced. "Janie, while I boil a pot of water to scald the feathers off, you and Benjamin chase down that fat young red rooster that started crowing last week. His time is due. Tonight he will never taste better. Where's Benjamin?"

"Never mind. I can catch that little red rooster all by myself!" said Janie and proceeded to do just that.

Most of the young fryers were accustomed to eating out of a handheld bucket, so it was an easy matter for Janie to hold out a bucket of grain, reach down and grab the chicken's feet, hoist it in the air, and carry it to the front yard, where Grace was waiting to wring its neck in a cold, surgical maneuver that she had done countless times since aged seven. She grabbed the fryer's neck, swung its body by its head in a vertical circle two or three times, then simply pulled off its twisted neck and dropped the fryer on the grass to let the now-headless victim flop around while its blood drained out. Then she dipped the bird by its feet into a bucket of scalding water on a workbench on the porch, deftly pulled its scalded feathers off, then carried it into the kitchen to her kerosene cookstove burner to singe off the tiny downy follicles that remained. Next step was to reach for her butcher knife to gut the fryer and cut it up into frying pieces.

Outside, Janie noticed Benjamin sitting alone in the cellar. "Benny, what are you doing down there?"

"Waiting to be punished," he replied softly. "I have broken Mama's butcher knife."

"Oh my!" exclaimed Janie.

"Oh my!" shouted Grace when she reached in the cupboard drawer and picked up the pieces of her broken knife. "Who broke my butcher knife?" There was only one suspect. "Benjamin! Where are you? Come here!"

"Mama, he's in the cellar!" shouted Janie.

Soon Ben looked up to see his mother standing over him at the cellar door, hands on hips, stern, angry, shaking her head, hovering over him like a menace. Ben looked down forlornly, dropping his head sideways, a chastened puppy.

"Benjamin Ray Bird, come out of that cellar and tell me what happened to my butcher knife!" she demanded.

He obeyed instantly, slowly ascending the cellar steps. No amount of cuteness or wittiness could help him escape the trouble he was facing. When he reached the top step, head bowed, Grace grabbed the hair on the back of his neck and pulled his face upward. "Look at me and tell me what you did to my knife, young man!"

"Mama, I am sorry, I have disobeyed you. When I went down to wait for the school bus today, I saw a cardboard box on the other side of the road, but Janie wouldn't get it for me and Jesse wouldn't get it for me, so when you started working on Janie's new dress, you were too busy to help me, so I went back and got the box—I looked both ways—then I borrowed the knife to cut on the box and turn it into Brody's barn, for the new cattle bottles I got at Granddad's last Sunday. And when I tried to cut out the side of the box, I cut into a hard metal thing and the handle just came off!"

"What's a Brody barn?" asked Janie.

"Janie, just stay out of this. Benjamin, this is the worst thing you have ever done! You have disappointed me so! Disobeyed me and hurt our entire family, because now I can't cut up the fryer and I don't know what to do about dinner."

"Why don't you just spank me and get it over with? Then I can run out to the pasture, where Daddy and Jesse are working, and get Daddy's pocketknife for you to use?" suggested Ben. He wanted to face his punishment and have it done.

"You just hush! I can't cut up a chicken with a pocketknife. And I don't have time to deal with your misbehavior. I've got to get a meal on the table. Benjamin, you sit right here on top of the cellar and stay there until I have time to deal with you. I've got to go in and get dinner."

"I'll go back down inside the cellar and wait there," Ben offered.

"No, I want you to sit on top of the cellar slab, in plain sight, where God can get a good look at you, and later, He can help me come up with the right way to punish you!"

"What's a Brody barn?" Janie again asked.

"Nothing," Ben replied. "It's just what I call a cardboard box."

"Janie, you need to come and help me set the table. I don't want you talking to Benjamin. I want him to sit there by himself and think about the bad thing he has done."

Benjamin's punishment had begun. He was in a sort of jail, isolated, waiting for trial.

*   *   *

Dinner was very different that evening. There was no fried chicken. Grace had used her sewing scissors to cut an incision from the fryer's vent into its body cavity, gut it, clean it, and drop it into a stewpot with seasoning and globs of biscuit dough for chicken and dumplings. Jesse was disappointed; he blamed his little brother. "Ben, you little skunk, your stupid behavior has cost me a fried chicken dinner!"

Ben was not allowed to answer. He was being shunned. Grace had sat him on a chair in a corner, and she put his food in a bowl on his lap. "You can't sit at the table with the family tonight," Grace told him, "and we don't want to hear a word out of you!"

Janie ignored Ben's problems and jabbered about her prospective new dress. "Mama, I want to wear my Sunday sandals tomorrow with my new dress!"

Daniel stated that he would take a can of fresh cream to town the next day and buy Grace a new butcher knife. Then he, too, ignored Benjamin's situation and ate the meal with gusto—he loved Grace's chicken and dumplings. Only Jesse, in good-son, bad-son mode, dwelt on the matter. "What a waste!" he said. "Mama, You shouldn't use a tender young fryer for chicken and dumplings. Chicken and dumplings are for tough old hens and roosters. There's nothing as good as good old young fryer fried chicken. Benny sure has hurt our family!"

Contrite, Ben wanted to tell everyone how sorry he was, but he was not allowed to speak. He hadn't the appetite to finish his bowl of dumplings, although he usually liked chicken and dumplings as much as his father did. He sat his bowl on the floor and began to sob quietly.

"Benjamin, if you are finished eating, then go outside and peepee," Grace ordered. "Then come straight back in the house and go to bed. And remember, we don't want to hear a word out of you."

And so Benjamin was kept out of the family circle for the rest of the evening. While Grace cleared the table and washed the dishes, Daniel helped Jesse and Janie with homework. From his cot in the bedroom, Benjamin could hear the activities; he had never felt so left out. Had he permanently lost his place in the family? Daniel and Jesse moved Grace's sewing machine into the kitchen for better light. Soon Ben heard the foot pedal driving the needle of his mother's sewing machine, *clickity-click, clickity click*, producing a soothing, rhythmic effect. He closed his eyes and began to feel Brody's weightless comforting arm reach around him as he drifted off to sleep.

Next morning, Grace arose thirty minutes early to put the hem in Janie's new paisley flour sack dress and iron it with her flat irons at the kitchen stove. Through morning chores, breakfast, getting ready for school, complimenting Janie in her lovely, new dress, the family functioned without Benjamin.

Passing in and out of the bedroom, no one noticed that Ben's cot was empty. Daniel poured the morning's milk production through the cream separator and confirmed that he would have a full can of cream to take to town. Jesse lamented that there was no piece of leftover fried chicken for his school lunch pail. Not until Daniel was off to town and Jesse and Janie were off to school did Grace go into the bedroom to make the beds and become aware that her youngest child was missing.

Had he run away? Had she been too hard on him? Or was he simply just outside on one of his usual early morning jaunts? She regretted her harsh and haphazard response yesterday to Benjamin's transgression. She looked in the clothes closet—he wasn't there. She looked under the bed. She walked outside and immediately noticed

Ben sitting on the platform near the top of the windmill, his head a few inches below the rotating blades. In instant panic, Grace stifled a scream, for fear that her scream might cause Benjamin to jump and fall off the platform or rise up and be decapitated by the rotating blades.

"Benjamin," she said, trying to sound calm, "what are you doing up there?"

"I am letting God get a good look at me, to let Jesus see if I am not any good."

"Honey, climb down and come inside the house. I saved you a biscuit and a slice of bacon. I will make you a bowl of hot oatmeal. I will put some honey and butter in it." She cherished those special times when everyone else was gone to their daily events, leaving her and her preschooler to share the morning. She said nothing about a spanking or further punishment. She realized that the family's shunning of Ben had really hurt him.

"I am sorry that I caused Jesse to lose his fried chicken dinner," Ben said soberly.

"When he comes home today from school, you can tell him you are sorry. See if he will forgive you."

"Do you forgive me, Mama?" he asked.

"Yes, Benjamin," Grace said, "but you must never do anything that you know will disappoint me ever again, whether it is disobeying your mother or behaving badly. It would break my heart."

"I won't, Mother," he replied. "I promise I never will." It was the first time he had ever called her Mother. He would rarely call her Mama again. Not quite so warm, not quite so sweet, not quite so nurturing as Mama, but totally respectful. She was clearly the enforcer of the family standards, the disciplinarian, Mother.

*   *   *

Benjamin was waiting at the mailbox when Jesse and Janie stepped off the bus. Janie ran ahead to tell her mother all the nice things her friends had said about her new dress. Soberly Ben approached Jesse. "Jesse, I'm sorry you didn't get your fried chicken dinner last night. I want to make it up to you. You can have my next three fried chicken dinners, plus five extra pieces. Do you want thighs, wings, or legs?"

"Life does not work that way, carrottop," said Jesse the sage. "Once you lose out on something, it is lost forever. You can't make it up."

"I did not know that," Ben responded. "I guess you won't forgive me then."

"Well, since you are my only brother, I guess I will always have to put up with you," Jesse declared and scuffed Ben's ears playfully. At least Benjamin took the scuffing as a playful gesture of affection and was relieved that his punishment was finally over. He did not realize that in his conscience, there now was an embedded supersensitivity that throughout life would influence him to subvert his needs and desires for the sake of others, else he could hurt them and alter the course of their lives as well as his own.

For if he was merely self-serving, he could be shunned.

He alone.

CHAPTER 19

Jesse Gets Saved

T he long and dreadful drought continued in 1939. Barely enough gentle spring rain came to provide the moisture that Daniel needed to get his crops planted in a timely fashion. Stunted cotton, corn, and sorghum were all "laid by" by the Fourth of July. The vegetable garden again flourished with its reliable subirrigation system; the tomatoes were the plumpest and sweetest in memory. The 1939 annual Dalkens family reunion in the Wichita Mountains was hardly a celebration of God's blessings, for everyone there who still farmed had sad reports on the prospects for a productive year.

In 1939, Vernon and Kirby did not spend the summer at Denim because two of Leona's office-cleaning jobs had been lost to bankruptcy. Consequently, she had been unable to save money for summer school. Nevertheless, Leona stayed on target with her dream by signing up for an individual research project through her major professor, earning three units of credit by conducting research on published child development studies through Altus Public Library's interlibrary loan department.

Kirby went to the cotton-chopping country with Grandpa Aaron to earn money for a fancy bicycle, and Vernon pushed a manual rotary lawnmower, scouring the residential neighborhoods of Altus, seeking lawn-mowing jobs.

One week following Jesse's twelfth birthday in early July, Daniel drove Jesse to the Jarrell Hereford Ranch on the Washita River near

Strong City to work six weeks for Lloyd Jarrell, a fifty-year-old bachelor, in a sponsored school 4-H project in which Jesse would earn wages to buy a Hereford show steer. Jarrell was a neighbor to Maudeen's brother-in-law, Ed Galloway, an old sheep man who had made the land run in 1892. Maudeen's eldest sister, Hetitia "Hettie" Swanfeather, had married Ed in 1907. They had three grown children who had all moved away. Maudeen showed deference to Hetitia because she was Maudeen's eldest sister, but they were not close. Hetitia was a trifle on the haughty side, being married to a prosperous, landowning sheep rancher in the midst of cattle country, with a large house with indoor plumbing and a watered green lawn and a big bay window with lots of house plants, something always blooming, and with lighted display shelves of crystal, china, commemorative plates, saltshakers and pepper shakers, silver, and pewter. Hetitia's house was the first in that part of the county to be electrified by the Rural Electrification Administration. She loved to host visitors with muffins fresh from her electric oven and ice tea with large perfectly formed ice cubes from her gleaming white refrigerator.

Grace would not have allowed Jesse to be gone for six weeks working and boarding at the Jarrell Ranch had her aunt Hettie not been nearby as a guardian in case things did not go well for Jesse under Jarrell's employment. "Honey, if things don't work out for you at Mr. Jarrell's, you run over to Aunt Hettie's house and she will deal with the matter," Grace told her firstborn. She was also consoled by their plan to visit Jesse each Sunday and take him to church in Strong City.

Daniel believed that Jesse's summertime job on the Jarrell Ranch would be a good learning experience. "I don't have enough chores to keep Jesse busy around here, now that the crops are laid by and the canning is done," he told Grace. "Jesse will learn to work with ranch cattle, using new equipment, and for him to earn money for a show steer will be rewarding."

Benjamin did not want Jesse to leave home for six weeks because of the empty space his absence would create. Janie insisted that she and Benjamin move their cots from the slab roof of the cellar to the porch because Jesse would not be there to keep the booger man away.

Jesse's first week at the Jarrell Ranch was exciting ranch work. On Monday, he and Mr. Jarrell rounded up a herd of forty cows with six-month-old calves ready to wean. Lloyd Jarrell was all business and a man of few words. Most of the day, Jesse was riding an old bay mare that was smooth and gentle. On Tuesday, the calves were separated and the cows were driven back to their main pasture.

Jesse's sleep was disturbed all that night by forty calves bawling in the weaning pen for their mothers. The next day, Wednesday, the steers were separated, and Jesse got to pick out his show steer from the entire herd. Mr. Jarrell allowed Jesse to pen his show steer separately and to start it out on a regimen that would prime it for fast growth, because Mr. Jarrell wanted Jesse's calf to do well so that the Jarrell Ranch might have the prestige to develop a good market selling show steers and show heifers.

On Thursday, they loaded the remaining steer calves in a long trailer and pulled them to the stockyards in Southwestern Oklahoma City. It was Jesse's first trip to the City. He would never forget the sights along Route 66: the towering skyscrapers appearing on the downtown horizon; the long line of livestock trailers waiting their turn to unload at the stockyards pens; the constant din of bawling cattle, the clamoring shouts of livestock sorters, the auctioneer's spiel; the stench of the nearby meatpacking plants, the burning hair, the stifling smell of rendered beef fat and vats of blood; and the enormous, plate-size porterhouse steaks Mr. Jarrell ordered for their dinner.

On Friday, Jesse and Mr. Jarrell vaccinated and branded the heifers. Jarrell showed Jesse how it was done: first, drive a calf into the squeeze chute and catch it in the headgate, then brand each calf on its right hip, and vaccinate it in the soft, loose skin on its neck. Soon, Jesse was adept at each part of the operation, keeping the branding iron at the right heat for a good, clean brand, breaking a vaccination needle only once. Mr. Jarrell was pleased with his new ranch hand and began to contemplate the day when Jesse finished school so he could hire him full-time. They then drove the heifers to a pasture on the back side of the ranch, some of the calves still bawling for their mothers.

On Saturday, Lloyd Jarrell gave Jesse a halter to put on his show steer, which Jesse had named Buster. Jarrell showed Jesse how to break the steer into leading and standing in a show-ring setting. Jesse began to anticipate winning his class, and perhaps the big prize, the county grand championship! Someone was going to win, and Jesse vowed to work hard with Buster and improve his chances. Mr. Jarrell speculated that Buster at least had the appetite to outeat its rivals and win it all.

On Saturday afternoon, Jarrell told Jesse, "Let's take the afternoon off and go catch a catfish for supper." So they sat in the shade of a big cottonwood tree on the banks of the Washita River and, using grasshoppers for bait, hooked three catfish that weighed almost two pounds each. Then suddenly, Jesse was taken aback when Jarrell stripped off to the buff and—exposing a small pale, sinewy, bow-legged torso with flat, tight buttocks—sauntered into the river. "Come on in, Jesse, this is our Saturday bath time."

Momentarily stunned with embarrassment, modestly caught between his soft, baby-fat days and the early stages of mysterious, rampaging puberty, Jesse allowed the thought of engulfing himself in the refreshing, cool water entice him into undressing in front of his boss, and without even covering his genitals with his cupped hand, he strode boldly like a mature, self-confident male into the current. In one short week away from his father and mother, one week of working like a man in a man's world, Jesse Daniel Bird had crossed a threshold. Only time and circumstances and psychological considerations would reveal what waited for him in the future.

*   *   *

On Sunday morning, Daniel drove his family to the Jarrell Ranch to bring Jesse fresh, clean work clothes and have Jesse accompany them as they visited worship services at Strong City First Baptist Church. Daniel had been spiritually restless attending the Denim First Methodist Church with all the Dalkens family. The Methodist fellowship was good and the Methodists were true believers, but to Daniel, the Methodist sermons simply did not convey the Lord's message strongly enough concerning repentance, confession, and salvation through faith in the Lord Jesus Christ. He was concerned that Jesse was about to join the Methodist Church. Although he had married a wonderful woman, a devout Methodist, he could not comprehend that his children might become something other than Baptist. There had not been a Baptist church in Denim since the Depression struck, for in hard times the Denim community could not afford to maintain two separate churches. When the impoverished Baptist minister resigned and moved away, the Methodist congregation invited the Baptists to worship jointly with them and offered to let the Baptist leaders officiate at the worship services on second and fourth Sundays. The arrangement hardly worked at all because, after all, the services were conducted in the Methodist church.

The worship service at Strong City Baptist Church was an eye-opener for Daniel's and Grace's children. Janie listened intently to the minister, Brother Nathan Jones, an ambitious, zealous ministerial student from Southwestern Baptist Theological Seminary in Fort Worth. Nathan Jones was a Bible-thumper, a shouter, a foot stomper and a jumper, a former gymnast and cheerleader at Baylor University, with tremendous stage presence and a ringing message of fighting off the devil at every corner. The Baptist General Convention's Home Mission Board paid Nathan to come to Strong City from seminary four Sundays a month to lead lost souls to Christ in life's short journey.

Janie concluded that Nathan the preacher was talking about an emergency situation in which bad people were in danger of going to hell right away. She could not imagine that her name was on the bad people's list, but sometimes she did have bad thoughts, such as wanting to steal a candy bar but not having the nerve to do it, so was that bad enough to send her to hell? Five-year-old Benjamin absorbed many of Nathan's religious phrases because he loved the sounds of the words but could not digest them as a message to him, for they rolled past him too quickly, and he did not feel the need to be saved from anything. What interested him most were the preacher's calisthenics. See preacher jump! See preacher shout! See preacher jump and shout!

Jesse was the child most under conviction. His first week at the Jarrell Ranch had allowed him to evade the soul-searching that had preoccupied him for several months, but now the exhortations of Nathan Jones were slapping him in the heart. Was he now mature enough to make a decision? Was he going to believe the preacher? Was he going to believe the Bible? Was he going to accept Jesus as his Savior? Or was he going to reject the message and risk going to hell? The worship service ended with an extended invitation for sinners to come to the front, confess their sins, and accept Jesus as their personal Savior. The invitational hymn said, "Come home, come home, come home, come home, ye who are weary, come home!" Brother Nathan noticed that Jesse was under stress, and like a good fisher of men with a nibble on the bait, he asked the congregation to sing the last verse of the hymn again and again:

> *Come home, come home, come home, come home,*
> *Ye who are we-ary come h-o-m-e,*
> *Earnestly, tenderly, Jesus is calling,*
> *Call - ing, O sin-ner, come home."*

Jesse wanted to go to the altar but resisted the call because he wanted to talk to his father about what to do; if he went to the front, would it require them to come to this church every Sunday? Jesse did not know if they would ever attend services there again.

"Daddy, the preacher was talking to me," said Jesse on the road back to the Jarrell Ranch. "I almost went to the altar. But should I do that? Because Strong City isn't our church."

"Son, you can make a public confession of your faith wherever you are. This week, your mother and I will talk about whether we should join the Strong City First Baptist Church. You don't need to join a church to become a Christian, but being active in a church helps you grow in your faith and stay on the right path."

When they reached the Jarrell Ranch and told Jesse goodbye, Daniel let Jesse keep his Bible for a week, with an admonition to study the Gospels.

With Nathan Jones's sermon still ringing in their ears, Daniel and his family remained affected by the preacher's fervency for the rest of the day. Still, no one was quite prepared for Benjamin's display of zeal just before dinner, when suddenly he jumped up on one of the benches at the dinner table and began to shout, pounding his fist into a folded copy of a catalog, "Ye must be born again, to wash away the sin, hi-ho the merry oh, you must be born again!" Then he jumped off the bench and began to stomp the floor. "Get out, get out, you mean old devil, and don't come back again. Get out, get out, I shout, I shout, or I'll throw you in your own fire and turn you into bacon!" Then he hopped around the table, singing, "Go home, go home, go home, go home, go home, you ugly old devil, go home!"

"Benjamin, slow down, or you'll run into the cookstove!" cautioned Grace, snickering. "Save your sermons for the chicken pen!" Daniel and Janie were laughing at Ben's antics as Grace added, "I hope the Lord has a sense of humor!"

"He must, indeed," said Daniel, "else He wouldn't have given us this little monkey!"

In the spirit of the occasion, Daniel asked young Benjamin to offer the dinner blessing. Everyone bowed their heads but peeked from under their foreheads to see what Benjamin would do. Without hesitation, he began, "Radishes, slaw, for olives, and other flavors, we thank Thee berry munch. Amen." Daniel shook his head. What could he say? Benjamin had paid homage to his dear, toothless old grandpa Aaron.

Before bedtime, as the family settled in, Daniel and Grace had a serious discussion about Jesse's situation and whether they should join the Strong City First Baptist Church. "Grace, honey, if Jesse makes a public confession of faith next Sunday at Strong City, don't you think we should place our membership there?"

Grace knew her husband well enough to know that he had already decided what they should do.

"You know I won't join a Baptist church, because Baptists won't accept my Methodist baptism," she reminded him, with conviction. "If Jesse gets baptized into the Strong City Baptist Church, go ahead and join with him," she said. "We'll go there as often as we can. Just realize that Strong City is about thirty miles from home, and we're not likely to be able to go there often. Hopefully, when we can't go to Strong City, you will continue to drive us to Denim Methodist so we can worship God with our loved ones."

*   *   *

Jesse's second week at the Jarrell Ranch was much more difficult for him than the first week had been. The enjoyment of working with cattle was lost, for Lloyd Jarrell had a weeklong project to build a barbed wire fence along a bluff in a bend of the Washita River where, throughout the years, he had had several cattle fall to their deaths. Digging postholes in the dry, hard dirt with a manual digger was backbreaking work, alleviated only a little by pouring river water into the holes from time to time to soften the hard-packed earth. Jarrell provided Jesse a pair of leather gloves, but they were not a good fit, and Jesse's palms were soon sporting several blisters that were painful and, when the blisters broke, became bloody. Hardened by years of outdoor toil, Jarrell performed most of the posthole digging himself, while Jesse lugged buckets of water from the river. Jarrell was impressed by Jesse's industriousness, working through his discomfort. By midweek, cedar posts were tapped into the holes and heavy strands of barbed wire were being stretched along the lines, tightened, and stapled to the posts.

Jesse coped with the drudgery of fence-building by concentrating on his religious concerns. "Mr. Jarrell, next Sunday, when my folks come to take me to church, I am probably going to turn my soul over to Jesus. What do you think about that?"

"Well, Jesse, a man needs to do what he thinks he needs to do," Jarrell replied. "It's a personal thing. I never got churched, myself. I always thought the Creator put me on this earth to run this ranch, and I suppose that's my religion, in a nutshell."

After dinner each evening, Jesse retired to his room, and from his father's Bible he read from the Gospel. He already knew John 3:16, the Gospel in a nutshell:

For God so loved the world that He gave His only begotten Son, that whosoever believeth in Him should not perish, but have everlasting life.

Jesse browsed through the chapters, concentrating on the words of Jesus highlighted in red. He found solace in the passage that said, "I am the resurrection and the life; he that believeth in Me, though he were dead, yet shall he live; And whosoever liveth and believeth in Me shall never die." He wrestled with certain scriptures that dealt with confessing one's sins, repenting, and asking for forgiveness. What were his sins? How much evil can be found in the life of a conscientious, well-behaved twelve-year-old? He rarely lied but often stretched the truth: Was that a sin? He worked hard, so he could not be punished for the sin of laziness. Was overeating a sin? He often ate too much, only recently devouring an entire plate-size porterhouse steak. He had no patience for others who did not apply themselves and do their best; he tended to blame the poor for staying poor. Was his critical impatience of others a sin? He wanted possessions: Was that wrong? He was beginning to covet Mr. Jarrells's ranch, becoming tempted to endear himself to Lloyd Jarrell in a deliberate ploy to entice the old bachelor to bequeath the ranch to him. Was covetousness a sin? He was beginning to desire girls; he wanted a girlfriend to kiss on and hug and perhaps lie down with—a certain sin!

Certain Bible verses threw Jesse into confusion. If only his father were available to help him clarify.

What does it mean when in the Bible Jesus says, "No one can enter the kingdom of God unless he is born of water and the Spirit." Was baptism necessary for salvation? Was the kingdom of God the same as heaven? The only way Jesse could deal with the confusion was simply to ignore or dismiss those passages that could not fit into the limits of his perceptions, and wait for a preacher to tell him how to understand. And so he studied on, on and on, seeking truths he could understand, preparing himself for his public confession of faith, hopscotching over difficult verses that did not fit his purpose. When he prayed, "Lord, I believe, please forgive my unbelief," and when he embraced the passages that he understood and needed, and when in clear conscience he ignored the rest, without realizing it he was joining multiple generations of true believers who throughout the centuries had picked and chosen certain Bible passages upon which their denominations existed, interpreting them in a certain comfortable way, and ignored or rejected other passages and other interpretations upon which other denominations existed, and members of each denomination were satisfied that they were bathed in the one true light.

*   *   *

Nathan Jones appreciated the long drive from Fort Worth each weekend to his dear little flock in Strong City, for it gave him time to hone his Sunday sermon, traveling alone, with God as his copilot, driving fifteen miles per hour above the speed limit, week after week, smoothly talking his way out of one speeding ticket after another. "Officer, I am in a hurry to do the Lord's work." Nathan weaved his thoughts and phrases together, aloud, grateful for the opportunity to draw on the knowledge he had learned in seminary that week, to practice and perfect his preaching skills on an adoring little congregation who waited dutifully to accept everything he said and did, believing as he believed that he was pastor-in-training for one of the future great congregations of the entire Southern Baptist Convention. And Nathan prayed as his mileage meter rolled on and on, "Dear Lord, please draw that nice, new family from Denim to our services again this Sunday morning. There is a soul to be saved!"

Opening prayer had been rendered, and the introductory hymn, "Bringing in the Sheaves," was in progress when Daniel Bird led his family into the sanctuary of Strong City First Baptist Church. They took their place in the same pew they had occupied a week earlier, with Jesse sitting closest to the center aisle. Janie sat between her parents, and Benjamin sat on the left side of his mother. Nathan Jones watched them arrive and mentally chalked up one for the Lord: the lad Jesse.

Nathan took his text from Matthew 13:47–50, the parable of the fishing net that was let down into the lake and caught all kinds of fish. When it was full, the fishermen pulled it on the shore, then collected the good fish in baskets, but threw the bad fish away. "This is how it will be at the end of the age," preached Nathan. "The angels will come and separate the wicked from the righteous and throw the sinners into the fiery furnace, where there will be weeping and gnashing of teeth!"

The heart of Nathan's sermon dwelt on the fiery furnace of hell, the weeping and gnashing of teeth, the eternal torment of the damned. "Oh, the endless pain and suffering, the scorching fire forever, the burning flesh that can never rest, and the eyes that can never sleep! All because sinners are too stubborn to accept Jesus, too proud to confess their shortcomings, too evil to surrender their sins. It makes no sense for someone to sit still and reject the message, too proud to say, 'I need Jesus,' too self-loathing to seek salvation. Look here, how many simple steps is it from where you are sitting to this forgiving altar? Let me count the steps."

Nathan placed his Bible on the speaker's stand and stepped down into the center aisle. He then started walking slowly, deliberately, toward the back of the sanctuary, counting the steps as he went. "One, two, three, four, five, six, seven, eight!" He paused at Jesse's pew and turned back, facing the altar. "Oh, how near it is, Oh how sweet the way, Oh how the love of Jesus can conquer all! But woe, how sad it is, how tragic, how *awful, awful, awful* to reject God's gift and turn away, never to be saved, forever to be damned in the fiery caves of hell!"

Before he finished his studies at the seminary, Nathan Jones would need to take a course in the subtle art of avoiding overkill. For a week Jesse had been ready to walk to the altar as soon as the invitation was offered. Unexpectedly, it was eight-year-old Janie who sat trembling, breaking into tears, frightened to death over Nathan's word pictures of hell. Nathan turned toward the back door. "Let's see, we were counting steps. How many more steps from this spot to the back door, to the outside world, to the uncertainty of tomorrow, to the car crash or the bolt of lightning or the disease that can send a sinner to his sudden grave?" He resumed his walk. "One, two, three, four, five, six, seven, eight! Eight more steps and you are out of here, away from God's grace, into the mainstream of sin and evil, with a travel ticket to hell!"

The worshipers were turned in their seats, looking back at Nathan, wondering what this flashy, striking messenger of God would do next. He mopped his brow, facing them, speaking quietly now.

"Dear hearts, let's think of the angels. Jesus says the angels will have a busy job of throwing sinners into hell. I am sure they don't want to do it. They love all people, just like Jesus does. They don't want any of us to be condemned. That's why they rejoice whenever a lost sinner turns to Christ. For sure, if only one sinner in this service gets saved today, a great host of angels in heaven will shout, and flap their wings, and sing hosanna, and dance in the air!" Suddenly Nathan dashed forward and whirled himself back to the altar, doing cartwheels, shouting "Hosanna!" every time his head popped into the air, and came to a stop with a great leap in which he turned and landed facing the congregation.

Following several gasps, the room fell silent. Nathan mopped his brow again then broke into the invitation hymn:

> *If you are tired of the load of your sin,*
> *Let Je-sus come in-to your heart;*
> *If you de-sire a new life to be-gin,*
> *Let Je-sus come in-to your heart.*

Nathan swept his arms open and beckoned. Jesse promptly stepped into the aisle and went forward, ready to proclaim his faith publicly. His father stepped into the aisle half a step behind him and strode forward. With the seat beside her suddenly empty, Janie jumped up and, crying openly, rushed to the altar and fell to her knees beside her father. In his mind, Nathan's internal calculator added not one (*ka-ching!*), not two (*ka-ching!*), but three (*ka-ching!*) new souls into the Lamb's Book of Life!

Nathan leaned down to Jesse and asked, "Young man, what is your name?"

"Jesse Daniel Bird."

"Jesse Daniel Bird, do you repent of your sins, and do you believe in Jesus?"

"Yes. I want Him to forgive me and save me, and I want to be baptized."

"Amen and Amen." Nathan turned to Daniel. "Sir, what is your name?"

"I am Daniel Jefferson Bird, a Baptist for twenty-five years. I want to transfer my membership from Hobart First Baptist Church."

"Amen and Amen." Nathan leaned down to Janie and lifted her to her feet. "Dear child, why do you cry?"

"I don't want the angels to throw me into hell," she wept. "I need to do what Jesse needs to do."

"What is your name?"

"Jane Eliza Bird."

"Jane Eliza Bird, do you believe in Jesus, and do you want Jesus to forgive you and save you, and do you want to be baptized?"

"Yes. I don't want the angels to throw me into the fire!"

"Amen!" Nathan looked up and addressed Grace, who remained in her pew. "Mother, don't you want to come forward and join with your family?"

"Leave her be," whispered Daniel to his new pastor. "She's a Methodist."

Nathan then turned and counseled Sister Sue, a middle-aged chronic repenter who came forward for rededication every time the Sunday service reached a certain level of emotionalism. Grace remained in her pew with Benjamin and appeared stoic, but her heart was twisted a dozen ways. She was rejoicing that Jesse had taken a stand for Jesus, and she did not mind that he was going to be a Baptist, if only he did not become so rigid and self-righteous as some Baptists tended to be. Grace loved her husband so much that she could take comfort in his enrichment of his spiritual life. She was concerned that Janie was too immature to comprehend that which had happened to her. *Janie has been brainwashed,* thought Grace. *Someday Janie will seek a redo.*

The worship service came to an end with Nathan's announcement that there was to be a caravan immediately to an area beneath the Washita River Bridge just east of town, where there was a water hole suitable for baptisms. Two deacons rushed to the site to clear out empty beer bottles, used condoms, and Sunday fishermen and to search the stream for snags and broken fishing lines. Nathan and Jesse retired to the pastor's study to don suitable attire: for Nathan, a pair of wading pants, and for Jesse, an extra pair of overalls Grace had brought just for the occasion. Poor, unpredictable Janie would need to get baptized in her Sunday dress, with a safety pin attached between her legs to keep the hem from floating up to expose her panties. She would wear wet clothing home today.

The congregation sang "Shall We Gather at the River?" as they marched en masse to the river, picking up a stray dog or two along the way:

Yes, we'll ga-ther at the ri-ver, the beau-ti-ful, the beau-ti-ful riv-er,
Gath-er with the saints at the riv-er,
That flows by the throne of God.

Nathan's performance in the baptism ceremony was beautiful. No calisthenics, no grandstanding. "Jesse Daniel Bird, I baptize thee in the name of the Father, the Son, and the Holy Ghost. Amen."

"Jane Eliza Bird, I baptize thee in the name of the Father, the Son, and the Holy Ghost. Amen."

Total immersion. For Jesse, all faith and seriousness. For Janie, total fright, gasping going under and gasping coming up. For Daniel, who stood beside Grace and Benjamin at the river's edge, gratitude to God that his children would be following in his faith. For Grace, maternal bystander, bittersweet trust that everything had happened for the best, and silent resolve that a jumping jackrabbit of a seminary student was not going to turn her into a Baptist.

For Benjamin, a big show, a lot of mystery. Daddy had gone to the altar to talk to the preacher, but Mother had not: that was not good. Ben could not understand why Janie became so scared and started crying in front of a bunch of strangers. For him, at this stage, there was nothing to fear. Hell was just a scary story, like trolls that lurked under bridges and the witch in the gingerbread house.

"If I should die before I wake, I pray the Lord my soul to take" was sufficient assurance for him, cradled in the bosom of innocent unaccountability. It was as though an eternal umbilical cord connected Ben back past his birth, back past his conception, back into a dimension where eternal life, gift of an omnipotent Creator, safely changes form but never ends.

CHAPTER 20

A Wider World

One might say that Benjamin Bird's formal education began before the age of two when his family moved into a two-room shack the walls of which were papered with 1932 newspaper headlines: "Dust Storms Continue." "Japanese Invade China." "Police Kill Four Marching Unemployed Ford Workers." "*Tarzan, the Ape Man* Movie Opens." "Hoover Says Downturn Is Over." "Kidnapped Lindbergh Baby Found Dead." "Dow-Jones Reaches Lowest 41.22." "Hoover Orders Bonus Army of Unemployed Vets Evicted." "Drought Persists." "Farmers' Protest Begins in Midwest." "Gandhi Begins Hunger Strike in Prison." "Babe Ruth Calls His Home Run in World Series." "FDR Wins in Landslide, Calls for New Deal." "Nazis Rise in Germany." "China Earthquake Kills 70,000." "Unemployment in USA Is 33%—14 Million."

Grace kept the headline about the murdered Lindbergh baby covered over with a 1939 wall calendar from the feed store. Benjamin studied the wall calendar closely, learning that there was a pattern to time—seven days in a week, thirty or thirty-one days in a month, twelve months in a year, new moons and full moons and four seasons, and one birthday per person per year. A person's entire life could be marked off a day at a time on only seventy or eighty or ninety calendars or less. For most people, less.

Although it would be years before Benjamin would understand fully the extent to which the world changed in 1932, his awareness

263

that important things were always happening set the tone for him to appreciate the history of his country and the events of his own time. His interminable curiosity and countless questions to his parents did little to quench his thirst to be knowledgeable, to understand events, to appreciate the full picture.

Because Daniel and Grace could not afford to subscribe to a newspaper or buy a battery-operated radio, they had no way to keep abreast of current events, except from gossip when relatives and neighbors gathered. But in August 1939, a traveling salesman stopped by and offered Daniel a one-year subscription to a weekly edition of the *Kansas City Star* newspaper and a subscription to *Capper's Farmer* monthly magazine in exchange for two-dozen eggs and an old car battery that had frozen and burst the previous winter. The weekly paper, which came in the mail each Wednesday, recapped the previous week's regional, national, and world news, with emphasis on the growing war fever developing in Europe. Benjamin nagged his father, mother, and brother to read the news articles aloud to him, and once they did, he could go back and read them himself, sounding out the hard words until he understood them, asking, "What does this word mean?" Once it was explained, he remembered. He kept the old newspapers folded and stacked under his cot.

Benjamin also stashed a growing stack of *Capper's Farmer* magazines under his cot and marked the pages that had articles or advertisements that contained photographs of cattle. He learned the breeds—black ones were Angus, red-white faces were Herefords, solid red and roan ones were shorthorns, black and white ones were Holstein dairy cows, yellow and brown ones were Jerseys. He claimed them all and named them identically to his favorite cow and calf bottles. He was a cattleman on the grow, a herdsman from the Bible, a Future Farmer of America.

* * *

When Jesse returned from his six-week sojourn at the Jarrell Ranch he would not allow Benjamin to mimic his pastor. "Brother Nathan is inspired by God to preach the way he does," said Jesse.

Nor was Ben allowed to feed Buster the show steer his special ration when Jesse and Janie started back to school, because Ben felt that the feed should be shared with all the other cattle. The special feed was too expensive to share, and Buster was so ravenous that soon the calf was nicknamed Budget Buster. Jesse's earnings at the Jarrell Ranch would be exhausted well before the county show. The show steer was kept in a pen beside the cowshed, where Ben checked on the level of its water tub several times a day and kept it topped off at the brim, and he brushed Buster often, just to have something to do.

*　　*　　*

When a special edition of the *Kansas City Star* arrived, reporting that Hitler's military forces had invaded Poland on September 1, 1939, that Great Britain and France had declared war on Germany and World War II had begun, Benjamin's world changed and the whole world trembled. Families isolated along the sparsely populated South Canadian River Valley in Rogers Mills County, Oklahoma, began to speculate when the United States would be drawn into the conflict. Would their men need to go fight in a war in Europe again? Would Daniel and Russell and Wally have to go into the army? Would the war last until Vernon and Jesse and Kirby and Jimmy and Benjamin and Donny and Gary were drawn into the fury?

Each Wednesday, about mailman time, Benjamin watched for the arrival of the weekly *Kansas City Star*, which included a battle sketch or two and European war zone maps in the war stories. Ben continued to agitate his father, mother, and brother to read the articles aloud to him, asking "What does this word mean?" less and less as time went on. He cut out war zone maps so that Grace could mix flour and water into paste and plaster them to the wall at Benjamin's eye level. He studied the maps and learned the names of the nations, and with his father, he began to hope that the maps that used arrows to show Hitler's forces pushing outward might soon show Hitler's forces being pushed back into Germany. He did not understand the war and its causes, but he knew that Hitler started it and it was bad, because a lot of people were getting killed.

Hell was in Europe.

* * *

When Benjamin was still only five years old, he learned that a rooster needed to jump on the back of a hen, push their tails together, and put "a blob of something like lotion" in her before her egg would hatch out to become a chick, and he knew that a bull needed to rise up on the tail of a cow and use his male thing to leave "a big blob of something like lotion" inside her in order for her to grow a baby calf in her tummy, because Jesse told him so. *Jesse knew everything.* Sometimes, when Ben watched a bull thrust his male thing into a cow Ben surprisingly was aroused with hardness down in his pants, and he discovered that he could feel pleasure and discomfort there in the same place at the same time.

It was at a 1939 picnic in Denim that Benjamin realized that when he was in the presence of his handsome, brash thirteen-year-old neighbor Jacob Jiggs, similar feelings of pleasure-pain could occur. In 1939, Denim Methodist Church sponsored a community-wide Harvest Festival fundraiser to send aid to missionaries in China who had been displaced by the Japanese invasion of Manchuria.

Families participating in the picnic brought hand-cranked freezers of homemade ice cream, melons, ice tea, covered dishes, hot dogs, and sandwiches to the event. Holiday activities included card games, community singing, patriotic readings, races, and games for the kids. Picnic tables were set up in the shade of the Denim gin, beneath the breezeway, in a wide covered alley where, during harvesttime, wagonloads of cotton were sucked up into the bowels of the gin. Tubs of free ice-cooled soda pop were located beside a table of food and refreshments. The church board designated James Dalkens as picnic coordinator, and the womenfolk in his family assumed the responsibility of serving the food and refreshments.

While his cousins and other neighborhood lads played catch, king of the hill, red rover, crack the whip, and ran races, Benjamin was confined to a picnic table near the food and refreshments. He was suffering from a serious sunburn on his face, neck, and arms, which he had contracted the previous day while meandering among the cattle all afternoon in stifling, sunbaked autumn heat. He had come in from the pasture feverish and nauseous and burnt red. Grace soaked him in the water trough for an hour, then rubbed him with lotion and put him to bed still running a fever. On festival morning, Ben was sore, suffering a headache, and fretful. When the Bird family arrived at the picnic, Grace said, "Benjamin, honey, whatever we do, we must keep you out of the sun. So sit over there at the table in the breezeway, where I can keep an eye on you while I help the ladies at the serving table, and I will let you eat all the ice cream you want."

Benjamin, who did not feel like circulating among his peers, accepted his mother's edict and said, "I would like to start with strawberry!"

And so Benjamin sat unobtrusively at a picnic table near the edge of the activity, and Grace brought him a scoop of ice cream in a small bowl, a small portion at a time, first strawberry, then a mixture of vanilla and chocolate, then a mixture of peach and banana nut. He ate slowly with a small flat spoon-shaped wooden utensil, licking the spoon in slow motion, to avoid an ice cream headache to add to his discomfort, and to avoid getting too full too soon. He found comfort in holding the chilled bowl to his feverish arms and face and was holding the bowl against his forehead, eyes closed, when suddenly he was startled by the husky voice of Jacob Jiggs.

"Hi, runt!" Jacob said. "Gosh, you look like a piece of bacon. What happened to you?"

Stunned, Ben did not answer. He was surprised and delighted that Jacob recognized him.

Carrying paper plates piled with food, Jacob, his nine-year-old brother, Jethro and three additional preadolescent lads sat down at Ben's table, Jacob directly across from Ben. His mouth agape, Ben stared wide-eyed at Jacob, the discomfort of his sunburn forgotten. Ignoring Ben, the group began to bolt down their food. Jacob's shirt was unbuttoned in the summer heat, his chest bare. Ben gazed at Jacob's chest, and as he stared at Jacob's nipples, a gripping arousal of sexual pleasure-pain began to stir in him. Jacob's nipples stared teasingly back at him. Ben wished he could touch them. To Ben, Jacob was even better-looking than he remembered. For a farm boy, such a beautiful face! Such thick shiny, dark hair! Such smooth, touchable skin! Such strong-looking hands! Ben longed to be touched by those hands. How breathtaking it would be for Jacob to reach across the table and smooth Ben's tousled reddish-blond hair or, like a pal, put his hand on Ben's shoulder. Trembling with nervousness, Ben dropped his ice cream spoon, and as he bent under the table to retrieve it he glanced at Jacob's legs across from him and for a lingering moment focused upon the bulge at Jacob's crotch.

He wanted to reach out and touch *it*—feel of it—but dared not. Then, in a sweat, he righted himself and unbuttoned his shirt.

Soon Jacob and his companions emptied their plates, and as they began to eat their ice cream, Jacob, always the center of attention, in a low voice with a bawdy tone, began to recite some of his favorite dirty jokes. Although Benjamin could not fully comprehend the jokes—most of them raunchy one-liners—Jacob's naughty inflection aroused him beyond anything he had ever felt before. One of the dirty stories in particular stayed with Ben for the rest of his life.

"Did you hear the one about a traveling salesman who got caught out in the country when night came and he didn't have any place to sleep? So he stopped at an old farmhouse and knocked on the door. The old farmer and his wife had already gone to bed, but their teenage daughter heard him knock and came to the door. 'I am looking for a place to sleep tonight,' he said. She answered, 'We don't have any extra beds, but it would be all right with me if you want to sleep with me.' 'Oh, I don't mind,' he said, 'if it is a good, strong bed.' So the traveling salesman went to bed with the farmer's daughter, and wouldn't you know it, they decided they would sleep better if they first had sex. 'Do you have a rubber?' she asked. 'No, but I have something just as good. Do you see this silk handkerchief? Feel how smooth and soft it is! I will put some lotion on it, and I will tie it on with a string.' And so they used the silk handkerchief with the lotion on it and had sex and got a good night's sleep. Then the salesman got up and left before daylight, before the old farmer woke up. About a year later, the salesman was on the very same sales route and stopped at the very same farmhouse, and the farmer's daughter came to the door, holding a three-month-old baby boy. 'That's a fine-looking boy you've got there,' said the salesman. 'He ought to be fine,' said the farmer's daughter. 'He got strained through a silk handkerchief!'"

Although they had heard versions of the traveling-salesman story before, Jacob's companions laughed loudly. In his serious innocence, Ben sought meaning to the story. After a short pause, he said, "I think it was the lotion that caused the baby!"

Jacob and his friends laughed louder than ever. Ben's sunburned red face reddened even more. "Benjamin, runt, you are all right!" Jacob exclaimed. "We are leaving to go skinny-dipping over at Spencer's pond. Do you want to go with us?"

Ben paused, then said, "I can't." Two words that potentially were his life's motto.

Jacob handed his ice cream bowl to Ben. "Here, runt, finish my banana nut for me."

Ben watched them leave, his eyes on Jacob, until the lads disappeared around the northeast corner of the gin. Although lost from his sight, in his mind's eye Ben went with them, imagined how the swimming party walked barefoot down the sandy country road to Spencer's place, helped one another through the barbed wire fence and crossed the pasture to a murky livestock pond, undressed, and plunged in. From the rear, Jacob had a perfect nude form, trim and tan and sturdy. From the front, Ben did not need to imagine the sight of Jacob's developing manhood—vividly he remembered being spellbound by it once before.

Ben's reverie was soon interrupted by the arrival of his mother. "Here, Ben, you need to eat this hot dog before you can have any more ice cream."

"Yes, Mother." He hid Jacob's bowl of ice cream on his knees under the table.

"Were those rowdy boys who were sitting here with you laughing at you and aggravating you?"

"No, Mother. They were my friends."

Grace returned to her duties at the food table, and Ben retrieved Jacob's bowl. He licked Jacob's wooden spoon clean and put in his pocket. He was going to take it home and hide it in his secret stash of special things, because Jacob had had it in his mouth and Jacob had had it in his hand.

*   *   *

"Jesse, why don't you ever run around with Jacob Jiggs?" asked Ben as the family drove home from the Harvest Festival picnic. "Isn't he your same age? He lives so close to us he could come over all the time and play catch with you, or go fishing or hunting, or just hang around, and maybe I could go along. It would be fun! You are always saying that Janie and I are no good to play with."

"You've got to be kidding!" Jesse retorted. "Jacob Jiggs smokes and he fights and he lies and he's got the dirtiest mouth in the county! If I was seen with Jacob Jiggs, it would ruin my name!"

"But wouldn't he act better if he had good friends? Couldn't you make friends with him and turn him into a good boy? Didn't the preacher tell you to live your life as a good sample to others?"

Jesse frowned and shook his head. "*Example*, Ben. The word is *example*! I do try to live my life as a good example to people I care about, you and Janie and all our cousins, and the kids in our church group! Jacob Jiggs is not on my list. Trying to help Jacob Jiggs behave himself would be like throwing a good plate of fried chicken into a hog pen!"

Benjamin frowned. "Jesse, you make me feel bad. I like Jacob, and I think there is good inside him, if you don't always tear him down. Our Sunday school teacher told us to let our light shine to show others!"

Daniel and Grace listened to the discussion between their practical, judgmental first son and their gullible, softhearted second son and decided to remain silent. Not so with Janie, although she did not understand why they were fussing over a strange neighbor boy, since she did not like most boys. Anyway, the discussion motivated her to sing "This little light of mine, I'm gonna let it shine, let it shine, let it shine, let it shine!" repeated again and again until they reached home.

*   *   *

In September 1939, Jimmy Dalkens started to school. He was not keen about it. The teacher would not let him roll his toy car back and forth across his desk. Recess did not occur often enough to suit him; he wanted only to go outside and throw and catch a ball. As he showed little interest in learning to read, his teacher sent his *Dick and Jane* reader home for home tutoring. When Benjamin visited one Saturday in early October, Jimmy showed him his school supplies—his pink eraser, his purple pencil, his red Big Chief tablet, his flash cards of numbers, his *Dick and Jane* reader—old stuff to Benjamin, who had learned to read at Janie's elbow and expanded his reading talents while practicing with the newsprint pasted to the walls of his home.

When Jimmy tried to read, "See Dick and Jane jump and run," Jimmy stumbled.

"J-u-m-p a-n-d r-u-n," Benjamin corrected him.

"Jump and run," read Jimmy. On the next page, Jimmy had another stumble, over the same phrase.

"J-u-m-p a-n-d r-u-n," repeated Benjamin. "Jimmy, 'jump and run' will always be 'jump and run,' no matter what page it is on," explained Benjamin, a little too authoritatively. After all, Jimmy was a year older than Ben.

Steamed, Jimmy doubled his right fist and hit Benny hard in his chest. "Benny, you throw a ball like a girl," he said. "You don't even know how to swing a bat! You're the only silly little freckle-faced fart in the whole family!"

Tears came to Benjamin's eyes, not because of the pain from Jimmy's fist, but from Jimmy's anger. Ben would need to learn the delicate art of helping others without incurring their resentment. It would not be an easy lesson to learn.

* * *

Rain! Rain! Rain!

In the fall 1939, abundant rains came and the drought finally ended, but it was too late for 1939 crop production. Daniel wrote banker Walter Williams that he had only five bales of cotton to har-

vest and that he would be unable to submit a down payment to purchase the farm, but with plenty of moisture now being stored in the
soil, he felt confident that in 1940 the crops would thrive and at least
he could make a down payment. Could Daniel be granted funds to
purchase seed for planting one last time? Grace was ambivalent about
buying their farm. While owning one's own farm was a good thing,
settling their family down on marginal land with low productivity—
alongside a deep ravine and a treacherous, rickety bridge—was not
something she wanted.

Walter Williams responded with a curt letter:

> *Your option to buy the farm has expired. A group
> of oil investors has bought it for the mineral rights.
> From now on, your sharecropping use of the farm
> will be extended year by year.*

* * *

Jesse spent nearly all his money earned at the Jarrell Ranch for feed
for his show steer, and it was not nearly enough. Buster the show
steer placed eighth in his class at the February 1940 Roger Mills
County Fat Stock Show, outclassed by barrel-bellied Hereford steers
from large ranches whose student 4-H Club owners or FFA owners
were students whose fathers actually fed and groomed and trained
their children's animals themselves in order to promote their registered herds through successful exposure in the competition. Buster
was nearly disqualified by his horns, for they stuck out in an angle
that cosmetically was anathema to the Hereford judge; Jesse had not
known when to place weights on Buster's horns in order to get them
to droop properly. "I don't see why an animal's horns should have
anything to do with the quality or taste of beef," grumbled Jesse, a
poor loser. Benjamin, who equally claimed Buster because he had
spent so much time watering him and combing him, did not believe
that cattle should have horns, anyway.

At the auction that concluded the show, Buster's sale brought
Jesse $30 over costs. Benjamin's heartache at seeing Buster loaded up

and hauled off in a trailer full of soon-to-be-slaughtered show steers was tempered when Jesse purchased a battery-operated, tabletop cabinet-model Zenith radio. A radio! The sounds of the world came crackling through static into the Bird household, providing instant communication and expanding Ben's world beyond imagination. The radio operated under the electrical power of the jalopy's battery, so Daniel or Jesse had to detach the car battery and set it on top of the cupboard beside the radio and make certain that overuse of the radio did not cause the battery to run down before it was regenerated in the jalopy.

Audible radio stations were sparse in Western Oklahoma in 1940. In the early morning hours, Daniel could arise and turn on a Wichita Falls station to get a broadcast of news, market reports, and weather.

Benjamin was up and at attention at the first crack of static; he sat on Daniel's knee or at his feet (unless Daniel was shaving at the mirror in front of the washstand), listening to every report and asking his father to clarify news reports when he could not understand. Sometimes Ben's questions shot forth so often that Daniel did not try to answer them all, and sometimes Benjamin was knowledgeable enough about the news that he and his father would engage in meaningful conversation.

Grace and Daniel enforced strict rules of engagement for the radio. It must be turned off at breakfast time and not turned on again until the kids were ready for school. They could then listen to music stations until the bus was seen arriving from the north, then Grace turned the radio off and Ben went outside to play. At noon, Daniel would come for lunch and listen to midday news, weather forecasts, and market reports, then during the baseball season, he would try to dial a broadcast of the St. Louis Cardinals baseball game of the day, to "see if old Diz is pitching today."

In midafternoon, Grace listened to her favorite soap operas, *Portia Faces Life*, *One Man's Family*, and *Stella Dallas*, which were broadcast from an Oklahoma City station whose broadcast power barely reached the Western Oklahoma area. When Jesse and Janie came home from school, the children surrounded the radio and listened to *The Lone Ranger*. They tried to memorize the introduction: "Out of the past comes the thundering hoofbeats of the great horse, Silver! The Lone Ranger rides again! With his sidekick, Tonto! Get 'em up, Scout! Hi-yo, Silver, away!" Every afternoon, for thirty minutes, the crooks and rustlers and train robbers in the Old West had no chance!

Then the radio was turned off until evening chores, homework, and after-dinner dishwashing were done so that their favorite programs would not be missed: *Lux Radio Theater*, *Fibber McGee and Molly*, *Jack Benny*, *Inner Sanctum*, with the scary, squeaking door. Then, by late evening, the only radio station that remained audible was from Del Rio, Texas, with its radio preachers and their prayer cloths and disc jockeys playing hillbilly and cowboy records: Gene Autry, Sons of the Pioneers, Ernest Tubbs, Hank Williams, Tex Ritter. The entire family enjoyed the music; the children learned the lyrics to many of the songs and sang along. One of the oft-played ballads at that time struck Benjamin to the quick: "Old Shep," a song about a boy and his dog, sung by Red Foley.

> *I was a lad and old Shep was a pup,*
> *O'er hills and mea-dows we'd roam.*
> *Just a boy and his dog, we were both full of fun,*
> *We grew up to-geth-er that way.*

As Red Foley sang of Shep growing too old to go on, the plaintive tone of the song opened Ben's heart to thoughts of his little friend Bran. Ben crawled under the table to conceal the tears that were welling up in his eyes.

> *Old Shep is gone where the good dog-gies go,*
> *And no more with old Shep will I roam;*
> *But if dogs have a heav-en, there's one thing I know:*
> *Old Shep has a won-der-ful home.*

Janie crawled under the table with Ben, herself brought to tears. She put her arm around Ben and patted his back in sympathy, as though old Shep and little Bran were one and the same and Bran's tragedy had just happened. Afterward, following a Hank Williams honky-tonk ballad, Ben and Janie emerged from under the table and soon were trying to dance to cowboy love songs. Ben learned new words from the radio, and added to Brother Nathan's words from the pulpit, Ben noticed that words sometimes were used in different ways. Words could be arranged to become stories, and stories could touch your insides, and words set to music had extra powers that stretched the imagination. Ben could have sat beside the radio and listened to it all day long and learned and learned and learned, but the electric power in the car battery would not last long outside the jalopy. So on days when the radio was off, Ben and Janie formed a club to act out their favorite stories and ballads. The club met in the cellar, and a club member could not enter until he uttered the secret password, *Trushay*, which Janie had copied from a radio commercial. Janie and Ben did not let Jesse join the club, or even tell him about it, because he was so bossy he would just take over and make them his workers.

CHAPTER 21

Family Affairs

At the age of thirteen, Olivia began menstruating, and although it was an annoyance to her, she considered it a validation of her arrival into womanhood: she was "more mature than her years." When she was fourteen, her breasts were fully developed, and she learned to alter the straps on her brassiere for best effect. Now, in early 1940, she was fifteen, a sophomore, telling her girl friends and male friends she was sixteen. She dressed like seventeen and longed to be eighteen so she could leave home and go to Hollywood and get discovered. Her parents would not allow her to date yet, but she was allowed to go on group excursions to area movie houses at Cheyenne or Elk City or Sayre or Shattuck on weekends only, if at least two other girls from their church were part of the group. The movie groups started out in compliance with the rules, but once out of sight, the teens usually reconfigured, and more often than not, Olivia found herself in the back seat with her boyfriend of the week. It was just too easy for this fifteen-year-old filly to kick the traces.

The movies! The movies! *The Gay Divorcee, The Night Is Young, Small-Town Girl, Libeled Lady, Live, Love, and Learn, You Can't Take It With You.* Olivia studied everything in the movies—how the starlets held their profiles, how alluring were their voices, how romantically they held their cigarettes and exhaled a gray cloud and made smoking seem almost like a sex act, how they held their lovers at bay then embraced their lovers and allowed their lovers to embrace them.

The kisses, the lingering lips. See the closed eyes, watch what the hands are doing, see where the noses go.

Olivia adeptly copied the hairstyles of the stars. She had just enough natural curl in her lush chestnut tresses to recreate a new hairstyle for herself each day of the school week. She had the prettiest hair in the county, and she knew it. She postured like Hedy Lamar and smirked like Bette Davis and smiled like Rosalind Russell and sulked like Joan Crawford and tried to sing like Judy Garland. Her favorite actress was Paulette Goddard because so often she was told she looked just like Paulette Goddard.

Several junior and senior girls who were not in her loop but were her rivals in attracting senior high school guys resented her "putting on airs!" Olivia tended to flit about when in the presence of males and was known to "accidentally" scrape her hand across a boy's body. "Shitty little prick teaser!" her rivals growled, and two sisters named Deidre and Pamsy Coppell openly threatened to stomp her if she tried to mess with their boyfriends.

Inevitably, Olivia went too far. A flirtatious girl cannot wink and flit about and affix her gaze on male bodies and ignore binding social mores without eventually incurring someone's wrath. Tragedy occurred one night at a high school bidistrict basketball game that Denim High School was hosting in March 1940. In training to become an official referee, Wally was timekeeper of the game. James and Maudeen were sitting in the stands behind Wally, while Olivia was flying solo, darting back and forth between her sophomore class's popcorn stand in the hallway (at which she was supposed to be working) and standing-room-only space at one end of the basketball court, where many young males in their teens and twenties were watching the game. Olivia found occasion to penetrate into the group of young males, weaving in and around them as though she were looking for someone specific who had been given incorrect change at the popcorn stand. Actually, she was presenting herself for their notice—not difficult to do. From her seat, Maudeen noticed her daughter's behavior and felt a premonition. If only one could be guaranteed that parents could teach a child the way that she should go and she would not depart from it!

At halftime of the closely contested game, several male spectators left the building to smoke cigarettes, and Olivia noticed two good-looking young men—strangers to her—who left via a side door. She followed them outside, approached them, and asked, "Would one of you nice gentlemen offer me a cigarette, please?" as though she were acting out a movie scene.

"Why, shore, honey, but tell me, what's in it for me?" replied Ronald Dayton, a roustabout from Elk City who, with his buddy, Tad Roker, had (unknown to Olivia) brought the Coppell sisters on a double date to the game.

Olivia took the cigarette in her hand, tilted her head upward, stretched her neck seductively, and replied, "Well, I should think that the opportunity to help a young lady is a reward in itself. Now, please, will one of you offer me a light?" She held the cigarette up to her lips and waited to grasp a hand. Suddenly she was pulled backward by a hard yank on her hair, and dragged to the ground.

"You little slut!" shouted Deidre Coppell, who, with her sister Pamsy, began to stomp Olivia in the stomach. "We told you to stay away from our boyfriends!"

Dazed by the fall, Olivia could not defend herself. Again and again they kicked her in the abdomen, then one of them jumped on Olivia and crushed her reproductive organs. She lay still, unconscious.

The two young men then forced their dates to stop the attack. "You have hurt her bad!" said Tad Roker. "Let's get out of here! She might be dead!" They ran to his car and sped away.

A small group gathered around Olivia. Someone recognized her and rushed in to tell her parents. Holding hands tightly, James and Maudeen ran to the scene. When Maudeen saw her child on the ground, seemingly lifeless, a long shrill wail escaped her—the heart-rending wail of a Choctaw mother. Wally carried Olivia to their car, and with James and Maudeen holding unconscious Olivia on their laps in the back seat, Wally sped thirty miles to the nearest emergency room, at Sayre Hospital.

When the doctor saw that Olivia had lost so much blood, he thought it was a miracle that she was not already dead. Bluntly he told James and Maudeen that he needed to rush Olivia into invasive surgery to remove ruptured, smashed tissue and cauterize the areas that were bleeding for her to have a chance to survive. She needed blood immediately. Wally volunteered and entered the emergency room with his sister. Within ten minutes, Olivia's ovaries and uterus—damaged beyond repair—were removed. Wally's blood was coursing through her veins. As he lay on a gurney during the transfusion, Wally gave thought not to Olivia's behavior bringing this disaster onto herself but on how his parents were mourning for their tragic daughter. If she survived, Olivia could never bear children.

Olivia's survival was in doubt for two days, as she drifted in and out of shock. Gradually, she regained consciousness and began to heal. She was released from the hospital after one week, then spent several days in bed at home. Grace, a born nurse, came and tended to her sister, changing her bandages every day. Benjamin was confused about what had happened to Aunt Olivia, because none of the grown-ups would talk to him about it. No charges were filed in the assault on Olivia Dalkens because no eyewitnesses came forth. She said she did not know who attacked her, or why, but her spirit was broken by the realization that her reproductive organs were gone. Maudeen encouraged her, "Get out of bed and make the best of the rest of your life, dear. You still have more to offer than most other girls your age!"

It took a new edition of Olivia's favorite movie magazine to revive her. The mailman delivered it on Monday before her sixteenth birthday, and as Olivia browsed through it, she saw a new hairstyle she immediately wanted to emulate. Sitting in front of the mirror, she saw that despite her surgical loss, she looked exactly the same, with an added tone of maturity that emanated from her experience with pain. Although she could never bear a child, there was a flip side: she could never be stymied by an unwanted pregnancy.

On her sixteenth birthday, April 20, 1940, Olivia was driven by Maudeen to the retail stores in Elk City, and her mother bought her three new dresses. The next Monday, she returned to school, but because of her continued physical tenderness, she was allowed to drive James's roadster to school instead of being jostled on the rough and bumpy school bus. She took advantage of her new independent mode of transportation by lingering in Denim after school each afternoon to drink a soda at Denim General Store, owned and operated by Geraldine Laird, a widow, whose only child, twenty-two-year-old Rory Laird, had just returned from Las Vegas, Nevada.

Rory Laird was a large heavyset, round-faced hustler whom Olivia thought looked like Orson Wells. He had been in Nevada since he had graduated from high school, working first as a bouncer at a Nevada brothel, where he enjoyed perks, then as an alleged hit man for the gambling underworld, according to some of his high school buddies in whom he had confided. Now he was back home, working as a cashier, sacker, and shelf stocker for his mother, while lawmen and others in Nevada wondered of his whereabouts. Olivia was attracted to Rory by his mysterious background, his size, his black hair combed straight back like Daniel's, and his winking, ogling eyes. Rory and Olivia began to spend time back in the storeroom, looking for something not out on the shelves.

The Saturday after the 1939–1940 school term ended, Olivia packed her best clothes and her cosmetics in two bags. About 9:30 a.m., Rory Laird drove up in the driveway at the old homestead and honked. With her bags in hand, Olivia darted out the door.

"Where are you going, girl?" Maudeen called after her. "What is going on with you and Rory Laird?"

"He's taking me to see *Gone with the Wind* in Las Vegas! We're eloping! Bye, Mama!"

"No, Olivia! You can't do this!"

"Yes, I can! I'm sixteen, the same age as you when you got married! So long!"

"No! No!" Maudeen wailed as Rory and Olivia pulled out onto the road. "James, come quick!" Maudeen yelled out to James at the barn. "Olivia is running off with Rory Laird!"

James hurried to the house. "I'll catch them and tan his hide," he said. But he could do nothing. Olivia had hidden his car keys.

*   *   *

Several significant developments were about to occur in Benjamin's young life, but Olivia's fast-paced drama dominated the family's concerns for several weeks. One week after Olivia eloped, Maudeen received a letter that contained a snapshot of Olivia and Rory Laird at a wedding chapel in downtown Las Vegas. Olivia wore a rented veil and a dramatic smile as she looked up adoringly into the eyes of her new husband. The letter:

June 13, 1940
Las Vegas, Nevada

Dear Mama,
We got married in a beautiful little chapel where movie stars have married. Rory has taken me to four stage shows already! He knows so many people in this town. I know we are going to do well here. He is going to give me money to take acting lessons. I have been offered a job as a cigarette girl in a neat little ruffled outfit, with a tray around my waist, which I would carry about on the gambling floors of this big fancy hotel. But I don't think I'll take the job, because the men in this town seem to like to pinch a lot, which I will not put up with. Rory is starting to work tomorrow for a gambling casino and hotel at the edge of town, where we will have our own little apartment. I wish I had paid more attention to how you cook your wonderful meals, but I probably won't try to cook much because Rory's job will take him out on the town every night. I'll write more later. I hope you are glad for my happiness.

Love,
Olivia Dalkens Laird

Maudeen let Grace read the letter, and Benjamin listened as Grace read the letter aloud to Daniel. Ben was surprised at how quickly Olivia's life had changed. Only three weeks earlier, he and Aunt Olivia had been playing checkers on the front porch. Now she was in a faraway place, a married woman doing many new things!

Barely a fortnight passed before Olivia returned in humiliation, riding a Greyhound bus from Las Vegas to Cheyenne, Oklahoma, then hitching a ride home with Mel McGregger. Maudeen was chopping weeds in her garden when Mel's rattletrap pickup stopped and Olivia emerged with her two bags of belongings. Maudeen shouted for joy. "Oh, honey, welcome home!" They ran to each other and embraced.

Olivia began to cry. "Oh, Mama, Rory has treated me so mean! He came home drunk every single night and beat me up when I would not do some nasty things he wanted me to do!" She pulled her hem up and showed her mother a deep bruise on her inner thigh.

"Don't cry, sweetheart. Your father and I will help you get a restraining order and an annulment. You can go back to school this fall like nothing has happened, and you can make something of yourself, I know you can!"

James and Maudeen took Olivia to an attorney to initiate legal proceedings to end the marriage, but legal action became unnecessary. In early August 1940, Geraldine Laird received official notice that her son's body had washed up on the shore of Lake Tahoe with a bullet hole in his temple.

*   *   *

Donna Belle Dalkens delivered her third boy child on June 14, 1940. Russell could not be prouder of his beautiful, healthy, loving wife and his three sons. Newborn William Monte Dalkens was the spitting image of his father, with as great a promise of handsome, sturdy athleticism as his muscular older brothers, Jimmy and Donny. His grandmother Maudeen and his aunt Grace had been on hand at his delivery; there were no complications. Nine-year-old Janie helped bathe her new cousin, and she bonded to little Will with such intensity that subconsciously she claimed him as her own. She stayed with Russell and Donna Belle for a week to help out with the new baby. Olivia was visiting friends in Shattuck, recuperating from her Las Vegas ordeal and insulating herself from the maternity scene.

Russell was embarrassed that he had not been able to afford a doctor. His expanding paternal responsibilities caused him to reevaluate his family's situation. Although he worked as hard as anyone and the rainfall in 1940 promised a bountiful crop, he concluded he was not a capable farmer. He planted at the wrong time, his mule team became lame, and his cows went dry in early May and did not breed back: his infertile old bull "shot blanks." All but four of Donna Belle's Leghorn hens had been carried off by varmints. Russell's cotton crop sprouted and came up to a good stand, but a heavy rain washed it all out, and he had no money to buy seeds to plant the cotton field again. Had it not been for hiring out for day wages to neighbor farmers a few days during planting time, he and Donna Belle would be completely broke. Their garden produced food for the table up to the middle of May, then aphids, squash beetles, grubs, grasshoppers, and tomato worms wiped it out. Fortunately, he had planted extra rows of Irish potatoes, producing bushels of tubers that he stored in the barn loft. Donna Belle did her best with what they had—mashed potatoes, baked potatoes, potato salad, fried potatoes, boiled potatoes, scalloped potatoes, potato soup. One day, Jimmy and Donny slipped up into the barn loft and began to see how far they could throw the smaller potatoes out of the loft or smash them against a wall. Once their prank was discovered, they got the hardest spanking they had ever experienced.

On the day their new baby was a week old, Russell told his wife, "Donna Belle, sweetheart, we are at the end of the line for us here. If I don't do something else, we will starve out, or we will need to go to the poor farm. I am going to write a letter to my old supervisor, Frank Liggett, at Porter Hill. When I left that job and we moved here, he told me I could always come back."

"If you have to handle dynamite to blast out the mountainside, I'd rather we live in a tent down by the river and live on greens and roadkill!" Donna Belle declared.

It took a week for Russell's letter to his old supervisor to make the rounds. From Porter Hill, it was forwarded to Denison, Texas:

June 28, 1940
Denison, Texas

Russ, old boy, it is good to hear from you. I am now supervising a construction crew on a big federal project that is building Denison Dam that is impounding Lake Texoma, a really big deal.

The Texoma project is capturing the entire Red River watershed, including the Washita River drainage, and all their tributaries.

We will be working here for years. I can use you today.

Get here as soon as you can.

Frank

Within twenty-four hours of receiving Liggett's letter, Russell had arranged to have his cattle shipped to the Oklahoma City stockyards auction; he packed a bag of work clothes, drove to Denison, signed up, and worked a half-day on his new job. Next day, he rented a house across the river in the town of Colbert, Oklahoma, and that weekend, he moved his family to their new home. Donna Belle regretted leaving her reliable support group, the Dalkens relatives in Roger Mills County, but she appreciated the advantage of having a regular income. Jimmy and Donny discovered a baseball field just a block away from their new home, found new friends instantly, and adjusted with ease. Within a week, Russell wrote his brother:

July 6, 1940
Colbert, Oklahoma

Wally, old boy, when are you coming? Let us know. There is a job here for you. This old $28 per week *comes in mighty handy! This job qualifies me for FDR's Social Security System. It is a great relief to know that Donna Belle and my boys will be taken care of if something happens to me.*

Russell Dalkens

Back at Denim, James advised Wally that perhaps it would be wise for him to move to the Lake Texoma construction project and sign on with Russell, since James and Wally and their families would likely need to move from Robert's old homestead in a year or two, anyway. Wally could not see himself working in construction for wages, drifting away from agriculture, no cattle, no horses. "I have been thinking of taking a trip over into the Texas Panhandle to look for a ranch-management job on one of those big spreads there," Wally told his father.

At the Bird household, Benjamin pondered the change taking place within the family, "I guess I won't get to see Jimmy and Donny very much anymore." He was somewhat downhearted, for he also sensed that the joy of his camaraderie with Uncle Russell, Tuff Nut to Tuff Nut, probably was over.

"Hopefully, we'll all get together at Thanksgiving," offered Grace, who knew the family ties would remain strong enough to survive the challenges of time and distance. It was Janie who suffered most from the sudden separation, for she loved her new little cousin, Will, with all her heart. Playing with dolls again to her no longer had purpose.

*   *   *

To Benjamin, the disturbing European war news on the radio sent him to the newspaper maps pasted on the wall almost every day. In May 1940, he traced the German advance across Poland and the Nazi seizure of Denmark, Norway, Luxembourg, the Netherlands, and Belgium and, in June, the fall of France.

At home, another conflict was underway. Jesse's plan to work again for Lloyd Jarrell that summer was delayed three weeks into June because the abundant rainfall that fell regularly throughout early spring caused a heavy growth of weeds in Daniel's cotton field, so Jesse and everyone else in the family—including Ben—chopped cotton, up and down one row after another. Janie was the slowest cotton chopper, for she paused often, staring into space, daydreaming. Ben, who had a small hoe with a broken handle, relished the task his father had asked of him. "We've got to clean out all the weeds and crabgrass without disturbing a single cotton stalk, because this is the first good chance we've had to get a good harvest, so everyone be careful and be thorough."

Ben basked in the knowledge that his labor was of value. He was near enough to the ground that often he easily pulled weeds by hand, speeding the task, instead of maneuvering the hoe around the cotton stalks; he pretended the weeds and crabgrass were Nazis and the cotton stalks were good people. Every row he cleaned was a battle victory in a war that had to be won.

Before the cotton-chopping was completed, Daniel began to notice that green bolls were beginning to fall off the plants, while other bolls developed a blemish, indicating an infestation of boll weevil larvae. Daniel did not have a strategy to combat boll weevils except prayer. Perhaps the Good Lord would intervene.

*   *   *

When Jesse began his summer 1940 job at the Jarrell Ranch, he propelled himself into the tasks with fervor, at a wage of two dollars a day, advancing his cowhand abilities from the previous summer's experience, and he opened up to Lloyd Jarrell more than he had done previously. "Mr. Jarrell, someday I am going to have a ranch like this," he declared. "I am going to work hard and save money and buy land and collect a good herd of cattle, and I am going to keep them fat so that they will be in good shape to raise a calf every year!"

"Power to ya'!" said Jarrell.

By Sunday, just before Jesse's family came to take him to church in Strong City, Jesse told Jarrell he was poring over the idea of not going back to school. "I can manage my own business, and I can handle money," he stated. "I can keep my own bank records, and I know when somebody is trying to cheat me. If I work full-time instead of going to school, it will just speed up the day when I can have my own place!"

Next day, Jarrell surprised Jesse by announcing, "Next Monday, I'm going to take a trip out west for a week, so I am leaving the whole operation in your hands. Do you think you can handle things until I get back?"

"Sure," Jesse said with confidence.

"If you handle things well while I'm gone, I am going to offer you a deal," said Jarrell. "If you are sincere in deciding not to go back to school, I will let you work here full-time from now on, and eventually—since I like you, and you remain a good, honest worker—when I get too old to work, I will give you what I have here."

Jesse was almost speechless. "Mr. Jarrell, I appreciate your offer! I just don't know what to say!"

"Well, if I were you, I would not tell your folks about your plans to quit school just yet, or about my promise to leave this place in your hands," Jarrell suggested. "I don't think they will understand."

"Mr. Jarrell, I won't lie to them," Jesse vowed.

"You don't need to lie. Just don't say anything until summer is almost over."

During the Sunday service at Strong City First Baptist Church, Brother Nathan kept his feet on the floor, for the most part, and delivered a provocative sermon about laying up treasures in heaven rather than on earth, *"where moth and rust destroy, and where thieves can break in and steal."* Safe and secure in assurance of his salvation, Jesse hardly heard a word of the sermon, for he was adrift in the dream of one day owning the Jarrell Ranch for himself. After dropping Jesse off at the Jarrell Ranch following church, Grace commented to her husband, "Jesse seemed distant today. Do you suppose he is not being treated right by Mr. Jarrell? Perhaps we should have brought him home."

"I wouldn't worry about that," Daniel replied. "Jesse is going through a difficult stage. A young fellow who is growing hair in his armpits begins to think he is already supposed to be a man when he knows he's not. Staying busy is probably the best thing for him, for now. When summer is over we will see how much he has changed."

Next day, Lloyd Jarrell packed a suitcase and drove away, with instructions to Jesse: "Just check on all the cattle every day, keep the fences mended if the bulls break through to fight, and don't burn the house down trying to cook yourself a big dinner."

Once Jarell was out of sight, Jesse saddled old Jodhpur, a favorite black gelding (named for a Tulsa polo player in jodhpurs who had tried to buy him with a bad check), and rode the length and breadth of the ranch. One day it would be all his! Did he deserve it? *Mr. Jarrell must think I do,* he mused. *It must be God's will. God works in mysterious ways, His wonders to perform. Thank You, Lord! Thank You, Lord!*

Jesse appraised "his" ranch, its pastures, working pens, and barns and made mental notes on how he would change things once the ranch truly became his. He launched a project to dig up the scattered prickly pear cactus plants and rid the pastures of all cacti and mesquite sprouts.

Lloyd Jarrell returned the following Monday and seemed unchanged. On Tuesday, they weaned the winter calves, and on Wednesday, they took the steers to the Oklahoma City stockyards auction. On Thursday, Jarrell noticed the piles of cacti and mesquite that Jesse had grubbed in his absence, and complimented him.

Throughout the summer, Jesse dutifully did everything Jarrell asked of him, and then some. As the weeks passed, Jesse began to drop hints of his plans to his parents as he accompanied them to church each Sunday. "Mr. Jarrell has offered me a full-time job, and I am thinking of staying on here full-time."

"But you need to finish your schooling," his mother protested.

"Well, I think the Strong City school bus passes by here," Jesse responded noncommittally.

"Jesse, you are not old enough to be out on your own," said his father.

"But I *am* old enough! I started shaving last week," Jesse answered. "And I have already been on my own. I stayed here a week by myself in late June when Mr. Jarrell took a trip, and I got along just fine. I cooked fried eggs and bacon for breakfast and fried potatoes and ham for lunch and ate bacon and egg sandwiches for supper."

"But, Jesse, you need to finish your education!" his mother repeated. "I have always believed that you are destined to do something special with your life."

Trying to sound casual about it, Jesse informed his parents, "Mr. Jarrell has said that he plans to leave me this place. You don't want to stand in my way of having a place of my own!"

Daniel and Grace were dumbfounded. Jesse would not lie to them, not about something so profound. But would Lloyd Jarrell lie to Jesse?

On the last Sunday before school was to begin, Daniel and Grace were determined to return Jesse home with them. "He is too young and immature to be making such a life-altering decision," declared Grace. Daniel doubted that Lloyd Jarrell would actually keep a promise to leave Jesse his ranch, and Daniel was hurt that Jesse would turn away from him for such a shaky prospect.

When they arrived to get him, Jesse had not dressed for church. He was astride old Jodhpur. "Get down, son, and come with us," said Daniel.

"I can't, Dad. Mr. Jarrell is gone on another trip. I can't leave things here unattended."

Daniel took a step toward old Jodhpur, to grasp the reins. Jesse and Jodhpur backed away, turned, and galloped into the pasture, Jesse waving his hat as a gesture of closure as he disappeared behind a shed. Grace began to weep. Watching everything from the back seat of the jalopy, Janie and Benjamin were wide-eyed, their mouths agape.

"I hate to see Jesse miss the start of school tomorrow," said Daniel. "This is a mistake that our son is making, but at this point, I don't know what to do about it. We can't just grab him and tie him up at home if he doesn't want to be there. Nor is he the first adolescent that has dropped out of school and chased a wild dream. We'll just have to pray that, in time, everything will turn out right."

"Drive us down the road to Aunt Hettie's and Uncle Ed's," Grace requested. "We'll ask them to keep an eye on Jesse until he gets over his foolishness."

Aunt Hettie was in bed with a migraine headache and did not come to the door. Ed Galloway was not there. Daniel drove his family on to church and back to their home near Denim in a sort of daze. Jesse had never caused them a problem, but now Jesse was throwing everything over for a pipe dream. Not for a minute did Daniel believe that Lloyd Jarrell would give Jesse his ranch. Little Ben with his cow and calf bottles was nearer to having a ranch than Jesse.

As soon as Jesse confirmed that his parents had left him behind, he returned to the house at the Jarrell Ranch and ate his lunch. As he finished his meal, he heard a vehicle come up the drive and stop. It was his great-uncle Ed Galloway. "Hello, High Pockets!" Ed addressed Jesse, using his nickname for lads who wore bib overalls. "I've come to talk to Lloyd. Is he here?"

"No, sir, Uncle Ed. Lloyd is gone on a trip out of state. He will be back later today or tomorrow."

"Oh, shoot! I needed to ask him something," said Ed. "That man can't stay away from those cathouses in Nevada. He makes three or four trips there every year!"

"What is it you wanted to ask? Maybe I can help you," offered Jesse.

"It has to do with a 160-acre piece of land that I bought off the Jarrell Ranch earlier this year, the quarter-section pasture next to my place. I don't get possession of it until the first of January, but I was wondering if Lloyd would mind if I moved some machinery in to have a stock pond dug so that I can try to catch some surface water to use as soon as I take control of the land."

Jesse was confused. "Do you mean that Lloyd Jarrell sold off a piece of this ranch?"

"No, no, not Lloyd," Ed clarified. "Lloyd don't own any of this place. It belongs to his uncle William Jarrell's estate, owned by two of Lloyd's cousins who live in Denver. Lloyd runs the ranch for them for a place to live and a percentage of the cattle sales."

"Oh."

"Well, as soon as he gets back from his frolic, tell him I'd like to move some equipment in to dig a pond."

"Okay."

For the next two hours, Jesse sat quietly on the porch and felt like a fool.

Lloyd Jarrell returned in midafternoon. Jesse met him at the driveway. "Lloyd, instead of taking you up on your offer to take your place here on this ranch someday, I have decided to move back home and finish school. Would you consider trading old Jodhpur and a saddle for some of my wages so I can ride home tonight and get back to school?"

"Sure. I hate to lose you, but I know you are making the right decision."

Jesse did not confront Lloyd Jarrell for deceiving him, for he did not believe he had. Jesse knew he had deceived himself.

* * *

Next morning, Janie and Benjamin awoke early and dressed in their new school clothes then waited on the front porch for the school bus, excited about Benjamin's first day at school. Grace had bought Ben a new pair of bib overalls and had made him a new shirt out of one of Janie's outgrown blue blouses, changing the buttonholes to the proper side and stitching crosses to close the old buttonholes. Ben did not care if it was a made-over shirt, and he did not care that all his other school clothes were Jesse's, Vernon's, and Kirby's hand-me-downs. He was proud of his new overalls, and he had already found that chewing and sucking on the tag end of the denim suspenders helped calm his nervousness about starting to school.

Suddenly, they heard *clop clop* on the rickety old bridge. "Look!" shouted Janie. "There's Jesse, riding that pretty black horse!"

Grace and Daniel came to the door and watched Jesse, tired and sleepy, ride up and dismount.

"This is old Jodhpur," he told his father. "I traded some of my wages for him. I think he is broken to harness. He can take turns with old Bill and old Hector pulling the plow."

"Good idea," said Daniel. "I'll take him to the barn and rub him down."

"Jesse, I have your school clothes laid out on the bed," said Grace. "If you hurry, you can sponge off at the washstand while I pack your lunch, and you can still catch the bus with Benjamin and Janie. *I am so glad* you will be available to tell Benjamin where to go on his first day."

Jesse was back. The family nest was intact. Grace's "I am so glad" was all that needed to be said.

PART III
Life Teaches, Benjamin Learns

CHAPTER 22

Benjamin Goes to School

In September 1940, when Benjamin Bird started his first grade at school, he was already reading at Janie's third-grade level. He did not seek to display his reading skill and the knowledge that he acquired from his reading ability, for Jesse cautioned him against it. "Carrottop, if you show off and act like a know-it-all, nobody will like you," Jesse pointed out. "You can answer the questions your teacher asks you, but don't jump up and down and raise your hands and wave for her attention, even if you know the answers to her questions and nobody else does. Your classmates will just hate you. Nobody likes a know-it-all."

Ben remembered when cousin Jimmy hit him in the chest for outshining him in reading *Dick and Jane*, and so he took Jesse's advice to heart.

"Also," advised Jesse, "let your teacher think she is the person who is teaching you everything. It will make her feel good about herself, and she will like you because she will be proud that she has taught you so well."

And so Benjamin sat on his hands when Miss Dean was teaching things he already knew, and Miss Dean understood his boredom because he answered all her questions correctly in a quiet, self-confident monotone; he read out loud perfectly, and he yawned sporadically while his classmates struggled with assignments. She decided to place him at a desk in the back corner beside a shelf of first- and second-grade storybooks, whispering him permission to read new books while his classmates were "catching up," occasionally placing a new storybook on his desk as soon as he finished the last.

Recess was a lark. His classmates, both boys and girls, flitted about the teeter-totters and swings and slides and water fountain and flagpole and laughed at just about everything that happened.

"Look, Jackie Joe is falling down on purpose!"

"Look, Donald is wiping his snot on Dale's sleeve!"

"Look, Jeanette is whispering a secret to Rowena. Everyone thinks she likes Vernal Ray!"

"Look, Benny is chewing on the end of his overall suspenders, like a titty baby!"

"Listen! Lonnie tooted! Don't breathe!"

"Look! Miss Dean is scolding Dudley for throwing dirt!"

"Jewel, be careful! You turned the swing loose too soon and almost hit Paula in the head!"

"Eek! There is a grasshopper on Yvonne's shoulder!"

"Children, do not teeter-totter so fast," scolded Miss Dean. "You'll break your legs!"

"Yuk! Miss Dean, you have stepped on Lonnie's bubble gum!"

Separating by gender, the students grouped into twos and threes for a trip to the outhouses just before the bell rang. Urinating into the trough in the boys' outhouse was a group activity. Ben applied the principle of not looking at anyone else while peeing. Jesse cautioned Ben not to go into the latrine when Jacob Jiggs and his buddies were in there. "They'll be smoking or talking nasty, so you'd best just stay away."

Lunchtime at school also was a time for fun. First, everyone marched into the cloakroom for their lunch pails or brown paper bags then marched in line to the lunch tables in the auditorium, where they laid their food out on paper napkins and began to munch, gobble, nibble, and swap.

"Nova, I'll trade my peanut butter cookie for your pickle."

"Who wants my buttered biscuit? It has brown sugar on it."

"Look, Wilbur has a fried chicken leg!"

Three of the girls had Shirley Temple lunch baskets. Jack Wheeler had a Gene Autry lunch pail, a Christmas gift from his grandmother. Several students, including Benjamin, had one-gallon lard buckets or syrup buckets, with lids that sealed so tightly that only strong boy fingers and thumbs could dislodge them. Ben would have liked a boiled egg every day, but the school superintendent announced a policy forbidding them because of the danger of food poisoning. Ben had always envied Jesse and Janie their lunch buckets, because he watched what his mother packed for them: a biscuit-and-bacon sandwich, or a peanut butter-and-jelly sandwich, or leftover fried chicken, a cookie or two, carrot sticks or a ripe tomato, a sealed Mason jar filled with fresh, sweet milk, and if she had time to cook them, fried fruit pies. Now he was a beneficiary of her culinary touch, and when he came home from school, he thanked her for the day's lunch bucket surprise, except on days when she had doused the end of his overall suspenders with Louisiana hot sauce to keep him from chewing on them.

The highlight of Benjamin's first month in school came when Miss Dean organized the class into a "rhythm band" with slightly frayed uniforms, including tasseled caps, passed down through the years. There were cymbals and triangles, tambourines and tooting horns, wooden blocks and bells, and one drum. The drum major—the carrier and beater of the drum—was chosen by competition. Which student could keep cadence while marching and staying in line all at the same time? Benjamin won the competition, hands down, thanks to Janie drilling him during their secret club sessions, marching to the radio broadcasting of "Alexander's Ragtime Band."

Eventually, when his classmates more or less caught up with Benjamin academically, the shared classroom experience of combining efforts to learn—studying together, collecting and pooling knowledge, expanding everyone's horizons, achieving group enlightenment—became to Ben a magnetic attraction that one day would draw him into a teaching career. His aunt Leona would understand, and so would his great-grandmother Lydia Dalkens. Those who can, teach.

* * *

Jesse's passage through adolescence occurred with hardly a bump and a brief rush of pimples. As a first child, he often displayed maturity beyond his years. He had enjoyed the privacy of having his own room when working at the Jarrell Ranch, and he attained his privacy at home by moving his sleeping cot into the storm cellar instead of leaving it in the southwest corner of the family's bedroom living room. Even during cold weather, he slept by himself in the cellar, with only a few extra bed covers, because the underground cellar was insulated from the cold.

Benjamin's cot was moved to Jesse's former corner, away from his parents' bed, and in his new location, he gained access to a section of the wall where relatively unfamiliar newspaper stories were pasted and where new newspaper maps could be posted.

Jesse's attitude toward school changed drastically for the better when Henrietta Hayes, a new student, enrolled in his class. She smiled nervously at everyone, hoping for acceptance. She was the prettiest thirteen-year-old Jesse had ever seen, and he made his move quickly, before his buddies stopped gawking. "Hi, my name is Jesse Bird, and I am running for class president. I hope you will vote for me. Can I carry your books to the next class? What is your favorite candy bar?" He played his advantage, the only fellow who had worked for wages all summer, and he cemented his boyfriend-girlfriend relationship with Henrietta every day with a Butterfinger candy bar bought from the senior class's fund-raising table.

Jesse and Henrietta learned to slip away behind the curtains on the auditorium stage during the lunch hour when no one was watching, linger in the darkest corner, and smooch, hugging and kissing and recklessly petting each other as though they were the first couple in history who could stir their hormones to a high fever without falling into a stupor.

Throughout autumn, a sporadic series of junior high school class parties, often centered on someone's birthday, took place on Friday nights at the home of the birthday person. While parents visited and played card games at the kitchen table, the adolescents gathered in the living room and played parlor games, the favorite being spin the bottle, with couples sitting together, someone spinning a soda bottle to see which couple the bottle would point toward, thereby selecting them to walk outside and around the house in the darkness, pausing to embrace and smooch until the next chosen couple took their place. Jesse developed a reputation for being quite the *smoocher*, with a sequence of girlfriends who tended to come and go at that age. He and Henrietta broke up quickly over religious issues; she was a member of the Church of Christ. Occasionally Benjamin had an opportunity to observe his brother's behavior without actually spying on him, and when Ben became aware of the ramifications of sexual arousal, he marveled that Jesse and his girlfriend could pet with such fervor without actually stripping off and making a baby right there on the spot.

* * *

Downtown Denim, Oklahoma, in 1940 did not have enough businesses to fill up one side of a main street block, let alone two. And yet Benjamin was excited each day as his school bus crept past the stores on its way to and from the schoolyard. Who would be in town today, taking care of business? There was Mrs. Laird's General Store, the only place in town to buy groceries and sundries. He really liked her ice cream cones. Next door was Pete's Barbershop, where Benjamin got his first paid-for haircut in late October 1940, after his mother's hair clippers broke. He had run to the barbershop during his lunch hour and was lucky to find the barber chair empty. Pete was a nice, quiet, unassuming man who did not get upset when Ben could not find the quarter in his overalls pocket to pay him; it was lodged against the crease. "That's all right, young man. I know your daddy. I know I'll get my quarter sooner or later." The quarter shook loose while Ben trotted back to the schoolyard, so he dashed back to pay the barber to save his reputation.

Ben noticed that there was usually something going on down the street at the cotton gin and feed store, or across the street at the blacksmith and garage. There was a small depot that served a passenger service for a two-car "doodle-bug" train that ran from a town in the Texas Panhandle past Denim and Strong City to West Central Oklahoma, but none of the Dalkens or Bird families had ever ridden on it, despite their obvious connection to those two towns. There was also a small dry-goods store and secondhand shop and a saloon and pool hall that sold legal 3.2 percent beer, not a strong drink, but strong enough if one drank a lot of it, a common practice throughout dry Oklahoma.

Ben and Daniel were in town one Saturday afternoon when two drunks were thrown out on the street for fighting in the saloon, and drawing a crowd, they continued fighting until one of them passed out or was knocked out—there was no consensus on that. Both were covered with blood from busted noses, facial scratches, and lacerated cheeks, but neither of them acted as though he felt pain. Ben wondered how anyone could become so insensitive to his own pain, let alone the pain of another.

Yes, Benjamin enjoyed the entire bumpy school bus ride, coming and going along several miles of rural farmland, past shinnery patches and sagebrush pastures, where he watched for cattle, becoming familiar with many he observed almost every day, except on afternoons when the bus's gasoline fumes gave him a headache and nausea and he had to lie down in an empty seat to keep from throwing up.

The highlight of Ben's school day was when he was on the bus with Jacob Jiggs sitting within his vision. On the morning school bus route, Benjamin learned to sit behind a pleasant, compliant obese girl named Lucinda Lines, who was in Jacob's class, because Jacob often sat beside Lucinda and flirted with her in order to lure her into sharing her homework. Ben studied the back of Jacob's head, his thick dark hair curling behind his ears, the tilt of his head as he shmoozed Lucinda. When he could see Jacob's hands, Ben stared at them, admiring the blue veins standing out from the smooth, tanned texture of Jacob's skin, his long graceful fingers and groomed nails surprisingly clean for a fourteen-year-old farm boy.

Benjamin knew that Jacob Jiggs had a bad reputation, but that did not keep Ben from yearning to be in Jacob's presence, to gaze at him and marvel at how handsome he was, how pleasing it was just to look at him and feel warm and contented on the bus with him and blush when their eyes met, and when Jacob actually said, "Hi, runt," to him, it was a guarantee that Ben was having a good day.

CHAPTER 23

Goodbye, Old Homestead

In 1940, the European War stretched toward America. In August, the German Air Force began to cross the English Channel to bomb British ships, factories, bridges, and cities. American ships hauling essential goods to England were vulnerable. In September, President Roosevelt transferred fifty overage destroyers to the British; many realized that, in a sense, the United States was already in the war. That month, Congress approved a Selective Service Training and Service Act, the first peacetime program of compulsory military service in history. All men between twenty-one and thirty-five were required to register. Benjamin read the news article in the *Kansas City Star* and recognized that Jesse was too young to serve, but was Daddy too old? The first registration in October resulted in the listing of 16,400,000 men, including Russell, Wally, and Daniel (who, in five months, would be overage). The first draft numbers were selected on October 29. Five days later, James Dalkens received the following letter from his nephew Rayford, who had decided it was time for him to return to his heritage, his father Robert's old homestead:

November 3, 1940
Pueblo, Colorado

Dear Uncle James,
My three sons have made a pact that if anyone of them got drafted, then they would all sign up and volunteer to serve together, so that they could look out for one another. Well, guess what? Jeff, who is twenty-two, has had his number called in the first draft, so Jeff and Johnny, who is twenty-one, and Harvey, who is twenty-four, volunteered together and are being inducted next week, and they go for basic training at Camp Pendleton. Their mother, Ella, is nearly crazy, and I ain't taking it too well myself.

I need now to plan what my boys might be coming back home to, God willing, so Ella and I need to put our roots down at the farm. We want to move right after the first of the year. The boys always liked to hunt and fish on the Canadian River, so it is my wish that we move back before they have their first furlough. I know this does not give you much time, but I can only think of my boys. Uncle James, I know you will be leaving the place in better condition than when you moved there, and for that, I will always be grateful. My brother Marshall and our four sisters have always had a special place for you in our hearts, as though you were our big brother. If you want to sell me some of your cattle when you move, and some of your workhorses, I will pay you the going rate.

Love,
Rayford

When James read Rayford's letter, it seemed to him like a letter of death. James sat down on a bench and felt like weeping for Rayford's boys, and for all the boys who might have to go to war, and for the families they would be leaving behind. He wanted to damn the lousy leaders of aggression who would not stop war. He mourned for the end of his dream, his heart and soul implanted in the old homestead. He mourned for his brother Robert, who had been in his grave for five years; he mourned for his father, John Jay Dalkens, who had given James the legacy of kinship to the soil and love of life and the strength and joy of family ties. James remembered one of the rare occasions when his father talked about his experiences in the Civil War, wounded during Grant's 1863 siege of Vicksburg, where John Jay's brothers tied their gangrenous brother to a log and floated him across the Mississippi River to safety and recovery at home in Louisiana. James understood why Rayford's sons wanted to serve together. In family there is strength.

*   *   *

One early afternoon at school in late November 1940, Benjamin got Miss Dean's permission to go to the outhouse to relieve himself. He rushed to the urinal, took care of his urgency, then pivoted toward the smell of fresh cigarette smoke and stared into a toilet stall to see Jacob Jiggs, now fifteen, rising from a toilet seat, his jeans and shorts down around his ankles, taking a last draw on a cigarette before dropping it into the toilet. Jacob's genitals, fully exposed, encircled by dark pubic hair, larger—much larger—than on the day two years earlier when Ben had been mesmerized in the cowshed, now mesmerized him again. Ben's gaze was frozen on Jacob's penis.

"Runt, you had better not tell the principal on me," Jacob warned. "I will get expelled if I get caught smoking again."

"I—I won't tell," Ben stammered.

Jacob pulled his jeans up and buckled his belt. "Why do you always stare at me? Do you think I'm a spook?"

"My eyes like to look at you," Ben confessed. "I don't know why." He turned to escape.

"Wait, I will walk back to the schoolhouse with you," said Jacob. "I want to warn you about something. I hate these damned cigarettes. They're just a trap. I already crave another one. They make me feel like a loser, which I will be if I get kicked out of school. Runt, do yourself a favor and never smoke a single one, or I warn you that you will crave it for the rest of your life."

"I won't," vowed Ben.

"Good! Let's shake on it!"

Awestruck, Ben was limp. Jacob clutched Benjamin's hand then patted him on his shoulder. Returning to his classroom, Ben felt an aftereffect from Jacob's grip on his hand and suspected that Miss Dean and all his classmates could smell Jacob's tobacco odor in his clothes. He did not care. He had touched Jacob's hand; Jacob's hand had touched him.

Later that afternoon, when school was dismissed, Benjamin was sitting by himself on the school bus when the older students boarded. Instead of sitting in the back of the bus, where the older students usually sat, Jacob sat down beside Benjamin and smiled at him. From the back of the bus, Jesse noticed Jacob and Ben sitting together but could not overhear their conversation.

"Thanks for not telling on me," Jacob told Ben. "Do you want to be my friend?"

"Okay. Sure!"

"Benny, everybody thinks I am a rat and a fool. For as long as I can remember, my old man has gone out of his way to tell me how worthless I am. Maybe I am, because I was fool enough to try to live down to his expectations. But there's some good in everybody, right? I like you, runt. You are not so quick to judge."

Benjamin sat quietly. Jacob handed Ben a fresh stick of Juicy Fruit chewing gum.

"Thanks."

Ben put the gum in his pocket and would keep it for weeks.

Jacob became quiet and stared out the window. Ben lowered his gaze and through the corner of his eyes with mysterious compulsion he stared upon the bulge at Jacob's crotch. His inexplicable attraction to Jacob was followed by spontaneous involuntary arousal; he yearned for something impossible and unfathomable. He could not begin to understand what caused his obsessive craving, but he knew that his craving was real.

*   *   *

Had Wally known how it would all turn out, likely he would have done it anyway. The time was overdue for him to make a move. He and Valdetta needed to be on their own. Russell had left farming and moved away. His cousin Rayford was moving back to take over the old homestead right after Christmas 1940. Wally's mother and father and Olivia were moving to the old Swanfeather homestead at Strong City. He had just noticed the want ad in the *Cheyenne Star*, and so in his father's roadster, he rushed with his family to the Texas Panhandle, to interview for the position before someone beat him to it. The Tolleson Hereford Ranch on Mammoth Creek in Lipscomb County needed a married couple to live on the ranch, the man to participate in all the ranch work, including managing the remuda—for horseman Wally, perfect! In addition, the wife was to cook lunch for Mr. Tolleson and his ranch hands—for Valdetta, a welcome task, if it meant she would be the lady of the house. Wally, who had no interest in military service, hoped that a ranch job might qualify him to get an agricultural exemption from the draft.

The Tolleson Ranch complex sat back at the end of a gravel drive that paralleled the east side of Mammoth Creek for almost a mile south from a county road. The meandering creek was lined with giant cottonwood trees, willows, and clumps of sumac and wild plum thickets. East of the drive were stands of little bluestem and sagebrush. The landscape reminded Valdetta of a Charles Russell painting in a wall calendar that she remembered from childhood, and she felt that she could raise her family there. Gary, now four, stared out upon the creek bottom, trying to absorb everything—the Hereford cattle grazing on the slopes, the wild turkeys and the litters of New Hampshire hogs browsing open range along the creek, with piglets of various sizes following a group of sows. *Hmmn, the ad didn't mention hogs*, Wally mused. *Cattle, yes. Horses, yes. Hogs, not so good.* As they approached the ranch complex, they came upon a small pasture of sheep, and as they drove through an open gate into a corral with several horses bridled and tied to hitching posts, Wally got the picture: the Tolleson Ranch had a diversified production program.

Booger Tolleson was trying without success to saddle a high-strung, half-broke gelding when Wally stopped the car. He got out, walked up to the gelding, and took hold of its halter. "This damned little nag is trying to get himself shipped off to the glue factory," said Tolleson.

"I see the problem," Wally said confidently. "This bridle is too tight, it is pulling the bit too hard against his tongue. Here, I will let it out a hitch."

Problem solved.

The gelding settled down as Wally stroked its neck. "My name is Wally Dalkens. My wife, Valdetta, and our son Gary came with me to interview for a job. I saw your ad in the *Cheyenne Star.*"

"I'm Booger Tolleson," said the rancher as he extended his hand.

"Mr. Tolleson, as we were coming up the road, I noticed a heifer lying down in the plum bushes. She was trying to calve, and it looked like she might be needing some help. Why don't I saddle this young fella and drive the heifer up into a pen here, where we can help her?" The manner in which Wally was asserting himself impressed Tolleson, who stood quietly aside as Wally saddled the colt and rode off into the creek bottom.

Booger walked over to the car and said to Valdetta, "Mrs. Dalkens, I'm Booger Tolleson. Why don't you and your boy go to the house and look it over while your husband helps me with a heifer? Or I should say, while I help him."

Valdetta took Gary in hand and walked through a turnstile onto a flagstone walk that took her to the back door of an old ranch house of native rock that had quartered the Tolleson family for three generations. Valdetta entered an enclosed back porch that was furnished with a meat freezer, a bootjack and a coat-and-hat rack, and an inner door that led into the kitchen. The house was wired for an electric system powered by a "wind charger" and had indoor plumbing with water supplied from a deep well with a storage tank located on a high slope across the creek. The entire two-bedroom, one-bath house with basement was furnished with ranch-style furniture that Booger and his wife, Flossie, left behind when they had moved into Follett six years earlier after their second son, Ranger, was born. Dabney, their firstborn, was nine.

"Boog, Shug, I have given you two sons, and now you owe me," Flossie had insisted. "Move us into town, where I can buy fresh bread every day if I want to and I can join a bridge club and a sewing club and a Red Hats Club and go to the beauty shop and not have to sweep dirt out of my house and smell the barnyard and listen to calves bawling day and night."

Booger had resisted. He did not want to break the family tradition of inhabiting the ranch day and night, and he did not want to drive the fifteen-mile, one-way trip twice a day. Nor did he want to dip into his financial assets to pay for a house in town. "Flossie, honey, we've got to preserve our savings for droughty years and for our old age."

"Boog, Shug, you know what I want and I know what you want, and I don't know anything duller than an old couple dying off with a pile of unspent money."

Booger did not want to give in, but he did, and Flossie got not only a new house in town but also new furniture, because she threatened to pull a Lysistrata.

Valdetta had never dreamed that she might soon be living in a house with electricity and indoor plumbing. She inspected every room and peered down into the basement, which spanned the entire south end of the dwelling. Gary found a box of old toys in one of the bedrooms and occupied himself while Valdetta gravitated back to the kitchen. It was a dirty mess, from being occupied by a series of messy bachelors or slovenly women, or both. Responsively she set to work, found a dishcloth and a pail and a box of detergent, and cleaned the cabinet counter and the dining table. Then she got a broom and began to sweep the worn, linoleum-covered kitchen floor. Having grown up in overcrowded shacks and starting her marriage in her in-laws' house, she could easily turn this dwelling into her family nest and be contented here for the rest of her life.

Before the day was over, that was exactly what she and Wally came to expect.

Tolleson watched Wally bring the stricken heifer into the lot, pen her and hold her in a working chute, and help her deliver a calf. "She never could have had her baby without some help," said Wally. "One of its front legs was turned backward. The little mama could not move it up into the birth canal. I had to straighten the leg and help her deliver the little critter. It is a nice bull calf!" Wally pulled the prostrate newborn out of the chute and released the new mother, who went straight to her baby and began to lick it clean.

"I think you have earned your first day's pay," said Tolleson as he followed Wally to a water trough and watched Wally wash his arms and hands clean from the heifer's birth mucus. "Let's go in the house and talk about my job offer with your wife sitting in, since this involves her being willing to cook noonday meals for me and my ranch hands."

Valdetta was sweeping the living room floor when Wally and Tolleson entered. "It looks like my wife has already taken hold of this place," Wally commented. "Honey, I think Mr. Tolleson is going to offer me a job, but it depends on you being willing to cook noon meals for the ranch hands. By the way, Mr. Tolleson, Valdetta is a real good cook. She has been taught by my mama."

"Wally, call me Booger. Mrs. Dalkens—"

"Call me Valdetta. I'll be happy to cook a big dinner for as many as show up, as long as there is meat in the freezer."

Booger sighed with relief. It seemed that at last he had found a married couple who would provide the help he needed to keep his ranch in the black. He was ready to seal the deal. "Not only meat in the freezer," he told Valdetta, "but I will give you a line of credit at the grocery store in Follett, which I partly own, which will cover your family groceries as well as the food for the noon meals. Plus, Wally, I will pay you $120 a month, with cost of living raises every year. Plus, I will pay payroll taxes to the Social Security Administration to get you on the Social Security retirement program. Plus a week's paid vacation every year. Plus, you can use the ranch's pickup for your transportation. Plus, if you do your job and don't start smoking and drinking and neglecting the work and you stay here working until you turn sixty-five, I will let you live in this house for the rest of your life."

Wally frowned. "Booger, the deal sounds real good. I don't drink and I don't smoke, and I don't mind hard work. There's just one thing: I don't know anything about raising hogs, and I'm not enthused about learning."

"You won't need to mess with the hogs. There is a big bulk feeder about a half-mile below us here and another feeder about a half-mile up the creek, and a grain elevator from Darrouzett delivers the feed. Every three or four months we pen a bunch of hogs and ship them out, because it seems like when cows make money, hogs don't, and when hogs make money, cows don't. So we run hogs here to beat the odds. By the way, I have been appointed to the Lipscomb County draft board. If the government allows agricultural exemptions, I don't think you need to worry about getting drafted, not as long as there's plenty of young single boys in this county who've got nothing to do but meander from one beer joint to another."

"Okay, deal me in," said Wally. "If Valdetta is willing, we'll take the job."

Valdetta nodded.

"Fine. When can you start?"

"I am helping my parents move to Strong City tomorrow," Wally said. "We will move our things here Sunday. I will be ready to go to work first thing Monday."

The two men shook hands. Valdetta smiled. There was no written contract. This was December 1940. In Lipscomb County, Texas, in December 1940, a man's word was his bond.

CHAPTER 24

Old Jenks and Young Ben

Maudeen had not kept in close touch with her Swanfeather relatives since she married back in 1907, when the Swanfeathers had moved back to Fort Towson, in Southeastern Oklahoma, but Maudeen had occasionally exchanged letters with all three of her sisters, including Heticia Hettie, the Strong City sheep grower's wife. Sister Vera May had married a Hugo attorney and moved to Kansas City, and sister Willa Beth had married Rufus Swamp, a shiftless Pushmataha County farmer who never worked hard at anything. Grace had never met any of her Southeastern Oklahoma cousins until she met them at her grandmother Swanfeather's funeral at Fort Towson in 1936. Jesse, then nine, remembered his great-grandfather Jenks Swanfeather as a brown-skinned old man in a leather vest and moccasins, wearing pigtails, who chanted a dirge commemorating the life of his departed wife to the beat of a tom-tom. Janie and Benjamin remembered him not at all.

In 1937, Willa Beth and Rufus persuaded her father, Jenks, eighty-two, cranky, eccentric, and in poor health, to move with them to his old homestead near Strong City, where they could raise turkeys and live rent-free. The place had been rented out for years to cattlemen who overgrazed it badly; the pasture was overrun with sandburs and broom sedge. The turkey operation made a modest profit in 1938, but in 1939, when the drought was broken by a heavy thunderstorm, Rufus Swamp stood idly in the kitchen door and watched his flock of young turkeys lift their heads to the sky and drown. Jenks Swanfeather cursed him for his laziness and, with a loaded shotgun in his hand, ordered Willa Beth and Rufus to move off his place. For the next year he lived alone, living on a small old-age pension check from the state but rejecting help from all quarters except Heticia and Ed Galloway, who checked on him every week or so and brought him groceries. He had been diagnosed with cancer in his urinary tract. For pain relief, they brought him peyote supplied by Ed's Mexican sheep shearer. "I would let him live at our place," Hettie wrote Maudeen, "if he weren't such an old grouch and didn't dribble on my Persian rugs."

In late 1940, when James and Maudeen vacated Robert's old homestead, Hettie persuaded her father to allow James and Maudeen to move back to his homestead, where they had spent a decade early in their marriage, three of their five children having been born there. Jenks Swanfeather agreed—on condition that James build him a willow brush arbor windbreak for him in the backyard beside an old *bois d'arc* tree, build him a fire pit there, and pitch a tent for him to sleep in. "There are bad spirits in the house," he declared. "I won't go in there again." What he did not admit was that because of his urinary incontinence, he decided to live outdoors, where his urine would soak into the ground and his body odor could partially dissipate in the fresh air, and where he could prepare to pass away lying down on the ground, as he believed his Choctaw ancestors had done. In addition to a fire pit beside the willow windbreak, there was a half-buried galvanized tub inside his tent, wherein kindling could be burned for warmth, with a hole cut in the roof of the tent to let the smoke dissipate. His daughters Hettie and Maudeen failed in their attempt to persuade him to occupy a bedroom in the house.

Maudeen became reconciled to take her father three plates of food each day, provide a basin of warm water for him to sponge himself, and supply him with plenty of fresh bedding.

When James moved from Denim, he sold all his cattle and horses to his nephew Rayford, not intending to farm anymore. He was sixty-two, inflicted with arthritis or rheumatism or gout, or a combination of them all. He had hidden much of his pain from his family because on the old homestead, Wally had done most of the hard work for him. James would try to earn income by using his carpentry skills to make wooden feed troughs, wooden toys, cabinets, benches, tables, and chairs, which he could sell at weekend flea markets, and he would help Maudeen raise turkeys for the Thanksgiving market. While James respected his father-in-law, he believed old Jenks was mentally imbalanced and there was no purpose in even talking to him. He would see to it that old Jenks had fuel for his fire pit, with blankets and cowhides and kindling for the fire tub for cold nights in his tent.

In Maudeen's return to her father's homestead, there was nostalgia about the decade she and James had raised their family there, but there were new elements. The house now was wired for REA electricity. With the money he got from selling his cattle, James bought his wife a new refrigerator, an electric iron, a toaster, a radio, an ice cream freezer, a curling iron for Olivia, and hanging from the ceiling in every room, an electric light bulb! No more cleaning the soot from kerosene lamp globes, no more trimming their wicks. On the dining room wall hung a telephone, connected to a four-party line. Their phone number was two "shorts" and one "long." Maudeen dashed to the receiver every time the telephone rang, whether it was her number or not. So did the ladies of the other three numbers. There would be no secrets in that neighborhood.

"Mrs. Dalkens, please get off the line. This call is for me!"

"I just wanted to know if there was some sort of emergency. I have organized a Ladies Helping Hands Club, so I need to know what's going on, to be prepared."

"No emergency, Mrs. Dalkens. Now please get off the line and let me tell Rudella what I heard about the Mortensons' breakup."

"Well, all right, but when you finish your call, please phone me back and tell me."

The move to Strong City provided Olivia an opportunity to redirect her life. She enrolled as a second-semester junior at Strong City High School in January 1941, with serious intentions to do her best with her schoolwork. She excelled in a combination speech-journalism class. She became the editor of the high school quarterly newspaper and won the starring role in the junior-senior high school play, a melodramatic murder drama. After Olivia's recent marriage and widowhood, the immature Strong City High School boys who drooled over her did not interest her. Instead, she went out of her way to make friends with her coed classmates, who considered her so beautiful and sophisticated. She spent hours helping them style and care for their hair, clean their complexions, trim and polish their nails, and color-coordinate their wardrobes. They idolized her and followed her around the school campus like ladies-in-waiting. Her friendship with them was genuine; she received a sense of satisfaction that she was helping them prepare for what likely was to be the forthcoming sole romantic period in their lives, when they would be courted by their boyfriends and future husbands.

One of Olivia's friends and classmates, Joanie Penteen, showed Olivia a picture of her twenty-one-year-old brother, Othel, who had been drafted. "I have written Othel about you, Olivia, about how pretty and smart you are, and he wants to exchange letters with you. Will you write to him, please?"

Olivia studied the photograph. Othel looked handsome in his neat army uniform, but Olivia wondered what he might look like in a pair of blue jeans or overalls. "Well, I am still sort of in mourning," Olivia said evasively.

"Please write to him, Olivia. He is serving our country, for goodness' sake!"

"Well, all right. But what can I say to someone I don't even know? Tell him to write me first, and I promise to answer."

And so the Dalkens transition to another community transpired relatively smoothly. James repressed his longing for the old homestead and turned to his woodcraft. Making things with his hands was good therapy—when the arthritic pain was not debilitating. Back at Denim, Grace suffered separation. Her parents had moved thirty-five miles away. Wally and his family were seventy-five miles away. Russell and Donna Belle were three hours away. Grace helped her cousin Rayford and his wife, Ella, settle into the old homestead, but she had difficulty communicating with Ella, who was a first-generation German American whose family had spoken German in their home.

"Rayford has started drinking a lot," confided Ella. "He is dying inside, with all his boys gone, and so am I. Grace, pray to God that our sons won't have to go fight a war against Germany. I have cousins there. I would lose my faith."

Daniel's and Grace's attendance at Strong City's First Baptist Church had been sporadic, at best, until her parents moved into the community. Now they attended regularly, because after church services, they visited James and Maudeen and Olivia and shared Sunday dinner. Grace usually brought fried chicken and baked bread and fresh garden vegetables. Maudeen baked a pie or a cake and cooked mashed potatoes and gravy, and unless the weather was terribly cold, with her new electric freezer, she made ice cream for dessert, usually vanilla, but if Maudeen had the fixings, it could be banana, peach, strawberry, chocolate, or Jesse's favorite—tootie fruity, containing pineapple, cherries, and nuts.

On their first Sunday visit to the Swanfeather homestead, Grace's children were surprised to learn that a strange old Indian man living in a tent in the backyard was their great-grandfather. "He is your mother's mother's father," explained Daniel. "Grandmother Maudeen's father is one-half Choctaw."

"What is his name?" asked Janie.

"Jenks Swanfeather."

"What is a *swanfeather*? How does an Indian get a name like that?"

Maudeen explained that according to the family tradition, when one of her ancestors was born generations ago, a white swan's wing feather floated down from the sky. Jenks sat on a cowhide under the brush arbor and watched them stare at him from the house and reacted angrily by bellowing at them to go away. Respectfully they retreated into the house and concentrated on their Sunday meal.

"I love my father," Maudeen said, "but in his condition, it is best just to leave him alone." After dinner, she prepared a platter of food for Jenks and asked Jesse to carry it out to the suffering old man. "Tell him who you are. If he understands, he will be glad to learn you are family." Jesse picked up the tray of food and bravely headed for the backyard. Benjamin's curiosity outweighed his apprehension and spurred him to accompany his brother. Janie was frightened and refused to go.

"Great-Grandfather, I am Jesse Bird, your daughter Maudeen's grandson. This is my brother, Benjamin. Here is your dinner."

Remaining silent, Jenks sat stoically on his cowhide, his shoulder draped with a red-and-black zigzag-striped Indian blanket, and did not acknowledge Jesse. Uncomfortable, nearly nauseous from the odor of dried urine, Jesse turned to go. Before following Jesse, Benjamin smiled at the old man and impulsively took a stick of Juicy Fruit chewing gum from his pocket and placed it on the old man's tray. Then, before departing, Ben raised his right hand and said, "How!"

Jenks chuckled and reached for his fork. "How, yourself," he said, smiling. "Why aren't you afraid of me?"

"I can outrun you, I think."

Jenks chuckled again. "Tell Maudeen to send me a saltshaker next time," he said. As Ben turned to go, Jenks asked, "Are you coming again next Sunday?"

"I think so. I hope so," Benjamin replied.

"Next time you come, please bring me a big paper bag full of sagebrush," Jenks requested, "and if you can find it, a pint of skunk berries."

Harvesting a bagful of sagebrush was not difficult for Benjamin, but skunk berries posed a challenge. "Daddy, what are skunk berries? And where can I find them?" Ben asked on their drive home from Strong City.

"They are fuzzy, smelly, red-skinned seeds from stinky little shrubs that grow along the side of the road," Daniel answered. "Why do you want to know?"

"Great Brownfather asked me to bring him some sagebrush and some skunk berries next Sunday," Ben revealed.

"I think he wants to burn stinky stuff in his fire pit to drown out the bad smells around him," Jesse speculated.

"Benny, he's a crazy! He'll scalp you!" said Janie. "You had better stay away from him!"

"Your grandmother Maudeen says he screams obscenities and beats on his drum half the night," said Grace. "Daniel, next Sunday, you should accompany Benjamin if he goes to Grandpa's tent."

"I don't think he is a threat," Daniel responded. "Jenks is a miserable, sick old man who is being eaten alive with the spread of prostate cancer. He crawls around on the ground because I don't think he can even stand up. I am not surprised that he has taken to Benjamin and Benjamin has taken to him."

"So stop at a skunk berry patch and help me pick him some skunk berries," Benjamin requested.

So they did, and the next Sunday, after church, Benjamin rushed out to Jenks as soon as they reached the Swanfeather homestead and presented Jenks with a paper sack of sagebrush and a pint jar of skunk berries. Jenks was sitting in his tent because a sharp norther had dropped the temperature near to freezing.

"Great Brownfather, here is the sagebrush you asked for, and a jar of skunk berries."

Jenks took a fistful of dried sagebrush and threw it into the fire tub. Immediately the tent was permeated with a pungent odor that masked the smell of dried urine. He tossed a handful of skunk berries against the inside wall of the tub, away from the flames, to allow them to scorch. A second acrid smell soon blended into the air.

"Maudeen says you were born with a hood on your head," said Jenks. "Is that true?"

"I don't know, Great Brownfather, I don't remember a thing about it."

"She said that you cried like a donkey, and the first time she changed your diaper, you peed in her face," he said, chuckling, then took a serious tone. "Choctaws think that being born with a membrane covering your head brings you big medicine, superpower, instinctive knowledge, the gift of prophecy, the heart to understand everyone, the ability to walk in others' shoes. You will grow up to think both like a man and like a woman. You will have the power to bring peace between struggling souls. From you, good will may spring forth and spread over others. Benjamin, I know this is true. Last Sunday, when your hand reached out and placed the stick of chewing gum on my platter, I felt your blessing. Now that you are near me, the pain in my belly is not so bad."

"I'm glad you're feeling better," Benjamin said, "but I don't know what you are talking about. I do not know Choctaw ways. I'm just a little bird. Can you teach me something about Choctaws?"

"Let me study the white smoke that is rising from the sage," Jenks said. "I will look for a sign for you." He gazed into the fire and lapsed into silence. Silently, Benjamin sat beside him for several minutes, then as the smoke began to burn his eyes, he withdrew quietly. Old Jenks seemed lost in another dimension.

*   *   *

Was old Jenks fooling Benjamin, was he fooling himself, or was there validity to his perception that Benjamin had a special destiny? Throughout the following week, when he was not in a near stupor from his pain or from the peyote, Jenks contemplated which elements of Choctaw heritage he should try to instill in his small fair-skinned descendent. Indeed, which elements of his Choctaw heritage had even survived within him? When his Choctaw father had abandoned his Indian wife and married his white mother, for love, and when Jenks had married a white woman, for love, they had willingly forfeited their tribal purity. His older, full-blooded Choctaw half-brother, Lacrosse Swanfeather, whom he loved, had criticized Jenks and his father for drifting away from the tribe. "The Great Spirit will punish you for turning away from the ways of our fathers," he had warned Jenks. "Your children will be weak in body and spirit and will suffer from their inability to harmonize with the natural world."

"Nonsense!" Jenks had replied. "There may no longer be such a thing as a full-blooded Choctaw. We have been mixed with Spaniards and Chickasaws and French and, especially, English for generations. Your mother, Wilma McCurtain, was considered full-blooded, but her surname is derived from an old Scotchman who married into the tribe in order to gain access to tribal lands. Lacrosse, my dear brother, your first name is French in origin, so don't preach to me about tribal purity. And as for having the ability to harmonize with the natural world, Choctaws do not possess a monopoly. I will teach my children and grandchildren what they should know, whether it comes from tribal heritage or common sense, or public school, or the Good Book."

Now, as his time was running out, what should Jenks share with his special great-grandson?

The following Sunday, Benjamin brought the old man another sack of sagebrush. "Thank you, Benjamin, for the sage. I will need no more. I will not live to see the grass turn green."

"Great Brownfather, next month, I will become seven years old. Whatever you tell me about Choctaw ways, I will always remember."

"Child, I have given this much thought. You are too young to grasp what I want to tell you."

"But I am already going to school. I can count to two thousand. I know all the nations of Europe! So tell me what I need to know and give me a chance to see if I can remember it."

"You sure are a stubborn little man. All right, I will tell you what this old Choctaw thinks you should know. You are growing up in a world that is changing beyond my ability to understand. My old house here on the homestead, built before Oklahoma became a state, is now wired for electricity and telephone. Maudeen thinks this is good, and so it is. But it is also dangerous, because the easier life becomes, the farther people are pulled away from the natural world. So remember this, Benjamin: do not lose touch with the natural world. You and your children will need clean water and fresh air and earth's bounty, but the danger of the modem age is that the cities and the machines and the new entertainments and inventions will pull you away from nature, and you won't even know what you are missing: the tranquility of the prairie, the beauty of the hills and sky, the romance of the woods and valleys."

"I believe that I can remember that."

"Oh, you do, do you? So in your own words, tell me, what do my words mean?" challenged Jenks.

Confidently, Benjamin responded, "Outdoors is better than indoors, country is better than town. And do not let new toys turn you into a toad frog."

Jenks chuckled. "You have said it better than I did."

"Great Brownfather, teach me something in the Choctaw language."

"I will teach you an important, all-purpose Choctaw phrase that you can use for many situations. Repeat this until you know it well: 'Nay-Boom Be-Man Tauntay! Nay-Boom Be-Man Tauntay!'"

"Nay-boom be an auntie! Na-boom be an auntie!" said Ben

"No, no! *Nay-Boom Be-Man Tauntay! Nay-Boom Be-Man Tauntay!*"

"Nay-Boom Be-Man Tauntay! Nay-Boom Be-Man Tauntay!" Benjamin said it correctly. Jenks was pleased. "Great Brownfather, what does it mean?"

"Sometimes it is a friendly greeting of good will. When you meet someone, you are saying, 'We may not have much, but let us make the best of it, thank the Lord for a good day!' Sometimes it can be a prayer asking for strength to overcome any problem. It can be a chant that calls forth extraordinary power for those whose hearts are pure, those who will use their power for the sake of others. It can be used to lay a blessing on someone else. It can also be used as a requiem, uttered over the body of a person who has just died, repeated over and over at the scene of death, before the body is removed for burial, to release the soul of the deceased from the dead body, so that it can soar with the Great Spirit. The person who is chanting the requiem should do so while beating a tom-tom, striking the drum each time the word *boom* is uttered. Benjamin, when I die, I want you to chant 'Nay-Boom Be-Man Tauntay' for me, sitting beside my body until the undertaker comes. Will you do it?"

"Yes, Great Brownfather, if I am here. You will need to die on a Sunday, after church, around noontime. But do you really want to die?"

"Yes. I have carried this pain long enough. Get my drum and chant for me now as I ask the Great Spirit to come for me soon about noontime on a Sunday."

For the next thirty minutes, Jenks stared into his fire tub, watched the pale-gray stream of sage smoke waft up through the hole in the top of the tent, while Benjamin sat beside him and chanted,

"Nay-Boom Be-Man Tauntay, Nay-Boom Be-Man Tauntay," striking the tom-tom reverently with each *boom*.

*   *   *

On the Saturday afternoon following Benjamin's seventh birthday, Jenks Swanfeather lapsed into a coma. His urinary tract had completely shut down. James and Maudeen carried him to the house and laid him down on a bed in a corner bedroom, bathed his sour old body, dressed him in clean clothes, then notified his children and his brother Lacrosse and summoned them to his bedside. Lacrosse arrived about sundown and sat at his brother's side all night. He believed that upon Jenks's death, his body should be taken to Southeast Oklahoma and be buried in an Indian cemetery, but he did not offer to pay the expense. Hettie and Ed Galloway agreed to have Jenks buried in the Galloway family plot in Cheyenne City Cemetery.

Next day, when Daniel and his family arrived from church, Olivia rushed out to tell them. "Our grandfather Jenks passed away about an hour ago. Daddy has called the undertaker. Uncle Lacrosse and Mother and Aunt Hettie have laid Jenks out on a bed. The other children are coming tomorrow for burial services in the Cheyenne City Cemetery."

The family embraced one another then gathered in the dining room, and James read aloud the twenty-third Psalm. Benjamin slipped out to the tent to retrieve Jenks's tom-tom, returned, and went into the corner bedroom unnoticed. As soon as James had finished reading the psalm, they heard the child's voice, faintly at first, then gathering volume. "Nay-Boom Be-Man Tauntay, Nay-Boom Be-Man Tauntay, Nay-Boom Be-Man Tauntay," he chanted, with a subdued beat of the drum with each *boom* emanating from the bed of the deceased.

"Isn't that Benjamin's voice? What is he saying?" asked Olivia.

"Benny told me Great-Grandfather Jenks had taught him a Choctaw chant," said Janie, "and asked him to sing it over his body when he died so that his soul could leave and go soar with the Great Spirit."

If Jenks did not believe in Jesus, the chanting will not do any good, thought Jesse, who had the grace not to say it aloud.

The chanting and the drumbeat continued. "Nay-Boom Be-Man Tauntay, Nay-Boom Be-Man Tauntay, Nay-Boom Be-Man Tauntay…"

"What is he saying? Whatever it is, it is getting on my nerves," said Aunt Hettie. "Uncle Lacrossse, is it Choctaw?"

"It is not Choctaw. It is gibberish!" exclaimed Lacrossse as the chanting and the drumbeat continued. "Jenks has played a cruel joke on the boy."

"Grace, go in there and make him stop," ordered Maudeen.

"Wait a minute," said Daniel as he walked to the door and looked in on Benjamin, who was sitting cross-legged at the foot of the bed, facing the deceased. "Nay-Boom Be-Man Tauntay, Nay-Boom Be-Man Tauntay, Nay-Boom Be-Man Tauntay, " Benjamin continued, cradling the tom-tom between his legs.

Daniel returned to the group and said, "Leave him be. Benny believes he is carrying out the last wish of his great-grandfather, and he is doing so with as much courage, compassion, and loyalty as any man could have. And right now, what Benjamin believes is more important than what actually might be the truth."

James concurred. "A seven-year-old in there with a dead body. You know, he's got to be brave. Folks, I'm not saying that we all neglected the old man, because there wasn't much old Jenks would let us do for him. But somehow only Benjamin got through to him, as though he realized what old Jenks was going through, as though he himself could walk in the old man's moccasins, and he reached out to help Jenks face the greatest challenge we will all have to face someday ourselves."

Grace arose and went into the corner room to sit beside her brave little youngster. The rest of the group sat quietly around the dining table, drinking coffee and postponing dinner until the hearse arrived. They listened to the simple, innocent, subdued soprano voice of the seven-year-old lad chanting for the safe passage of their loved one, looking death in the face and not turning away.

*   *   *

Grace's overprotective tendency toward Benjamin might have saved his life on the last Monday in February 1941. He awoke with severe pain in his abdomen, a distended belly that was too painful to touch. Grace had read an article in a quarterly magazine about the causes and symptoms of acute appendicitis and concluded immediately that Benjamin was in crisis. "Daniel, we have got to get this child to a hospital at once!"

Daniel was hesitant. They could not afford a hospital bill. Perhaps Benjamin was only constipated. "Try some mineral oil," he suggested.

Grace's motherly instinct would harbor no delay. "Daniel, we have got to get this child to a hospital! Now!"

Had they delayed, it might have been too late. The surgeon reported that had they not arrived when they did, Benjamin's appendix would have ruptured in a short time, flooding his abdominal cavity with poisonous infection. The surgical nurse stripped him and swabbed his abdomen down with alcohol and applied ether. Ben gagged and lost consciousness almost immediately. Later, he would remember the walls and roof of the hospital crashing in upon them all, everyone screaming, equipment smashed, *din, din*, the whole world being sucked into a chasm. Of course, it was hallucination caused by the ether. He also remembered drifting in weightless, formless suspension, floating up to a corner of the ceiling, watching the surgeon make the incision, grasp an intestine, and slice off the tiny appendix infected by a poorly chewed, fermenting pinto bean lodged there since Sunday dinner, when Ben ate too fast in order to get to dessert—a small bowl of chilled, sliced peaches topped with whipped cream.

As Ben floated suspended against the ceiling and watched the surgeon seal the incision, a bright light shone around Ben and a sweet, grandmotherly angel held his hand and kept his heart pumping until he slowly descended and returned into his body, descending into a deep unconsciousness that lasted until he awoke hours later in a hospital bed in a children's ward, suffering a staggering headache and uncontrollable nausea until the effects of the ether gradually subsided. Through numbing dizziness, he saw a swirling image of his mother holding a damp washcloth, mopping his brow and catching his vomit in a bedpan and gently so gently mothering him back to consciousness.

Benjamin remained hospitalized for four days, totally bed-ridden, a perfect, smiling, cooperative patient for the nurses who attended to him, although one morning defensively he accused them of spilling water in his bed.

Daniel applied for and received a grant from his state representative's office to cover the hospital bill. When Ben was dismissed, the hospital staff gave him a ceramic owl penny bank and a shiny quarter to put into it.

Back at home, Grace changed his bandages and continued to hold him bedridden until his stitches were removed; he was not allowed to walk, because in those years, the medical practice was to keep surgery patients nonambulatory until after their stitches were taken out.

After a week, Ben's stitches were removed; his incision was healing satisfactorily. Grace helped him out of bed and discovered that Ben could not walk: his leg muscles had collapsed from lack of exercise.

For the next week, the family worked with Ben and his normal strength returned, but overly cautious, Grace held him out of school for three weeks. Janie brought him homework every day, which Benjamin mastered in short order, with time on his hands to wonder about his out-of-body experience in the operating room in the hospital, which he likened to certain recurring dreams he had been experiencing during the night and during his afternoon naps. In Ben's recurring dreams, he often went soaring and drifting several feet off the ground, with arms outspread, rising over treetops and rooftops and fences, escaping the pull of gravity. Ben's dreamed sensation of being weightless and airborne and the memory of being out of body during surgery led him to conclude that he, Benjamin Ray Bird, was not just a flesh-and-blood entity—he could exist outside his body.

C H A P T E R   2 5

Going to War

In March 1941, Olivia received a short letter from Othel Penteen introducing himself; the letter included a wallet-size snapshot of him in his military uniform. He asked her to send him a photo of herself so that he would have something to remind him of the nice things back at home for which he was serving his country. How could she say no? She sent Othel a provocative snapshot of herself in a halter top that Rory Laird had taken of her standing beside a boulder with a backdrop of ponderosa pines in the foothills outside Las Vegas, Nevada. In April 1941, Othel wrote Olivia a warm note asking her to go on a date with him to the movies at Elk City when he came home on a short furlough in May. She accepted, and when he came home on leave, she was pleasantly surprised to discover that Othel was at least as attractive as his photograph, a pleasant companion whose quiet sincerity and sense of responsibility reminded her of the qualities she had always found attractive in her sister's husband, Daniel. They kissed several times on their first date. By June 1941, their weekly letters were laced with romance. Othel was going to be stationed hundreds of miles away, and Olivia felt she could be safely sweet with him without making a permanent commitment.

*   *   *

In May 1941, when the school term ended, Jesse harnessed his horse, Jodhfur, to a two-wheeled cart and went about the neighborhood collecting scrap metal. The repair garage in Denim was purchasing the scrap iron and shipping it to the Gulf Coast, where British agents were buying it to send to England, to use in their war against Germany. A year earlier, scrap metal was being shipped to Japanese agents on the West Coast, but Japan's aggression in Asia throughout that summer and Japan's alignment with Germany and Italy in the Axis Alliance in September 1940 set the stage for a worldwide war, for the Axis powers, each intent on military expansion, pledged mutual assistance in event that their aggression caused other nations to enter war against them.

Benjamin tried to comprehend America's increased concern over Japanese expansion in October 1941, and his world expanded considerably. The *Kansas City Star* provided maps of trouble spots in the Far East and the Pacific Ocean, and Ben asked his mother to paste them to the wall beside his cot. The news articles, which he read with his father's assistance, confused him. "Daddy, what are the Axis countries going to do? Are they going to fight their enemies with axes?"

"No, son, the Axis countries have chosen to help one another as the war spreads and other countries start fighting against them. It will be the Axis powers against the Allied powers."

"Oh, I see. The countries choose up sides, like us kids do when we play Red Rover."

"President Roosevelt is concerned that Japan plans to attack our possessions in the Philippines, Guam, and Midway Island," Daniel explained.

"Why are they our possessions?" asked Ben. "How did we get them?"

"We won them in the Spanish American War in 1898."

"So we don't want Japan to take them away from us?" contemplated Benjamin. "We fight wars and take things but we don't want anybody else to do the same thing?"

"It's more complicated than that," explained Daniel. "What we've done is for our national security."

The drift toward war continued throughout autumn 1941. In the Atlantic Ocean, the United States Navy undertook convoy protection of American merchant vessels carrying goods to Britain as far as Iceland, and the president asked Congress to authorize the arming of US merchant vessels and permit them to carry cargoes to nations fighting Germany, who resented America's drift from neutrality. An American destroyer, *Kearney*, was torpedoed and damaged by a German submarine on October 17, and on October 30, the US destroyer *Reuben James* was sunk by a German submarine in waters near Iceland. The newspaper maps of war activities became too numerous to paste on Benny's wall, so he began stacking the maps under his cot.

In November 1941, Grace baked four-dozen peanut butter Christmas cookies and mailed them to Dewey Hargrove, whose ship, the USS *Oklahoma*, was stationed at Pearl Harbor in Hawaii. "Do you want to include our final payment to Dewey for the items we took when we moved from his parents' farm?" Grace asked Daniel. His 1941 cotton harvest had been the best yet; not only had Daniel paid the government loan in full, he had also paid off the final balance on their longstanding debt to Jabour's Grocery in Roosevelt, bought a new shorthorn herd bull, and renewed their subscription to the *Kansas City Star*.

"Yes, we'll send him a check for $150, and that will pay us up with our young sailor friend. We'll be debt free!"

*   *   *

On Sunday, December 7, 1941, in an effort to bring peace between two deacons who had been competing bitterly for the same tract of rental farmland, Brother Nathan Jones of the Strong City First Baptist Church took his sermon text from the sixth chapter of the Gospel of Luke:

> *Love your enemies, do good to them which hate you,*
> *Bless them that curse you, and pray for them*
> *which despitefully use you.*

*And to him that smiteth thee on the one cheek
offer also the other; and for him that taketh away
thy cloak forbid not to take thy coat also.*

*Give to every man that asketh of thee; and of
him that taketh away thy goods ask for them not
again.*

*And as ye would that men should do to you, do
also to them likewise.*

"Do unto others as you would have them do unto you" might or might not work between God-fearing Baptist deacons but cannot possibly pacify aggressive nations, as America learned before nightfall that fateful day. The Daniel Bird family and the James Dalkens household were finishing a bountiful Sunday dinner at the Swanfeather homestead when the telephone rang, one long, sustained emergency ring that summoned everyone on the party line. Maudeen rushed to receive the call. "It's Mrs. Logan. Mr. Logan just heard terrible news on the radio! Japanese airplanes have attacked our Navy at Pearl Harbor!"

James went to his radio and turned to a news station. Everyone gathered around the radio and gazed upon it as though they were watching the images that the news reporter's words conveyed. The attack had begun at 7:55 a.m. Honolulu time and was continuing. Three US battleships were sunk, one was grounded, the USS *Oklahoma* capsized. Altogether, nineteen ships were sunk or disabled, and over 2,300 military personnel were killed.

"This is war," James muttered. "No doubt about it."

"Othel will have to go overseas, I just know he will!" Olivia wailed dramatically.

Daniel drove his family home, all of them in stunned reaction to the Pearl Harbor attack. Grace's concern about Dewey's situation on board the USS *Oklahoma* brought tears. "We need to hear from Dewey," she said.

Next day, President Roosevelt announced that a state of war existed between the United States and the Japanese Empire, whereupon Germany and Italy declared war on the United States. Grace wrote Dewey a short note. "Dewey, God protect you! We are desperate to hear from you. Please write!" The dreaded answer came two weeks later. The box of peanut butter cookies for Dewey was returned unopened. A special edition of the *Kansas City Star* arrived on December 17, containing an updated list of the missing in action at Pearl Harbor and a list of the known dead. Dewey's name was included on the list of the latter.

*   *   *

After December 7, 1941, the old Hargrove jalopy never started again. Daniel cleaned the carburetor, changed the spark plugs, bought a new battery, installed a new ignition, cranked and cranked, but nothing worked. So when Dewey's Christmas package was returned unopened, Daniel used the $150 check and made a down payment on a used green 1937 Ford two-door.

The celebration of Christmas 1941 across America was dented by the absence of military personnel, who were being shipped overseas. By Christmas, the Japanese had invaded the Philippines and had taken Guam and Wake Island. The price of chocolate, pineapple, and coffee skyrocketed, and soon price controls and rationing were underway. Grace received a ration book limiting how much of certain items her family could purchase. Sugar became scarce; she used molasses for sweetening. Butter was rationed; she churned more butter than ever and shared with neighbors who had no milk cows. In the Dalkens clan, the shortage of coffee was a constant crisis; they were English in origin, but tea would not do. At school, the children were encouraged to buy war stamps, ten cents each; filling out a card, $1. Five $1 cards could be exchanged for a $5 war bond. Patriotism flourished. Anti-Japanese and anti-German sentiment was on the rise.

In June 1942, bride's month, Othel Penteen came home on a short leave and asked Olivia to marry him before he was to be shipped overseas. Hesitant, she said, "We do not really know each other."

"But we don't have time to wait," he declared. "This war will take a big chunk out of our lives."

"But I still have a year left of high school," she said.

"Married girls can go to school," he declared.

"I have already been married," she told him.

"I know that. It doesn't matter," he replied.

"Othel, I can never bear children," she confessed.

"I know that. We will adopt," he countered.

Olivia should have told him that although she was fond of him, she was not in love with him, but instead, she doubted that she would ever have a chance to marry a nicer man. She admired him and understood his urge to share the intimacy of marriage with her in case he did not survive the war; at least he would have the memory of their honeymoon. Then, too, there would be benefits: the prestige of being a soldier's wife, the possibility of financial assistance, life insurance payoff in case he did not return, discount shopping at a federal post exchange. His absence might make her heart grow fonder.

And so Olivia and Othel Penteen became statistics in a national phenomenon of hasty GI marriages. Without any of their family present, they got married in the Roger Mills County judge's chamber and honeymooned for two days and nights, bouncing on an innerspring mattress in a motor hotel on Route 66 in Shamrock, Texas. James and Maudeen accepted the news with subdued consternation; their lovely daughter had acted hastily again. Othel's mother, who did not like Olivia because of her past, was livid. To placate her, a Jehovah's Witness, Othel promised to declare himself a conscientious objector so that he would not be sent into battle. Two months later, he was in England, driving fuel transport trucks from the docks to military installations in the fog at night without lights on, through total blackouts, on narrow winding roads in an unfamiliar country where people drove on the left side of the road. A photograph of his wife, Olivia, was clipped to his dashboard.

*　　*　　*

It was the second Saturday in September 1942, one week following the beginning of the school term. Benjamin was relocating his cow-and-calf bottle ranch to an area behind the chicken house, at the request of his mother, who was tired of having dozens of empty old bottles lying around on the north side of the house. Ben was stretching strands of twine along an imaginary fence line of sticks when a shadow suddenly hovered over him. It was Jacob Jiggs, who had emerged from the deer crossing that spanned the great ravine between the Jiggs and Bird farms. Ben jumped with surprise, then smiled warmly when he recognized Jacob, who placed his hand on Ben's shoulder. Jacob's touch thrilled him.

"From our porch I saw you playing out here behind the chicken shed, Benny, and I thought I should come over and ask a very special favor of you," said Jacob. "Don't talk loud, because I don't want your parents to know I'm here."

"My daddy and Jesse are over at Rayford Dalkens's place, helping him haul some corn in from the field. Mother and Janie are inside, doing some sewing," said Benjamin. "What happened to you this week? I noticed you missed the last two days of school."

"I dropped out," Jacob said. "I hitchhiked to Elk City and joined the army. I leave next week for basic training."

"But you're not old enough to go to the army!" Ben protested.

"I lied about my age," Jacob confessed.

"But why?"

"You've got to promise not to tell."

"Jacob, if you tell me a secret, you know I won't tell."

"I know. That's why I am telling you my deepest secret. I am in love with Henrietta Hayes. I wake up every morning thinking about her sweet face, and I go to sleep every night dreaming about being in bed with her. The problem is, she won't have anything to do with me. At school, she won't even talk to me. She thinks I am scum, because of stupid things I have done in the past. So I am going to make myself over. I am going into the army, and I am going to turn into a hero type and make her proud of me. And this is what I want you to do: I want you to write me a note every two or three weeks and let me know what is happening with her, what she is doing, who she is running around with, what she has been wearing, how long her hair is, everything you can describe. I know you are smart enough to write letters."

"Mother and Daddy won't let me send letters to you," Benjamin said bluntly. "They won't let me get mail from you."

"That is why I am going to send my letters to you at school. I will send you stamped, self-addressed envelopes to use. When I get a good picture of myself in my uniform, I will send it for you to slip into Henrietta's purse or book bag. Maybe I can gradually win her heart. Will you do it for me, little buddy?"

"I will try," Ben promised. "But I have a deep secret too. I will tell you, if you promise not to tell anyone else, because people will think it is really bad."

"I promise," said Jacob. "If I can trust you, you can trust me. What is it?"

Ben looked down. With deep embarrassment, he confessed. "Ever since that day, right over there in that cowshed, when you nearly peed on me, you asked me if I liked the looks of your *thing*, and you asked me if I wanted to touch it, and I have not stopped thinking about it. So that's my secret. I want you to show me your *thing*, and I want to touch it."

Through several moments of tense silence, Benjamin did not look up.

Recalling the incident, Jacob was regretful. "That was one of the stupid things I never should have done. I am so sorry, little buddy, to have affected you like that. Please forgive me."

"I just want to look at it and touch it," Ben said. "Please."

"Benny, I told you I am trying to turn over a new leaf. If I do what you are asking of me, it would be *so wrong*. You need to forget it. It must never happen."

"All right, then," Benjamin replied. "I know there will be so many things in life that I want but can't have. Jacob, I will pray for you every night when you are in the war. And when you come back home, maybe I won't be so messed up."

"There is nothing wrong with you, Benny, but you need to match up with somebody your own age. Life can make us want to do many foolish things. When I was your age, I wanted to be a boar hog, because a boar's *thing* is shaped like a long corkscrew and I always thought that would be so wild! As far as I know, hogs are the only animals that actually do screwing!"

Benjamin laughed. They shook hands and parted.

Jacob's first letter to Ben arrived at Denim Public School two weeks later. The principal turned it over to Benjamin and asked why he was writing to Jacob the dropout. "It's my defense project," said Ben, "writing to service men to keep up their spirits."

September 19, 1942

Dear Jacob,

 I got your letter at school. Mr. Selmon asked why we were writing.

 I said war project. I saw HH in the hall at recess. She wore blue today. Her hair was pretty and long. She is pretty. You have good taste. All the girls are trying out for basketball and cheerleader next week. I will let you know. Be careful.

       Love,
       Ben

October 3, 1942

Dear Ben,

 Thanks for writing. I am going into paratrooper school after basic training. It will give me a chance to do good. Enclosed is a picture of me in my dress uniform that you need to slip into Henrietta's book satchel. Do you think I will look good to her? If you get caught, just tell her the truth.

       Love,
       Jacob

October 16, 1942

Dear Jacob,
This little spy did good. I put your picture
in HH's purse during lunch hour today. Nobody
watches a guy like me. I liked your picture. Can you
send me one?

Love,
Ben

*   *   *

The first large-scale American involvement in the war against Nazi Germany occurred in late 1942 in North Africa, where British forces under the command of General Bernard Montgomery were trying to drive German and Italian forces under General Erwin Rommel off the African continent. Rayford Dalkens's sons, Jeff, Johnny, and Harvey, participated in an amphibious operation commanded by General Dwight D. Eisenhower, their unit landing on November 8, 1942, at Casablanca on the Atlantic coast of Morocco. Benjamin attempted to follow war developments by studying the newspaper maps in the *Kansas City Star*, but war correspondents were hampered by news blackouts of major military operations, so the folks back home were left to wonder and worry about what could be happening to their sons, brothers, husbands, cousins, and neighbors in the war operations. For many, the suspense was unbearable. Rayford Dalkens drank heavily during the intervals when he could hear nothing from his sons, when he knew they were in the thick of battle.

A brief letter from Harvey Dalkens to his parents on the anniversary of World War I Armistice Day was gutted with censored sections, large groups of blacked-out sentences, but Rayford and Ella could read between the blacked-out lines. Their sons had been in battle and had escaped injury, but the war was only beginning. How could they and their sons endure such painful apprehension?

On November 15, 1942, Ella Dalkens walked all the way from the old homestead to Daniel's and Grace's, arriving shortly after breakfast. "Rayford did not come home last night," she fretted. "He has been drinking a lot ever since our boys were shipped overseas, and I am afraid he has crashed his pickup into a ditch somewhere. I was going to see if he might have run off the old bridge below your house, but I am afraid of what I might find. I wonder if Daniel could—"

"Of course, I will go find Rayford and bring him home," Daniel replied. "Ella, you sit down and rest, and Grace will bring you a fresh cup of coffee. Do you know where Rayford goes to buy his whiskey?"

"In his shirt pocket, I found a receipt from the service station over on Highway 33 across the state line, the store that has a sign on its roof that says, 'Eat Here and Get Gas.'"

Driving out upon the road, heading south toward Denim, Daniel did not bother to stop and look beneath the bridge, for they would have heard a crash had Rayford's pickup driven off into the chasm. When he reached Denim, Daniel drove slowly and looked about and noticed Rayford's pickup at the gin, parked beneath the suction hose that, during cotton harvest, pulled the cotton into the bowels of the gin. He found Rayford stretched across his pickup seat, soused, snoring, reeking of rye whiskey.

"Rayford, wake up! I have come to take you home."

"Ella, have we heard anything from our boys?"

"Ella isn't here. This is Daniel. Ella's waiting at our house for me to bring you home."

Slowly Rayford roused, got out of his pickup, and stumbled to the wall of the gin, where he leaned over, vomited, urinated, and began to weep. "Daniel, I have this deep fear that my boys are going to get killed in the war. I can't stand it!"

"Rayford, get in my car and I will drive you home. We'll come back for your pickup when you get to feeling better."

"I hate to cause you any trouble."

"You are not causing me trouble, Rayford, but you are driving your dear wife crazy. You have got to control your drinking. Be as strong as your sons are strong as they face the enemy. Draw on your inner strength."

"I guess I don't know how to do that. I don't seem to have inner strength. Where does it come from?"

Daniel helped him in the car and turned toward home. "I can only speak for myself. I find strength through my faith. You and Ella need to go to church. Your church is the filling station for the soul."

"But I pray all the time. I pray to God to protect my boys, but I keep seeing Harvey and Jeff and Johnny blown to bits! And so I hit the bottle…"

"Well, I won't preach to you, Rayford, but if you don't get ahold of yourself, you are going to die before your sons do. Count your blessings, man. You have the old homestead in your possession. You have a loving wife, and you have three fine, courageous sons. So stop being afraid of what might happen to them. Fear is a deadly enemy. It destroys more men than bullets do."

"You are right, of course. Daniel, thank you for being here."

CHAPTER 26

Good Uncle, Bad Uncle

Russell and Donna Belle's fourth child, another son, was born in October 1942. His name was Robert Alan Dalkens, because Donna Belle and Russell had hoped for a daughter, and they had selected a name, Roberta Alana Dalkens. Robert would be called Bobby Alan. His genes held the athleticism of his father and his brothers, although he looked like his grandfather Morrison Lee, who, in retirement, had come to live next door to his daughter and her family in Colbert, Oklahoma. Bobby Alan would be introduced to the Dalkens clan on Thanksgiving weekend 1942, because they would all be gathering at Wally's home on the Tolleson Ranch in the Texas Panhandle.

Wally was proud to host his family, proud of his home, proud of his job, proud of being on his own, proud of his son Gary and his lovely wife, Valdetta. Valdetta was having a problem pregnancy, however: sporadic, early labor pains. Her doctor told her to stay in bed until February 1943, when she was due to deliver. And so Maudeen and Grace spent actual Thanksgiving Day at the Swanfeather homestead cooking dishes to take to Wally's for the weekend, when Russell's family would visit the Tolleson Ranch and they would all be together again. Wally had shot a wild turkey tom and was thawing out a huge beef roast for a Saturday feast. Maudeen and James would arrive at Wally's on Friday so that Maudeen could prepare the meat dishes.

Benjamin spent Thanksgiving night with his grandparents so that he could travel with them to Wally's, where he and Gary would have an extra day to play together. This was the first time Benny had been alone with his grandparents, and he felt a bit uneasy, for he could never quite comprehend what his grandmother thought of him. He loved her because his mother loved her, but there was always a sense that a personality clash was hovering under the surface of their relationship.

Next day, on their trip to Wally's, James stopped at Uncle Ed's and Aunt Hettie's sheep ranch for a brief visit. Ed had asked James to construct an extension on his shearing shed and James was going to measure the site and estimate what the project was going to need. When Benjamin emerged from the car, Uncle Ed's sheepdog snarled at him. "Benny, that dog thinks you are a varmint because of your size," said Granddad Dalkens, "so you'd best go with Grandmother into the house and visit with Aunt Hettie."

Ben followed the ladies into the house quietly and uneasily; this was not a child-friendly atmosphere, either outside or inside. Hettie Galloway said she loved well-behaved children but she had never found one. To her, children were best not to be seen and not to be heard. She had borne three of her own, but apparently, only their accomplishments had been dear to her, since their successes reflected to her benefit. Each of her children had only one child each, for much of the same reason. They visited seldom, and that was enough for all. None of them were there for Thanksgiving.

Maudeen, on the other hand, basked in her offspring and her grandchildren and excitedly told her sister Hettie about Russell's new son. To her, having grandchildren was a clear accomplishment in which she excelled over her competitive sister. "We have our ninth grandson," she bragged, "Russell and Donna Belle's fourth boy. I think they are going to grow a basketball team! They will be at Wally's tomorrow. We will be missing Olivia, for she is spending Thanksgiving weekend with her in-laws. She isn't happy about it, but family obligations have to be respected. Right, Hettie?"

Hettie was not listening. She frowned as she noticed Benjamin, wide-eyed, hands in his pockets, wandering about, looking at the shelves and cabinets of knickknacks, figurines, crystal, doilies, china, travel souvenirs, silver, and pewter. "Maudeen, that child is making me nervous. Make him sit down."

"Benjamin, sit in that chair by the dining room door and don't touch a thing," Maudeen ordered.

"No, not that chair," Hettie interrupted. "He will wipe snot on the fabric. Make him sit on that wooden chair by the bay window."

Respectfully Benjamin sat down in a straight wooden chair and waited patiently for their trip to Gary's to resume. In a low monotone—ostensibly so that Benjamin could not hear—Maudeen proceeded to tell Hettie about Valdetta's problem pregnancy. "We're all just worried to death," she said. "Valdetta thinks she tore something loose one day when she was carrying a pot roast to the dinner table. Her doctor says her baby is due in mid-February, so she has to stay in bed for more than two months. We are hoping for a girl. Grace's daughter, Janie, is our only granddaughter so far. Wally and Valdetta haven't told little Gary anything about the new baby yet, in case things don't turn out right. Hettie, please pray with us that Valdetta will deliver a beautiful, healthy child."

Benjamin was sitting only eight feet away, and of course, he heard every word. He felt that Gary should be told about the new baby because it was going to be Gary's sister or his brother, and he should have a chance to prepare for it.

Benjamin's reunion with Gary was a joy ride, literally. Within thirty minutes after Ben's arrival, the cousins were on horseback, riding freely across the prairie. Nearly two years younger than Ben, seven-year-old Gary, hyperactive and fearless, reined an old brown mare named Bumpy along a trail that paralleled Mammoth Creek. Bumpy was a kid's horse that dutifully and patiently went through whatever paces her young master challenged her to do, in exchange for being let out of the boring corral. Ben rode behind Gary, holding on to saddle straps to keep from bouncing off; he fell in love, not with the rough-riding horse, but with the spaciousness and the mystique of the ranch. They traveled two miles before coming to a fence. Gary rode into the midst of a herd of Herefords, forty cows and two young bulls and two-dozen identically colored, white-faced calves.

"When I get big, I am going to have prize calves and show them off in a big show ring and win all the ribbons," Gary boasted, "and when I am grown, I am going to be the judge because I will know everything about the cattle business because my daddy is a rancher and he will teach me everything." Gary's future was set. He was confident.

How convenient, thought Ben, feeling a touch of jealousy.

"Nay-Boom Be-Man Tauntay," said Ben.

"What?"

"May your plans come true," said Benny. "You are so lucky to be growing up on a big ranch. God must really like you to put you here where you can ride and ride and ride without bumping into anything. Gary, are you wanting a baby sister or a baby brother?"

"No, I want a puppy. For Christmas, Daddy has promised me a puppy."

"No, your mother is having a new baby in February. Do you want it to be a boy or a girl?"

Gary answered, "I don't know anything about a new baby. I have been asking for a puppy!"

Gary was confused, and as soon as they returned to the ranch house, he went right to his mother's bedside. "Mama, Benny is telling me we are getting a new baby. What's he talking about? What about my puppy?"

Valdetta was upset. She realized that Ben had overheard Maudeen tell someone about her health crisis, and Valdetta feared that Maudeen might be judging her harshly for having a problem pregnancy. Maudeen quickly diverted attention to Benjamin. "Hmmn, little pitchers have really big ears! I simply asked Hettie to say a prayer for your safe delivery, Valdetta, dear, and the little snitch was listening in. Benjamin, why did you tell Gary something you knew you were not supposed to tell?"

Benjamin felt a burning condemnation hovering around his heart. Grandmother was accusing him of doing something horribly wrong. "I—I thought Gary had the right to know that he was going to have a little brother or little sister," he said contritely. "He will want to give the baby a birthday present." He knew he should not argue with his grandmother; it was an argument he could not win.

"It was none of your business, you little busybody," Maudeen charged. "I knew we should not have brought you without your mother. Now you apologize to Valdetta about gossiping about her, and you and Gary go back outside and stay out of my way in the kitchen."

"I am sorry," Ben said, laden with guilt.

He and Gary spent the rest of the day exploring along Mammoth Creek. Ben tried his best to stay out of Maudeen's presence until his family arrived around midmorning the next day. Russell and his family also arrived about an hour before the delayed Thanksgiving meal was served. Benjamin could hardly wait to greet his cousins, and especially his uncle Russell.

"Hello, Tuff Nut!" said Uncle Russell.

"Hello, Uncle Tuff!" replied Ben, smiling.

"What do your straight As on your report card look like?" asked Uncle Russell.

"Boring," replied Benjamin. "I got an A- in spelling. Some silly English words don't sound like the way they spell."

"A B would drive your mother into a fit, I suppose," said Russell.

"And a C would drive me out of the family," Ben quipped.

"A D would banish you to the Sahara Desert," Russell speculated.

"And an F would turn me into a stink bug!" said Ben.

Russell laughed; he appreciated Benjamin's attempt at humor.

At dinner, Wally carried Valdetta to a sofa in the living room, where most of the family members had brought their plates full of food. James offered a blessing for the food and the preparers; asked guidance for Vernon and Kirby, his two missing grandsons; and thanked the Lord for the handsome infant Bobby Alan.

After the meal was consumed and the leftovers put away and Valdetta returned to her bed, the family gathered outside for photographs to be taken. The *four musketeers*—Jimmy, Benny, Donny, and Gary—posed for their annual photograph with the ranch's huge hay barn as background, whereupon they ran into the barn, climbed into the loft, and spent most of the afternoon making a hideout in the hay. Janie resumed her infatuation with Donna Belle's toddler, Will, and kept him pampered and entertained for the rest of the visit. Wally took the men to the remuda corral and showed off the saddle horses, proud as though they were his own. Russell and James were pleased to see that Wally had found his *niche* and seemed to be situated for life.

Daniel and Jesse returned to Denim in the late afternoon to do the milking and evening chores; James and Maudeen would deliver Grace, Janie, and Ben to Denim on their return to the Swanfeather homestead the next day.

That evening, after a meal of leftovers, Donna Belle and Grace made a large pallet of quilts and blankets on the basement floor for Jimmy, Benny, Donny, and Gary to sleep on. The boys had played hard and were tired. Benjamin and Jimmy took turns telling stories until Donny and Gary fell asleep; soon, all four of them were slumbering.

Before retiring, Russell took Grace aside for a confidential conversation. "Sis," he said, "on the job, I have been having dizzy spells up on the scaffolding. I told my foreman about it, and he sent me to a doctor, who diagnosed vertigo and gave me some pills to take. But I think my dizziness might be caused by that concussion I suffered when I broke my leg in my last football game at Hobart, because the headaches are the same as I had back then, including brief blackouts when I can't focus on a thing."

"Russell, you ought to change jobs," said Grace. "Ask your foreman to let you do something less stressful that will keep you on the ground."

"But I can't do that," he replied. "If I don't work on the scaffold, my pay will be cut in half. Sis, for the first time in my life, I am making decent money for my family. The kids have good clothes. I bought Jimmy and Donny new baseball gloves, bats, and cleats, things otherwise I could not afford. With Will and Bobby Alan coming along, I just can't cut back. Donna Belle deserves the best of things, and it's my responsibility to provide. She doesn't know about my dizzy spells, so I am telling you this in case something happens to me. She would get insurance and monthly Social Security income, so that takes some of the worry away, but if she has to raise our four boys on her own, she will need some help."

Russell paused for a moment and stifled a potential sob. His hands were shaking. Grace took his hands and covered them with her own.

"Donna Belle's father lives next door to us now," he continued, "but he is too old to help, and he plans to return to Alabama to live with his sister. Dad and Mother would devote themselves to help with the boys, I know, but have you noticed how hard it is now for Dad to get around, let alone do physical things? And Mother, bless her heart, she would do her *Helping Hands* thing, and she would just take over, and that would not be good for Donna Belle. So I guess what I'm trying to say is, if, God forbid, something happens to me before my kids are grown, I'd like to think that you and Daniel would somehow be there for her and the boys. I have not said anything to Daniel, but I remember what a giving soul his mother, Clara, was, and I know that he inherited her compassion. Daniel's influence would be good for my sons."

The portentous tone of Russell's conversation made Grace tremble. "Russell, when you start feeling dizzy, grab ahold of something and take deep breaths to keep oxygen flowing to your brain!"

"But if I can't stay conscious, I won't be able to hold on to anything, and if I fall, I will be a goner. So I am trying to be responsible, and I am genuinely sincerely asking if you and Daniel would be there for my wife and kids!"

"Of course we would do what we could, my dear brother, but lift your spirit and let your mind dwell on watching each of your sons grow up to be as good a man as his father, and we will just pray that God will watch over us all and take care of all our needs!"

Grace and Janie slept that night on the living room sofa's pull-out mattress, with little Will curled up against Janie. Grace lay awake for an hour, unable to get Russell's concerns out of her mind. In the darkness her eyes drifted to the living room window, before which the children's winter coats were tossed on chairs that formed an outline in silhouette resembling the form of a man's body lying in a casket.

Next morning was frosty and bitterly cold, so after breakfast, the boys returned to the basement and used their pallet as a wrestling mat, taking turns wrestling one another, an activity in which Jimmy and Donny indulged in almost every day. "I have to let Donny win ever once in a while," said Jimmy, "or he gets too mad to see straight." Unexpectedly, Benjamin considered the competition a lark, like a box full of puppies romping together, and he laughed his way through one loss after another. Not one of them could exert himself without flagellating, and they could not hear the farts without laughing. Ben could not match the strength of any of his cousins except young Gary, and when he held Gary down, his advantage did not last because Gary got angry and bit him on his forearm. Benjamin laughed through the pain and let Gary turn him over and pin him down.

A crisis occurred when Donny and Gary were matched, because neither of them knew how to lose without losing his temper. Donny pinned Gary down easily and held him down, while Gary writhed and snarled, then burst into an angry scream, and began to cry loudly.

The basement door opened. "What's going on down there?" asked Donna Belle.

"We're just wrestling, Mama," Jimmy explained. "Gary got mad because he thinks he always has to win!"

"Benjamin, you should not wrestle! You will reinjure your back!" shouted Grace from the top of the stairs.

"Mother, it is too late! Everyone has already beat me!" Ben laughed. "But don't worry, I will not wrestle for a living!"

"Play something else! Play May I! Take baby steps and giant steps across the room and back and stop fighting one another!"

The cousins decided to don their wraps and go outside to explore the creek and the hillsides, looking for mastodon bones, gold nuggets, arrowheads, agate stones, animal dens, and hidden treasure. The sun had burned off the frost, and the temperature was rising.

The 1942 Thanksgiving weekend at Wally's home created lasting memories. When his uncle Russell loaded his family for the return trip to Colbert near Lake Texoma, Ben stood at the driver's side of Russell's vehicle and waved goodbye to Jimmy and Donny.

Russell reached out his open window and shook Benjamin's hand. "Keep up the good work, Tuff Nut," he said.

"I'll see you later, Uncle Tuff!" Ben answered.

"I'll see you later, little Nut," Russell replied.

Despite the awkward incidents with his grandmother that Benjamin had experienced at the beginning of his first visit to the Tolleson Ranch, he would do it all over again. Indeed, he hoped to return at every opportunity, for he was drawn to the pristine atmosphere along Mammoth Creek, the western aura of the sage-brush-covered hillsides, the open skies and the presence of animals, both domestic and wild. He recognized and valued the mystique of the land, far more than even Booger Tolleson could comprehend.

*　　*　　*

December 7, 1942

Dear Benny,

　　Enclosed is a Christmas Card to Henrietta that I want you to slip into her things. I signed my name to it. If she catches you, tell her that I love her and I am going into paratrooper school. The dollar is for you to buy yourself something for X-mas.

Love,
Jacob

December 20, 1942

Dear Jacob,

　　Today is the last day of school before Christmas. I took a big chance trying to put your card into HH's lunch sack and she caught me. She asked am I the one who put Jacob's picture in her bag. I said yes because he likes you and I said I would. She said you look nice and she thinks you are doing good, but she has a boyfriend for now, who would get mad if she writes you. She said maybe later. Thanks for the dollar.

Love,
Ben.

*   *   *

What of Dexter Dalkens in prison? A virile man among sexually driven men without women. Dexter was one of the more aggressive alpha males who bullied weaker inmates into submission.

He signed up to work in the prison's woodworking shop, where he carved wooden figurines with Western motif, such as horses, boots, longhorns, cowboys, spurs, wooden Indians, tomahawks, polished and varnished and very salable in the prison gift shop. One day, with five years to go on his sentence, one of the closely monitored knives assigned to him disappeared, and this caused other inmates to view him cautiously as a secretly armed and dangerous man one did not want to upset. Dexter often drifted near the thin edge of trouble, but his need for the outdoors and his love of working with animals found him successfully striving to qualify to work as an orderly at the prison livestock farm, where he trained horses and worked with cattle and gained prestige as one of the major organizers and participants in the annual Oklahoma State Prison Rodeo.

On Christmas Eve 1942, James and Maudeen, who were spending the holidays with Russell's family at Colbert, traveled to McAlister for a supervised visit with Dexter at the state penitentiary. Although they were pleased to see that Dexter was in good health, it was a painful experience to find their firstborn locked into a lifestyle of incarceration that seldom brings out the best in one. They presented him with a small collection of Western pulp fiction, which he had always enjoyed. They could see a threatening cold and wrinkled expression in and about Dexter's eyes that caused them to realize that prison life creates in one a different humanity. He had aged several years.

Maudeen attempted to establish a casual atmosphere for the visit. "Dexter, I received a note from Leona last week," she said, "with some good news about her and your sons. The war has created a teacher shortage throughout the country, which has led the state of Oklahoma to liberalize the certification of teachers for the duration, so through the placement office at her college, she has been hired to teach a third-grade class at Washita Public School in Caddo County, in a village six miles west of Anadarko. The district school board officers have already moved her to a two-bedroom frame house near the school, about half a block from the school and the grocery store. Washita School goes through twelfth grade, so Vernon and Kirby can finish their schooling there. Isn't that wonderful!"

"Yeah, I guess so," said Dexter. "I have lost track of how old they are. What grades are they in?"

"Vernon will be sixteen in April, and he is a sophomore," said Maudeen. "Kirby will be fourteen next month. He is in eighth grade."

"How tall are they now? Do they look anything like me?"

"Vernon is as tall as his mother," said James, "and looks like her. Kirby is about the same size and is built like my late brother Robert. But he has your hawk eyes. They would love to hear from you, Dexter. You need to write them, general delivery, Washita, Oklahoma."

"They don't need to hear from a jailbird," Dexter replied. "I am trying to get my sentence reduced for good behavior and get a parole, and when I get out, I am going to become a fishing guide on Grand Lake in Northeastern Oklahoma. All I will need to get started is a bass boat and a tent and some fishing gear, then as soon as I get released and get set up, I will contact my boys and take them fishing."

Dexter did not ask about Leona or comment on her. Actually, at that very moment, Leona was humming an upbeat melody for the first time in a long time. Having moved into her modest Washita residence, wherein her sons would share their own bedroom, she was unpacking her books and her dishes and her teaching aids, putting clothes away, watching her sons carry their fishing poles down the road to the bank of the Washita River just a quarter mile away. Leona rejoiced. She now had a regular salary, barely at subsistence level, but at least she could plan a budget and she could set money aside to cover summer school expenses. She could finish her degree! She felt liberated, liberated from abject poverty, liberated from the negative influences in Altus that were threatening the future of her sons.

Altus was not a corrupt town, not a cesspool of evil, just an average town that had its own share of scoundrels. Vernon and Kirby had spent too much time on Altus streets loitering among the loiterers, and Leona had been unable to do anything about it. Vernon worked two evenings a week setting pins in a downtown bowling alley. If Vernon had been corrupted by the bad influences abounding in the pool hall and bowling alley, he was clever enough to hide it from her. But Kirby! Kirby was always open to suggestion, vulnerable, fun-loving, and lustful. He practically lived in the Rack-It-Up Pool Hall and became hard to beat at pool and billiards. His proficiency kept money in his pocket, and he bought so much candy his teeth began to decay. Thank goodness he inherited his love for fishing from his wayward father; at Washita, Kirby would now spend hours baiting hooks on throw lines and catching catfish along the banks of the Washita River. Leona promised to cook everything the boys caught.

*   *   *

When Leona moved from Altus, she tried but failed to persuade her father, Aaron, to move to nearby Anadarko, where boarding rooms were available; Aaron refused to move that far from Clara's grave at the Altus Cemetery. He had returned later than usual from his fall cotton-picking expedition to West Texas, and he postponed his post-Thanksgiving visit to Daniel's until Christmas and postponed his customary psychosomatic illness until the day after Christmas, when Daniel would have time to go across the Texas-Oklahoma border for a fifth of whiskey for his medicinal toddy.

After Christmas 1942, right on schedule, Aaron's visit to Daniel's was followed by aches and chills, a trip to the border, and hot toddy. Aaron recuperated on Benjamin's cot in the corner, where the natural light from the window was too faint for him to read the last chapters in the book of Revelation to fulfill his commitment to read the entire Bible each and every year. Respectfully, eight-year-old Benjamin came to his grandpa's rescue; he sat on the cedar chest at the north window and read aloud the last chapters—17 through 22—which included a passage in chapter 21, wherein the author describes heaven or the holy city as a great city 1,500 miles square, with walls two hundred feet thick, a city of pure gold, with streets of pure gold. Benjamin skillfully sounded out the big new words he did not know. As Aaron lay quietly and listened, the elderly man's lips moved in anticipation of every word; most of them he remembered because he had read them so many times.

"Thank you, Benjamin, for finishing my Bible reading for me this year. You did very well."

"Grandpa, going to heaven sounds pretty nice," offered Ben, "to see such a gob of gold, but I don't think I would want to live there very long. With its high thick walls, it sounds too much like a shiny jail! I want my heaven to be all natural and wide-open, like a prairie, with springtime and green grass and new baby calves everywhere. Should I pray a lot and ask God for a special place like that?"

"Benjamin, be careful you don't upset God. To be on the safe side, study the Bible and follow the Word."

CHAPTER 27

The Year 1943

January 5, 1943

Dear Benny,

Happy New Year! I loved your last letter. As soon as Henrietta breaks up with her boyfriend, let me know. Give her this snapshot of me taken in my swim trunks when I won the swim competition over my whole unit. Don't you think I'm in pretty good shape? My unit will be shipping out to —— next ——.

I think this will be a good year.

Love,
Jacob

January 13, 1943

Dear Jacob,

I hate to tell you HH is not in school here anymore. Jesse said she got p.g. and has moved to El Reno with her boyfriend to get married. Can I keep your picture? You look so good in your swimsuit. I am sorry about HH. But don't worry, you are

349

so good-looking you will find someone easy. Every
time you pull your rip cord, say 'Nay-Boom Be-Man
Tauntay!'

Love,
Ben

*   *   *

On Saturday, January 16, 1943, the death notice took a roundabout path. Donna Belle's father, Morrison Lee, tried to telephone Wally Dalkens at the Tolleson Ranch, but the rickety telephone line was grounded somewhere, so he directed his call to the Tolleson residence in Follett. Booger took the call, grimaced at the message, picked up his Bible (he never studied it, but in a crisis, he was comforted by holding it to his chest), drove to the ranch, and delivered to Wally the tragic news: working Saturday overtime on a high scaffolding on the project to build a railroad bridge across the Red River below Denison Dam, Russell Dalkens had either blacked out or lost his balance and fell seventy feet to his death. Donna Belle was distraught. The Dalkens family needed to go to her right away.

Flossie Tolleson came to stay with bedfast Valdetta and the child Gary while Wally delivered the tragic news to his family and helped them through the heartbreaking experience. When Wally arrived to tell Grace that her beloved brother had been killed on his job, Grace knew before Wally even got out of his pickup that he was bringing dreadful news.

"It's Russell, isn't it?" she asked.

Wally nodded. "He fell to his death this morning about eight thirty."

Grace shrieked, stumbled to the bed, and buried her face into her pillow, weeping uncontrollably. Daniel went to her, placed his hand on her back, and patted her gently. The children watched their parents in stunned silence as they absorbed the news. Janie then fell to her knees at the foot of the bed, and in response to her mother's heartbreak, she began to sob. Jesse bowed his head and prayed that his family would have the strength to cope with the tragedy, prayed for the salvation of Uncle Russell's soul, and prayed for the wisdom to understand God's will. *Why would God take a young father who had four sons to raise?*

Benjamin's empathy for the suffering of others expanded greatly from observing how family members coped with his uncle Russell's accidental death and burial. He watched his mother recover her composure, for the sake of setting a strong example for her children. She stopped sobbing but could not keep her eyes dry or her chin from quivering. He watched her pack church clothes for herself and for Benjamin. She was accompanying Wally to the Swanfeather homestead to break the news to their parents, then they would travel to Colbert in James's roadster. Benjamin, nearly nine, was coming along so that he could be with ten-year-old Jimmy and eight-year-old Donny, to help them cope with the trauma of losing their father. *Cope, cope.* Daniel, Jesse, and Janie were staying home to do chores, then traveling a day later for the funeral.

When James and Maudeen received the news of Russell's death from Wally and Grace, James staggered to his knees, shaken beyond measure, and pounded the floor with clenched fists.

"Noooo-o o-o," he cried. "It can't be!"

Grace threw her arms around his shoulder. "There, there."

Maudeen's response was instinctive: a nerve-shattering shriek followed by a sustained wail, shrill and sharp to the heart, the wail of a grieving Choctaw mother. She tried to pull her hair, but Wally restrained her.

Benjamin could not bear to see his grandmother so distraught—she who had often seemed cross and thoughtlessly impatient with him. He went to her side and hugged her around her waist, then he and Wally each took her by the hand and led her to a chair. Olivia cried quietly and helped tend to her parents. She loved Russell, but she had never been close to him; he had married and moved away when she was only five years old. Dutifully she helped pack their clothes, made sandwiches for the trip, and shared the driving to Colbert with Wally.

Tightly fitting in James's roadster, the family found comfort in one another. As they traveled across South Central Oklahoma, they shared their favorite memories of Russell, as though their memories could make him seem alive. James allowed that Russell—unlike Dexter—had never given him a serious discipline problem.

"Why, no," Wally agreed, "Saint Peter is going to have a hard time finding a blemish on Russell, of any kind whatsoever."

Silently, slowly, Benjamin absorbed the reality that his beloved role model was gone, he who had made sure that Benny would not be left out. Russell had seen to it that the *three musketeers* would be the *four musketeers*; he had recognized that Ben's achievements would come not from his muscles but from his intelligence, and Russell's supportive encouragement had helped Benny feel good about himself and face life's challenges with confidence.

The family's thoughts turned to foreboding for what the future might hold for Donna Belle and her sons. "She will need help," said Maudeen. "We will all need to live close by. We will need to help her raise those boys. She must not move to Alabama to be near her father's relatives. She must never remarry. I could not stand to see another man take Russell's place."

Olivia offered the possibility that if Donna Belle wound up in hard straits, she and Othel could raise Will and Bobby Alan as their own. Grace revealed to them her conversation with Russell on Thanksgiving weekend at Wally's, when Russell requested that she and Daniel *be there* for Donna Belle if something should happen to him. "He had a premonition," said Grace.

Aware that his family was threatened by new and potentially divisive forces of change, James began to contemplate a strategy. In the few years he had remaining, what could he do to hold his family together? As they crossed the Washita River Bridge near Paul's Valley, he was struck with the fact that the old Washita River Valley strung them together like a cord, from the Strong City community where he lived; to Leona, Vernon, and Kirby's new home near Anadarko in Caddo County; to the Washita River arm of Lake Texoma, where Donna Belle and her sons were awaiting their fate.

Donna Belle would be receiving an insurance settlement that should be large enough to purchase a small farm. During the next several months, he could help her find a suitable farm, which Daniel could operate until Donna Belle's sons were mature enough to take over. Living nearby, Grace and Daniel would be a great help to Donna Belle raising her sons. Ideally, her new farm should be located near Anadarko, near Leona and his grandsons—to tighten the family circle.

The Swanfeather homestead was about to be sold to settle the estate, so Maudeen's portion could be used to buy a small house in a town near Donna Belle's farm. James could do carpentry work or open a small repair shop, and Maudeen could cook in the school lunch program or open a small laundry or whatever.

Arriving at Colbert, the family found Donna Belle heavily sedated, sitting in a rocker, holding three-month-old Bobby Alan, who was drowsily fretting because his digestive system was upset by the sedatives that were passing to him through his mother's breast milk. Donna Belle acknowledged each of them with a mournful sob as each of them leaned down to embrace her.

Three-year-old Will, who recognized them from their Thanksgiving together, asked, "Did you bring Daddy? Where's Daddy? When is Daddy coming home?"

Grace took him aside and told him, "Janie is coming tomorrow. Tomorrow you can play all day with Janie."

Morrison Lee and neighborhood ladies were taking care of household matters. The dining table was overflowing with love offerings of food dishes prepared by sympathizers from Russell and Donna Belle's rural Methodist church.

"Where are Jimmy and Donny?" Ben asked them.

"They're over at the baseball field," he was told. "Go east a block and you will find them."

Benjamin found Jimmy and Donny fully engrossed in a game of work-up, running the bases and batting again and again without fanning or being thrown out, besting all other players who were their contemporaries from all over town. Ben was struck with his cousins' concentration on the game—hadn't they just lost their father! Their vigorous activity seemed to be their way of coping; instead of denying their loss, they were ignoring it, filling the void with frenzied physical activity.

Sitting through the funeral service next day was, for Ben, a heartbreaking experience. Dry-eyed Jimmy sat beside his granddad in the little country Methodist church two miles outside town, sniffled, but would not look at the open casket. Donny sat beside his uncle Wally and chewed on his fingernails, his gaze also directed away from the coffin. Sitting beside his brother Jesse, Benjamin succumbed to his personal grief, wiping his tears on his shirtsleeve as he looked at the body of his beloved uncle laid out in a new dark suit he had never worn before. *Why am I crying when his own sons are not?* he wondered. *Don't they realize they will never again have their father?* During the brief funeral sermon, Ben began to move his lips, silently uttering, *Nay-Boom Be-Man Tauntay, Nay-Boom Be-Man Tauntay,* unobtrusively clicking his thumbnails together with each *boom,* as though he were participating in the release of Russell's soul from his now-useless, handsome, lifeless body.

The service ended with a tenor—the choir director—singing *a cappella* the family's religious theme song, "In the Sweet Bye and Bye," as friends and coworkers, then relatives and close family members, passed by the open casket. Ben held Jesse's hand as he took a final look at his uncle's face, uttering one last silent *Nay-Boom Be-Man Tauntay,* keeping Jesse's hand as the procession walked outside to the freshly dug grave site in the picket-fenced cemetery shaded by giant post oaks behind the church building. The congregation held together like a single animate being as pallbearers and funeral directors carried the casket to the grave site and rolled it onto its stand. After a brief reading of scripture and a final prayer, the casket was rolled down into the grave, and the pallbearers—all first cousins of Russell—tossed clods into the grave, the service's final punctuation.

Indelibly, the event would be stamped in Benjamin's memory: Granddad turning away from the grave, collapsing to his knees in grief, being uplifted by Wally and cousin Rayford; Donna Belle being helped—practically carried—to the funeral director's limousine by the minister and Daniel; Olivia and Grace embracing each other, sisters in mourning. A clump of female relatives surrounded Maudeen, flourishing tear-dampened hankies, consoling her as she wailed, "Why me! Why my dear Russell, my dear and precious baby! Why me! Why me!"

Jimmy and Donny stood beside the grave, picking up clods and throwing them against post oak tree trunks to watch the dirt shatter. Ben continued to wonder about their stoic failure to grieve. Was it because they were ignorant and innocent of future uncertainties they might face without their father's guidance? Or was it that their father had already instilled in them the confidence to face the future without him? Benjamin looked up into the branches of the tallest post oak, under which Russell's grave was sheltered, and noticed a brief flurry of rustling leaves.

Was that Uncle Russell's spirit rising into heaven? So long, Uncle Tuff! To your reward! Thank you for helping me feel important!

The procession returned to Donna Belle's house, where during the funeral service, Janie and Will had stayed and played and where a covey of church members had remained to care for the infant Bobby Alan and prepare for the brief family reunion, with friends and relatives filling the home with supportive hugs and subdued laughter and paper plates full of tasty foods, holding reminiscences and cups of coffee, admiring Russell's and Donna Belle's sons, stirring from room to room and place to place like a game of musical chairs, where all the walls were lined with folding chairs from the funeral home. The post-funeral visitation lasted into early evening, when everyone but the immediate family departed. Then the walls closed in on Donna Belle and her fatherless children.

*   *   *

Valdetta Dalkens delivered a healthy, beautiful daughter on February 14, 1943, Ladena Lynn Dalkens, six pounds, two ounces. James and Maudeen went to see her before she was a week old. Maudeen beamed over their second granddaughter. Said James, "One life ends, another begins. Blessed be the name of the Lord!" Gary drew a picture of a spotted Shetland pony for his baby sister and otherwise left her alone until she could react to him. Wally liked to hold his lovely little daughter but changed no diapers.

Back at Colbert, Morrison Lee stayed with his newly widowed daughter until she could find direction. Donna Belle accepted her father-in-law's suggestion to use Russell's life insurance to buy a small farm where she could raise her sons in a safe, healthy environment in the midst of Dalkens relatives. She depended on James to find a suitable location and wished that the move could take place during the summer so that Jimmy's and Donny's change of schools would go smoothly. James and Maudeen began to spend weekends with Leona and her sons at Washita, using her home as a base of operation from where he could search for a farm for Donna Belle. In June, while Leona attended college summer school, they stayed with Vernon and Kirby and scoured Caddo County for a suitable farm.

In June 1943, Olivia Dalkens Penteen graduated from Strong City High School. She would have been salutatorian had she not transferred so many credits from Denim. Her journalism instructor gave her a letter of reference, for which she received a job offer to be a cub reporter for *The Lawton Constitution*. She and her sister-in-law, Joanie Penteen, moved to a small apartment in Lawton, just two blocks from one of the main gates into Fort Sill Military Reservation, where Olivia could shop on discount as an army wife at the post exchange. Her first months at the newspaper were spent answering telephones and writing ads for the want-ad section. Soon Joanie became homesick for her boyfriend and returned to Strong City, but Olivia remained in Lawton because it was modern enough to have many amenities and she saw opportunities there. She hoped Othel could transfer to Fort Sill when he returned from Europe. Her letters to him were loaded with family news:

July 17, 1943

Dearest Othel,
Your sister Joanie has moved back to Strong City to be near her boyfriend. They are really serious about each other, and I think they will get married

as soon as he finds a job. Good luck to him in finding work in Roger Mills County!

I am still taking phone calls and writing want ads at the newspaper, but the editor says I can write some freelance articles and submit them for consideration for publication.

My dad and mother have used her share of the Swanfeather estate settlement to buy a little two-bedroom frame bungalow in Apache, a nice little town in Caddo County about fifteen miles southwest of Anadarko. They are staying with Vernon and Kirby at Leona's in Washita until Leona finishes her summer college courses, then they will move to Apache. Dad has found a 140-acre farm for Donna Belle to buy; it is located ten miles north of Apache. She has signed the papers but does not gain possession until the current owner, Sid Withers, harvests his crop and moves away this autumn. The place has a two-story, four-bedroom house for her and her sons, and down the road about a quarter mile, the farm has a three-room, mother-in-law cottage for Daniel and Grace's family. Daniel will operate the farm until Jimmy gets old enough to take over. They will move during the Christmas holidays so that the kids can change schools between semesters.

Darling, you will be so proud of me when I tell you that I am volunteering two nights a week at the USO. All the soldiers at Fort Sill seem to be homesick, so volunteers bake them cookies and play music for them and give them a cozy place to get away from their commanding officers for a little while. I go there with Mrs. Jakes, our landlady. I help her coordinate the refreshment table and mostly just keep the coffeepot going. It is my little part in the war effort!

Sweetheart, I miss you so much! When you finish this letter, please kiss the lipstick kiss I place here below my name.

Love,
Olivia Penteen

*   *   *

Daniel's crops that summer promised a fair harvest, but the prospect seemed anticlimactic. He had learned how to get the most out of the sandy, wind-swept field, realizing that the best he could produce was not going to be very much. As early as July 1943, he had decided that instead of moving his animals and farm implements to Caddo County, he would sell Hector and Bill and all his cows and his farm implements in a public auction, hoping to raise enough capital to buy a used farm tractor and a small herd of younger, more productive milk cows for Donna Belle's farm.

During the summer months and into the fall school term, Grace remained anxious to move to Caddo County to be near her parents and to help her dear sister-in-law raise her four sons. Meanwhile, changes were taking place in her own children that concerned her deeply. Jesse turned sixteen in July, and when school started in September, he stayed preoccupied with girlfriends. Grace appreciated his enthusiasm about being in school, where his girlfriends were, but she was concerned that his grades were noticeably below his potential to achieve. He had launched a campaign to convince his father to let him use the family car on Saturday nights, and Daniel was gradually giving in to the pressure.

Janie was nearly thirteen, and early puberty was turning her into a lithesome, moody young lady, pretty as a princess but unsure of herself and a head taller than most of her contemporaries; she often slouched and stooped to appear shorter. She heard, "Janie, stand up straight!" several times each day. She had bouts of mild depression that brought inexplicable inertia, followed by a rush of high energy. She could take sheets of newspaper and cut out a dress pattern for her size, and if she had the material, she could use Grace's sewing machine to put a new dress for herself together in short order. She asked her mother to let her hair grow out; she would not wear her hair short with bangs again. One day she would experiment with a touch of rouge and face powder then next day be turned off by the very thought of it.

Benjamin, now nine, was changing too. Although he had hardly grown at all for the past year, there was nothing babyish about him any longer. The day before school started, he put all his cow and calf bottles into a gunnysack and dragged them to the family dump ground in a wash in the back of the pasture. He was not through with pretending, however. He was now in fourth grade, and his new teacher, Mrs. Spurlock, scheduled a talent show in last period each Friday, if the class had done well enough that week to be rewarded. Ben planned to sing songs he had learned from Jesse's radio and steal the show! He started paying attention to the appearance of his clothes and his hair. He kept his fingernails clean and actually polished his school shoes at least twice a week.

Ben's first performance was a headbanger. He walked to the front of the class with a swagger and belted it out, as uninhibited as though he and Janie were playing show business at home in their clubhouse down in the cellar:

> *Drink-ing beer in a ca-ba-ret and was I hav-ing fun*
> *Till one night she caught me right, and now I'm on the run.*
> *Lay that pis-tol down, babe, lay that pis-tol down,*
> *Pis-tol- packing Ma-ma, lay that pis-tol down!*

Benjamin knew all four verses and sang them with gusto, each louder and more animated than the last. The class roared with applause! Mrs. Spurlock wondered about the propriety of her class of nine-year-olds celebrating a honky-tonk song. Clearly, Benjamin was the hit of the show. "What are you going to sing next week, Benny? You big star!" His popularity skyrocketed within the fourth grade and also the second and third grades, because his song had carried across the hall. Actually, his fame spread clear across the entire east end of the school's elementary section, and he was inspired to top his own performance the following week.

For the following Friday's talent show, Benjamin went all out. He selected a heartrending ballad that had once brought sobs to him. If only he could sing about old Shep with tears in his voice only, he could touch even the most calloused classmate. When his turn came, nervously he arose from his desk and walked solemnly to the front, cleared his throat, and clasped his hands:

> *When I was a pup and old Shep was a lad,*
> *O'er hills and o'er bellies we'd roam—ooops!*

The class roared with derisive laughter! Mortified, Benjamin slunk back to his seat, his face red as his Big Chief tablet. He dropped his head, so embarrassed he wanted to pull his head down into his overalls bib, a chastened terrapin. How could he ever survive such a blooper!

On the school bus ride home that afternoon, he recalled Great Brownfather's admonition. Ben had let his urge for fame and popularity pull him away from his natural personality—he had turned himself into a toad frog. The incident brought him a nickname, Pup, with variations, and relentless teasing—to the point of bullying—which caused him to look forward to moving away at the end of the fall semester.

Unexpectedly, Benjamin received a three-week reprieve from school and from the ridicule and bullying when a polio scare swept across Southwestern Oklahoma. A sudden rise in the number of cases of infantile paralysis led health authorities to issue a series of warnings about suspected sources of the disease and precautions to take to avoid the often-deadly illness, although its causes then were unknown and there was no vaccine or proven treatment. Hundreds of children contracted polio throughout the nation each year, and many died. Parents were warned to keep their children away from crowds, swimming pools, movie theaters, unwashed fruit, coal smoke, over-exertion. Children were urged to wash their hands and face at least three times a day and wear bags of foul-smelling asafetida around their necks to ward off germs, should germs, and not viruses, cause the disease.

From a nearby county, two boys near Benjamin's age died of polio within two weeks after the fall school term began. "Daniel, we are pulling Benjamin out of school until cold weather sets in," Grace announced after reading an article in the *Cheyenne Star* reporting on the epidemic. "Benjamin doesn't have a strong resistance. I don't want to take a chance with him circulating among so many children."

Daniel recognized that his wife was overreacting, but he remembered the guilt he felt when he was reluctant to take Ben to the hospital for an emergency appendectomy, so he drove Grace to school, where she arranged with the principal and with Mrs. Spurlock to homeschool Ben for several weeks. Jesse and Janie, who would be protected by asafetida bags hung around their necks, would bring Ben daily homework assignments.

Ben was torn. On one hand, he did not want to be branded as a weakling. On the other hand, the unrelenting ridicule, teasing, and taunting he was experiencing since his talent show blooper had become unbearable for one so sensitive. He was hurt and confused. Most of his male classmates had been close buddies since first grade. One year they were all chums, with their arms slung over one another's shoulders, next year they were careful not to display any affection, lest it be misconstrued as weak and shabby girlishness. His classmates could see how embarrassed he was; why, then, did they want to hurt him? Was it because they were jealous that his first performance had been such a sensation? Was it because they had resented the fact that he was always ahead of them in their studies, finishing assignments almost before they could get started? Was it because he had once been the class's drum major? Was it because children recognize that if they can mark a victim, it might protect them from becoming a victim? Was it because Ben's male classmates, who were spearheading the bullying, had a primal instinctive suspicion that there was something covertly perverse in Benjamin? Children who taunt and bully can be among the cruelest animals on earth.

Ben's homeschooling went as expected. Ben did all assignments in short order then dawdled with time on his hands. Grace sent Mrs.

Spurlock a note for an extra stack of books for Ben to read, a good idea that did not work, because he had already read them all. "Read them again," said his mother. "The stories might seem different to you now."

Bored, Ben drifted into a phase of acting like a semi-invalid, lolling on his cot, browsing through his stack of *Capper's Farmer* magazines he had accumulated under his bed. Secretly, Ben had kept the snapshot of Jacob Jiggs, posing in his formfitting swim trunks that had been intended for Henrietta Hayes. He kept it hidden in his magazines, and during his sojourn from school, he often gazed at it, his mother unaware. Jacob had stopped sending Ben letters once Henrietta had gotten pregnant and moved away. On the school bus, Ben had heard Jethro Jiggs comment that his brother had been sent to England for advanced paratrooper training. Jacob's pose in his skintight swim trunks was not intended to be provocative, but to Benjamin the photo intensified his crush on the handsome young soldier. The black-and-white snapshot clearly and distinctively reflected Jacob's masculinity, including his broad shoulders, his flat, muscular midsection, and the bulge at his crotch, which preoccupied Ben's imagination and stirred his recollection. *Henrietta Hays is a fool,* he thought, *if she could not see how desirable Jacob really was. She should have saved herself for him!*

For an imaginative lad who could turn a collection of empty bottles into a vigorous, thriving cattle ranch, daydreaming about Jacob Jiggs was profoundly easy. Fantasizing, Ben could place himself in Jacob's presence, anywhere, day or night. He could absorb himself into the photo, touch the trophy, put his arm across Jacob's back, feel his bicep, rub against his thigh, squeeze his buttocks, lock onto the waistband of his swim trunks, pull them down.

No, don't imagine that. Too gross.

In his mind, Ben could travel remotely, leave his preadolescent body behind, zoom across the Atlantic, descend upon an army barracks in England at night, drift down onto Jacob's bed, touch his sleeping heartthrob's cheek, waft below the covers, linger a moment at Jacob's throat, plant a kiss, creep down to his chest, caress his nipples, absorb the warmth of his abdomen, nestle in his navel, weave down through a pubic forest, drift past his organ (*too worshipful to touch!*), sink down between his inner thighs, and like a leech, attach to his scrotum.

But no, not that. Too crude.

In his fantasy, Ben could imagine *becoming* Jacob Jiggs, standing proud and nude and erect for public inspection, Mr. America, Mr. World, the perfect Adonis, cameras devouring him from every angle, while breathless women line up, one of them lucky to be selected to bear his child. *But no, not that.* If Ben became Jacob, how could he bestow love upon himself?

Ben could imagine that he was neither Jacob nor Benjamin but the chosen woman, as beautiful as Jacob was handsome, perfectly formed, two perfect creatures stealing away to a secret place to become absorbed into each other. *But no, that was unsatisfying.* He did not want to ever be a woman. He wanted Jacob to always be Jacob and he, Benjamin, to always be Benjamin, with the hope that his fantasy of them being together somehow, someday could become real.

In his ultimate fantasy, the one most often visited and most often experienced at night near the thin edge of sleep, paratrooper Jacob Jiggs hangs high in the sky, his parachute fully unfurled. Ben clings to him, face-to-face, full frontal, Ben's arms around Jacob's neck, Ben's cheek nestled against Jacob's throat, Ben's legs encircling Jacob's waist, Ben's genital zone rubbing, pressing, tingling, tantalizing, maximizing their connection, Ben totally melded with Jacob. Together they are drifting and soaring, soaring and drifting, barely descending, never, never reaching the ground.

CHAPTER 28

Selling Out

"But, Mother, you've got to let me go back to school this week!" Benjamin pleaded on Monday morning in his third week of quarantine. "Janie says that on Wednesday, the whole elementary school is walking over to the movie house to see *Sergeant York!* I've never seen one movie, Mother. Don't you want me to learn about movies and learn about the Great War? I know I will understand the movie. Daddy, tell her what is more important, hiding me from polio germs or letting me grow up like a normal person?"

Daniel knew that Benjamin was making a valid point; keeping him out of school because of the vague threat of polio was not a wise thing to do. But Grace's position was anchored by her intuition; Daniel kept silent as Grace held her ground. That Monday, Benjamin stayed home, looked out the east window, and watched the bus come to pick up Janie and Jesse, who, before boarding, took off their asafetida necklaces and hid them under a rock.

Next day, Maudeen visited and critically applied her own motherly intuition. She observed Ben on his cot, listless, picking at lint on his blanket. "My stars, Grace, if you don't stop smothering that child, you're going to turn him into a sniveling little pansy! You might just as well go ahead and wrap him up in a baby blanket!"

Stung by her mother's criticism, Grace relented. Next day, Benjamin returned to school, just in time to accompany the elementary student body to the Rialto Theater to see *Sergeant York*. His

364

fourth-grade class sat near the front, where it was hard to focus on the images on the screen without getting eyestrain. Benjamin left the theater with a headache and a lasting impression that military conflict was hellish and that most soldiers were brave and stupid. For nearly two hours, he had watched trench warfare, families torn apart, bodies torn apart, artillery explosions, snipers, horse-drawn canons, dead bodies everywhere, mankind imposing such hell upon itself, stupid, stupid, stupid!

As the students were walking back to the schoolhouse from the theater, suddenly one of the boys impulsively shoved Ben down from behind, and hazing him resumed with a vengeance.

"Get out of our way, you mangy little puppy!" "Sick puppy!" "Polio puppy!" "Puppy poopy!" "Poopy puppy!" "Arf! Arf!" "Woof! Woof!" "Yowl! Yowl!" "Whine! Whine!" "Sweet little puppy, looking for a bone to suck on? Here's a bone, right here in my pants!" "Hey, everybody, do you want to see a queer puppy! Here he is! His name is Benny. Want to watch him lick his own ass?"

The bullying ended abruptly as Mrs. Spurlock pounced upon them and made everyone form a line. Benjamin was blanketed with total humiliation. He might have tried to fight one of them, but there were half a dozen. For the first time in his life, he had been called a *queer*! What did they know? He had never told anyone about his secret attraction to Jacob Jiggs. Did it show on his face? Was it the way he walked? Was his speech a giveaway? He had always projected an image of wide smiles, gentle friendship, and sunshine—should he become gruff and haughty?

During study period later that day, Mrs. Spurlock took the boys who had been aggravating Benjamin out into the hall, one at a time, to ask them why they were picking on him. Most of them could not or would not say. "It is hard to put into words," said one. "There is just something weird about him that really turns us off!" For a few days after Mrs. Spurlock took the agitators aside, the hazing declined. Ben was relieved to be back in school, but coping with the bullying was a nightmare that would not end until he moved away.

*   *   *

On September 25, 1943, Daniel was cleaning some of his implements along the garden fence, preparing for his upcoming farm auction, when he was startled by a black military sedan thundering across the bridge, speeding toward the old homestead. It was not a hearse, but it had that effect. Immediately he dropped his tools and walked toward his car. Grace was on the porch, tossing out kitchen scraps to Purrpuss, Calico's only surviving descendant (a great-grandkitten); she saw the ominous vehicle and took off her apron. "We need to get to Rayford's and Ella's right away," Daniel said. "I'm afraid they are about to receive some terrible news!"

Had World War II come home? Unknown to their folks back home, Harvey, Jeff, and Johnny Dalkens had participated in the successful liberation of Sicily in August 1943 and were in the amphibious landings at Salerno, Italy, on September 9, the day after Italy accepted the Allied terms of unconditional surrender. German troops, who still controlled a large portion of Italy, put up strong resistance at Salerno until September 18, when they withdrew to defend their positions elsewhere. Had the Dalkens brothers survived unscathed?

The military courier brought tragic news to the old homestead. On the third day of the Salerno operation, a German artillery shell exploded into a redoubt the Dalkens brothers were occupying. Four American soldiers were killed, including Harvey, who was disemboweled. Johnny suffered a hip fracture, spinal and cranial injuries, and multiple lacerations. Jeff was kneeling behind a stack of provisions and escaped the shrapnel, but the percussion burst his eardrums and he suffered a severe concussion as the blast threw him against an embankment.

Daniel and Grace arrived to console and assist their cousins Rayford and Ella in their terrible moment, but what could they do but weep with them and offer to do their farm chores while they mourned and joined the legion of parents who collectively lost 322,188 sons and daughters as a result of the war.

Initially, Rayford's spirit was crushed. His sons were his life. Harvey had been his firstborn son. Would Johnny ever walk again? Would Jeff recover from his hearing loss and his emotional collapse, a posttraumatic condition that, in World War I, had been called shell shock? Ella Dalkens knew that she had to become the bulwark of her family; she would become strong where Rayford was weak. To her relief, Rayford stopped drinking. He stayed home. He stopped farming. Ella believed he showed symptoms of a stroke. She took over. She inquired of the government where Harvey was buried in Italy; she needed to know where to direct her prayers. She made plans to take Rayford on a train to a military hospital in San Antonio, where Jeff and Johnny were to be sent for treatment, recovery, and rehabilitation.

Benjamin did not know Rayford's and Ella's sons, but he grieved for them, imagined what combat had been like for them, more violent and destructive than even the bloodiest scenes in *Sergeant York*. For several days, he had no stomach for war news or war maps. He did not want to know where Salerno was. He did not want to see another war movie, ever. Especially, he did not want to know if paratroopers were engaged in the Italian campaign.

*   *   *

Donna Belle was disappointed that she could not move her sons to their new farm until their fall semester ended at Colbert Public School. Her father stayed with her until late September, when he moved to Alabama to live with his sister. The day before he left, he counseled his widowed daughter. "Donna Belle, you are still a young and pretty woman. If a good man is drawn to you, you'd do best not to turn him away. Although he might not hold a candle to Russell, a second husband can be a godsend for you and a valuable stepfather to your sons."

Maudeen planted a different seed. "Donna Belle, sweetheart, please don't ever remarry out of desperation," she said one day when she and James were on one of their regular visits. "I have seen so many young widows make bad decisions because of loneliness and financial need."

As for James, he evaluated Donna Belle's situation purely from a pragmatic, nonromantic perspective. She was receiving monthly checks for the support of her four sons from the Social Security

Administration, and it was James's understanding that the checks would continue for each son until he turned eighteen or finished college. "Thank God for Social Security!" he said. "Thank God for FDR! Thank God for the New Deal!"

From eleven-year-old Jimmy's perspective, not to worry, he was to become the head of the household. "Mama, as soon as I watch Uncle Daniel farm our land a year or two, I am sure I can take over," he said.

Donna Belle kept her own counsel. She would never consider matching up with another man, because Russell would always stay fresh in her life. She had shared heaven with him already. Physically she could see aspects of him in each of their sons. Shortly after she and Russell had married, they went to Lawton and had a large portrait made, a traditional pose in which Russell, wearing a herringbone gray suit, was sitting in a white high-backed wicker chair. Standing beside him, her hand on his shoulder, Donna Belle smiled warmly in a light, ruffled dress, her bobbed hair in precisely sculpted waves. The portrait hung on the wall above the headboard of her bed. It was the last thing she looked at each night when she retired. Sometimes in her dreams she and Russell were reliving that happy day when the portrait was made, perpetually young. Sometimes she dreamed they were on an idyllic horseback ride through the Wichita Mountains. She believed that someday, when she died, they would be reunited, ageless, painlessly free of heartbreak, loneliness, and toil.

* * *

Aaron Bird arrived for his year-end visit with Daniel's family on Thanksgiving Day 1943 earlier than usual because of their impending move to Caddo County. His year-end maneuver for a whiskey toddy began the following day, but Aaron rallied from his psychosomatic chills Saturday morning when he learned that Daniel's family was going to attend Sunday services at Strong City First Baptist Church for the last time. He wanted to attend church with them; he could relapse on Monday.

One of the church's families, the Dithers family, was under great stress because of the admitted infidelity of Roscoe Dithers, a former deacon, with a prostitute. Trying to address the issue, Brother Nathan preached against the "sins of the flesh," the need for commitment in marriage, and the glamorization of the sinful lifestyles of Hollywood. The impressive young pastor took his text from 1 Corinthians.

> *Do you not know that your bodies are members of Christ?...*
>
> *Do you not know that he who joins himself with a prostitute becomes one body with her? For as it is written, "The two shall become one..." Because of the temptation to immorality, each man should have his own wife, and each woman her own husband... If they cannot exercise self-control, they should marry. For it is better to marry than to be aflame with passion.*

And from the first chapter of the book of Romans, wherein Saint Paul describes what can happen when men give in to sexual wickedness:

> *Therefore God gave them up in the lusts of their hearts to impurity, to the dishonoring of their bodies among themselves, because they exchanged the truth about God for a lie and worshiped and served the creature rather than the Creator...*
>
> *For this reason, God gave them over to dishonorable passions. Their women exchanged natural relations for unnatural, and the men likewise gave up natural relations with women and were consumed with passion for one another, men committing shameless acts with men and receiving in their own persons the due penalty for their error.*

In his fervency for enlightenment of God's children, Brother Nathan hit the scale of sexual sins, from fornication to adultery to divorce to covetous idolization of movie stars to homosexuality, but bypassed bestiality, a potentially sensitive topic here in the midst of farming country, and masturbation, in which Nathan himself sometimes engaged. Roscoe Dithers, the inspiration for his message, was absent. Brother Nathan prayed earnestly for the success of the sermon, for he identified with Saint Paul, who said, "I wish that all men were as I am," which Nathan interpreted as having a low sex drive. Nathan's fatiguing studies in seminary, his extensive training for gymnastics and long-distance running drained his libido to the point that he seldom dated, postponing any thought of marriage, which likely postponed his rise to his deserved ministry of a great congregation.

The sermon caused Jesse to ponder his situation. Currently, he was really sweet on Melinda Forsythe, a sophomore, and he felt certain that his father was going to let him start driving the family car on dates before they moved away. Considering his pepped-up teenage libido, he was a candidate to fornicate. Now Nathan was telling him not to do it: he would get in trouble with God.

Janie, on the other hand, did not want to think about anything sexual. She was concerned about the changes taking place in her body, and she hoped to evade the responsibilities of becoming a woman as long as possible.

Grace had not appreciated the sermon. She felt she did not need an unmarried, inexperienced Baptist minister to help her instruct her children about sex: sex was to be confined to marriage, and all sexual activity outside marriage was dirty and degrading, and disease prone, and that was that!

On the drive home from church, Janie sat in the front seat between her parents; Benjamin sat in the back seat between Jesse and Grandpa Aaron. The sermon had spawned in Ben a dozen questions and subconscious resentment that his family's Christian standards would find his secret, passionate daydreams about Jacob Jiggs evil and dirty. "Can someone tell me why Brother Nathan says that people need to marry in order to get rid of passion?" he asked with a slight tone of recalcitrance.

"Brother Nathan didn't say that, stupid!" Jesse retorted.

"Yes, he did," Ben insisted. "He read from the Bible that it was better to marry than to burn up with passion!"

Daniel chuckled quietly, and Aaron shook his head. Only little Benjamin the upstart would come up with such an interpretation. "By the way," Ben continued, "what is the difference between passion and desire and lust? Won't all three give you a *hard-on*?"

Grace gasped. "Daniel, stop the car and give that child a spanking! He knows better than to talk like that!"

"Grace, Ben asked a serious question," Daniel replied, "and I think he deserves for you to give him a serious answer."

Grace sighed. Why did such a sensitive, naughty topic arise from a youngster who was not yet ten years old, who was a physical type not likely to attain puberty for another four or five years? Grace struggled to explain. "Benjamin, *desire* is an attraction a person feels toward someone worthy of his love, and *passion* is the intensity of that desire when mutually shared. *Lust* is unhealthy desire directed toward someone unworthy or unqualified for sharing that desire, which makes it evil and ugly and dirty and sinful."

"What if Jesse sneaks around and has sex with his new girl-friend, Melinda, since he really, really likes her? Would that be passion or lust?" Ben wondered.

"Jesse knows not to do such an evil, dirty thing," said Grace. "Only married couples may make love. I trust Jesse to wait until he is married."

Jesse pinched Benjamin hard on his leg.

"What if Jesse gets a crush on one of his buddies and they start feeling passionate toward each other and they go ahead and do something *homosexive*, like those men Brother Nathan mentioned from the Bible?" asked Benjamin. "What would it hurt?"

"The word is *homosexual*, you little nut!" snarled Jesse. "I would never have filthy sex with a stinking, dirty guy. So just shut up!"

Grandpa Aaron affectionately touched Benjamin's hand and said, "Child, the Bible clearly says that God intends sex to be enjoyed only between a married man and his wife, and certainly never between people of the same sex. The Old Testament calls homosexuality an abomination and calls for those who engage in it to be put to death! God expects us not to yield to temptation."

Recalcitrant still, Benjamin sighed with exasperation, turned to his grandpa, and said quietly, "Grandpa, I will make a deal with you. I promise not to have sex until I marry a girl, no matter what I might desire, if you promise not to ask Daddy to go across the state line tomorrow to buy you some whiskey medicine."

Grace was brushing Janie's hair away from her eyes and did not concentrate on what Ben had just told his grandfather. Daniel heard it, and winced. Grandpa Aaron fell silent, turned and stared out the window, pained in his Achilles' heel. When they reached home, Daniel took Benjamin aside and scolded him for hurting his grandpa. "Benjamin," he said, "you needlessly hurt your grandpa's feelings. Don't you know that there is so much pain that just naturally occurs in this old world? There is no good reason to unnecessarily add to it with hurtful words. Grandpa has lived a hard life and deserves a little concession at least once a year."

Next morning, before anyone else arose, Daniel drove to the state line and bought his father a fifth of whiskey. When he returned, Aaron was sitting in the rocker beside the heater, a blanket over his shoulders. Daniel took him a hot toddy. "Here, Papa, you'd better take this preventative. You know there might be a hard winter coming on, and you had better bolster yourself for it."

Contrite, Benjamin went to his grandpa, hugged his neck, and smoothed wrinkles out of his blanket.

*   *   *

Daniel's farm auction occurred on the second Saturday in December 1943, and it came near to tearing Benjamin's heart out. Right up to the auction, Benjamin pleaded for his father not to sell any of the cows. "Why can't we take them with us, Daddy? Nobody else will appreciate them like we do. They're all good cattle!"

"That's beside the point, Ben. Donna Belle's farm has only a small pasture. She and her boys will need a fresh milk cow in the springtime and another fresh milk cow in the fall, for their own table. We need to wait to see how many cows her pasture can sustain before we can add our own. At least we are taking the chickens. You can stay friends with the chickens."

The auctioneer had a booming voice that blanketed the moderate crowd of bidders and curious attendees; his voice echoed from the far side of the ravine so clearly that it sounded like someone was copying him. Janie came outside to watch the auction, wearing a pretty pink winter coat, but becoming upset at the strangers who stared at her, she went inside and stayed there. Jesse had a tablet and tried to tally up the sales returns unofficially as the bidding transpired, but a clerk from the Strong City National Bank was handling all transactions. Grace kept hot coffee and cookies available on the porch. A dry cold front had rolled in during the night; the auctioneer was not going to keep the crowd together very long. First to be sold were consignments from neighbors, items printed on the sale bill so there would be enough prospective bargains to draw a crowd. When Daniel's farm equipment came before the auction block, Benjamin tried to see who bought what, but the proceeding went too fast for him to keep up.

It was the sale of the farm animals that tore Benjamin up. Old Bill and old Hector were now well over ten years old, and although they were still a fine-looking pair and could do a full day's plowing, they were short in the mouth. They brought less than their wagon and harness. "Old Bill and Hector are on their way to the glue factory," Jesse said. His horse, Jodhpur, warranted crowd interest. He was beautiful, saddled, available for prospective buyers to ride out to the mailbox on a test ride and back again. "Jesse, why are you selling old Jodhpur?" asked Ben, who wondered why Jesse seemed to have no affection or loyalty for his horse. "Why, you could ride him all the way to our new home! If I had my own horse, I would ride him off to Texas before I would let Daddy sell him to some old whipper," he declared.

"I am hoping Daddy will let me have the money from Jodhpur for a down payment on my own car," Jesse replied. "I have already saved $17.50 from selling possum, skunk, coon, and badger hides I have trapped down in the river bottom."

The sale of the roan shorthorn bull did not disturb Ben because the burly herd sire had been a nuisance, breaking through fences to fight neighbor bulls, tearing up stanchions and feed troughs, and hazing small calves. Ben was glad to see him go. But when the cows went on the auction block, it felt like Ben's very family was breaking up. Old Red was the only surviving cow from the original group; all others were daughters of the originals or heifers of the daughters of the originals, all of whom Ben personally had bucket-fed as babies and pampered and watched grow into productive members of the herd. He did not want to know who bought them, so he drifted away from the auction, went to the porch, and helped his mother serve coffee and snacks to the attendees.

Once the sale ended and the buyers began to back their trailers up to the loading alley, to avoid watching his cow friends being hauled off, Ben dashed out past the chicken house and fled to the back of the empty pasture, where he had discarded his cow and calf bottles. He retrieved them from the trash and lined them up in a row single file and aimed the line northward. In his make-believe mind, he was taking his own livestock to open range, where he was filing on free land, using the 1864 Homestead Act to establish a great ranch that his children and grandchildren would inherit so that none of them would ever have to scrounge a meager living out of dry ground or be forced to sell cattle that should not be sold. If only he had been born at the right time...

*   *   *

Daniel spent the week following the auction (the last week of the school semester) in Caddo County, staying with James and Maudeen so that he could help James prepare Donna Belle's farm for their occupation. Back in October, when the previous owner vacated Donna Belle's property, James ignored his gout and his rheumatism and his arthritis and became busy tearing down a cavernous, dilapidated old barn for material to rebuild a smaller, more compact barn for Donna Belle. Then he used the leftover barn lumber to build chicken houses for both Donna Belle and for Daniel's farmyard a quarter mile down the road. Finally, the last of the best of the barn lumber was used to add a small lean-to room for Janie onto the three-room cottage where Daniel's family would live. For the first time in her life, Janie would have the privacy of her own room.

The three-room cottage—now a four-room cottage—was small for a family of five but larger than the two-room shack Daniel's family had lived in during the past seven years. It faced the west, only about fifty feet from a north-south county road. Its front door opened into a small living room that had two doors, one on the north side, opening into the kitchen, and one on the east side, opening onto a screened-in porch. On the porch's north side, a door opened into Janie's newly constructed room. The porch was to be closed in with lumber from the barn project, but James and Daniel ran out of time to get it done before the Bird family would be moving in; cotton ducking partially covered the porch's windows. Daniel went to Anadarko, bought a new kerosene heater, and installed it in the living room. An electric light and a wall plug outlet were located in each room. They would need to use their wooden icebox until Daniel sold a new crop to have the money to buy an electric refrigerator, but that would eventually happen. Then how much more modern could one get!

On the ninth day before Christmas, James and Daniel rented a truck, drove to Colbert, and moved Donna Belle and her sons to their new home, with her following behind the truck, with her sons in their family car. Coming through Apache, they stopped at James's and Maudeen's bungalow for a late lunch, then Maudeen accompanied them on out to Donna Belle's farm.

About eight miles north of Apache, their route passed Thaxton Public School, which the children would attend, and four miles beyond the school was Pine Ridge Missionary Baptist Church and Cemetery and Beiber's Gas and Grocery Store, each of which would become important in the lives of the community's new residents. Donna Belle's farm home, known locally as the Sid Withers Place, was one-half mile north of the country store, with the Birds' cottage halfway in between. Donna Belle had seen her new place only once before, on the day that James had brought her to sign the realty papers. She had noticed that despite its forty years of age and its need for paint, her two-story house was the most impressive house in that community.

A twenty-acre tract opposite Beiber's Store had been sold off from the Withers quarter section to Jud Withers, a descendant, and his wife, May. They had lived in the back of their feed store located in the corner opposite Beiber's Store until they had moved to California after having been voted out of the Pine Ridge Missionary Baptist Church for dancing in a street dance at a carnival in Carnegie. The expulsion action had been led by the community's stern patriarch, the late Grandpa Barnaby.

"Boys, run upstairs and pick out your room so that we will know where to set up your beds," said Granddad James as he and Daniel began to unload the truck. Donny and Jimmy darted inside and upstairs. Having first pick, Jimmy selected the north bedroom, which incorporated the stairway landing, not realizing that it would be the coldest room in the house, with a north window, no furnace, and walls with no insulation. Donny's south room contained the warm brick chimney that reached from the heater below to the roof above.

Soon the brothers were out exploring the empty barn and its empty loft. They marveled at a small flock of pigeons that had taken up residence in the rafters and ledges in the loft.

"Pigeons are fun to watch," said Jimmy.

"Fun to catch," said Donny, "and good to eat!"

Fifty yards north of the barn, there was a two-acre stand of Catalpa trees, planted for a windbreak and woodlot by the previous owner, but now grown up in tall weeds and a plum thicket.

"Wow! Our own jungle!" said Jimmy. "Let's explore it and open up a trail!"

With Maudeen's management, Donna Belle's household was in place by nightfall, including her kitchen dishes and utensils in the cupboard, and in her bedroom, her portrait with Russell hanging on the wall over her headboard. Two neighbor ladies who had driven by and noticed new neighbors moving in brought a big pot of beef stew and a pan of warm corn bread. They introduced themselves as the Barnaby sisters. They were the curious, outgoing, self-appointed welcoming committee of Pine Ridge Missionary Baptist Church, and they invited Donna Belle and her sons, "Come worship with us next Sunday." It was a fitting encouraging gesture to a young widow who would need all the help she could get from her late husband's caring family and from warm and friendly neighbors.

*   *   *

Their last day at Denim Public School was a noticeably different experience for Jesse, Janie, and Ben. Jesse received sweet goodbye notes from three recent girlfriends. Janie's class had a going-away party for her and presented her with a small pink makeup kit. Benjamin's class made no special notice for him, but some of his former chums who had been bullying him treated him decently and shook his hand, as though to absolve themselves from their recent cruel behavior toward him. At any rate, their favorite target was moving away, and each of them worried that he might be the next target.

The days leading up to their move to Caddo County were stressful for everyone. The cows were gone. Grace "borrowed" milk from Rayford and Ella, a gallon at a time. Daniel was away, preparing their new home for them. Jodhfur was gone; Jesse walked to the river bottom and gathered his empty traps. Janie looked forward to living near little Will and Bobby Alan, and from her latent motherly instinct she contemplated how she would assist Donna Belle in taking care of her toddlers, but she was nervous and teary; she could not explain why she feared the change that was imminent. Benjamin was told they would have no room in their new home for his collection of old newspapers and magazines, so he went through them all, cutting out his favorite feature articles, photos, maps, and news stories, placing them in an old shoebox, with his secret, hidden swimsuit photograph of Jacob Jiggs.

On the eighth day before Christmas, James arrived with the rented truck, and Daniel followed in his '37 Ford. Before bedtime, everything was packed and loaded except their beds, the crate of chickens, and mixings for a bowl of mush for breakfast. Shortly after daylight, on the seventh day before Christmas, the two-vehicle caravan rolled out on the county road, James and Jesse in the truck, leading the way. Daniel stopped at the mailbox to leave a change-of-address note then turned onto the county road and, for the last time, rumbled across the rickety bridge. "Don't look back," he told his family. "Only look ahead."

Grace closed her eyes as they crossed the bridge, then released a deep sigh of relief. *Good riddance to the hardscrabble farm, goodbye to the dreadful, rickety bridge,* she thought. *Too bad it took Russell's death to dislodge us from this desolate land. We will help Donna Belle get her sons up and on their own, then God willing, Daniel and I can find a path to a better future for ourselves. Perhaps God will plant an ambition in Daniel to try something better than sharecropping. Then someday I can become a nurse.* Grace did not look back.

But Benjamin did. On his knees in the back seat, looking through the rear window, he tried to implant everything for his life of memories: the little two-room frame shack, his happy home, the only home he remembered; its newspapered walls that stimulated him to learn to read and indicated how large and sometimes sombre and always exciting the world was; the front porch, where a lot of happy things happened with kittens and games and Bran; the cellar and the windmill and the chicken house and the outhouse, all of them exactly in the right spot; the cowshed, where he made so many calf friends and shared chores with Daddy and Jesse; the cowshed, where he first saw, *really saw*, Jacob Jiggs; the garden that had sustained the family for seven years and the mailbox that had brought good news and bad; the deep ravine and the rickety bridge that had brought Bran and then had taken him back; the steep hill where Mother crashed their jalopy into the embankment and, in her mind, turned him into an invalid; now all out of sight as the caravan crested the hill and passed by the Jiggs mailbox.

Benjamin turned from the back window and stared out the side window so that no one could see the tears running down his cheeks. Jacob was gone from his life. He would never see him again and would never hear from him again. As time passed and life gained complexities, daydreams of Jacob would become harder and harder to construct. Was this why God willed that the family had to move away, to remove Jacob from his life? To save Ben from a life of homosexual yearning? Perhaps he would never feel that way about another male ever again. Perhaps this was God's way of cleaning the slate. Perhaps from now on Benjamin could be normal, free from joyous, sensuous, rapturous, lustful adoration of a certain unattainable flesh-and-blood same-sex person. Thank God if he could be normal.

Daddy had said, "Only look ahead." Benjamin needed to turn over a new leaf and rid himself of characteristics that made him seem queer, whatever they were. Should he smile less? Should he smile with a sneer? Should he exercise to try to build up his muscles? Should he go out for every sport, no matter how nonathletic he was? Should he hang out with guys who chased girls? Should he always have a girlfriend, actually pick one, hold her hand and hug her and kiss her and try to really love her? Should he spit a lot? He might try to swagger and curse and pick fights and be a bully.

Or Ben might simply be his natural self, Benjamin Ray Bird (1934–????), and like untold numbers of closeted homosexuals, hide his yearning and be something less than happy.

CHAPTER 29

A New Leaf

O n December 21, 1943, Jimmy and Donny were playing in their front yard when they saw the rented truck coming, with Daniel's green 1937 Ford following close behind. "They're here! They're here!" They were so excited they dashed to the road as the truck passed their house, and Daniel needed to slow down to keep from running into them.

Benjamin waved and yelled, "Hi, Jimmy! Hi, Donny! We're moving in!"

Jimmy and Donny sprinted closely behind the two-vehicle caravan as it pulled off the county road and stopped beside the cottage. Immediately Jimmy told Benny about their "jungle" woodlot.

"Trees! Trees!" shouted Ben as he jumped from the car and noticed along the fence row paralleling the county road, for about a hundred yards toward Beiber's Gas and Grocery Store, a stand of black locust trees tall enough to provide good, shady places to play in the summertime, thick enough to hold birds' nests and hideouts, to hide foxholes and forts, to find all sorts of bugs and snakes and small animals. Two large locust trees were located just south of the cottage, near enough to provide summer shade on the cottage roof and exactly the right distance apart to stretch a hammock.

As the men began to unload household items and carry them into the house, Donny told Ben, "This is my house, Benny, but you can use it till I grow up. Then I'm going to live here and raise rabbits and racing pigeons and billy goats."

Donny's claim to the house caused Ben to pause and reflect. It was true. This could never be his home, except for a temporary time, because it belonged to Aunt Donna Belle and her sons. When could he ever feel at home again?

"Let's go explore!" said Jimmy, and off the three musketeers went, down a path to Donna Belle's house, past the barn, and over into the catalpa woodlot, where Jimmy showed Ben their secret fort—a two-foot hole in the ground, buttressed by a rim of excavated dirt—not much of a fort, but good enough for boys their age (Jimmy, eleven; Ben, nine; Donny, nearly nine, all with good imaginations). Then they raced down a lane east into the forty-acre pasture, on to the back side of the pasture, where a natural drainage ditch found a gathering of willows growing slantwise because of Oklahoma's nearly constant wind, slanted so that the boys could not just climb them but also actually run up their trunks and jump off into deep sand.

"This will be a good place to go camping," said Benjamin.

"Let's go find some big rocks to build a campfire pit," said Jimmy.

Then off they went to find whatever they could find. *Living here will be fun,* thought Benjamin, keeping up with his cousins. Jimmy and Donny were gifts to him from his uncle Russell, constant playmates, rough and tumble.

He knew they liked to wrestle and play baseball and he was not good enough to excel at either, but he welcomed the experience. He would become a true *Tuff Nut.* Before returning to the cottage, the three boys explored every corner of the farm, including the southwest corner opposite Beiber's country store.

"This store is sure going to be handy," said Donny. "I wonder if they have a lot of candy..."

The sun was setting when the boys returned to the cottage. Everything was unloaded and in place. Grace's large kitchen table and benches were in the center of the north room, circled by the wooden icebox, cookstove, washstand, and cupboard, crowded but snug. Maudeen and Donna Belle had brought a big pot of beef stew,

which sat in the center of the table, with a stack of soup bowls waiting for the evening meal. An electric light bulb dangled over the
table and bathed the room with a brightness that Benjamin could
not believe—no more flickering yellow kerosene lamplight, no more
smelly, sooty, oily lamps!

"Perhaps as soon as the war is over, we will be able to buy a new
refrigerator, electric range, and toaster," said Grace, "as soon as Uncle
Sam can stop making jeeps and guns and tanks and fighter planes."

There was not enough bench space for everyone to sit around
the table, so the three boys sat on the floor, with their legs crossed
Indian-style, and slurped their soup, Ben in the middle. "This is the
life!" said Jimmy. "Aunt Grace, can Benny spend the night with me
and Donny?"

"Not tonight," Grace replied. "Tonight we all need to fit into
our new places. Benjamin will need to put his things away before
bedtime. Where's Janie?"

"She's in her little room in the back of the house," said Jesse.
"Will is helping her put her things away."

"I'll go get her," Ben volunteered. He was eager to see Janie's
room and find his own space. As he scampered through the door
into the living room and through another door into the screened-in
porch and opened the new door into Janie's room, he smelled the
fresh white paint of her windowsills and doorframe and baseboards.
New wallpaper with a design of small pink climbing roses covered
the walls, hung two days earlier by Maudeen while the menfolk
were moving people to Caddo County. A single bed, freshly painted,
was pushed against the east wall. It was Olivia's old bed, for which
Maudeen no longer had room. Grace had given Janie sole use of the
dresser, where she was putting away sundries, undies, and cosmetics.
A small table lamp with a lacy white shade sat on the dresser.

"Janie, you have a nice room," said Benjamin, glad for her,
unaware that Janie's room created a barrier between them that had
not been there before. "Mother wants you to bring Will into the
kitchen for supper. We're having beef stew. It is really good!"

Ben returned to the kitchen and squatted down against the wall,
between Jimmy and Donny, to finish his stew. He saw his grandpar-

ents, parents, Jesse, Janie, Will, and Donna Belle, holding Bobby Alan, crowded around the table, yet there was a feeling that someone was missing. Aunt Donna Belle sat stoic, slouched with weariness, leaning down to feed spoonfuls of stew to Bobby Alan. She looked as though she had not smiled in months, but there was a firmness to her expression, a resolute determination to endure. She had four fine sons to raise, in tribute to her beloved late husband. Like Ruth's loyalty to Naomi in the Old Testament, her husband's family shared their devotion to her cause.

*　　*　　*

Their first night in the cottage was a celebration of electrical lighting. Before bedtime, Benjamin read two stories from *Children's Illustrated Bible Stories*. Daniel filled out an application form to compete for a temporary job conducting the 1944 farm census. Grace mended one of Jesse's shirts, hand-stitching and sewing on buttons without eyestrain. Janie stayed in her room with the door closed and kept herself in secrecy. *Do I want to put red polish on my toenails? Do I want to comb my hair over to the side, like this?* Ah, the joy and relief of privacy! It was cold in Janie's room, and on the screened-in porch, where Jesse was organizing his personal belongings in two covered cardboard boxes, sitting on the double bed that had been his parents but now reluctantly he would share with Benjamin. Thank goodness the years on the cots were over. Jesse's boxes would be stored under his side of the bed. Benjamin's box, containing personal things like marbles and pretty rocks and buckeye seeds, report cards and school pictures, newspaper clippings and Jacob's photograph, socks and shorts and undershirts, would stay under his side of the bed.

Grace and Daniel were going to sleep on a fold-out "duo-fold" in the living room, given to them by Maudeen, who had no room for it in her Apache bungalow. Grace and Daniel would attain their first bedtime privacy since moving to Denim seven years before. Grace's cosmetics and Daniel's shaving materials were to be kept on the top shelf of the kitchen cupboard. There was a place for everything, if convenience could be made to seem an irrelevant luxury.

At bedtime, Grace filled a hot-water bottle and put it in Janie's bed to warm the covers, then she placed two bricks on top of the kerosene heater until they were burning hot; she wrapped them in towels and placed them in Jesse's and Ben's bed to warm their feet. Then she tucked in all her children with every spare cover she could muster, for it was turning sharply cold outside, with snow flurries. Benjamin settled in next to Jesse and pulled his head under the covers. He would sleep restlessly and move around too much for Jesse to tolerate, but what could Jesse do but bear it? They were stuck in a drafty, screened-in porch under a pile of covers for the night.

Next morning, the third day before Christmas, they awoke to find five inches of snow had fallen during the night. Jesse and Benjamin's bed was covered with a light blanket of snow that had filtered in through the ducking covering the windows on the screened-in porch. They grabbed their clothes and darted into the living room and dressed beside the heater, where they found that Janie had abandoned her room as soon as her hot-water bottle turned cold. She had brought her covers to the living room and snuggled up on a pallet beside the fire.

"Son, we'll need to go down to Donna Belle's place and kick through the snow to find enough barn lumber to close in the porch today," Daniel said. He often called his firstborn *"Son,"* but never Ben, an unconscious oversight noticed by no one except Ben.

Jesse was cross. "Daddy, you and Mama can have your darned bed back tonight, and I will sleep on the duo-fold. I cannot sleep with Ben. He kept putting his cold feet against my legs, and he twisted and turned all night. He would not keep his hands off me!"

"I did not!"

"Yes, you did, in your sleep! You're going back into the corner onto your old cot. You're just a cot person, anyway. You are so uncivilized you don't know how to sleep in a bed!"

"Jesse, don't be so gruff with your little brother," scolded Grace.

"You'd be gruff too if someone woke you up every five minutes! Does this place have a storm cellar? If not, I am going to build one, where I can have a place to sleep in peace, like I did back home."

"Jesse, this *is* home," Daniel said. "We are here until Jimmy and Donny can farm this place. So we will make the best of it. We'll close in the porch today, and Jesse can sleep on the duo-fold, and Benny… well…"

"I want my old cot," said Benjamin. "Just put it in a corner somewhere and forget about me. I'm just a cot person, anyway."

Grace could not remember both of her sons being out of sorts at the same time. It must have really been a bad night. She decided to adjust their attitudes with a warm breakfast of cinnamon-flavored oatmeal, hot biscuits with butter and honey, and several pieces of hickory-flavored slab bacon. After breakfast, Daniel went out to the hand pump for fresh water and discovered that it had frozen up during the night. He returned to the house with his water bucket full of snow. "We'll need to melt snow on the heater to make water for a few hours, until the sun comes out and thaws out the pump."

Benjamin bundled up and took a pail of snow water and a can of grain out to the chicken house, where eight hens and the current rooster, Red Robert, were getting accustomed to their new accommodations. They were not to be let outside today because of the snow. "Hello, girls. This is cot-man speaking to you. Welcome to your new home. Red Robert, I haven't heard you crow yet. You might as well get used to the idea—you will never leave this place alive. So make the best of it. By the way, I've got good news for springtime. There is a row of trees along the road, with thick weeds and grass where you can hide your nest and hatch your own babies. What more can you ask?"

As Ben plodded back to the house in the snow, he looked northward and saw Jimmy and Donny in their front yard rolling up snow for a snowman. "Hey, Benny, come and help us build a snowman!" Jimmy yelled from a quarter mile away, distinct and audible. *Wow, how sound carries in cold air!* Ben ran into the house and asked, "Mother, Jimmy and Donny have asked me to come play with them. Do I need to ask every time I go, since it is so close?"

"Well, it is a good thing to let your mother know where you are."

"In case I get a call from the president?"

"Yes, of course. Put on your mittens!"

"I have outgrown my mittens."

"Wear Jesse's. He never wore them."

Before that day ended, the three musketeers built the largest, ugliest snowman in that part of Caddo County and threw a thousand snowballs at it, trying to knock off its head. Benny got tired of throwing snowballs, but Jimmy and Donny were completely into it, so Ben threw and threw with them, until Aunt Donna Belle called them in for a lunch of hot chocolate and chili. Afterward, they stood at the living room window and watched a neighbor, Ollie Colver, pass by on his farm tractor to make ruts so cars could get to town. His wife was nine months pregnant, and he did not want to be snowbound with her a single day.

The boys then went upstairs to Donny's warm room and played basketball, playing *horse*, competing to see who could throw a small potato into an empty chili can from four or five feet away.

*   *   *

By nightfall, Daniel and Jesse had enclosed their screened-in porch, not insulated, but now snug enough to open all the inside doors to let the heat from the living room heater permeate throughout the house. Janie claimed sole possession of her room and told her brothers they were not welcome there unless she asked them, although in cold weather she was going to leave her door open for heat to come in. Ben's cot was placed against the inside wall in the southwest corner of the closed-in porch, and he seemed satisfied. He wanted to paste papers and maps on the wall alongside his cot but did not ask to do so because this was Donny's house and Donny might not like it.

Jesse had adapted his battery-operated radio to electricity, and the family was pleasantly surprised to learn that more than twice as many clear stations were available to them than before. The house rang with Western music until bedtime, when Jesse brought covers to the duo-fold and made himself a nest.

Next morning, the second day before Christmas, Grace and Donna Belle began preparations for an extended family Christmas dinner at Donna Belle's. Olivia was coming on a Greyhound bus from Lawton. Missing from the affair would be James and Maudeen, for the roads were clear enough for them to fulfill plans to take a motor trip to Wally's for Christmas; Maudeen was anxious to see how her infant granddaughter, Ladena Lynn, was developing.

Daniel returned the rental truck to Anadarko and paid the rental bill. In his first significant driving experience, Jesse followed in the family's green 1937 Ford. Donny, Jimmy, and Ben wanted to accompany Jesse, but Grace denied them, saying, "We need to give Jesse an opportunity to get more driving experience before he has to worry about chauffeuring the likes of you silly gooses."

Daniel and Jesse returned by way of Washita, where they visited with Leona, Vernon, and Kirby, inviting them to come for Christmas dinner. "Have you heard from Papa since he visited with you at Denim on Thanksgiving?" asked Leona.

"No, but he told me he was looking forward to the Christmas Eve dinner at Altus First Baptist Church and the choir's Christmas cantata, so I guess he is contented there, at least for now."

"What food dish do I need to bring for the Christmas meal?" she asked.

"Grace and Donna Belle went grocery shopping yesterday, so we'll have plenty. Just bring yourself and your boys."

Vernon had paid $25 for an inoperable old car and had scrounged parts for it in a salvage yard at Anadarko. He tinkered with it enough to get it running, but it had slick tires and a weak battery and a suspicion of sediment in the gas lines. "Uncle Daniel," Kirby said, "if we don't get to Donna Belle's by noon, that means we have broken down somewhere between here and there, so you might need to come looking for us."

"Nonsense!" Vernon retorted. "Why, I could drive my neat little auto clear to California!" Thus began Vernon's adventures with a long series of used cars, none of them in good condition, but all of them fun for him to work with; he would never own a new car.

Leaving Washita, Daniel and Jesse then drove to Apache and picked up Olivia at the Greyhound bus station. They were surprised to see that she had gained considerable weight, but they were kind enough not to mention it. "I'm afraid I couldn't bring any Christmas gifts," she said. "I got behind on my rent and had to use almost all my last paycheck to catch up." She did not reveal that she also had been splurging on new clothes in her new size.

Olivia and the Birds spent a pleasant evening at Donna Belle's, playing cards, checkers, and dominoes. Then near bedtime, they walked home, with moonlight illuminating the trail, snow crunching under their footsteps. Olivia slept with Janie in her room, after spending an hour sitting at the mirror showing Janie hairstyling and cosmetic makeup techniques. "Aunt Olivia, I have missed you," Janie said as they settled under the covers.

Next day was the day before Christmas, and all through the family, not a gift had been bought.

Grace and Donna Belle had spent all their grocery money on a turkey and trimmings for Christmas dinner. Donna Belle's monthly Social Security check had been delayed because of her change of address. After having paid the bill for the rental truck, Daniel had only five dollars left in his pocket. Daniel's money from his farm auction had been held up by the banker until all the personal checks that buyers had used to pay for his sale items could be cleared. If either of their checks did not come in the mail today, well...

While waiting for the mail, Daniel decided to take Jesse, Jimmy, Donny, and Benjamin to the back of the pasture, to an old abandoned public road that for several years had grown up in saplings, including red cedars of various sizes. A small bridge over a ditch had collapsed on the road during the depths of the Depression. Caddo County Commissioners Court had received New Deal WPA funds to rebuild the bridge, but because no one lived along that stretch of the road, there was no traffic demand; it was never rebuilt.

"Boys, we will claim a tree on the basis of public domain, so pick one out," said Daniel. "Just remember, you will need to carry it home." Jimmy chose one that was too tall for their living room ceiling, but Jesse and Donny wanted a smaller, thicker one, whereupon Jesse settled the matter by sawing his choice down. "Don't let it drag in the snow," Daniel cautioned, "or it will lose its needles!" So they took turns carrying the tree, one holding its trunk, another holding up the other end.

When they returned, they learned that the rural carrier had driven past their mailboxes without stopping. No checks in the mail! "What will we do?" wailed Janie. "How can Christmas happen without gifts? Can't someone come up with any money for gifts?" Jesse did not offer the $17.50 he had collected selling pelts that he had trapped on the Canadian River; it was earmarked to apply to the purchase of his first automobile. Benjamin still had his dollar that Jacob Jiggs had sent him the previous Christmas, but he could not offer it without revealing his secret. In her purse, Olivia had only thirteen cents and a return ticket to Lawton.

Daniel turned to Olivia and handed her his five-dollar bill. "Olivia," he said, "of all our family, you are the only person who has the flair to go in to Anadarko with a five-dollar bill and bring back presents for everybody, including Leona, Vernon, and Kirby, who will be here tomorrow." He handed her his car keys. "You'd better get a move on, before the stores close!"

Olivia loved the challenge. She went alone and headed for the TG&Y variety store. Three hours later, she returned carrying her purchases in a single brown paper sack. "I'll wrap your presents while everyone else is at the Christmas Eve church service," she said. The Barnaby sisters had stopped by again and invited them. "Bring all the kids! Santa will have a bag of goodies for everyone!"

There are Santas, and again, there are Santas, thought Ben, a Santa nonbeliever who kept quiet about it because he did not want to upset any of his cousins.

Pine Ridge Missionary Baptist Church was not only a fundamentalist congregation; it was also a community center of Barnaby relatives, Barnaby neighbors, and relatives of Barnaby kin. To have two new families move into the neighborhood less than a mile from the church was the most exciting event in months. Daniel's family and Donna Belle's family arrived together. The church building was a forty-year-old wooden-frame building with a beaded ceiling and beaded walls, a single large room with an open side room for overflow crowds, used for Sunday school classes but unused for overflow crowds since Grandpa Barnaby's funeral in 1939. The pews were hand-hewn benches with slatted backrests.

The pulpit was a small stage with a handmade wooden lectern. An old upright piano was located on the left side of the stage, and a banner containing the church covenant hung on the front wall. Electrical wiring was fastened to the ceiling, with two overhanging lights above the congregation; a single bulb dangled above the pulpit. A large coal-burning stove in the center of the main aisle heated the entire building.

The Birds and the Dalkenses entered just as John Barnaby, the song leader, was about to begin the service. Holding Bobby Alan, Donna Belle sat down first, with her sons, on a bench near the center of the room, followed by Grace, Daniel, Janie, Ben, and Jesse next to the aisle. All eyes were on them. John Barnaby's wife, Bea, from the welcoming committee, promptly arose and introduced them.

"Folks, this is widow Donna Belle Dalkens and her four wonderful sons, and Donna Belle's brother-in-law and sister-in-law, Daniel and Grace Bird, and their three children. They have moved onto the old Withers place. Mildred and I stopped by their place and invited them to the service tonight, and we are so happy they have joined us!"

"Welcome to Pine Ridge," said John Barnaby. "We were about to sing some Christmas songs. It would be a miracle if one of you ladies could play the piano. Mrs. Beiber, our regular pianist, fell and broke her hip last month, and ever since then, we have been *a cappella*."

Daniel responded. "My wife plays by ear," he said. "She does pretty well with most of the church hymns. Grace, would you like to accompany the singing?"

Grace was shocked and embarrassed. Later, she would chastise her husband for putting her in a spot. Her mother's old upright piano had been moved so many times it had lost its tuning, and she had not touched it in years. Reluctant, she said, "I have not played for so long I don't know if I can!"

"Please come forward and play for us," John Barnaby requested. "They say that playing an instrument is like riding a bicycle. Once you know how, you never forget."

Then inexplicably, a sense of *déjà vu* came over Grace, as though this moment had already happened one night years ago and she had played well. Bathed in a sense of *this is what I am destined to do*, she arose and walked to the piano. John Barnaby gave her a list of Christmas hymns, and the program transcended what anyone could have anticipated. The Pine Ridge members were born singers, and Grace's chords were the very thing they needed to ring in a memorable celebration of the birth of Christ.

Benjamin was astounded. He had heard his mother pecking at Maudeen's dilapidated old piano, but nothing as impressive as this. His mother had never had a piano lesson, but she could play like an angel. *Surely, she is touched by a guardian angel,* he thought. Each hymn was more wonderful than the last: "Silent Night," "Hark the Herald Angels Sing," "O Little Town of Bethlehem," "It Came Upon a Midnight Clear," "Away in a Manger," and "Joy to the World!"

Benjamin looked down his row. Everyone was singing. Daddy was singing in his monotone bass, off-key, but drowned out by the decibels from the crowd. Donny and Jimmy and Janie were singing, and so was Donna Belle, with an expression of peace of mind that Ben had not seen in a long while.

Sitting on Jimmy's lap, Will was waving his arm in time with the song director. Ben looked behind him and noticed two boys about his age on the back row singing and smiling and waving at him. He waved back. He turned to Jesse, who was singing, and whispered, "What do you think of this church?"

Jesse whispered back, "This is a good church. Everyone is friendly. Mama is doing well!"

The songs were to be followed by a nativity skit from some of the children. Grace returned to her seat amid rousing applause. "Mrs. Bird, the church really appreciates you," said John Barnaby. The nativity skit was short and sweet and half-narrated by Mildred Barnaby the prompter, because the children participating were too nervous to remember their lines. Then Santa (Hubert Langford) burst through the back double door with a "Ho! Ho! Ho!" and a large bag full of sacked goodies. Small children squealed, and large children smiled as though they were in on a secret, and parents watched their children watch Santa. Each bag held an apple, an orange, two Brazil nuts, three walnuts, four pecans, several unshelled, parched peanuts, and several pieces of hard, multicolored, ribbon-shaped Christmas candy. Each person received a bag, and there were enough bags left over to take to Mrs. Beiber and other shut-ins in the neighborhood. Janie took an extra one for her aunt Olivia.

After the service ended, the people lingered and gathered around their new friends, while some of the men went outside to heat up their family cars. Several expressed their gratitude to Grace and expressed hope that she would attend next Sunday's services and play piano for them again. Daniel beamed because he could already see that Grace would have difficulty refusing to join such a warm and friendly congregation.

Benjamin was approached by a lad his age. "Hi, I am Denver Dover. What is your name?"

"Benny Bird. Pleased to meet you. What grade are you in?"

"Fourth grade at Thaxton Public School. What grade are you in?"

"Fourth grade too. We will be in the same class!"

"I am glad. This guy standing next to me is my cousin, Alvin Madison. He's in fourth grade, but he goes to Apache Public School."

"Howdy," said Alvin, a short curly-haired ten-year-old.

Jimmy and Donny stepped from their row into the aisle. "This is my cousin, Jimmy Dalkens, who is in fifth grade," said Ben, "and his brother, Donny, who is in third grade. Jimmy and Donny, meet Denver and Alvin."

And so, just like that, five preadolescent boys from the Pine Ridge community formed a bond of friendship that would hold together for the next five years.

When the Birds returned home, they found that Olivia had gone to bed in Janie's room, a sack of Christmas presents protectively placed under her bed. Dramatically, she had brushed her long chestnut hair away from her scalp, like a halo or crescent across her pillow.

"Shh," said Janie. "Aunt Olivia is asleep."

"Aw, she's not really asleep," said Jesse.

"Yes, she is," Janie replied.

"Then let's look in the sack to see our Christmas presents," said Jesse as he stooped to pick up the sack.

Suddenly, Olivia raised her head and shouted, "Don't you dare!"

Janie screamed. Jesse and Benjamin laughed at Janie, and so did Olivia.

The next day, Christmas Day 1943, Vernon's rehabilitated old automobile, coughing and blowing exhaust smoke, rolled into Donna Belle's front yard just in time for them to participate in opening presents. What could Olivia have bought for everyone with only five dollars? Wrapped in colored Sunday funnies newsprint, tied with plain cotton string, for her nephews, twenty-five-cent clear glass molded miniature figurines: Vernon, Jesse, Kirby, and Jimmy each got a glass car; Ben, Donny, and Will got songbirds, and little Bobby Alan a bunny rabbit, which Donna Belle took away from him because she was afraid he would try to bite it and break it in his mouth. Subtotal, $2.

For the ladies—Grace, Leona, Donna Belle, Janie, and Olivia herself—dainty handkerchiefs made from a single remnant of fine *madras* cloth, colored in irregular stripes of many colors, cut and hemmed on Grace's sewing machine, each slightly different because of the variant stripes. Subtotal, $2.

For Daniel, a tin coffee cup with a blue enamel coating. Subtotal, 65¢. With leftover change, 35¢ worth of bubble gum for the kids.

It was a Christmas to remember, with presents for everyone, and with everyone imbued with a spirit of joy and sharing that was without price. "Gee, with my tin cup, I could take it to a street corner and beg up another five dollars for next year!" Daniel joshed. Everyone laughed, except Benjamin.

He thought it sad that his father, the great provider, temporarily did not have a dime.

Next morning, Daniel found a crumpled dollar bill in his overalls pocket. *Where did it come from?* he wondered. It remained a family mystery.

*   *   *

The surrender of his gift dollar bill from Jacob Jiggs was a step toward freeing himself, Ben believed. Now he needed to get rid of Jacob's provocative swimsuit photograph. As soon as the ground thawed out from the hard freeze that came with the snowstorm, Benjamin dug a hole under the locust trees along the road, wrapped the photo in wax paper, and placed it in the bottom of the hole. He thought of tearing it to shreds but just could not do it. Deliberately he did not notice which tree he was under, in case he was tempted to retrieve it. He filled the hole and covered the site with leaves. Burying the picture seemed almost like a funeral. *Nay-Boom Be-Man Tauntay,* he thought, *release me from my desire. Nay-Boom Be-Man Tauntay, release me from my need. Nay-Boom Be-Man Tauntay, release me from my abomination.*

*   *   *

A few days later, another type of closure took place while Benjamin was wrestling with Jimmy and Donny. Their wrestling matches took place almost every day, always with the same result. Ben never came close to besting either of his cousins, but he remained steadfast in his determination to *be a man and take his medicine.* Donny and Jimmy knew they could whip Ben easily, and it seemed to him that they were becoming rougher and rougher with him. Resentment was smoldering within him, and it became connected to an unspoken character issue Ben had harbored against them ever since their father had been killed.

Suddenly, Benjamin just blurted it out. "I don't understand you two! You must have something missing! You're not all there!"

Jimmy bristled. "What do you mean, you little smarty?"

"When your daddy died, I cried and cried. Your daddy and my daddy are the two best daddies in the whole world. But I didn't see you cry, neither one of you. You must not have a heart!" Ben said it with a sob, knowing his words would anger them, and his tears came.

"That's just all you know!" Jimmy retorted. "When Grandpa Lee told us that Daddy fell off the railroad bridge, he told us to be strong so as to hold up our mother. So I didn't let her see me cry. But I cried a lot, in the dark, under my pillow. And I cried again this Christmas, after I went to bed. So you just shut up about it!"

"What about you, Donny?" asked Benny.

"I didn't cry, and I'm not going to cry, because I am just so mad!" said Donny through clenched teeth. "I am mad at God for letting Daddy fall down and die, and I am mad at Daddy for having such a lousy, risky job!"

Suddenly, Jimmy slapped Donny hard across his jaw and said, "Don't you be mad at Daddy, you little fool! You better cry!"

Shocked with pain and blind with rage, Donny clenched his fist to take a swing at his brother. But suddenly a great sob escaped him, and all his anger and all his stifled grief came gushing forth, purging months of unexpressed grief and weeks of hidden fury and days of numbing anguish. Then all three of them fell to their knees, their arms around one another's shoulders, their heads together like little lost puppies, crying together until finally Donny was drained of his anger.

Minutes later, resilient as only children can be, they were still on their knees, engaged in a game of mumblety-peg, arguing over whose turn was next.

End of Volume 1

Acknowledgement

T he Bible passages quoted in this volume are from the King James version and the Revised Standard version.

Hymns dating back for generations were profoundly moving to those who faced hard times in the Dust Bowl years during the Great Depression of the 1930s. The lyrics of these old religious songs still resonate:

Amazing Grace, by John Newton in 1725
In the Sweet Bye and Bye, by Sanford Fillmore Bennett, 1868
Enough for Me, by Elisha A. Hoffman, 1873
Let Jesus Come Into Your Heart, by Lelia Norris, (1862-1920)
Softly and Tenderly, by Will L. Thompson (1847-1909)
Shall We Gather at the River, by Robert Lowry, 1864

Two highly popular songs contemporary to the fictional time of Benjamin Bird are *Old Shep* by Red Foley and Arthur Williams (1933) and *Pistol Packin' Mama* by Al Dexter (1940s).

About the Author

M. D. Gage is an Emeritus Professor of History at Tarrant County College in Fort Worth, Texas. He received his BA and MA degrees from the University of Oklahoma. He has published several research articles in regional historical journals and an extensive series of weekly articles on local and regional history published in the *Fort Worth Star-Telegram*. In retirement, Gage operates a registered Simbrah cattle ranch in Clay County, Texas, near Larry McMurtry country.

CPSIA information can be obtained
at www.ICGtesting.com
Printed in the USA
LVHW040912080419
613325LV00003B/191